WITHDRAWN

EAST OF THE SUN

A JACE SALOME NOVEL

EAST OF THE SUN

TREY R. BARKER

FIVE STAR
A part of Gale, Cengage Learning

GALE
CENGAGE Learning·

Farmington Hills, Mich • San Francisco • New York • Waterville, Maine
Meriden, Conn • Mason, Ohio • Chicago

GALE
CENGAGE Learning·

LIBRARY OF CONGRESS CATALOGING-IN-PUBLICATION DATA

Names: Barker, Trey R.
Title: East of the sun : a Jace Salome novel / Trey R. Barker.
Description: Waterville, Maine : Five Star, 2016.
Identifiers: LCCN 2016024382| ISBN 9781432832322 (hardcover) | ISBN
    1432832328 (hardcover) | ISBN 9781432832360 (ebook) |ISBN 1432832360
    (ebook) |ISBN 9781432834722 (ebook) | ISBN 143283472x (ebook)
Subjects: LCSH: Policewomen—Fiction. | Correctional personnel—Fiction. |
    Police—Texas—Fiction. | GSAFD: Mystery fiction
Classification: LCC PS3602.A77555 E17 2016 | DDC 813/.6—dc23
LC record available at https://lccn.loc.gov/2016024382

First Edition. First Printing: December 2016
Find us on Facebook– https://www.facebook.com/FiveStarCengage
Visit our website– http://www.gale.cengage.com/fivestar/
Contact Five Star™ Publishing at FiveStar@cengage.com

Printed in the United States of America
1 2 3 4 5 6 7 20 19 18 17 16

ACKNOWLEDGEMENTS

No one is an island. It is the same with writers, though there is only a single butt in the chair. I started writing in the 7th grade and none of the millions of words I've written have been written solely on my own. A bevy of people contribute to keeping my behind in the chair. For help in so many different ways, I'd like to thank Craig Johnson, Elaine Ash, Alison Evans, Midland County (TX) Justice of the Peace John Barton, Bureau County (IL) Deputies Jordan Sommers and Mackenzie Kruse, Sandi Loper, John Purcell, Eric Campbell, Elicia Dunn.

As ever, if it's right, blame them. If it's wrong, blame me.

One of the greatest tragedies in life is to lose your own sense of self and accept the version of you that is expected by everyone else.

—K. L. Toth

CHAPTER 1

—whiskey tango foxtrot! I'm bored. Ain't the road guys doing nothing tonight?—

The voice over the radio, a faux-British accent that more than one jailer liked to try on occasionally as an homage to Zachary County sheriff's office records manager James Balsamo, was shot through with exhaustion borne of the tedium of emptiness.

—on Christmas Eve? No way; they're with their families—

—or mistresses—

—or both—

From her seat at one of the booking computers, Jace Salome's eyes widened.

Corporal Kleopping laughed. "Wait for it. In 5 . . . 4 . . . 3 . . . 2 . . . 1 . . ."

—can the chatter—

—uh . . . yes, sir—

"Had to be Urrea, didn't it?" Kleopping shook his head. "Never heard a British accent until you've heard a Tex-Mex do it."

The collective chuckle slipped away as quickly as west-Texas melted snow. The deputies went back to the nothing that had occupied them so far on this Christmas Eve. This was the dead shift, working 11 p.m. to 7 a.m. six days on and two off, and this was their third night on. For the first time since Jace had pinned a badge on her chest eight months ago, there hadn't been a single arrestee. More than one hundred and sixty thousand people in the county and on any given night there were about forty cops, between county, the one big city, and the smattering of small towns scattered over the county like high notes from a jazz trumpet. Yet somehow there hadn't been a single arrestee brought to the jail.

"Oh, man." Rory banged her head against the desk. "I hate wintertime overnights. Even worse on Christmas."

Booking had eight officers, six of whom were part of the Emergency Response Team. Tonight, Jace and Rory were the booking officers. Jace wasn't certified for ERT and wasn't sure she wanted to be. The duty struck her as requiring a taste for violence she didn't have.

"Why can't we put up some lights or a tree or something?" Jace asked.

Rory mimed a string of lights around her neck, strangling her.

"Ah. Right."

Deputy Sassy Laimo, a woman with a vague mustache who'd been with the department about a decade, shook her head. "Been here nearly a year, Salome; figure it out already."

"Barely nine months and she knows what she's doing," Rory said. "Mostly." Rory chuckled but it died when Laimo opened her mouth again.

"Yeah? If she's so smart, how come she hasn't yet figured out her lover Bobby is selling ganja to all the inmates?"

Rory laughed. "You jealous, Laimo?"

Jace looked at Laimo. "Inmate Bobby? No, he's not. That's inmates jealous that he's a trusty. Jailhouse scuttlebutt."

"Sure, whatever you say."

"Okay, so our guy's speeding, right?" Rory's voice suddenly boomed in the booking hallway. "And I'm writing out his ticket—"

Kleopping snorted. "That's right . . . the newly minted part-time road deputy." He winked. "Soon to be Cop of the Year for Rooster County."

Everyone in the long hallway hooted, though Rory stared them down and eventually pulled a wallet out of her pocket and flipped it open. The Rooster County badge gleamed. "That's right, bitches, Rooster County. RC 30 on the radio. Listen for me. So I'm writing our guy a ticket and I notice a crap-load of machetes. In the back seat. Like . . . twenty? Thirty, maybe? So I say, 'What are those for?'

" 'I'm a juggler,' our guy says. 'Use 'em in my act.' "

"You get his phone number?" Laimo laughed, a brittle sound that reminded Jace of breaking twigs. "Book him for the New Year's Eve party."

Rory's eyes went wide. "Never met a juggler before, so I say, 'Yeah? I'd love to see it.' Our guy gets outta his car and starts juggling. Grabs three machetes and tosses 'em straight up. Crazy, right? Three and then four and five, and finally he's got seven machetes going. Our guy ain't even breaking a sweat. He's got 'em going overhand and underhand and behind his back and everything else. It's like freakin' Barnum and Bailey right there on I-20.

"So while he's doing his thing, this other car drives by, real slow . . . like grandma slow. Driver leans out the window and says, 'Shit! I gotta give up drinking and driving . . . I could never pass that sobriety test.' "

The booking hallway was silent for a beat before it exploded in a chorus of laughs and catcalls and shouts of "liar," and "bullcrap." A couple of jailers threw wads of paper in Rory's direction.

"That's a load," Jace said.

With a wink, Rory put a hand over her heart. "God's honest truth."

"Whatever." Jace grinned while her fingers idly tapped out a jazz riff.

"Wait." Rory, bug-eyed, looked at the clock. "I think it moved."

"Don't toy with us, Bogan," Laimo said.

"No, really, I think it did. Another thirty . . . forty . . . hours and we'll be done for the night."

One of the guys, Jimmson, said, "So there's a horse cop—"

"We don't have a horse division." Rory winked at Jace.

"Got enough horses' asses for it," Jace said.

The room boomed with laughter.

Rory jumped up and clapped like a cheerleader in love with the quarterback. "Oh, break it off in their bee-hinds! She made a joke, you guys. You hear that? An actual joke."

"Nine months . . . one joke." Kleopping grabbed Jace's hand and raised it, a triumphant fighter. "Late to the party but at least she's here . . . finally."

Jimmson waited until the room was quiet and continued, laying his story out theatrically. "One day a seven-year-old little girl drives past this horse cop on her little Schwinn."

"Don't make Schwinns anymore, dumbass."

Rory stuck her tongue out at Laimo. "Let him tell his story. You can tell the one about electrolysis next."

"Fuck you, bitch."

"Willya let me tell it? This seven-year-old passes the horse cop and the copper notices she don't have no taillight so he pulls her over."

"No taillight? On a bike?" Rory cocked her head. "This is what you're going with?"

—control . . . B-boy inner—

The voice over the radio—a guard in B Pod—sounded tired. On quiet winter nights, when bad boys and girls stayed home to try and keep the chill out of their bones, and the hours were molasses-slow, attention wandered and it became difficult to stay awake. Eventually everyone sounded tired. A few seconds later, from the far side of B Pod, everyone heard the muffled thump of the inner door opening and then closing.

—control . . . B-boy outer—

Again, the pause, then the pop of the lock, then the door closing.

The inner door led directly into the pod. The outer door led directly into the hallway. The area between those two doors was called the go-between.

"Got a prisoner moving?" Kleopping asked Rory.

"It sound like something else?" Laimo asked.

"Ooh, Deputy Laimo, don't yell at my stripes." Kleopping didn't actually rub his corporal's stripes, but close. He was in charge of booking and ERTs for the dead shift. "When's Bibb back? I can't stand how Conroy does the job."

Sergeant Bibb was the dead-shift control-room sergeant and before he left for a forced vacation, Bibb had militantly begun announcing any and all movement of inmates. Guilt plagued him, every moment of every day, because of the beating Jace had taken in a go-between. Conroy, manning the control room while Bibb was gone, mostly didn't follow Bibb's new policy. The new way of doing things drove nearly everyone crazy at first with the amount of radio traffic, but ultimately, deputies had gotten used to it.

And were thankful for it.

Because no one wants what happened to me to happen to them.

"Couple more nights." Rory sniffed the air. "Until the aroma of microwaved burritos will once again fill the jail like . . . like . . . I don't know, like something."

"Dirty sweat socks?" Kleopping said.

"Willya let me tell it?" Jimmson glared at everyone. "So the cop says, 'Did Santa give you that bike for Christmas?' The girl, see, she laughs and says, 'Yes, sir.' The cop writes her a ticket and says, 'Next time, tell Santa to put a taillight on it.' The girl takes the ticket and says, 'Did Santa give you that horse?' 'Yes, ma'am,' the copper says. 'Well,' the girl says, 'next time tell Santa the dick goes under the horse—' "

"Not on top," everyone finished together.

"Yeah, okay . . . you probably heard that one."

Another round of laughter bounced up and down the long, narrow booking hallway. Sound reverberated off the metal doors of the holding cells, off the metal benches with D rings bolted to them, off the concrete walls. In the booking area, everything except the two computer desks was made of metal or concrete or bolted to concrete or metal, which meant every sound was amplified and multiplied. Usually, on a busy night, the hallway was such a cacophony that Jace went home with a headache. But tonight, the booming silence made the hallway feel more dangerous than usual.

When the electric lock on the metal door between booking and the main hallway popped, the sound thundered through booking like a cannon on a lonely hill. Jace jumped, then crushed her annoyance at herself for being startled.

"Still scared?" Laimo's voice was overly sweet, a confection designed just for Jace.

"Shut up, Laimo." Rory's voice was as hard as Laimo's had been soft.

"Piss off."

Kleopping glared at them. "Both of you shut up."

Rory leaned close to Jace. "Hate to say it, but the wench is right. You been here a while." She held up a single finger. "You should tell more jokes," and then a second, "and you shouldn't be scared by the door locks."

"Ain't 'a-skeered'a nothing." Jace did it in her best imitation of Rory.

14

"Oooh, ain't you a tough sister?" Rory nodded at the visitor who'd wandered in from the main hallway. "Well, well. What's the haps, Caps?"

The man, Caucasian and well into his forties, strolled to the desk and plopped two well-manicured hands on it. "*Nada, nada,* Bogan. How you?"

"Passable."

The man turned to Jace. "You Salome?"

"Yes, sir."

He held out a hand. "Simon Shelby. I'm with the task force."

"Task force?" Jace's stomach tightened.

"Force Chrome."

"Uh . . . okay."

"Drug interdiction?"

"Uh . . . okay."

"The regional multi-jurisdictional drug interdiction task force?" Shelby smiled. "Any idea at all what I'm talking about?"

Jace felt the color rise in her cheeks.

"She's a newbie worm."

"Gotcha. Listen, I made a bust a few days ago you two might be interested in. Cat named Tomas Salazar. Brother of Enrique. Or should I say: brother of dead Enrique."

Jace kept her face blank, trying to crush down the memory of Salazar. During the Badgett investigation, Salazar had made his presence known to Jace and Rory by trying to run them over with an SUV. After they'd tracked him down, she and Rory bled him dry for information. In return, and hoping for an ongoing source of info, Rory had let him skate on the vehicular assault charge. Salazar had later been killed by a man named Badgett, who had presented Jace with a hacked-off ear as proof.

"I popped Tomas with decent weight. Not a career bust, but good enough for some free beer at Doll's. We got to talking and pretty quick you guys' names came outta his yap. Name dropping. Trying to get some rhythm for the delivery I interrupted. Deputy? You okay?"

"I get nervous when a dealer I've never met is tossing my name around."

Shelby shrugged acknowledgement. "True, that. But you've got no worries with me."

"A Texas Ranger said that to me once."

He cocked his head. "I did hear tell of that. Look, I'm just a drug guy down by the end of his road. Ain't working up no sweat over anything. In fact, I brought you a gift. Salazar said you two did his brother a good turn. He wants to pay back the family's honor. Mexican *machismo.*" Shelby handed Jace a slip of paper. "That'll be a good bust for the two of you to have."

"What's this?" A date, a time, a highway, and a vehicle description.

"Shipment."

Rory's eyes were wide and excited. "Drugs."

Shelby nodded. "Weed, crank, knock-off pharma. All from Mex."

"Coming to Zach City?" Rory asked.

"Far as I know."

Jace's gut fluttered and a surprising bit of excitement sat lightly in the back of her throat. "We can't arrest people on the street; we're just jailers."

"Jailers with information. Parley with someone who can make the bust and roll that into some credit." He winked at Rory. "Or pop it in Rooster. Word will get back."

"You could ride with me. Pull it down on a traffic stop." Rory grinned. "Either we get it ourselves or bank the credit."

"True, that. Never know when you might need it. Or when some itty, bitty tiny piece of info you have puts someone else's entire case together." Shelby stared at Jace. "Deputy? What's on your mind?"

"Nothing. I'm good. I . . . just—"

"What's the problem?"

"No problem." She handed the paper to Rory. "Why didn't you keep the info? Drug busts are your thing, not mine."

His sigh felt like a breath from the desert. Dry and dusty, ancient. "I'm getting old, Salome. Too old to worry about who gets what credit. I keep that info? Hell, then I've got to find the damned truck, stop it, make the bust, do the paperwork. Bah. The only credit I'm interested in now is my twenty years' pension. Six weeks, three days—" a quick look at his watch—"four and a half hours. You two got a career up ahead of you. Besides that, doesn't matter how hard I try, I absolutely will trip over Salazar's dumb ass again and he'll ask me if I gave you guys the message." He stared at her. "Plus, you straight up did the right thing with Badgett. I know there are cops getting their mail in the Huntsville state pen behind all that bullshit, but I got no sympathy for them. You did right by all of us."

Jace choked back her surprise. "Doesn't feel like it sometimes. From some cops."

Shelby leaned in close. "Fuck. Them."

Rory nodded. "Straight up."

"You sleeping at night?"

Not all the time, she wanted to say, but she knew what he meant. "Mostly."

His eyes narrowed. "Uh huh. Well . . . go get that bust." He handed each woman a business card. "You guys call, you need me."

"Thanks . . . uh . . . Captain."

He grinned. "I ain't no captain; I work for a living. Few more weeks, anyway."

"Thanks, Simon."

"I gotta tell you, I'm intrigued by the tattoo." For a long, discomforting moment, his gaze was heavy on the base of Jace's throat. "Half a heart? When my daughter was a junior in high school, she and her boyfriend both had a necklace with half a heart. Put 'em together and all was right with the world." He winked. "Got a high-school boyfriend?"

Self-consciously, she covered the tattoo with her hand. "I'd probably remember."

He shook hands with them. "Sucks ass to work on Christmas, but at least you get time and a half. Have a good one."

When he was gone, Kleopping shoved his cell phone in his pocket. "No tour tonight."

"What's up?" Jimmson sat against the wall, eyes closed.

"Well, before tonight's tour, Dr. Ernesto R. Cruz apparently took the visiting administrators out."

"Shouldn't'a had a tour on Christmas Eve anyway," Laimo said.

Kleopping shrugged. "Holidays do not wait on millions of dollars. Some sort of deadline for paperwork and blah blah blah."

Jimmson looked at his fingernails. "Sort of funny to think of our little jail doctor spreading all over the state—"

"Like a fungus," Laimo said.

"—snatching up new jails."

"Anyway," Kleopping said. "No tour because I guess they got—"

"Rolled by hookers?" Rory said.

"Drunk, Deputy. So no tour, which is fine with me. Probably tomorrow."

Rory rolled her eyes. "Guess they should'a come before they got—"

"Rolled," Jace said.

"Drunk." Rory gave Jace a half-smirk. "All those administrators from all over the state drive me batty."

Laimo snorted. "Short-ass drive."

"Shorter than your 'stache, anyway."

"Let's keep it professional." Kleopping stared hard at everyone.

"Hey, Corporal." Rory winked. "Aces, that's us. The most professional shift at Zachary County. Top-shelf professional all the time."

Jimmson laughed. "Going to Hell for lying, Bogan."

"Not just administrators and sheriffs, either," Kleopping said. "Lt. Beem told me there's been a Mexican cop in here a couple of times."

"A *federale*." Rory whistled. "I guess Dr. Cruz is going big time."

"Wouldn't mind seeing a Mexican badge," Jimmson said.

Rory giggled. "Badges? We don't need no stinking badges."

"That's not how the quote goes, idiot," Laimo said.

"Kiss my—"

—so . . . how many cops does it take to throw a suspect down the stairs? None. He fell, I swear, Your Honor, he just fell—

This time, the laughs were subdued even as they slipped out like cracked mortar from between bricks.

"Day late and a dollar short," Rory said.

"Short of actual comedy."

"Holy balls." Rory's eyes grew wide. "Two jokes? Not just one but *two*? In one night?" She went to Jace's side, tilted her head back and stared into her eyes. "Who are you and what have you done with Deputy Jace Salome? And don't lie to me because you work here and I'll find out who you are."

A moment later, Sgt. Dillon's voice came over the radio. *"Officer Urrea, that's the funniest one yet. Why don't you come to my office and tell me where you got it?"*

—uh . . . no, thanks, sir . . . I'm pretty busy here—

—control room . . . M-medical outer—

19

Everyone listened. There was no thump of the door being opened.

—*M-medical outer*—

Still, the lock was silent.

"Conroy." Kleopping barked into his radio. "Medical outer. Now."

"Can't wait for Bibb to roll his big ass back in." Rory sighed.

A moment later, everyone heard the outer door open. There was a pause and then the officer, the same guard who'd come out of B Pod minutes earlier, asked for the inner medical door.

Laimo snorted. "Prisoner's lying. Wants his fix or a cushy bed."

"They don't all lie, Laimo." Jace spoke through a mouthful of annoyance.

"Yeah, they do. You'll figure it out if you last long enough."

Rory whistled. "She'll last longer than you. I got ten bucks says so."

"That's all? Better stop spending your quarters on Skittles; gonna leave you toothless and broke."

Rory stood, hands clenched to fists, chest squared, feet planted.

"Rory." Jace touched her hand.

"Tougher than you when I'm sleeping," Laimo said.

"I *am* asleep," Jace said. "Can't we get even one arrest?"

It was a lie. Jace hadn't slept worth a crap since her beating, though the nights had gotten better lately. She usually managed some sleep, though it was inevitably interrupted by broken images; dreams of a small house up on cinder blocks, windows broken and doors hanging from destroyed hinges, walls with holes, and stains of brown paint everywhere. Bright orange sun, a morning sun, blasted through the windows and tattered curtains and she knew, with dead certain dream-knowledge, that those windows faced west.

She woke from that dream, every time, with cotton in her mouth, her skin soaked in sweat, a barely remembered jazz tune that Mama danced to in her head, and all she wanted was to shove the dream away and burrow deeper under the comforter.

"Jace?" Rory's voice was hushed. "You okay?"

Jace shook her head clear of the dust storms. "Right as the rain."

"Ain't rained in like . . . I don't know . . . a year. News keeps talking about the drought? Ringing any bells?"

The silence, unnerving as cold steel against a throat, fell again. Kleopping gently banged his head against the wall while Laimo scraped old polish from her nails. At the far end, a new guy, assigned badge 410, went back to his car magazine. Another new guy, badge number 429, scribbled madly in a small notebook. Another officer came through the sally-port door, stubbing out a cigarette butt while he hummed some twangy country song.

And still the clock never moved.

". . . need my meds . . ." The voice was muffled but angry and it came from the medical pod, just on the other side of one of the many sets of doors that dotted the booking hallway.

"Told you." Laimo looked up from her nail polish and smirked. "Looking for meds."

"Bite my ass." Rory blew her a kiss.

". . . that ain't right . . . it ain't fucking right . . . I need my meds; my doctor prescribed them." The same voice, still muffled as though from some great distance, but angrier now, loaded with menace and righteousness.

Jace glanced nervously at the medical-pod door.

"Calm down." Rory tapped Jace's foot with her own.

"Yeah, yeah. It's nothing. I'm fine."

"Well, you ain't fine, but you're right, it's nothing. An inmate upset he can't get some aspirin or something." Rory didn't even

21

bother looking toward medical and Jace had no idea if her friend was actually unconcerned or simply trying to appear unconcerned.

"You wanna see me dead? 'Cause that's what'll happen. I need my 'script."

The voice was sharper now. What was missing from the conversation was the guard's response. Jace knew, from both the academy and the few months she'd already put in, the guard would be talking slowly and calmly. Probably his hands were up, palms out, trying to ease the inmate's agitation.

Rory kept her eyes on the computer screen. "Nothing going on you need to worry about. Just another agitated inmate. You've seen it lots of times, worm, nothing new. It'll be fine."

"Why do you keep saying that?" It came out sharper than Jace expected.

"Because you're getting scared."

"It's going to come to blows in there."

"Maybe, but it's not your fight. You don't have to worry about it. And even if it does, it'll never end like Thomas."

"Do not say it won't happen again. Do not."

"Jace, listen to me." Rory grabbed her friend's head and turned it until they were face to face. "An inmate will not be killed in this jail on this night."

"You can't promise that."

Rory sighed. "You're right, I can't. But I believe it. How's that?"

—zebra 2! zebra 2!—

"Son of a bitch." Jace's heart dropped into her stomach and she felt it all at once: the adrenaline, the fear, the anger, the sudden certainty she'd chosen the wrong profession. She stood, sweat exploding on her skin and her heart revving in her chest like Art Blakey pissed off and drumming to save his life.

"Sit down." Rory said it as a command.

22

The facility-wide alarm exploded, its blast as piercing as an ice pick to the eardrum.

"Let's go." Kleopping's emergency-response team members were already moving, their faces stone. He opened the armory closet and deputies moved in and out, jaws tight, getting their equipment.

Jace whispered, "This guy is gonna get killed."

"Jace, it's not—"

"It is just like Thomas, damn it, and Stimson and Rissley and all the rest."

When Rory slapped her, a rocket went off in her head and blew out the screaming alarm. "Sit down and take a breath, sister." But even as she ordered it, Rory stood. Her face was flushed. Rory gently cupped Jace's chin. "Don't sweat it, worm."

"I am not a worm anymore."

"My mistake." She indicated the booking computers, the fingerprinting machines. "You're intake tonight. That fight isn't your gig."

"But—"

"Not. Your. Gig."

—*zebra 2 . . . zebra 2*—

Jace's mouth dried at the sound of the officer's voice. The deputy, whoever he was, wasn't bored anymore; he was scared to death. Zebra 2 was the internal call for the ERTs.

"Kill the alarm," Kleopping said into his radio.

—*get me some help*—

The guard's voice rose into hysteria.

—*get me some help goddamn it*—

—*he's killing me. Goddamn it help me*—

Kleopping keyed his radio and barked, "Where are they, Conroy?"

Jace could imagine Conroy's eyes sweeping the multitude of monitor screens mounted on the wall of the control room. Every pod, every holding cell, almost every inch of the jail was covered by a camera.

—*uh . . . medical . . . yeah*—

"You sure?"

—*yeah, uh, I'm . . . I'm sure. Medical*—

One of the ERTs tossed a hard look at Kleopping. The corporal shook his head.

—*all call from control: lockdown. Lockdown until further notice*—

Louder. Jace remembered the chaos louder. Her memory, always a tricky thing, told her it had been louder when she'd been on the floor beneath an ERT shield. Yells and shouts and confusion. The noise of emergencies. Tonight, from this side of the doors and experience, the sound seemed dull and almost bored.

"Kill the alarm!"

Her cheek flared where the shield had jammed her to the floor a few months ago. Her bladder ached at the memory of pissing herself.

The radio exploded.

—*A Pod locked*—

—*B Pod locked, one inmate in medical*—

"For God's sake be—" *careful,* Jace tried to say.

"Shut the fuck up, worm." When Laimo banged the bottom of her ballistic shield on the concrete, the sound cracked like a whip. "Can't hear squat with you bawling like a titty baby."

Tight-faced, Kleopping looked at Jace and put his finger over his lips. She felt like a complete idiot.

—*we're locked in D Pod*—

—*kitchen is locked*—

Kleopping slammed the armory door. Then he put himself at the front of the ERTs and led them to the medical door.

With a spit of anger, he keyed his mic. "Damn it, Conroy, shut off the alarm. I'm not going to tell you again." Starting with Kleopping and moving down the line, his crew bumped fists. Then Kleopping took a deep breath. "Medical war."

The lock popped, a sound both jarring and comforting, and then everything was over. The ERTs were gone. The alarm died. The M-Pod war door slammed shut. The radio went quiet and the sudden slam of silence drove a stiletto blade into Jace's brain.

CHAPTER 2

"The hell is this, then?" The howl was made worse because it was muffled. "Takes six of you bastards to beat me down? Doctors selling drugs to johnnies and you let that go but you gotta come for me?"

None of the ERTs answered, per their training. Dead silence, which had been one of the things that unnerved Jace the most when they burst into the pod after Thomas's death.

"Hah! Gonna take more than that!"

Boots pounded against the concrete floor and shields banged. Something shattered on the floor.

"It ain't right. It ain't fair. It ain't—"

Sudden silence. Nothing from the inmate, nothing from the ERTs.

Jace, her breath shallow and frightened, looked at Rory. The woman was transfixed by the medical-pod war door. Her fingers held the desk's edge so tightly they were as pale and colorless as wax. *It's what she wants.* Jace swallowed. Not necessarily the violence, but certainly the blasting heart and hyperawareness, the sense of being alive, that comes with the adrenaline dump. Rory wanted to get in there and do whatever needed doing, for keeping control of the jail, but also for the electricity of the physicality.

—*control room from 419*—

—*419 go ahead*—

—*situation secure. Repeat. Situation secure. Cancel zebra 2–*

Jace hadn't realized she wasn't breathing until she started again. Situation secure meant everything was fine, just as Rory had said. They weren't calling for an ambulance or the JP. Nor were they calling for the detectives or the Texas Rangers to come investigate an in-custody death.

—all call from control: cancel zebra 2. Repeat . . . cancel zebra 2—

"It's fine." Jace was fully aware she was whispering. "Everything's fine."

Rory squeezed her hand. "Told you."

Jace laughed, slightly embarrassed. "Yeah, you did. That's why you're the veteran and I'm the worm."

A few minutes later, the door leading to the medical pod popped open and the ERTs came through, babbling and laughing and retelling the call they'd just been through. Jace recognized the banter as the aftermath of the adrenaline high. She'd felt it herself a few times. It was the last bit of nervous energy that had no place to go.

"You see that guy's eyes?" Jimmson grinned. "Big as truck tires."

Laimo threw Jace a hard eye. "No jailers to arrest tonight, worm. No cops to tear down so I guess we don't need you."

"Shut the hell up."

"Insubordination, worm. Be careful who you mouthing off to." Laimo's eyes brightened. "Son of a bitch was scared outta his mind, wasn't he?" Her laugh smeared her face the color of radishes.

"That's funny to you?" Jace stood, but Rory's hand, deftly on the back of Jace's belt, held her.

Laimo snorted out another laugh. "Ease off, worm. Ain't no big thing."

"A bit of *schadenfreude* to make your world better?"

Laimo frowned. "The hell are you talking about?"

27

Jace's hands clenched. "An ego so big and world so small that you stand on the shoulders of whoever you've shoved into the shit?"

"It was the guy from B Pod. Scared so badly he pissed himself," Badge 429 said.

"Yeah, did you get a load of the smell?" Laimo gagged as she kept laughing. "God awful."

"Now it's people pissing themselves that's funny to you."

When Jace stepped from behind the computer desks and squared off, Laimo drew up to her full height, a couple inches shy of six foot. She spoke slowly and leaned into Jace's face. "Just as funny as when *you* pissed yourself."

Jace cocked her right arm.

"Do it, worm, and let's see where the cookie crumbles."

Rory grabbed Jace's hand and held it tight. Jace yanked but Rory held on. "Not tonight."

After a minute of tugging, Jace stopped. She sneered at Laimo's ballistic shield and baton. "Easier to laugh when you're the Man, isn't it?"

"Kiss my ass, you self-righteous bitch. You don't know anything about being police." Laimo's eyes rolled down to Jace's boots and back up. "Ain't even got no real uniform."

Jace wore the hunter green and tan of the Zachary County sheriff's office. Laimo, and every other member of the ERT, wore black.

"You just a worm, Salome, and you ain't done nothing."

"She's got a few dents, Laimo." Rory pulled Jace back. "She's a hard rookie."

"She's crap." Laimo glared at Jace. "Sucking off a ranger and double-dealing behind our backs. Didn't any of us get arrested until she came along. Badgett was doing righteous work." Laimo spat on Jace's boots. "She ain't one of us, Rory, and long as you with her, you ain't one of us, either."

"Righteous?" Jace grabbed the woman's collar and drew back her fist. This time Rory didn't stop her. "He was killing inmates for their land, you bitch."

"Deputy." Kleopping's voice snapped through the air. "Release your fellow officer."

No one moved.

"Now."

Grinding her teeth, Jace let go. Smoothing her uniform, Laimo chuckled as she walked away.

"Whatever this is *will not* happen in my booking hallway. You want to beat each other silly, do it outside. But remember this, whoever's standing at the end—and I suspect it'd be Jace—gets the write up and the suspension."

Laimo spun toward Kleopping, anger on her lips.

"Got something to say, Deputy?"

Laimo flexed her jaw. "No."

"No, what?" Kleopping kept his eyes hard on her.

"No, *sir.*"

"Everyone get back to work. Shields and batons cleaned. Holding cells cleaned. Floors swept and mopped. Laimo, write the report. A fully detailed and realized report. No short cuts. It'll probably take you a while."

As the deputies spread out, anger burned Jace's blood as hot as her own piss had when the ERTs stormed A Pod and slammed her to the ground the night Thomas died. Hearing Laimo laugh about a man's degradation infuriated her.

"Sounds like you're *persona non grata* around here." Jace toweled off her boots. "At least when you hang with me."

"With Laimo? She's an idiot and if you paid me a million bucks, I couldn't possibly care less about what she thinks."

"She's not the only one, though." Jace tapped the breast pocket of her uniform shirt. Inside was one of the flyers she frequently found stuffed in her locker. Tonight's had a hangman game on it, with most of a stick figure filled in and four spaces for letters beneath it. Three of the spaces were filled in with letters from her name. *J. A. E.*

"Been a few days since the last one," Rory said. "They're getting bored."

"Maybe."

"They wanted to see you lash out. You're not playing ball." Rory wrote an imaginary note. " 'Doesn't play well with others.' "

In the aftermath of Thomas's death, the Badgett case had led to a number of officers being arrested around the state. In her own shop, there were deputies who blamed Jace. She'd been yelled at, threatened, spit at, and twice physically attacked by some of the very officers with whom she worked. At first, in the days after the arrests, the hangman flyers—and worse—had come every day, carefully shoved through the lower air vent in her locker and decorated with full color pictures of dead rats and children killed by pedophiles and sometimes a Photoshopped version of her, dead and bloody.

"Troglodytes."

Jace blinked in surprise. "Troglodytes?"

"Cave dweller? Mouth breather?"

"I know what it is. I'm just surprised you know. That's a three-syllable word."

"Yeah, well, troglodytes—" Rory counted syllables on her fingers. "Don't scare me."

While they talked, Jimmson came over, his face flushed a serene red with a nicotine-stained, yellow-toothed smile in the middle of it. His breath was long and deep.

"Any fun?" Rory asked.

"You betcha. But we got him down pretty quick. He was all mouth. Didn't want to play."

"Deputy get hurt?" Rory asked.

Jimmson grunted. "Croft? No. I'll never understand why he wanted to be a deputy. Scared to death of everything. Can't do shit by himself. He hates everything about the job."

"Doesn't hate the badge. The badge is what it's all about."

"Yeah, I guess. No, he didn't get hurt, God knows how. Neither did Doc Wrubel. The guy—Mercer—was pissed in a big way, though. Needed some asthma meds and Wrubel said no. Hadn't been approved yet." Jimmson shrugged. "Mercer never hit anybody. Pushed the computer off the counter. Broke a stethoscope, too. Wrubel was talking to him and probably would'a had the guy talked down. Croft panicked, but it broke up the night for us, didn't it?"

Swallowing, Jace asked, "What'd you do with him?"

"Medical holding, at least until tomorrow morning. Cruz will decide where he goes. Didn't have to strap him down or anything. Once we got him on the ground, he was fine. He even thanked us for not hurting him."

When the ERTs entered a pod, everyone went hard to the floor—guard, inmate, visitor—and were held there until the ERT commander sorted out the situation.

"Because of meds." Jace shook her head.

"You know how it works," Rory said. "Might not be pretty, but that's how it is."

"I know, but come on. Asthma meds?"

"Cruz is a control junkie." Jimmson squeezed his legs together. "Has to approve everything."

"It's a harsh methodology," Cruz had once told Jace. "It is how we have to do things. Think of it this way: if the clients have been taking their prescriptions, then those drugs will still be in their system and they can afford to miss a day or two, and anyway, so many of our clients bond out within two or three days. Now, if the clients haven't been taking their prescriptions, maybe they don't like the side effects and I will not force anyone

31

to take medication if the situation isn't life-threatening. Or maybe they can't afford them and want the county to pay for it."

"Man, I'd hate to get sick up in here." Rory shook her head.

"Rules is rules, Rory-Bory." Jimmson had about a decade behind the badge. He winked at them. "You look unhappy with that, Jace, but do you wanna be on the hook for making medical decisions? Hell, no. I love having medical staff. Hand the inmate over and let those guys deal with it."

"Still, that's gotta suck if your head's banging around," Rory said.

"Yeah." Jimmson squeezed his legs together. "Gotta run. Excitement always makes me want to pee."

"Better stay away from sex, then." Rory laughed.

"I'm married; sex is dead to me."

Jace sat behind her computer, punched up an internet radio station, and found Miles Davis. *"Kind of Blue,"* she said to Rory's blank stare. "Don't worry, I'll teach you."

"Ain't interested."

Jace grinned. Rory said jazz wasn't her thing but she was slowly coming over.

"You know, I'd bet even money half the ERT calls are for medical."

Jace shook her head. "He ought to be able to get asthma medicine."

"I know. But jail medical problems are contagious; you've been here long enough to see that. One inmate needs an inhaler and suddenly everyone does. One inmate needs antibiotics and suddenly everyone does. Doesn't matter what it is, everyone catches it."

Jace and Rory had become pretty good friends over the last few months, but there were still aspects of working in a jail, a job that warehoused human beings, that offended her. "Some people really need those things. They're not all looking to trade or sell."

Rory grinned. "You see who was last through the door going in?"

"Yep."

"And first coming out?"

"Yep."

Laughing, they whispered at the same time, "Laimo."

Rory tore open a package of Skittles and held it out to Jace. "Wanna eata?"

"Passa thanka."

Rory popped a handful into her mouth. "Mmmm . . . all the deliciousness of high-fructose corn syrup."

"Whatever, Etta."

Rory cocked her head. "Huh?"

Jace laughed. "Nothing."

Eventually the clock rolled past three a.m. Jace waited for arrestees who never arrived and played more music, alternating between jazz for herself and classical for Rory. The other deputies tried to stay awake or at least not sleep too obviously, some of them occasionally humming a Christmas carol. Laimo worked on her nail polish and let her head loll against the wall. Jimmson worked on one of his new radio-controlled airplanes and slowly built from pieces to plane. Kleopping was intent on his schoolwork—a master's in criminal justice. Someday, he wanted to be sheriff. There was little noise beyond the music Jace and Rory played. The entire booking area had gone silent, a cemetery encased in concrete walls and metal furnishings bolted to those walls.

Into the blanket of silence snapped the electric lock of the door leading directly to the medical pod. A youngish man, call him late thirties, came in.

"Dr. Wrubel," Kleopping said.

Rory looked up, curiosity ripe on her face.

Wrubel, the assistant doctor who worked mostly overnights, had a short conversation with Kleopping, both faces locked in tight smiles. Eventually, they shook hands and Wrubel headed back to medical. When he caught Rory's gaze, he altered his path.

"Jailer."

"Quack."

He tossed her a small bag of Skittles. "Thanks for last week. And Merry Christmas."

She eyed the Skittles suspiciously. "These are full strength, right? Not like the drugs you sell on the side."

"Shut up," he said with a laugh.

"Last week?" Jace asked.

"Quack here was handing out meds that weren't working. Had himself a hard time with two or three johnnies." Rory puffed her chest out. "I had to save the day for him."

"Yeah, *that's* how it happened." Wrubel shook his head. "Bad drugs. Or people have tolerances built up or whatever. Happens sometimes. Give them to the patients and they don't do anything. At least with the heroin withdrawals, it's not about the drugs." His voice deepened in imitation of Dr. Cruz. " 'Cold turkey and aspirin. Maybe some soup if they can keep it down. That, Dr. Wrubel, is the Cruz Medical protocol for heroin withdrawal.' "

"A little dope-sick spiritual medicine," Rory said.

Wrubel shrugged. "Well, it's inexpensive and it teaches a moderately painful lesson. Always looking to save money and teach lessons."

"So . . ." Rory jerked a thumb toward medical.

"Mercer wanted his asthma inhaler." He shrugged at Jace's blank look. "Hasn't been approved. I'm sure it will be tomorrow morning."

"But you're a doctor," Jace said. "Do it now."

"I'm also an employee of Cruz Medical and we do things a certain way."

"Don't sweat Cruz," said Rory. "With any luck, he'll get himself a pile of new state contracts, make millions, and be out of our hair. Pretty soon, too, I betcha. He had another tour tonight. He canceled it when everybody got rolled by hookers."

Wrubel's eyes grew wide. "What?"

"No, they didn't," Jace said. "They did get drunk, though. Hey, Mercer said doctors were selling drugs to johnnies."

Wrubel licked his lips. "Guess I missed that. Just a pissed-off inmate. All kinds of crap comes out of their mouths."

"Had a pissed-off johnny give me winning lotto numbers one time. Except they were letters. *K. I. S. S. M. Y. A. S. S.*" Rory laughed. "Anyway, maybe you'll get lucky and get to be head quack around here when Cruz's new contract goes through."

"Maybe. He and I talked about it a few months ago but he won't say much now—said he didn't want to jinx the whole thing—but he's pretty upbeat." Wrubel shook his head. "Ought to be. He gets the contracts he wants? Millions. Won't be doctoring much after that . . . take too much time to count all his money." He took a deep breath.

"Quack? You okay?"

He shrugged. "Nothing. You know . . . contracts and whatever. A little fear of the unknown, I guess."

"Contracts won't have anything to do with you, will they?"

"Not directly, no, but if Cruz Medical grows, it'll breed bureaucracy, you know? That's why I left the UT medical system. Too much paperwork, not enough doctoring. Don't get me wrong—Cruz is great at corporate leadership. I just don't want to be part of a giant corporation."

"Not smart enough?"

"Hah. Exactly. I've got a friend in town and all he does is

family medicine. Doesn't even always get paid. Sometimes they pay in fresh eggs or fresh ham or whatever."

Rory cocked her head. "Sooooo . . . about ninety billion years of medical school for . . . breakfast?"

"Tough to pay off student loans that way, I'd think," Jace said.

Wrubel dropped his voice. "No student loans . . . didn't actually go to med school." He flopped his stethoscope around. "Not even real. It squirts water."

The grin went out of his voice and eyes quickly, and he took a deep breath. "ERTs shook me up, I guess."

That's not it, Jace realized. His face belied his words. His hands played at the corner of the booking desk and he continually licked his teeth.

"Anyway, thanks for last week."

"Later, Sawbones."

"Later, Warden."

He disappeared back into medical and the door closed behind him like a metallic fist.

From across booking, Kleopping whistled to get everyone's attention. "Doc Wrubel said thanks. Said you guys did a great job. Jimmson, you got a special Merry Christmas thanks from the inmate. Said thanks for not cracking his skull."

"I'd'a cracked his skull." Laimo sniffed.

"Hard to do from the back of the line." Jimmson never looked up from his plane.

"Cruz will want the report first thing this morning so get it done, Laimo."

When Rory saw Laimo headed for her computer, she lingered.

"Move," Laimo said. "Some of us have real police work to do."

"Shouldn't take too long." Rory kept her voice low. " 'Dear Diary, I was the last one in and the first one out. I did nothing

36

and helped no one, but don't I look good in my black uniform.' "

Laimo's eyes flashed and her nose flared. She stood, her hands clenched, and waited for Rory to move. Eventually, Rory did, joining Jace against the wall.

Viciously, Laimo snapped off Jace's jazz and began pounding on the keys.

"Okay." Badge 429 took a deep breath. "So our two girls are speeding down the road."

Rory groaned. "Man, I thought we were done with this."

"What the hell is this guy's name?" Kleopping asked. "Does anyone actually know him?"

The guy colored. "I'm Travis. Stokeley? That's not funny."

Rory nodded. "Yeah, it is."

"So anyway, these chicks are flying. 80 . . . 90 miles an hour. There's a brunette driving. She says to her blonde friend, 'Do you see any cops following us?' The blonde turns and looks and says, 'Yeah. He's coming up fast.' So our driver says, 'I can't afford another ticket. Are his red and blue flashing lights on?' The blonde says, 'Yes . . . no . . . yes . . . no . . . yes . . .' "

Everyone laughed but beneath it, Jace caught Laimo's glare and it left her with the impression she and Rory had just been put on a list. Jace tried to look casual and easy in her own skin.

"By the way." Jace edged a bit closer to Rory. "Troglodytes don't scare me, either . . . much."

CHAPTER 3

On shift the next night, Christmas night, Deputy Jose Urrea
kept his hard, brown eyes on Jace. His forehead crinkled like
the skin of a pea while the fingers of his right hand played at a
scar just under his lip. The man stood about six foot two and he
carried that bulk effortlessly. He walked toward her easily, with
just a bit of street rolling through his hips.

"What's the problem, *chiquita?*" His voice was low so that
only they could hear.

Jace stood behind the jailer's desk in B Pod. It was tonight's
assignment and so far, it had been quiet, though they were
moving a little slow locking down the lower tier of prisoners.
"What makes you think I have a problem?"

Urrea chuckled. "Moving slow like my old Gramps. Got some
heavy-duty bags under your eyes. You really tired or maybe you
smoked up some *mota.*"

"*Mota?*"

"The sacred herb. If you sucked down a blunt, I won't tell
. . . the Lord above knows we all need some every now and
then, but you drop dirty and you will have a problem."

"So . . . can I buy some of your piss? I assume it's clean."

"Clean as a whistle . . . at least that's what my supplier says.
And for you? I'll sell it wholesale."

"Don't want to line your pockets at co-workers' expense?"

"Line my pockets? I'm barely paying my bills. Mom can't
work anymore and my bro lost his job a couple months ago."

He pantomimed tightening his belt. "Getting scary at the Urrea household."

"Damn, I'm sorry to hear that. Have to increase your piss sales, I guess."

"So how much can I put you down for?"

"No *mota* for me, Urrea."

"No? Or no *mas*?"

She stared at him. "My particular vice doesn't run to weeds."

Near the stairs, where a handful of inmates paid half-hearted attention to the TV, one inmate stared from inside his cell with a goofy grin on his thin lips. *What do you want, buddy,* Jace wondered. But even as she thought it, her gaze moved to the upper tier, which was already locked down for the night. After a few seconds, she looked back at the inmate's cell. His name was Anthony Tate and he now sat regally on the stainless-steel toilet with his jail-issue orange pants at his ankles. His eyes laughed at her before going back to his comic book.

In spite of the embarrassment of seeing a man on the toilet, Jace felt a swell in her chest. *I'm catching the signs,* she thought. A few months on the job and, just like Rory said would happen, she was beginning to notice the little things. In this case, it was an inmate who'd never given her a moment's thought who had suddenly decided to favor her with a sloppy grin.

Dillon called them "curiosity ticklers" but Rory called them "hot spots." "See, I used to have a dog," she'd said once, "and this mutt would lick and lick and lick until he had a hot spot. Then Mom and I would have to get some medicine and put it on his paws and watch him so it would heal. Huge pain in the butt. But I got to where I could spot the difference between regular licking and hot-spot licking."

"Regular licking?" Jace had asked.

Rory had colored a deep red. "Yeah, you know, regular lick-ing . . . the fun kind. Anyway, if I saw the hot-spot licking I could do something about it before it happened."

Recognize those jail hot spots, Rory believed, and a jailer would be able to solve most of the small problems before they became big problems.

The hot spot now was that he was off the toilet, pants hitched at his waist, comic book gripped tightly, but Jace hadn't heard a flush. These toilets, built to withstand riots and fires and endless attempts to take them apart for escape or weapons or boredom, flushed with the fury of an artillery barrage.

Urrea came up behind her. "What's your vice, then, it ain't weeds?"

"Corona and Daniel's. Barbeque."

"I dig it. Maybe we'll scrape us up some sometime."

A bit of heat washed into her face. "Bed?"

"Well, I'm not sure we know each other well enough, but I'm up for it."

"The inmates, you ass."

He frowned. "Hmmm . . . all those inmates be a lotta people in the bed, but I'll try anything once. We can film it and put it on the internet and make millions."

Jace laughed and headed for the cells. Within a few minutes, nearly all the lower tier inmates were in for the night. A few doors had already closed, pulled by the inmates, while a few others were still open. As they did every night, a few inmates joked with her. A few gave her polite good nights, a few others mumbled. Initially, those mumbles had scared her, but now she ignored them. Inmates who wanted to hurt a guard wouldn't mumble about it, they'd just get to the hurting.

Jace closed and yanked on every door because sometimes the inmates stuck a playing card between the door and frame and the door only appeared locked. The computer that controlled the door locks always caught an open door but even if it didn't, there was nowhere for the inmate to go. There were two secured doors just to get out of the pod, countless more secured doors between the hallways and the World. Besides, the jailers didn't leave the pod after lockdown. Any inmate who was outside his cell after lockdown found, rather than freedom, the discipline pod.

Well, the master of his ship, even he stuck in the middle of the ocean and cain't do not but sail . . . he still the master of his ship.

Preacher used to say that, about Jace's mother. Maybe, in the jail, it was exactly that simple.

About halfway down the tier, the inmate who'd been on the toilet stepped from his cell into the pod, shirtless, his arms flexed like a body builder. Jace thought she smelled a bit of burned cannabis coming out of his cell.

"Wanna go to a gun show?" He flexed his biceps again.

"They have shows for BB guns, Tate?"

The man's face, his eyes red and almost sleepy-looking, broke apart in surprise. "What?"

As soon as she said it, she was angry with herself. She wasn't a jailer who casually tossed insults at inmates or who routinely verbally abused them. Treating them that way, she believed, would boomerang back someday.

She shook her head in an unspoken apology. "Come on, Tate, get in the cell."

His arms came down. "The fuck is your problem?"

Can't just recognize hot spots, Jace, have to not cause them.

This particular hot spot, growing hotter by the moment, she had absolutely caused.

Her voice cool and calm, Jace put a step or two of distance between them. She kept her eyes on Tate, rather than showing weakness by looking for Urrea. "It's too late at night for whatever this is going to be. Let's just call it good and everyone walks away."

"Walk this away, bitch."

It happened quickly, but later Jace would revel in knowing that she'd seen it coming. She didn't see it soon enough, but she did see it. Tate rocked back on his right foot and jerked something from behind his back. In a single, quick motion, he drew back and threw it.

She was unafraid, which surprised her.

That's his T-shirt.

This was the inmate who hadn't flushed and now that shirt, soaked in urine and feces, flew right at Jace, but hit Urrea when he stepped in. A thick, wet plop.

"Son of a bitch." His voice was a bellow. He fell backward away from them, the shirt and the feces plastered to his face and chest.

Jace moved instantly into Tate's laugh. She grabbed the guy's right arm, still extended from the throw, pivoted to her left, and used his momentum to spin him all the way around until he was facing his cell. As Tate stumbled, she planted a foot squarely against his butt and shoved him into the cell. He crashed to the floor while she calmly closed his door and pulled it twice to make sure it was locked.

Urrea stood there, the shirt on the floor, the stain and stink of it all over him. "Oh, man, this is bullshit."

"Well, some kind of . . . anyway." She didn't want to laugh, but once it got started, it was impossible to stop.

"Wha'choo laughing at?"

"Pretty funny, boss."

Urrea glared into the inmate's cell window, then walked away. "Yeah, funnier for you than me."

"Well, like Shelby said, 'True, that.' "

A half hour later, Urrea had showered and changed. Both of them sat staring absently at the pod TV. On it, a man pleaded with them to send money. For $19.95, plus shipping and handling, they would get not one, but four buckets of cleaning solution, guaranteed to clean anything anywhere anytime.

"Hah. A little late." Urrea grinned.

Jose Urrea had stepped in and taken that hit. For her. Early on, just after the officer arrests, he had shunned her. Lately, the color of his clouds had changed. They'd been tinged with purple and edged in the scarlet of anger, but now were shades of a soft blue.

"I guess I'm buying the Corona, Jack, and barbeque for a while, huh?"

After a long moment, during which he sniffed himself intensely, he chuckled. "True, that. But when I can afford to, I'm buying at least one round."

"Why's that?"

His laugh slipped into a darker, edgier place. "You faced off that freakin' cow."

" 'Freakin' cow'? Is that an idiomatic Spanish expression? Castilian, perhaps?"

"Idio—? What? No, hell, no, I'm from Texas." He frowned. "Wha'choo talking about? I mean Laimo. You didn't even care who she is."

"Who is she?"

"Major Jakob's daughter."

The woman in charge of the crime lab; third or fourth in command of the entire sheriff's office. "Crime lab is under operations . . . the road deputies."

"*Sí.*"

"Well, that was stupid on my part, huh? For career advancement." Not that Jace had any inclinations toward working the road.

"Might have—"

—*control lockdown . . . lockdown*—

Conroy's voice tripped over its own fear and half a second later, as though Conroy had actually been paying attention, the general alarm exploded to life. That same shrill, piercing sound that Jace hated. Her heart jumped into her throat as she jumped out of the chair, and her skin heated to a white-hot laser. Her eyes snapped almost automatically to the second tier and then down to Urrea.

"They're all locked up." He spoke gently. "It's not this pod. We're good; you saw to that."

"And if I got it wrong?"

"You didn't. I trust you completely."

—*zebra 4. Control, it's a zebra 4. Get a bus rolling. Now*—

Jace's teeth came down hard on her tongue. Zebra 4 was a facility security breach. A bus was an ambulance. Something was terribly wrong.

—*all call from control: lockdown. Facility lockdown*—

—*A Pod locked*—

Urrea nodded and she keyed her mic as she took a sweeping look at all one hundred cell doors in the pod, then double-checked on the computer. Green lights, locked doors, across the board. "B Pod locked."

—*locked in D*—

—*E Pod locked*—

—*Females locked*—

The voices over the radio were concerned but efficient, each one quick on the heels of the previous one but waiting until it was their turn. Except now there was a break in rotation. Medical didn't report and Jace's breath froze.

—*medical?*—

Still nothing and Jace's breath burst raggedly from her nose. She took a few steps toward the pod's inner door. "Something's wrong. Something's—"

"Take it easy."

—*medical locked*—

But there was something unsaid, something left out, a lie by omission by the officer in medical. Jace heard it in the hesitation.

—*Ad-seg locked*—

—*booking only one prisoner, she's in holding*—

—*kitchen empty*—

Conroy's voice bellowed from the control room.

—*medical?*—

There was a short pause.

—*Dr. Wrubel is not in medical. Repeat . . . Dr. Wrubel is on premises*—

—*zebra 4 at B Pod. 248 on scene. One from B Pod, one from A Pod*—

Her head and Urrea's swiveled toward B Pod's main doors. Whatever the situation, it was right outside those doors.

"Go."

"But—"

"You've got it. You know what to do."

"I don't."

Urrea smiled, gently and genuinely. "Trust yourself, Salome. Trust me that I know what I'm doing to send you. Go help Doc Wrubel. He's a good man. He's one of us."

Jace ran toward the inner door. Before she got there, the electric lock snapped. She bolted through and the outer door opened before the inner had closed completely.

"Sheriff Jace?" The trusty stood near the wall, just outside the B Pod outer door, holding a mop and pale as lace. "What's going on?"

"Inmate Bobby. What the hell are you doing out?"

He raised his mop. "Every night, you know that."

"Did you see it?" Her mind raced, faster than what she could understand. What should she do? What would Rory do? What the hell had happened? "Who else was here? Out here in the hallway?"

45

"Nobody, Sheriff Jace."

"Nobody passed you? No one at all?"

"No, Sheriff Jace. I came from around that corner." He pointed toward the distant main hallway.

"Damn it, stop calling me that. It's Deputy Salome. Who did this?" Her head seized on the empty hallway, filled with only one person. "Did you do this?"

"Me?" Inmate Bobby swallowed. "No, I didn't even know him."

Jace shook her head. "Damn it. Get in the go-between and don't move." Jace radioed for the go-between. When it popped, the trusty went inside and the door closed hard behind him.

Forty feet away lay Doc Wrubel. Blood pooled around him and Jace wondered how it could seem so tender, as though it were nothing more than a sanguine halo radiating from his chest and shoulders to above his head. Both eyes were open but, thankfully, neither of them saw Jace.

And the alarm clanged on and on.

CHAPTER 4

There was so much blood.

As endless as the screaming alarm.

When Jace was young, a radio man had lived at the Sea Spray Inn. Bruce Haden had wanted to be a world famous jock, but eventually had settled into the skin of a newsman. By the time he was 35, he'd been hired by a local AM station, a 50,000-watt behemoth whose news department had never been out of contention for best in the region and top ten across the state. He'd been offered the city-council meetings, meetings of the school boards, the hospital or parks-district board meetings, all of which were safe, easy-to-cover beats that had semi-regular hours.

But those weren't the beats he wanted.

He'd grown up poor on Zach City's south side and had seen more than his share of cops slamming into neighborhoods with sirens wailing, red and blue lights beating the darkness into submission. They came for domestic batteries, knifings at the nearby bars, raids on bathtub gin distillers, murders, suicides, robberies and burglaries, raids on shooting galleries, all manner of depravity. As a young girl, Jace had loved listening to Haden's stories of crimes and criminals. She loved the sheer number of people he'd met and interviewed and—when a freakish blast of summer rainstorms caused massive flash flooding—his stories of helping get people into boats and out of flooded homes.

Long after Mama had been killed by a drunk driver in Lubbock, Haden had played babysitter for Jace. On that Saturday night, Haden had been called out for a train that had slammed into an old station wagon and killed all four teenaged passengers. With no one to watch over Jace, Haden had taken her. His voice shaky with what she now understood as fear, he'd told her to stay in the car and at first she had. But curiosity, stoked by the storm of blue and red flashing lights and uniformed officers and paramedics and official-looking men and women with sleep heavy on their faces, had forced her out of the car. She had wanted to see the accident and smell the carnage and feel the tragedy.

The car had been a mangled, two-piece disaster. Part of it had lain near the point of impact. Another part was impaled on the front of the train. Other bits and pieces were scattered throughout the empty field, and fluids—oil, gas, transmission fluid, radiator fluid, the beer that had been in the cooler—covered everything.

All kinds of fluids but no blood. Nor any bodies.

Was that how it was when Mama was killed? Had the drunk been going fast like the train and smashed Mama so hard her body was flung into nothingness?

Later, Haden said the scene had been covered with blood and body parts. He'd told her she'd willfully not seen it. Jace had thought about that over the years. Maybe Haden was right. Maybe, in those dead teenagers turned into jigsaw puzzles, Jace had seen Mama and so blocked out everything. Maybe, if memory made the train crash as bloodless and antiseptic as possible, it would somehow lessen the pain of Mama getting hit by a drunk who, when caught miles down the road, casually told officers he'd hit a deer somewhere back up the road.

How far did you crawl, Mama? Did you a find a creek and, in an attempt to cool the blast furnace of pain, slip in? Or maybe you found a pile of fallen trees and, in a moment of mindless desperation, burrowed beneath it.

Either way, Mama was gone and a few years later, Bruce Haden was, too. He had moved on to local television news and died in a helicopter crash while heading back to the station after filing a story about cattle rustling from deep in the Zachary County hinterlands.

Now Doc Wrubel was dead and for a split second, Jace thought there was no blood, just as there hadn't been with the teenagers and the train.

Jace was third on the scene, just behind Laimo and the road deputy who'd stumbled across Wrubel's body. That deputy, name of Craig something, bellowed into his radio to get the bus here and get it here now.

But it was over and all of them knew it. Jace had no idea about the injuries, but she saw his empty eyes. Glassy and shocked as though he wanted to ask, "How did this happen? Haven't I been a good man? How did I die here, on this stained concrete floor?"

Jace keyed her radio. "Control, can we get the alarm off?" The sound slashed at her brain.

Laimo said, "And a detective."

The road deputy nodded. "And whatever command staff is here."

The alarm died with a thundering reverberation.

—Adam 1 is on his way. So is Major Jakob . . . she was in the building—

The deputy moved Laimo and Jace both backward a bit. "Mark it off from A Pod to D Pod, then get on the other side of those lines. You—" he pointed at Laimo, "at D Pod, and you at A Pod. No one gets past those lines unless they're paramedics, administration, detective, or lab rat. Keep a list of who does go in, what time they went in, and what time they came out."

Laimo stared at the road deputy. "The hell you think you are?"

The roadie nodded. "Sure, whatever you want. Your jail, your problem." He waved and stepped over Wrubel's body. "Enjoy."

Panic exploded on Laimo's face but was gone quickly, buried beneath a shrug. "Your name's already on it. First on scene, your scene to handle. I'm just assisting. I better not get bogged down in whatever shitstorm this is going to be."

"Whoa," the deputy said. "Don't knock me over with that ambition."

Jace stared at Laimo, completely unsurprised. This was a new version of her being last one in and first one out when the ERTs hit medical the previous night.

"Assist your ass to D Pod. And you get to A Pod."

Jace nodded, her throat as dry as a concrete sidewalk during high summer, while the rest of her body swam in sweat. *This isn't happening, not again. There can't be another dead man in this jail. Not while I'm on duty.*

"Asshole." But Laimo's tone was small and hinted at some inner fear.

Good. I don't want to be the only one scared to death.

"Do we—" Jace wiped her lips with the back of her hand. "Do we stay when the detectives get there?"

The road deputy shrugged. "Who knows what they'll want. They'll tell you. Get to it."

Walking away, Laimo hollered at Jace. "Nobody ever died here until you showed up."

The deputy's eyes snapped toward Laimo. "Shut the hell up before I put you back in the middle of all this." His eyes, as deep as silver alloy, pummeled her.

Jace opened her mouth but he held up a silencing finger. When Laimo was near D Pod, he shook his head but offered that same evil grin. "She's an idiot and tramping through the blood will put her deep in this scene, regardless of where she's posted."

On the floor, weaving in and out of the colored stripes that led to various pods, there was the heel half of a left-shoe print, then a gap, then another left-shoe print, all leading toward D Pod. "Don't let her get under your skin, Salome. Some people need to crap on everyone around them so they lose the smell of their own stink." He pointed toward A Pod. "Now get down there and remember, write down everyone's name and their times by the clocks on the wall."

Jace swallowed. "Cataloging scene access?"

"Yeah. Some dumbass who believes his or her badge gives access to everything is going to drop by for a look-see. Your job is to keep the scene as clean as possible."

He was right. In her short time in the jail, she'd handled a few scenes that had attracted jailers and more than a few road guys and even a lab wonk or two. There had been a couple of beatings, a horribly bloody female on female rape, and a home-brew booze experiment that went devastatingly awry when the hooch exploded and burned the inmate over three-quarters of his body. At every one of those scenes, small crowds had appeared as though summoned by some quiet god of chaos who pointed the way to carnage.

"I don't even smoke and I could use one of Laimo's cigarettes," Jace said.

He chuckled. "Control access, save the scene, let the detectives notice. They won't say anything but they know who is who in the department. Or when they come to you breathing fire about a scene so messed up they can't pull any evidence, you'll hand them the names and be done." He winked. "Plus? Cops don't usually want their names written down anywhere so they'll move along." He thought for a moment, then offered his hand. "By the way, I'm Ezell, Craig Ezell."

She shook. "Jace Salome." She took a deep breath. "Doc doesn't need an ambulance."

"No." Ezell keyed his radio. "Control. 10-22 the bus."

—say again—

"Disregard on the ambulance. 10-79 instead."

—10-4—

10-79 . . . the JP.

"Damn." Jace made sure she didn't step in the blood—from Wrubel, from the teenagers laughing in the Rambler just before the train struck, or from Mama—and headed for A Pod.

CHAPTER 5

The main hallway at the Zach County jail was scarred; a hard skin broken by the violence of men and women.

Most of the beige paint had long ago been flayed from the walls. What was left had been dulled to a matte smear by time and the press of bodies. Just below an average man's waist, the paint had been scuffed and broken by shoes, duty boots, hand trucks, and all manner of items. Above the waist, the paint was marred by the reach of batons once used against unruly inmates or by the metal of locked handcuffs banged against the wall by bored inmates. Occasionally, the concrete itself was scarred. Regardless of how hard that skin was, the inmates and cops who sometimes fought against each other believed themselves harder.

Hard boot falls sounded, carried and amplified, like the house trio at a small jazz club, by the concrete. When Jace heard them, something deep inside her tightened. The road deputy, Craig Ezell, gestured at her to calm down, though he took a deep breath and smoothed out the lines in his uniform shirt.

Sheriff James Bukowski came around the corner, his face lined with the mileage of too many years behind a badge. An unlit cigar hung from a corner of his mouth. "Salome." It was a pitbull bark. "What'd you do this time?"

In one of their first meetings, he'd lit up a cigar in the jail and then ordered her to write him a ticket. That he did, just because it gave him a laugh, made her uneasy. But he'd also shown her the thin investigative file from the Lubbock County sheriff's office about her mother's death. So while he made her nervous, he also comforted her in a way she couldn't quite define.

He was a tall man, better than six feet, and carried his weight easily. He looked wiry, almost thin, but she'd heard he was hell on wheels in a fight. His conversation was normally peppered with profanities but also long silences. His eyes were dark, his hair salt and pepper with more pepper every day. Worn, black jeans hung easily on his hips, as though denim and man were comfortable with each other, while his black shirt, new with *Zach County SO* embroidered over the left breast, seemed stiff and uncomfortable. His boots, like always, were jet black. Black was his favorite color.

"The man in black."

He chewed on his cigar. "The one about the suspect falling down the stairs was funny."

Jace frowned, confused, until she remembered Urrea's joke. "Yes, sir."

"You tell one?"

"Couldn't think of one."

"Uh-huh. Let me know when you do."

"It'll probably be about an insomniac sheriff who wanders the halls of his own jail at all hours of the night."

"Yeah . . . that shit ain't no joke." He craned his head to see around her to the dead man. "You see it?"

Like you did last time, he left unsaid.

"No, sir."

With a nod, he raised the crime scene tape again and stepped through. She checked the time on the wall clock and scribbled it down on her paper. Next to that, she wrote the sheriff's name and badge number, and noted that he was going into the scene rather than coming out.

From a good distance back, he looked the scene over for a few minutes, his cigar clamped tightly between his lips. Jace saw his head specifically follow Laimo's bloody footprints to Laimo, then back to Wrubel's body. He leaned against the wall, as she saw him do so often in the early hours of the mornings, when his insomnia had the better of him and there was no relief save for the halls and the thump of his boots against the floors. His head up toward the ceiling, he took a deep breath. His lips moved, but he was silent. Finally, he heaved himself from the wall.

"The bloody footprints?"

Jace swallowed. "Uh . . . yes, sir?"

"Not yours."

Going the other way, Jace almost said. "No, sir."

"She's an idiot." He shook his head. "Shouldn't'a said that. Forget it. She's not an idiot, she just . . . well . . . I don't know."

"She's cruel, Sheriff." Jace stared straight at him. "She laughs at weaker people. She takes glee in people hurting. I'll never understand that kind of person."

The old man eyed her. "Maybe she covers her fear in cruelty."

Jace shook her head.

"Tell you a story . . . when I started out? Scared to death. So I laughed at people all the time. Made me a big man and put the fear a little further away." He stopped, pulled a bit of tobacco off his tongue and flicked it to the floor. "Later when I got tough, I just beat on people instead of laughing."

The sheriff let that hang between them, a bloody carcass dangling by a butcher's hook. Eventually, he shrugged and said, "We all have our own ways of coping, I guess."

"That'll never be me."

"Yeah? You better than me, Deputy?"

"No, sir, I'm not saying that. I'm saying I won't be her. I will never laugh at someone who's weaker than me just *because* they're weaker than me."

He stared at her for a long minute, his eyes hard and narrow. His lips cracked a tiny smile. "See that you don't."

"Good thing that cigar's not lit, Sheriff," she said as he walked away.

He snorted. "Get another ticket. I gotta be written up." His boots echoed through the concrete hallway. "Suppose you wanna do that, too."

"If I'm not busy with something important . . . painting my toenails or something."

"Nice lip, Salome."

By the time Major Jakob, the major in charge of the crime lab, arrived fifteen minutes later, Jace had threatened to write down fourteen names: four jailers, seven road officers, and three random people whose job Jace had no clue about. All of them had slunk away but not before trying to peer around her to get a glimpse.

"You do the taping?" Jakob asked, running a finger along the yellow crime-scene tape.

"Yes, ma'am." Jace had strung the tape wall to wall just beyond the A Pod outer door before Bukowski arrived. It was a good forty feet from the body. Laimo had done the same on the far side, creating a zone empty of everything except the dead man and the road deputy.

"Good. Who are you?"

"Jace Salome."

Something flashed across Jakob's mild face. Frowning, suddenly feeling the paranoia of being a worm, Jace lifted the crime-scene tape for her.

"J-A-K-O-B. Lincoln 1."

Jace blinked. "Excuse me?"

"My name is spelled J-A-K-O-B; badge number Lincoln 1."

Jakob stopped about ten feet from Wrubel and spoke to Ezell

for a few minutes before dismissing him and then directing a trio of scene techs who'd arrived from the other direction. They became a sandstorm of activity. Flashbulbs exploded like heat lightning from deep inside that sandstorm and the thin, not-quite metallic snap of tape measures filled the hallway.

Her phone rang. "Salome."

"Hey, worm."

Jace breathed a sigh of relief. "Hey, sister. What's up?"

"Just wanted to tell you, we got another body in the jail. Dr. Cruz."

"It's not Cruz, Rory."

"Got it from a reliable source."

"Better pay your source more. It's Doc Wrubel."

"Doc? How do you know that?"

Jace wet her lips and turned away. A head popped around the corner up the hallway, but the officer didn't bother coming toward the scene. "Because I'm standing right here."

Rory's heavy breathing stopped. "No crap?"

"No crap."

"You do it?"

"Not funny."

Rory gave a half-chuckle. "Hah. It's damned funny but you won't realize it until tomorrow. You okay?"

"I guess." She licked her lips again, then wiped them off. "I mean—whatever. Yeah, I'm fine." *I've got as much steel as those lab techs who don't even seem to notice the dead man at their feet other than to mark and measure.*

"Jace?"

"Don't worry about it. It's my prob—"

Jakob's voice boomed down the hallway, but because of the echo, Jace had no idea what she had said. She looked and saw Jakob jabbing a finger at the bloody footprint. The techs hustled to photograph and log the prints.

"Wow. Who's that?"

"Major Jakob. She's running the scene. Laimo and me are doing scene access, if you can dig that, and Laimo screwed the pooch."

"Wait . . . Laimo screwed it up? That's almost hard to believe."

"Be nice."

"Uh . . . no?"

"Well, Laimo walked through the blood and carried it all the way down the hallway."

Rory laughed.

"First name I had to write down was Sheriff Bukowski's."

Rory's laugh boomed through the phone. "Holy hell, Jace, how the hell do you stumble into this crap?"

"If you can figure it out, I wish you'd tell me because I'd rather *not* stumble into this crap."

"Sounds like we're going to need a stress breakfast again."

"Long as you're buying."

"I ain't the worm."

"Jeez, already, how long am I the worm?"

"Until they hire someone new and you get some seniority."

"They've hired like . . . I don't know . . . five new jailers since I got here."

"Oh. Right. Forgot about that. Then forever, I guess. See ya at seven, worm."

Shoving her phone back into her pocket, Jace watched the techs work. They'd work until the justice of the peace got here, at which point he would do his thing and release the body. Then the techs would move back in and get back to evidence collection.

Urrea popped his head out of B-Pod's outer door. Just a tiny bit, just enough for her to see him. He pretended to take pictures, then rubbed his thumb and forefinger together: *Take pictures I can sell,* he was saying.

Jace ground her teeth until she heard her jaw pop. She pointed at Urrea and then at the murder scene. *This should be you,* the gesture said, *not me.*

"I'm just the worm," she mouthed.

"Exactly," he mouthed back.

CHAPTER 6

"You okay?"

"Not even close." She whirled on Rory. They were in the locker room, grabbing their personal gear before heading out. "And don't you ever, *ever* say no one will die in this jail. Ever again."

"Yes, ma'am." Rory looked toward the floor. "I'm really sorry about that."

"You should be. Damn it." She sat heavily on the bench, willing the tears not to come. Maybe Gramma was right; maybe this job was too much for her. Maybe Jace simply wasn't cut out for a job where people routinely died, where she routinely saw the anguish and despair of it.

"I know that look."

"Stop it." Jace closed her gym bag. "It's not any look and it doesn't mean anything."

"It is a look and it does mean something." Rory sat next to her. "Listen to me: This is a tough job, no shit about that. But you couldn't quit even if you wanted to. The sheriff already refused your resignation. What makes you think he'll take it now?"

"First of all, I wasn't thinking of resigning. Second of all, if I did want to resign, Sheriff Bukowski has no say over that; I'll just quit showing up and send all his gear back FedEx. Third of all . . ."

"Yeah?"

"It just . . . it scares me, okay?"

Rory gave her a quick hug. Her voice was as soft as a pleasant night. "I know. We're all scared sometimes."

"You?"

"Of course not." She tried an ill-fitting grin, then threw it away. "Don't quit, Jace. This is the greatest job in the world. The hardest, too, maybe. Don't quit yet. Next week, if you want, I'll write your resignation for you."

"You can't write."

"Fine. You write it and I'll bring the Skittles. Just promise me you won't quit this week; that's all I ask."

Jace nodded as a knock sounded on the locker-room door. "You guys decent?"

"Not a single day in our entire lives."

Dillon came in. "Always with the comedy jokes . . . and yet, hardly ever funny." He shook his head. "Jokes after a murder. We are twisted individuals, indeed." He looked at Jace. "Detective Von Holton wants to talk to you when you sign on tonight. First thing. But also, you need to come in an hour early. Mandatory debrief."

"With Von Holton?" Jace asked.

"With me. It'll be fine. Generally we did pretty good. Only one big problem."

Rory mimicked Laimo's walk through the bloody scene.

"Easy, Bogan," Dillon said.

She saluted. "Yes, sir."

"Who's Von Holton? I don't think I know him."

"A detective," Dillon said.

Rory looked at Dillon, then at Jace. "One of the flyer boys."

Jace ground her teeth.

"Flyer boys?" Dillon frowned. "That mean what I think it means?"

"Doesn't mean anything, Sergeant."

61

"Don't lie to me, Salome."

"I would never lie to you." She held three fingers up as though she were a Girl Scout. "Probably."

"Tonight," Dillon said again. "Hour early for debrief, then Von Holton, and if I find one of those flyers that you guys think is 'nothing,' I'll take care of the problem myself. You understand that?"

"Yes, sir."

After he left, Rory said, "I think you oughta kick his ass."

"Dillon's?"

"Von Holton's, dummy."

Jace tried to laugh it off. "Luckily, Miss Violence, I didn't ask you."

"Miss Violence? I like that. 'Today's contestants for Miss Universe include Miss Violence, well-schooled in the art of offensive defensiveness and more than willing to bring about world peace by kicking a two-by-four up your ass.' "

Jace chuckled. "I guess my question would be how does she look in heels and a ball gown?"

Rory struck a quick pose. "Marvelous, I'm sure."

"Ladies," someone said through the closed door. "Can I have a word?"

"The popularity of Miss Violence is overwhelming."

"Enter, if you dare." Rory's voice rang out, girlish and coy. "Oh, crap, Doctor. Sorry, we were just having a laugh. Just . . . Well, damn. I'm really sorry about Doc Wrubel."

Dr. Ernesto R. Cruz was just under six feet. Lean but decently muscled and always tan, as though the Texas sun, summer or winter, sought him out. "Me, too. He was a good man."

Until Dr. Cruz came along, the Zachary County sheriff's office had kept most medical in-house. They had a doctor with privileges at Zach City Memorial, but he wasn't on site and his usual treatment was to take the inmates straight to the hospital.

Dr. Cruz had convinced the county commissioners he could provide better and less expensive medical treatment. The Zachary County jail hadn't been Cruz Medical's first contract, but it had been their largest to that point. Cruz was a good doctor but an even better hand-shaker and his company now had contracts at jails throughout west Texas and eastern New Mexico. He still counted himself the head doctor in the Zach County jail, though his time in the facility had gone from forty hours per week to something closer to ten. That was the reason he'd hired Doc Wrubel.

Cruz's right hand curled around a manila folder with Wrubel's name at the top while his left thumb moved urgently from fingertip to fingertip and back again. After a moment, he offered Jace his left hand. "Deputy."

Jace shook the man's damp hand.

"You were there, right? You saw what happened?"

"No, sir. I heard the alarm and was directed to the scene. I saw Doc down and—"

"He was dead?"

Jace hesitated, uncomfortable beneath the man's penetrating eyes. "I'm not a doctor—"

"Sure, right, I know. But—" He stopped himself with a deep breath. "My apologies; I'm not doing this well. Doc Wrubel . . . Francis . . . Frankie . . . was my friend. I'm not asking for any medical distinction; I just want to know . . . if he was dead."

"Sir, yes, I believe he was. I'm sorry. I didn't know him very well, but he seemed like a decent man."

"Thank you for that; it is appreciated. And he was; for all his problems at the end, he was my friend and I'm heartsick over this. I know that sounds stupid."

"It doesn't sound stupid at all," Rory said.

"I controlled scene access on the A-Pod side. Major Jakob got there pretty quick with her guys and she dismissed me after the scene was processed."

Cruz nodded thoughtfully. "Okay. Thank you. I am so sorry you had to see something like that, Deputy. I know it's part of our job, but violent death is not the kind of thing you get comfortable with."

"Not even close," Rory said.

Cruz said, "What can you tell me about the incident with Mercer? The inmate? Were either of you on that detail?" His gaze, intense and troubled, scuttled back and forth between the women.

"We were working booking," Rory said. "We weren't in medical. We heard him yelling but didn't see—"

"He did it, didn't he?" Cruz interrupted her quietly, as though he didn't want to give voice to the thought. "Mercer killed Frankie because of that incident."

Jace shook her head. "I'm sure the detectives will look at him—"

"Damn it." The man clenched a fist. "I should have let him approve that inhaler. Frankie was an extraordinary doctor, deputies; he was more than capable of approving those. I had great plans for him when the new contracts get finalized. Supervising doctor at any jail he wanted. Or a regional supervising doctor if he wanted."

Jace frowned. "Dr. Wrubel wanted a bigger job?"

Cruz shook his head. "Not at all. He told me over drinks at a Zach JuCo basketball game last week that Cruz Medical was getting too big. Too corporate. He wanted to get back to pure medicine. That was my plan. I would take care of all the paperwork and regulatory garbage and he would do nothing but doctor. Heal the sick and hurt."

"That sounds exactly like him."

"Yeah." Cruz blew out a long, tired breath. "Damn, I'm going to miss him. He was a good man and a good doctor."

"Then why couldn't he approve the inhaler?" Jace asked. "Seems like that would have avoided the entire problem."

Cruz looked at Jace, his head cocked slightly. His left thumb, back and forth and back again over his fingertips, stopped suddenly. "That was my judgment. I am, ultimately, the man responsible for every medical decision; therefore we will proceed how I believe best." He lowered his head. "But also? Because I'm a control freak. These—" his arm swept the breadth of the jail. "Are my patients and I find it extremely difficult to give them to someone else's care. It took me three years to even decide to hire another doctor." A deep red flushed his cheeks. "I'm still working on letting go."

"Doc Wrubel said you guys had a difference of opinion on medical things," Rory said.

Surprised at Rory's disclosure, Jace kept her eyes on Cruz. The man nodded immediately.

"Sure. Ask any two doctors about a single issue and you'll get ten opinions. We all have huge egos and quite a bit of narcissism, and on a great many things we have a difference of methodology."

This time, Jace spoke up. "He also said you weren't getting along too well."

The man's eyes filled with hesitation. "Well, we'd go up and down, you know? Today, we hate each other. Yesterday, we were best buddies. Tomorrow, who knows? Nature of our relationship. We were still friends, though, don't doubt that. He's been to my house I don't even know how many times for dinner. Been to basketball games together and more than a few bars."

"But he had some problems lately?"

With a dismissive shake of his head, he said, "Nothing, Deputy Salome. Just adjusting badly to working overnights. That's a tough schedule. So . . . Mercer? That's our guy, right? Because of the inhaler?"

Jace hesitated, caught Rory's eye. Rory shook her head slightly.

"Well, like I was saying, I'm sure the detectives will want to—"

"Right, I know, but who would you arrest?"

"Well, I don't know if—"

"It's bad in most jails, deputies. Twenty years ago, just before I started working in jails, the smaller jails dealt with drunks and maybe the occasional pregnancy and sometimes bipolars or maybe a schizophrenic." He looked at the line of lockers along the wall. "It's every day anymore. Psychotics, paranoids, withdrawal from massive drug use, heart conditions from massive drug use, alcoholics, deliriums, STIs on an unimaginable scale." When he looked back at the women, his face seemed more haggard.

"Yet you keep working the jails," Jace said.

He smiled, half-embarrassed. "I do. Just because they're inmates doesn't mean they're not people. Some of them are bad and should be locked away forever, but some of them made a mistake and are just trying to get it back together. Unfortunately, the medical staff has been lied to so many times, we have to stick to the rules unless it's a life-threatening emergency, you know? A guy comes along and says he needs asthma medicine, but the catch is, he demands *his* medicine specifically. He'll say his doctor ordered it special or something. He doesn't want our meds. Why do you suppose that is?"

Rory snorted but it took Jace a second to see it. "Yours is the medicine it's supposed to be."

"And theirs frequently isn't. You're exactly right. It's one of the ways illegal drugs are smuggled into jails. Look, inmates are allowed—and I even encourage them—to bring their own meds. Saves us and Zach County money. Whatever they bring, we don't have to pay for. So we have protocols in place: has to be in a prescription bottle with the inmate's name on it, has to be current, has to have the doctor's name on it. We check all that stuff and check the pills in the bottle against the PDR, but sometimes illegal drugs make it inside. Brought by guards or officers, by administrators." He shrugged. "Even doctors and nurses, sometimes."

"Good money, though; all these county and city contracts? Sounds like some happy coin."

Cruz shook his head. "You've been listening to the wrong people, Bogan. Not anywhere near as much money as people think. Every agency I deal with believes they know better than me. They also believe I charge them too much when I'm cost cutting every day. I'm so close to the bone now I'm afraid the back of Cruz Medical's going to break. But the money's not why I do it. I do it because I'm a doctor. Just so happens I'm a good administrator. The more jails I can get under contract, the more people I can help." He glanced at his watch. "I'm bringing a few administrators through this afternoon. I'm pretty sure it's already a done deal, but they want to see systems in action."

As he spoke, Jace noticed his right hand for the first time. It was oddly misshapen, with at least three of the four fingers bent upward just a little. Cruz noticed her looking and held the hand up in front of his face.

"Childhood accident. With a car door. I don't remember much about it except it hurt like hell."

"I apologize for staring, Doctor; that was rude of—"

He waved it away. "I've come to grips with it, Deputy, trust me. It was a long time ago and I'm just fine." He touched the manila folder he carried. "Only have one of the initial reports, from a road deputy, and he obviously doesn't have any idea who might have killed Frankie."

"I have no idea about any of that. Like I said, I was ordered to—"

"Control access, yes, you said that. What I'm wondering is, what do you think? Mercer?"

"Ain't our gig, Doctor," Rory said, with just a hint of annoyance. "That's the detectives' thing. Mine and hers, right now, is to get some stress relief. I know that sounds awful, but that's what we do. Then, tonight, when we come on duty, we'll have to deal with Detective Von Holton so he can do his report and get a debrief about how the jailers handled it. But right now . . . we're done with a terrible shift and we'd like to go home."

Cruz blew a long, hot breath through his nose. "Right, right, I understand. Sorry about all the second degree, I just . . . There is no reason Frankie should be dead." He ran his bent fingers through his thinning hair as his brows knit in a tight frown. "God, sometimes I really hate this job. Sometimes I really do."

"I hear you," Rory said.

"Please," he said. "Do everything you can to help Detective Von Holton. I want to know who killed my friend."

"Absolutely," Rory said.

"Absolutely," he repeated as he walked away. His shoes clicked, then the sound disappeared when he slipped through the door.

"Seems nice enough," Jace said.

Rory shrugged. "He's always been kinda pushy, but I've never had a problem with him."

"He's pretty upset, though."

Rory fixed an eye on Jace. "That's some high-powered observational skill you got there, Worm."

"Years of practice. Someday, if you apply yourself, you might be—might be—this good."

"Call me Jace Junior. Hey, you're going to come with me to Rooster, right? To make the bust? Stop the van, make the bust? From Shelby's information?"

They headed down the hallway and were outside in just a few steps. Two incoming office staff wore Santa hats and Christmas sweaters.

"Merry Christmas," Rory said.

One guy flopped his hat. "You, too," the other said.

At their cars, Jace shook her head. "I appreciate the offer, but that's not my thing. I'm not interested and even if I were, I don't have the training."

Rory snorted. "Hah. Traffic stops are easy. I love 'em."

"Cops get killed on traffic stops."

"Not this cop. I love 'em; I could do 'em all day long. Look, I-20 runs right through Rooster. This'll be easy. "Jace opened her mouth to protest, but Rory waved it away. "Don't spoil my fun, Jace."

"Silly me, not wanting you to get killed."

"Good call, sister."

Jace climbed into her car. "You do what you want, but it's probably too dangerous to do alone. A highway stop, a drug dealer, and the information coming from a dealer who we know has a penchant for violence. Make sure you've got some backup."

"Penchant?"

"It means a taste for violence."

"Ah. Nice word." Rory winked. "So do I."

"That's what scares me."

CHAPTER 7

A half hour later, Jace and Rory strolled into Alley B's in sloppy jeans, T-shirts with the sheriff's office logo, and light coats.

Alley B eyed them. "I'm guessing you want one of your nasty breakfast sundaes. Your mamas wouldn't be happy 'bout your nutritional choices."

Rory snorted. "Mama's who taught me to drown the troubles of a shitty shift in ice cream."

"Nutritional choices?" Jace sniffed loudly and crinkled her nose at the fetid odor of greasy eggs and fatty bacon. "Are you sure that's the lecture you want to give?"

Alley B glared pleasantly. "Ain't nobody ever died in my place."

Rory pointed toward the parking lot. "They die out there. Why do you think there's always a tow truck lurking in your lot? Waiting to hook up a car for a grieving family."

Alley B chuckled. "Kiss my ass, bitches. And Merry Christmas."

Normally, Saturday morning crowds were thick but this was Christmas Day so there weren't many people, mostly the same single business people who drowned their lives beneath the weight of 24/7 business deals. They looked uncomfortable in their weekend attire, as though they weren't themselves unless clad in their tailored suits of armor. They jabbered away on cell phones or furiously tapped out text messages.

Within minutes, the ladies were deeply into their sundaes.

Vanilla ice cream and bananas, layered with fudge and nuts, whipped cream, and a handful of Skittles on Rory's. But the sundaes didn't come close to covering the taste of the night. They ate silently and when she was done, Jace stuck her spoon into the last of the banana. It stood straight up like a mythic sword stabbed challengingly into the dirt.

Alley B sidled up to them. "You guys okay?"

"Right as the rain." Jace nodded.

Alley B glanced out the window. "Rain? This is west Texas, honey; it don't rain here."

"Who's the new boy?" Rory asked, nodding toward a small boy behind the counter. "Looks like he's about twelve. You pick up some slave labor off of Craig's List or somewhere?"

"He's ten and he's my grandbaby. Thinks he wants to be a chef."

"So you hired him here?" Jace grinned. "You don't do any chef-ing here."

"Short order is still cooking."

"Well . . . sort of," Rory said.

Finished with her breakfast sundae, Rory tossed an eye toward the busboy. He zipped to the table and grabbed the empty bowl, but Rory held it tightly until he looked at her. "You tell your grandmother you need a raise."

His eyes brightened. "Yes, ma'am, but you know how she is." Then he dashed into the kitchen.

The ladies sat in silence awhile, as though each was afraid to broach the subject. Jace hadn't known Wrubel particularly well, but he and Rory had been friends. Jace had seen a few deaths in her life, of friends and relatives, and just wanted to wait her friend out. Maybe she'd want to talk, maybe she wouldn't.

"Sooooooo," Rory finally said. "Selling drugs to johnnies."

"Yep."

"And Cruz saying he had problems at the end." Rory blew

71

out a hot breath and shook her head. "I know he smoked his weed. Damn it, maybe this didn't have anything to do with an inhaler."

Rory banged a hand hard against the table. Alley's grandson looked up, mimed eating another sundae. Rory shook her head. He went back to wiping down tables. "You think he was selling drugs to inmates?"

"I don't know, Rory, but this is not what I wanted for Christmas morning."

A man appeared at their table, his face red. "No? And what would that be?" He coughed into his hand. "It is impolite to overhear conversations and that was not my intention. I apologize."

The man had a rugged face that was, though softer, much like the sheriff's. Both were lined with age and worn by wisdom both good and bad. But this large man, looming over their table at probably better than six feet, was heavy where the sheriff was thinnish, and where the sheriff seemed perpetually tired, this man, his green eyes holding her and Rory tightly, seemed melancholy.

"Dr. Vernezobre." Rory stood formally. "How are you?"

"Miss Bogan, I am well, though I am tired these days." The man bowed slightly to both women and offered his hand, in turn, to each.

"Dr. Vernezobre, you've been tired as long as I've known you."

"Which has been quite a number of years now, has it not?"

Teeth, tinged yellow but perfectly straight, peeked out when he smiled, but Jace felt another wave of sadness wash across her.

"It has, sir. This is my friend, Jace Salome. She is a jailer."

"Another of Zachary County's finest. It is a pleasure to meet you, Miss Salome." She rose and when he took her hand—

unexpectedly—he kissed it without a trace of sexuality. "An interesting name, I would think, given its heritage."

"I've had a few comments about it."

"Are you the dancing woman from the book of Mark?" He grinned. "Or Wilde's *femme fatale?*"

With a smile, Jace took her hand back.

"Well, she doesn't have the looks or the brains for that whole *femme fatale* thing," Rory said. "But she probably does dance some. Mostly on tables. Nude. Drunk. Like that."

He chuckled and when Rory indicated the booth, he sat only after the women had. Alley B's grandson immediately appeared with a glass of water. "Thank you, my boy."

"Yes, sir."

The doctor, a giant of a man but with such gentle edges that Jace couldn't help but feel comfortable with him, turned his gaze upon her. "I must confess, Miss Salome, I know your *abuela*. She is a fine woman." He winked. "Though a bit of a warrior when she plays her dominoes."

Jace startled. "You know Gramma?"

"Indeed. I have for many, many years. She and I once frequented the same social club, a lovely place which many nights had Cuban jazz. Your *abuela* was quite a lover of jazz, if I remember correctly."

"You do, sir. My mother was a jazz fan, too. She danced." Jace's face flared with hot blood. "She used jazz in her routine, I mean. 'Embraceable You,' 'Sophisticated Lady.' Gramma and I still go hear jazz whenever we have the chance."

"Alas, not often in Zachary City. Perhaps, next time there is an opportunity, both of you ladies will accompany me?"

Jace nodded, color flushing her cheeks. "That would be lovely."

He smiled but remained silent and in that silence, Jace clearly heard his labored breathing. Eventually, he focused his eyes on

Rory. "Dr. Wrubel. It is extremely sad."

"You heard already?"

"Indeed. I know them both. It is, after all, a small medical community, Miss Salome."

"Please, sir. Jace is fine."

With a pleasant grin, he winked. "As you wish . . . Miss Salome. Miss Bogan, do you know what happened?"

"I don't, sir. It doesn't have anything to do with me."

"It was in your facility, was it not?"

"Yes, sir, but it's a big jail. I was somewhere else. Miss Salome was there, though."

His deep-set eyes, so full of sadness, moved to Jace. "Can you tell me what happened?"

"I'm not sure anyone can at this point, sir."

He nodded thoughtfully. "Certainly, I apologize for asking. It is, of course, none of my business. Perhaps I can venture this question: Did my friend suffer?"

Jace hesitated and knew he saw it. She touched his hand. "Sir, I don't believe he did. I believe it was quick and painless." She felt like a fool for telling a doctor that stab wounds with a ragged homemade shank to the chest were quick and painless but she didn't know what else to say.

"You are quite a good liar, Miss Salome, and I mean no offense by that. In your line of work, I should think that would come in handy." He took a deep breath and it amplified his somber face. "I know he was in pain. More than that, I suspect he hurt. Lately his demons had gotten the better of him." He drained half of his water glass in a single swallow. "It has been many years since his mother passed. His father took his own life after fighting the depression of the loss of his wife. His older brother wrestled with methamphetamines as Jacob wrestled with the angel."

"I do believe Jacob won, Doctor."

"Well, it is a nuanced story, but this time, Miss Salome, Jacob did not get his blessing. Francis was alone, and he worked with the inmates to bring them a peace his brother never found. I think helping them also brought him a measure of peace. A peace that for a while he even tried to find in self-medication."

"He was addicted?"

Rory and Vernezobre both shook their heads.

"Just the weed," Rory said.

"And I'm not sure I would say . . . well . . . I don't want to say he was addicted to anything. He and I never discussed it. I broached the subject two or three times but he did not respond."

"So how do you know he had issues?"

"Dr. Cruz told me more than once that he and Francis had discussed meds when some had come up missing. Dr. Cruz believed Francis self-medicated. As I said, his demons were legion and I believe they were getting stronger. That's why he worked so hard to help others." His eyes flashed and his massive hand clenched to a fist. "And now one of those he tried to serve has killed him."

"We don't know that, sir."

"I believe we do, Miss Bogan." He leaned across the table to bring the three of them closer together. "You know Francis and I had a love of theater in common. He and I both loved big theatrical flourishes. More than once during intermissions did Francis horrify me with stories of angry inmates. Threats. Even physical assaults."

Vernezobre lowered his head into a hand and it reminded Jace of her grandfather, tired from fighting his cancer. Grapa had put his head in his hands, as Vernezobre did now, and had said to Gramma, "I think I'm done." The next day he stopped his treatments and two days after that, he was dead in his own home.

The doctor said, "So many inmates. Although I admire the

job you ladies do, I cannot understand how you find whatever it is inside you to allow you to do it." He cleared his throat. "Francis told me that nearly every new patient angrily wanted what they thought they were being denied."

"Which was what, sir?" Rory asked.

"More medicines and more procedures. More tests. It is the way of our medical system: more of everything." Vernezobre took a deep breath. "I have no desire to harm any man, but there must be justice for Francis's death." A pained look shot through his eyes. "He told me there had been an incident with a man named Mercer."

Rory nodded but said nothing. Catching something in her eyes, Jace held her tongue as well.

"Before his final shift, Francis told me Mr. Mercer had threatened to kill him. Mr. Mercer told my friend he would send him to his God."

"Doc Wrubel told you that?" Jace sat back against the vinyl booth seat. Could it be this easy? Was Mercer so stupid as to fight with the doctor, threaten him, and then kill him?

"Francis told me this man would harm him and now Francis is dead." He hesitated, as though he wanted to say more.

"Doctor?"

"Miss Salome. Sometimes, in the course of civility, acquaintances mention one thing or another and in truth, that information probably should not pass lips."

"Doctor, we are not interested in insider information; we're interested in who killed your friend."

The man, his aristocratic skin darkened by genetics and a lifetime spent in the Cuban or West-Texas sun, nodded. "Thank you for your discretion. I do hate to leave such a weight on her shoulders, but I have been informed that the nurse, Ms. Shortz, was . . . perhaps . . . asleep on duty."

Rory grimaced. "Maybe that's how Mercer got into the hallway."

"Dr. Wrubel told you that?" Jace asked.

He shook his head with a quiet dignity. "I will not divulge that, Miss Salome. Nor on the stand when Mercer is convicted for Francis's murder. They should not have spoken when school was out, but they have helped and I will keep their names secret."

Rory grinned. "No problem, sir, no problem."

"I trust you will get this information where it needs to go? I am thankful I had the good fortune of seeing you two this morning, only hours after Dr. Cruz called me with the news." Vernezobre stood and offered his hand to both women. "I am sorry for interrupting, ladies. I am just an old man who is grieving the loss of a friend. It was a pleasure to meet you, Miss Salome. Perhaps I shall see you when Cuban jazz again fills the air of Zachary City."

"It was good to meet you, too, and maybe we'll share a trumpet or piano."

"I look forward to it." He inclined his head toward Rory. "Attempt to bring her, as well. She and culture should become acquainted."

When he was gone, Rory stared at Jace, a grin playing at her lips. "Already solved. Over ice cream, no less. Von Holton's gonna love you."

A buzz of giddy excitement rode through Jace. This investigation, hers only tangentially, was finished before it was even begun.

"Superficially, it's about Mercer not getting an inhaler." Jace pointed toward where Dr. Vernezobre had been. "But if Wrubel was self-medicating, wasn't he probably also selling . . . just like Mercer said?"

"Hang on; we don't know for sure he was self-medicating,

okay? He smoked some weed and I know that because he told me. But I don't believe he was into anything harder than that. And I sure as hell don't believe he was selling. But even if he was, Mercer's our guy." Rory motioned to the grandson. When he came over, she ordered the number 2: two eggs, two sausage, two toast. "Scrambled eggs and hot sauce, please. Wheat toast."

The kid, his eyes wide that she trusted him with her order, nodded and dashed to Alley B. Alley B listened, then looked at Rory and questioningly held up two fingers. Rory nodded.

The case was over, as easily as that. Yet if that were true, then why did Jace feel the need for a second stress-management sundae?

"Damn," she whispered.

CHAPTER 8

A bit later, Jace stood at her apartment door, the key as talisman.

Frost on windshields and trees naked of leaves and all the Sea Spray tenants wearing heavy coats and knit caps, and yet Jace Salome stood here drowning in sweat. It was a simple thing, putting a key in a lock, turning that lock, and opening a door. There should be no terror, no panic or dread. It should be a simple matter of unlocking the brushed-brass knob and the two deadbolts—one old and one new—and going inside.

Yet almost every homecoming to the apartment Grapa had built from two hotel rooms stacked atop each other and that gave her a duplex-type residence resulted in this battle. She stood on this spot, watched the key shake in her hand, and worked feverishly to convince herself that Will Badgett was not still in the apartment.

She always got inside and then felt like an utter fool for the ritual. Yeah, it was getting better. Each day her ritual shortened by a breath and she found a smidgen more strength to charge in and reclaim her home. Yet during that moment when she did hesitate, she wondered if she'd ever be who she was before Will Badgett.

You changed me, you bastard. You came into my life and changed it fundamentally and I still haven't figured out how to deal with that or what it means down the road . . . if anything.

Jace swallowed, gritted her teeth, and unlocked the door. She rushed in, closed the thing tightly behind her, and shot the deadbolts home.

"Nobody here, Jace. No one at all."

"Well . . ." Preacher's lazy voice came to her from her small living room. "Somebody's here."

Jace bit the inside of her lip and tasted a spill of warm blood. *Not now,* she thought. *Preacher, I love you but get the hell out.*

It wasn't just Preacher. It was Gramma, too. They sat on her couch, beneath Jace's towering poster of Wonder Woman plastered on the wall. Preacher had a handful of her jazz CDs spread on the coffee table, reading liner notes to Dave Brubeck's *Time Out,* while Gramma read the back cover of a DVD about patrol tactics.

Jace took the DVD from her grandmother. The woman looked at her, sadness in her eyes. "Rory let me borrow it," Jace said by way of apology. Gramma's silence bothered Jace more than if the woman had spoken.

For a long moment, no one spoke. Jace saw the silent messages flashing back and forth between them. Years of days and nights together, of dominoes and drinking with the rest of their little cohort—Jace called them the Hot Five because it had been Grapa's poker buddies and he'd so dearly loved Louis Armstrong's trumpet. The Hot Five was one of Armstrong's first groups. Grapa, Gramma, Preacher, Hassan, and Galena had spent so many years together there was no language required. It was a silent language Jace could only rarely understand.

This morning, Jace understood all too well. "You heard."

Gramma nodded. "You need to quit."

"No."

"I hate that you work there. It's all violence and death and blood and horrible people."

"Now, it ain't all like that for our little baby girl." Preacher shook his head. "Jace be helping people, too."

Gramma jerked the *Time Out* CD out of his hands. "Violence and death. Guards killing inmates and now inmates killing doctors." Gramma paced the apartment, like a mother waiting up for a daughter not home yet as the rain makes the streets slick and dangerous. "Hell, you already can't sleep."

"I sleep just fine."

"You sleep like shit and we both know it." Gramma tapped a wall. "Too thin. You were sleep-talking last night." Gramma put her hand beneath her chin, her sign of confusion and concern. "But not about your mother. Or Badgett."

Last night, it had been especially vivid; the house on cinder blocks, the house with the fluttering and tattered curtains, with the windows broken until they were nothing but glinting bits shaped like jagged teeth, with the door long since stolen, with the dirty cream walls stained by slashes and splashes of brown paint, with the floor covered in dirt and weeds and used condoms and syringes, while a blistering morning sun blasted up over the western horizon.

She'd dreamt, again, of the house she didn't understand.

"What was it, honey?" Gramma came to Jace and hugged her fiercely. The warmth of her hugs always knifed Jace's heart.

"Just a bad night."

"I can get'cha some sleep helpers, you need." Preacher winked. "Some candles and incense. Get'cha some books on relaxatin' and some'a them nature albums. Rivers and oceans and whales singing and I don't know what all."

"They're CDs now, Preacher," Gramma said.

"Hah. Not even CDs anymore, it's all downloads, but I get what you're saying."

"Warm milk will help, too." The old woman smacked her lips.

"I thought you preferred letting Mr. Daniels help you."

The woman nodded. "I do, but I'm retired and you have a

real job to worry about." There was just a slip of silence and Gramma added, "A job I wish you didn't have."

"Gramma, please. I like my job and I'm good at it."

"Yeah, but people die at your job."

"People die at all kinds of jobs. Hell, motel clerks get killed all the time." She pounded her chest. "At least in my job, I get to catch the people who do the killing."

"What?"

"I know who killed Dr. Wrubel." *At least, I think I do,* she left unsaid. "And, yeah, I saw his body and I saw the blood and it was awful and made me want to throw up and come home so you could sing to me but I figured out who did it and I'm going to help our detectives prove it and lock him up forever."

"And that makes it better? Seeing all that nastiness is better because you can lock someone up forever?"

Jace ground her teeth until her jaw was bright with pain. "Damn it, Gramma, this is my job. And yeah . . . I think it does. It makes it easier to live with what I've seen if I know the bad guy goes to prison. That's justice."

Clearly surprised, the woman stepped back and cleared her throat. "I apologize, Jace. I didn't mean to start another argument. I just . . . well, I love you and I worry about you. I just want you happy and safe, and—cop or not—I'll always want you happy and safe and I'll always love you."

Jace pulled the old woman back to her and hugged her hard. "I'm sorry for that. I love you, too. You are my heart." She hesitated, then she goosed her grandmother. "Besides, if I piss you off too badly, who's going to clean my apartment?"

Grinning and twisting away, Gramma snorted. "You are bad, Jace, nothing but bad."

Preacher looked at Jace, his serious, Sunday-morning sermon face on. "Do you need us to stay?"

She wanted them to, thought she might need them to. But

she also wanted to sleep without them. This was the job she'd chosen and this was part of the cost. She would sleep alone, after the ritual of her second bedroom, to prove to herself she could.

"I'm okay. Thank you." Gramma was out the door first, humming as she headed down the second floor balcony to her own apartment. Preacher hesitated at the doorway. "You got that face on."

"What face?"

"Robison's face."

Preacher's son's face. Robison's face.

"You maybe wanna go look for him?"

Jace averted her gaze and eyed the Wonder Woman poster on her wall. It was the early heroine, and in the picture, she stood slightly cocked, her head angled up as though looking into the heavens. She wore the bulletproof bracelets and had the magic lasso at her side. "They changed her."

Preacher frowned. "What's that?"

"She was an Amazon princess. She was a superhero because she was a superhero. Beautiful and intelligent and strong and all her super powers were hers alone."

Preacher was confused.

"They took that away from her. Later on they said her powers came from the gods."

"It all comes from God, babydoll."

"You know what I mean." She sighed. "People got her and changed her."

"Ever'body changes ever'body, babydoll. Cain't meet someone or know someone or love someone without leaving a part of yourself with them."

Jace took a deep breath, her eyes on the closed door to her second bedroom.

"Jace?"

"How long has Robison been gone, Preacher?"

The old man thought for a while. "Well, it was the beginning of the school year. Ain't but about Christmastime now. 'S just a few months."

Twenty years, actually. Robison was Preacher's son and he'd disappeared while walking to school just after the start of his first-grade year. Preacher believed, with a fervency Jace found both disconcerting and comforting, Robison would be back soon. Somewhere deep in his dented and tired brain, when times were good, Preacher believed his son had gone to visit his mother. When times were bad, Preacher believed Robison had gotten lost and just needed finding.

"You're a good father, Preacher. Good night."

"Good morning, babydoll."

Chapter 9

The apartment was empty.

Preacher and Gramma were gone. Will Badgett was not here. He was not in the kitchen or the bathroom. He was not downstairs in either of the bedrooms, and the upstairs living room where he'd beaten her so savagely before soaking her with pepper spray had been cleaned months ago. The blood-stained carpet had been torn out and replaced by hardwood floors, and the head- and fist-shaped holes in the walls were long since patched.

In the far bottom corner of the Wonder Woman poster, Thomas's booking photo stared at her. He didn't look scared in the picture, like he had later when he begged Jace to save him. In this picture, he looked bored; a guy who'd missed a court date and been caught driving with a suspended license.

A few days, that look said, *and I'll be right with the law.*

Jace stripped quickly, her naked skin cold in the apartment's winter air. She touched the tattoo at the base of her neck. It was half of a heart and in her head, though she knew it was stupid, her mother had the other half.

Maybe time for a new one?

Maybe Thomas's eye? Just a reminder?

In her hand, she clutched last night's flyer. She took a deep breath, and opened the door to her second bedroom.

The flyers filled the room.

Spread across the walls like arms waiting to grab her and

smother her. From the floor up, every wall, creeping onto the ceiling. Some askew and crooked, some perfectly aligned or in deliberate rows. They trailed and spun, wound and hopped, with the walls of eggshell crème paint peeking out from beneath, between, and behind. The intensity gave her vertigo and her stomach rolled as though she were standing on a precipice. Enormous rats and dickless rangers, deputies and rage, dead and bloody cops. Worms. Children. Pictures of handcuffs, too, symbolic of those who'd been arrested and of her being immobilized and unable to get away. Words cut from magazines, arranged haphazardly into threats and intimidation, promises of retaliation. Over and over again was her departmental photo, staring back from everywhere, enlarged and violated, savagely sliced, painted with blood. That picture had also been ruined with black marker and nearly lost beneath crude drawings of female genitalia.

But also of huge penises emitting a steady stream of piss onto her face.

It was a reminder, like Laimo's words, that Jace had pissed herself when the ERTs had exploded into A Pod the night Thomas died.

It was a reminder, like Laimo's words, of the most humiliating moment in Jace's life.

Later, when her dreams took her, she squirmed. Eventually she cried.

Her young-girl dreams had been soft and gentle and always had horses. Her teenager's dreams were built on edges sharpened by Mama's death. At first, her sheriff's-deputy dreams had been exciting and nerve-wracking yet always with scores and legions and brigades of other cops backing her up. Since Badgett, her dreams had become corrupted; they were incomprehensible nightmares. Lately she found herself in the unrecognized shack repeatedly, but also in the A Pod go-between and it was sometimes difficult to tell the difference between the two. In the shack, there were holes in the walls and windows broken, and in the go-between there were non-existent bars on the doors. The lurid colors, oh so reminiscent of Rory's Skittles, that spewed from the dream streetlights antagonized her, too. Brick-hard reds and liquid greens and yellows that came through the broken windows no matter how hard she tried to keep them out. Electric purples and oranges that reminded her of a wet downtown on a night someone might die. Downtown Chicago, maybe, Detroit or Kansas City.

Frequently, she stood in the middle of the dream-shack, surrounded by bent syringes and handcuffs and flyers and the empty aluminum cans of 40s. She stared at a sun that she knew was rising up from the west and had no idea what the hell that meant. She sweated a harsh fear because the shack, which was sometimes the shack and sometimes the go-between and sometimes both at the same time, scared her.

But on this night, in this dream, there was something new. This night, there was a bobbing laughter that Jace immediately recognized.

Laimo. Laughing at a man's degradation, and even though Jace's eyes popped open and she was fully awake and sweating and fearful, Laimo kept laughing a laugh that sounded like a train skidding to a stop on the rusted rails that cleaved Zachary City in half.

What surprised Dream-Jace about the laughter was that she heard it at all. She realized, in that split second when she recognized it, that part of what had been scaring her all these months was when she dreamed of the house, she dreamed silently. Her dreams had always been full of music and conversation and sound. But this dream, of this place, was as silent as an empty stage.

Would it be less scary with Clifford Brown? With the Yellow-jackets or Jazz Crusaders? Maybe with the hard bop of Sonny Rollins or Wayne Shorter? Or was there simply no way to make that house any less scary?

When she woke, the taste of Laimo's laugh still in her throat, the early-afternoon daylight fighting valiantly with Jace's thick curtains, she was unsure if Laimo was laughing at Mercer or at her.

CHAPTER 10

Later that night, after the debrief and roll call, Jace stood at the doorway to the detectives' bureau, what everyone called The Pulpit. She swallowed down a throat full of burning nerves and entered.

There were four or five desks in the room and all of them were drowning beneath paper and pictures and color-coded file folders. It made the already small room feel even more cluttered and overworked. The far wall was hidden behind memos and Wanted posters and parolee update sheets and an endless ream of random bits of paper. When she'd been here last time, there had been a five-dollar bill pinned to the wall with a note beneath it asking if anyone could identify the bill. Now the bill was a twenty and Jace still thought the joke was weak.

It was almost 11:30 p.m. and the street outside the two windows was surprisingly quiet, though bathed in saturated colors burning from neon signs: blues and reds, purples, greens, the occasional orange. Usually, people and cars filled those streets, from squad cars and cops to work release inmates coming or going to drunks from the bars that lined the street opposite the jail. There were also inmates freshly released and shaking off the dirt of custody as well as free people sucking down a last cigarette before reporting to spend a few days or weeks or months at the county-run hotel.

"Deputy," Major Jakob said. "Thanks for coming down."

"Yes, ma'am." Jace hadn't expected to see Jakob and it ratcheted her nerves up.

Next to the major sat Von Holton. That man, though Jace hadn't known his name, had been the detective in the room when she'd first come here after Thomas's death. He'd been brusque and accused her of not staying in the pod with her partner, thus allowing that partner to get hurt. Like a dog pissing on a hydrant, he'd sprayed and intimidated her with his territorialism.

"We gotta stop meeting like this." He smiled, putting Jace in mind of a bulldog baring teeth.

"Yes, sir."

"I'm not a sir; I work for a living."

He motioned her to a chair but she'd been in that chair before. The padding was worn thin and one leg was shortened. The detectives used it to make people uncomfortable. Jace chose a different chair. She caught the tiniest smile on Jakob's face.

Von Holton eyed her. "I told you to sit there."

"Actually, you didn't tell me anything at all, but I prefer here, thank you."

He sucked his teeth. "Let me ask you: can you see through the ice?"

"Excuse me?"

"The ice beneath you is pretty thin. I just wonder if you know that."

Beneath her? Jace spent more time thinking about the ice around her—the deputies who froze her out—rather than ice beneath her.

"Do you know what I mean when I say we have to stop meeting like this?"

Jace ground her teeth and tried to shake away the feeling that the room was growing around her, leaving her small and meek and scared in the chair. *That's what he wants. He doesn't like you.*

He wants to hurt you. He is a bully. "It's a little foggy, to be honest."

"Ah, well, let me burn some sunshine through, then. Every time I see you, you're involved with death. Thomas's. Now Wrubel's. Always death with you. Being around that much death would give me a complex."

Jace pictured this man in the orange jumpsuit of general population. *He's a bully one step removed from the inmates and you've faced them down for months now. Don't let this guy freak you out.* She'd staved off the inmates—sadists and brutalizers and sexual degenerates and garden variety bullies—by making them believe she had no fear, even as her stomach twisted into Gordian knots. When she glanced at Major Jakob, the woman's eyes flicked and a single eyebrow rose in a question mark.

Jace plunged in. "It doesn't seem to have bothered you so far."

His eyes bulged. "What?"

"Four shootouts, Detective. Three dead suspects, one of whom was in custody and pulled a small gun from between his buttocks that, apparently, the pat-down missed. Two high-speed pursuits, one of which ended in the death of an old woman who happened to be in the wrong place at the wrong time. That body count's twice as high as mine. Tell me again what kind of complex keeps you awake at night?"

Instead of boiling over, he grinned. "Well, you ain't the scared worm you were last time. Got yourself some info. Found some jail balls, too."

"Detective."

"Apologies, Major." He said it with a phoniness that irritated Jace. "But I've had some dealings with Deputy Salome here." He glanced at what Jace assumed was Wrubel's case file. "And last night, as it turns out, she was pretty near where this innocent man was attacked and murdered, and she did nothing to stop it."

Jace stared hard at him. "A few months ago you yelled at me because I was outside my pod. Now you're yelling at me because I was inside my pod. Which is it, Detective? Where do you want me?"

"That's the fluidity of police work, Deputy. You gotta figure out where the trouble is going to be and make sure you're there." He winked at her, again with a phoniness that irritated Jace. "Reminds me of the old joke: How many cops does it take to screw in a light bulb? Only one but he's never around when you need him." Von Holton laughed.

"Very funny, sir. I'll have to remember it."

He glared at her. "Tell it next time you guys are being comedians over the radio."

"Detective? The murder?"

"Oh, don't worry about it, Major, it's a done deal. This is Jace Salome, the *wunderkind* of the Zachary County sheriff's office. Investigator *extraordinaire*. She's the one who sniffed out the dirty cops and got us back on the path to righteousness." He slammed a meaty fist on the desk to punctuate his words. "Hallelujah."

"Well, the sheriff figured as long as you weren't doing the job, someone ought to."

Von Holton laughed off her insult. "Nice try. You wanna dig your way under my skin, get a bigger shovel."

Jace shook her head. "Sir, I'm not trying to get under anyone's skin."

That single eyebrow still played on Jakob's face while Von Holton's eyes worked Jace over like a pugilist with a weaker opponent. "Get on with the interview.

"Yes, ma'am." Grinding his jaw, Von Holton shuffled his papers until he managed to tear one. He stopped, carefully aligned them, and looked at Jace. "I have a few questions, Deputy."

"Anything I can do to help, Detective."

"You were in the pod and Urrea ordered you to go to the scene."

"Yes."

"The inmates were locked down?"

"Yes."

"Wrubel was dead when you arrived?"

"Yes."

"You were ordered to control access?"

"Yes."

The irritation was plain on his face. "Anything to add to those answers? Or aren't you capable of anything except monosyllabic grunts?"

"Respectfully, don't—"

"Piss on your respect."

"Respectfully, if I'm asked yes or no questions, I give yes or no answers."

Tension lay between them like two performing musicians caught on opposite chord changes.

After clearing his throat, he began again. "Who are your suspects?"

"Mercer."

Von Holton blinked rapidly, like he had something stuck in his eye. "You wanna think about that?"

"No."

"Why him?"

"Because of the problem with meds the night before. The ERTs had to be called." She left the rest unsaid, unwilling to sully Wrubel's name before she had a chance to ask a few questions.

The detective shuffled the papers and produced one, which

he waved like a single at a stripper. "Because of this?"

"Well, I don't know what you're waving around, but if it's the incident report, then yes, because of that."

"Well, bless me, why didn't I think of that?"

Boiling blood filled Jace's cheeks. She turned away from Von Holton, not wanting him to see he had embarrassed her.

"Tell you what, why don't you run that phenomenal lead down for me. Find out where Mercer was and where he was supposed to be. And while you're at it, find out why he did it and where the murder weapon is."

Jakob leaned back in her chair. "The murder weapon was in the man's chest, Detective."

This time, Von Holton's face flood with hot blood and Jace kept a satisfied grunt to herself.

"I think you focused on Mercer too quick, Deputy," he said. "I'd say we've got another three hundred or four hundred suspects available to us."

"You're wrong."

"Everyone in the jail at the time is a viable suspect."

"Wrong."

"Why?"

"Because most of those viable suspects were locked down. You said yourself that the inmates were bedded down and you were right. So it's ten or twenty suspects at best. Only those trusties who were free to move around when the murder happened."

"The prisoners could have gotten out of bed."

"Out of bed, out of their cells, *and* out of the pod? No."

"Are you questioning me?"

Jace wished Rory were with her. This was the kind of grandstanding bullcrap that Rory loved to get in the middle of. If she were here, Jace might feel better about swinging back at this blowhard. As it was, Jace's nerves, already like high-voltage lines down and sparking, made her want to throw up. "Trying to think logically, sir."

"For the last time, I am not a sir; I'm a detective."

"Really." It was not a question.

"What about cops, Salome?"

"What about them?"

"Couldn't they have done it?"

Jace frowned.

"A cop in particular, maybe?"

"I'm a little lost here, Detective. What are you asking me?"

"Never mind. Wrubel was stabbed, right?"

"Yes."

"How'd he get knifed?"

"It wasn't a knife; it was a shank."

"Same difference."

"No, they're not."

"Yeah? And you know that how?"

"Training and experience."

Von Holton rolled his eyes. "I've got me a few days' worth of experience, too."

"Not in the jail, you don't. The jail isn't your kingdom, it is mine."

"Please, I've—"

"How many shanks have you seen in the last few months? In your entire career? I've been on-duty nearly a year and I've pulled twenty or more out of cells and off inmates' persons. Knives look like knives. Shanks look like shanks."

"What's the diff—"

"There was no finished handle, Detective. The handle was taped."

"Could have been a broken knife."

Jace bit back a laugh. "I defer to your experience."

"Okay, a shank versus a knife. That doesn't really matter."

"Sure, it does. A shank means probably an inmate."

"Which puts us back at three hundred suspects, just as I said. What about bribes?"

"Are you offering me one?"

"Jailers take bribes all the time. How many times have you turned a blind eye to sex or a beat down and gotten a few extra bucks in your pocket? Or maybe a little manliness up between your—"

"Major." Jace turned to Jakob. "I'd like to file an official complaint for sexual harassment against Detective Von Holton. I'll need a union representative and at least two members of the administration for a preliminary hearing."

Von Holton snapped his mouth shut, his eyes glistening with venom. Jace ignored him and kept her gaze on Major Jakob. The major stopped writing on her yellow pad and set her pen aside. Eventually, she raised her head and tugged on her ear.

"Certainly, Deputy. Once we are done with this interview, you can fill out the paperwork in my office."

Von Holton glared at Jace and busied himself with making notes. "Still going after cops, I guess."

"Do you have an investigation-related question, Detective?" Jakob asked. "If so, get to it."

"Absolutely, Major. I think it is more than possible that an inmate could bribe a jailer and get out of their cell."

"And then?"

"Then the inmate goes into the hallway and knifes—excuse me, shanks—Dr. Wrubel."

"If an inmate gets out of their cell, by whatever means, they're still in the pod," Jace said.

"Another bribe to get out of the pod," Von Holton said.

"At which point they're in the go-between."

"For God's sake, another bribe, then. Or one giant bribe. You're playing games with me, Deputy."

"Not at all, sir. But let's say somehow a prisoner gets to the hallway; how does he manage to time everything so that Doc Wrubel is there when he wants him dead?" Jace sighed. "I guess I'm not sure why you're so convinced a guard did something wrong."

"Me? You investigate bad cops, not me."

Biting back a foulness from deep inside her, Jace stood and moved behind the chair, and hoped her iron grip on the thing didn't show. "Look, I'm sorry you're floundering in your investigation, Detective, really I am. I'd hoped we could find Doc Wrubel's killer together but that might be asking too much. You can flog me all you want, but that doesn't change anything. I saw what I saw and know what I know. Sitting here trying to beat me up because you're pissed at me isn't going to solve this murder."

"Floundering? You think I'm on the wrong track?"

"To be on the wrong track, you have to at least be on a track. Once you find that track, let me know and I'll be glad to take another look for you. Your murderer is Mercer. Period. Are we finished?"

The only sound in the room was Von Holton's breathing. "Take another look? I don't need you looking over my shoulder." His nostrils flared. "Get the hell outta my Pulpit, worm."

She hesitated, then pulled the newest flyer from her pocket. It had been hanging in the vents of her locker when she'd arrived tonight. After smoothing it out, she laid it softly on the table directly in front of Von Holton and Jakob. "If you want to dig your way under my skin, get a bigger shovel."

Von Holton's eyes caught the flyer and immediately came angrily back to her.

CHAPTER 11

"Laid it right out there, huh?" A touch of barbeque sauce leaked from Rory's mouth during their dinner break. Her tongue flicked out to lick it away but was just short.

Jace wiped Rory's face. "You should have seen him."

"He didn't expect you to have it."

"He oughta see my second bedroom, then."

"What?"

Jace waved it away. Rory asked about the complaint forms and the preliminary hearing, but Jace shook her head. "I was just mouthing off."

"The hell you say. You should file. The guy's an ass, Jace; he needs to be taken down a peg or two."

Jace brushed away cracker crumbs from her uniform shirt. They'd had Brooks Barbeque delivered early in the night and warmed it in the microwave. "Sure, but not by me, he doesn't. I'm on dangerous enough ground already; I don't need the ag-gravation, either in my head or my career."

"That's the best place for it." Rory licked her spoon clean.

"Head or career?"

"Yeah."

The ladies gathered up their trash and dumped it.

"So, this career you're talking about. I'm not sure I've ever heard you mention a career before."

With a shrug, Jace said, "Not a big deal, Rory."

"Okay. Except a few months ago, you went into Dillon's office with your resignation all typed out nice and neat."

"Yeah, well, that was then. It's different now."

"Why?"

Jace grabbed a paper towel, wet it, and wiped down where they'd eaten, and thought about her answer. When Chief Deputy Cornutt, now dead, had first handed her a shiny, new badge, Jace had been unsure of the entire affair. It had almost been a lark, applying for the job, and a part of Jace had thought this might well be nothing more than another in a long string of bad jobs she would keep for five or six months before moving on to something else. The problem was that the next job was never better and frequently it was worse. This job, that required her to store people like pallets of goods shipped from China, turned out to be something else altogether.

When Gene Thomas's death had hung in everyone's head and the weight had begun to focus on Jace, she wanted nothing more than to disappear into the forever of a summer sandstorm. But now she was almost a year into the gig and everything was different. In those first, terrified days, the job had seemed like an unknown monster that would probably eat her alive. It was still a monster and always would be, she knew, but she believed she was beginning to recognize it even if she wasn't quite sure yet how to fight it.

"That whole drama was a little embarrassing. Resignation and facing off with the sheriff and whatever."

"Drama Queen 101. It's what I like best about you."

"And here I thought it was my razor sharp wit and lovely eyes." Jace dumped some quarters into the soda machine. A gigantic Mountain Dew rattled down the chute to her. "I think I like this job."

Rory said nothing for moment. Then she grinned. "Yeah? And you might be halfway good at it someday if you learn the lessons I'm teaching."

Jace nodded emphatically. "Right. Whatever Rory says, do the opposite."

"Ah, that wit, razor sharp as a cheese-covered noodle."

Jace raised her eyebrows. "Cheese-covered?"

"Whatever. Listen, sister, you are good at this job and you should like it. I've told you before, being a copper is the greatest job in the world."

"And the worst."

"And the worst."

"So if I want to keep this gig," Jace said, "I probably shouldn't make enemies of people like Von Holton."

A couple road deputies wandered into the break room, nodding at the jailers but deep into their own war stories.

"Don't worry about Von Holton. Think of it this way: he already hates you."

"Golly gee . . . thanks."

Rory keyed her shoulder mic. "Control . . . 456 headed back to post."

—10-4—

Together, they strolled through the main hallway, Rory stepping neatly on the purple lines on the floor that led toward the female pod, while Jace had been assigned to the investigation at Von Holton's demand.

"What I'm saying," Rory said, "is that he hates you and there ain't thing one you can do about that. If you found the murderer and gave him to Von Holton with a signed and videotaped confession, Von Holton would still hate you. It's the way of the world. He's a throwback who probably doesn't believe women should be in this job—"

"Barefoot and pregnant."

"With a bushy 1970s hoo-ha."

"Yuck."

"Probably also believes the police are always right, no matter what." Rory held up a finger. "One: you're a chick." She held up a second. "Two: you brought down a bad poh-leece." A third finger popped up. "Three: you made him look bad in front of Major Jakob and I wish I'd been there to see it. Fourth: you gave him the murderer. Now it's his job to prove it. Besides, you're not in his chain of command so who gives a crap? What can he do to you?"

Jace was worried less about what he'd do to her than what words he'd put in other deputies' ears.

Rory stared at her, her head slightly cocked.

"What?"

"You crack me up. You're sitting in the interview with him and slamming him eight ways from Sunday, hauling out those jail balls I told you you'd discover, and now you're standing here terrified you're going to foul up your job. You are about as bipolar as anyone I've ever met. Up down up down."

Jace laughed it off. "A girl can have multiple faces, can't she?"

"No problem . . . Sybil."

"Thank you . . . Etta."

"Huh?"

"Nothing."

They stopped at the turn where they'd part company.

"Tell me about Major Jakob."

Rory looked sideways at Jace. "Pretty interesting she was in that interview. She wasn't in there for Laimo. Wasn't in there for Craig, either." Rory shrugged. "I know she's queer for chicks on the job. Not sexually, I mean. She believes there need to be more women in this line of work and from what I hear, she'll go balls to the wall for any women she thinks deserve it."

"She ever do it for you?"

Rory's eyes focused sharply on Jace. "What're you saying?"

In the blast of Rory's gaze, Jace was suddenly uncomfortable, as though she'd stepped on a tripwire she hadn't even known was there. "Not saying a thing. I'm just curious. You're telling me she's helping me out somehow and I'm just wondering if that's the kind of help I want."

"Straight up, sister, straight the hell up."

Still feeling the tripwire against her shins, but maybe less taut, Jace nodded. "Good, I'll take all I can get."

"She's great at what she does. Her lab is constantly at the top of crime labs in Texas. People send her evidence from all over the state. They do all kinds of superstar DNA stuff. She's worked with the FBI a few times, too. Some of her computer guys, Vance is one of them, do ICAC forensics and always get their bad guy."

"ICAC?"

"Internet Crimes Against Children. Child sexual exploitation. All computer-based crimes. Kiddie porn. Like that."

"Wow."

"Pretty good for a hometown girl. She's on the talk shows sometimes." Rory nodded. "She's impressive as hell, Jace, and you want her thinking you're a good guy."

"A good guy with breasts."

"Boobs or not boobs, if you're a good cop, she's a supporter. But yeah, if you have that extra chromosome, she's your supporter."

"My own personal, living, breathing sports bra."

Rory laughed. "You been to see Bibb yet?"

Jace waved the Mountain Dew and a five-pound bag of peanuts. "Going right now." She glanced at her watch. "He texted me and said he's coming in tonight. Idiot. His last day of vacation and here he's coming back."

"Oh, hey, almost forgot. Changed my schedule in Rooster so I'm on when the truck comes through." She waved the tiny piece of paper Shelby had given them. "Gonna stop that truck and have some fun. Sheriff said you could ride. It's gonna be a blast."

"I'll pass on hanging with Cop of the Year, thanks."

Rory eyed Jace, her frown deepening. "This is going to be a great bust and even if we can't find him, it'll be fun driving around with you. You can see what it's like to work the road."

Jace stopped walking. "I don't know, Rory. I just . . ."

"What?"

"I'm not a road cop, Rory; I'm barely even a jailer."

The truth was, Jace had thought about maybe someday being a road cop, in an unreachable fantasy way, like having a perfect date with *Young Man with a Horn*–era Kirk Douglas. But when it came down to it, Jace wasn't sure she had the stones for that job. She certainly didn't have the training and maybe that scared her more than anything. She'd been on the bad end of a big bust and it had nearly killed her. She had no desire to jump in that particular swimming pool again anytime soon.

"Oh, bullshit. You're twice the cop most anyone else in this jail is . . . the obvious exception being me." Rory grinned and winked. "Look, I'm not trying to turn you into something you're not; I'm just trying to have some fun with my best friend. And maybe trying to help her see that she's better than she thinks . . . expand her horizons some."

Jace nodded and headed for the control room, thinking that expanding her horizons was exactly what Von Holton was trying to do to her.

CHAPTER 12

On the way to the jail control room, Jace got stopped by an inmate named Doug Kerr. He worked as a medical trusty and had fairly good run of the place.

"Hey, Salome. What's shaking?"

"Living the dream, Kerr, living the dream."

He laughed, his gigantic arms wrapped around his body and his hands holding the opposite shoulder. He ran better than six feet and had hardly an ounce of fat on him. *He'd be a monster in a fight,* Jace thought. *Have to call ERTs for that one.*

"Hey, grapevine word is you're working Doc's death."

"Grapevine, huh?"

"Usually solid."

"You know anything about it?"

The man shrugged. "Eh . . . what do trusties ever know for sure? Ever'body who talks to us got some agenda or other."

"Hearing any agendas last couple of days?"

The smile left his face and his eyes, leaving them empty and cold. It startled Jace, made her back up a step and raise her hands slightly. But he never squared up or clenched his fists.

"Hearing a thing or two."

"Yeah?"

He said nothing. Silence bounced off the concrete walls.

"Kerr?"

"Look, keep me outta it, okay? I just wanna do my time and boogie down the road. I got my medical technician schooling almost done. I'm'a get me a good job, get my ass on the straight and narrow." He grinned. "Got me one boy already and another coming. They gonna need me around. Gonna get straight behind all this child support, get me a job with Cruz. Hey, who better to work a jail than someone been in one? Right?"

"Sure."

"Well, word is Wrubel wasn't as clean as ever'body likes to think. Maybe he was selling a little on the side. You know he and Cruz argued about missing meds a few weeks ago."

"He's selling out of the pharmacy?"

"Maybe, but what do I know from nothing? Maybe outta the pharmacy, maybe offa the street."

"Was he using?"

Again, the unreadable shrug. "I don't know. Maybe . . . maybe not." He headed off down the hall. "Anyway, just thought you should hear what I'm hearing."

Jace watched him go, distrust as heavy in her gut as the barbeque.

CHAPTER 13

Five minutes later, Jace sat in the jail control room, what the dead shift jailers called the Pig Pen. The last two weeks, though, with Sergeant Bibb on vacation, the Pig Pen had actually gotten cleaned. The cleaning staff had done the job every night, which they didn't do when Bibb was around. As long as he was casual about the remains of his tacos and his peanut shells and his half-finished cans of soda and energy drinks, the cleaning crew was firm in their avoidance of the room.

However, on his two annual vacations, the cleaning crew—civilians rather than trusties in this sensitive part of the jail—would go in vengefully. The carpet was deep-cleaned and all fifteen computer screens, strung five across and three tall along the wall beyond the controller's desk, were as clean as if they'd come out of the box ten minutes ago. The green lights of locked doors and red lights of unlocked doors, embedded in the touch screen which was itself embedded in the main desk, were bright and easy to see. With everything so clear and clean, the room seemed a foreign land; bright-eyed and pulsing with energy where with Sgt. Bibb it was always dark and dirty and smelled vaguely of back alleys and cattle pens. To Jace, the sterility of the clean Pig Pen was boring.

This windowless room was the nexus point for all jail security. No doors or gates, with the exception of individual cell doors within the pods, opened or closed that the control room sergeant didn't orchestrate. She chuckled. This was also the place from which Bibb frequently watched Jace's behind as she walked the hallways. Not just her, of course, but all the women. It was like being under the constant, intense gaze of a teen-aged boy. Yet because of that very constancy and security, she became comfortable. Bibb was a 41-year-old pubescent who had a fixation on rear ends and ate like a college boy, but there was no one Jace wanted watching those monitors more. His very fixation meant he always had an eye on the deputies whom he considered *his* jailers.

Right now, the second shift controller sat behind the desk, eyes hard on all the screens and doors. The radio crackled over a loudspeaker hung in the corner and a stream of communication poured from it.

—*control adam outer*—

—*10-22 on the transport*—

—*booking two males 10-76 . . . about two minutes out*—

—*10-4*—

—*436 from 472*—

—*472 go*—

Jace marveled. It hadn't been that long ago that she heard every word over the radio but understood none of it. Now she understood almost all of it but with that understanding came a deafness to it. Most of the words slipped away even before the speaker finished uttering them. She heard only what she needed to hear.

"There he is," the second shift control sergeant said to her. On the black and white screen, Jace saw Bibb wandering slowly along the main parking lot, a grocery bag in his hand.

She laughed. Meeting or not, Bibb always had his snacks.

In the days and weeks after Jace was attacked, Bibb had blamed himself. If he had paid closer attention, he believed, Will Badgett would never have been in the jail. "That son of a bitch never gets in? He don't beat on you."

"Sarge," Jace had said over and over. "He beat on me at my apartment first, *then* at the jail."

"Well . . . whatever. One less beating."

That was his drunken apology on her doorstep at the Sea Spray two days after she got out of the hospital. The blame that burned in Bibb's head made him much more conscientious of his job. He watched foot traffic and listened to radio traffic much more closely. It was both maddening and comforting.

In fact, it was that very militancy that helped Bibb take a vacation. His supervisor had a bevy of complaints about Bibb's demands to know every step at every moment. Traylor was the jail administrator and he had insisted Bibb move his vacation from his mother's January birthday to Christmas with a vague supervisory pressure.

The day after Christmas and a dead guy on the floor. Welcome back, Sarge.

On cue, Bibb's voice crackled over the two-way intercom from the jail's back door. "Let me the hell in."

The second shift control-room sergeant popped the lock and on the desk, a red locked-door light became the deep green of an unlocked door, then changed back to locked-red when Bibb closed it. Jace stepped out of the Pig Pen and waited.

"The hell is this happy horseshit?" Bibb asked when he rounded the corner a few minutes later.

"Welcome back, Sarge. Merry Christmas."

Growling, he slammed a meaty fist against the Pig Pen's door. It banged closed with an explosive thunk. "Damn door oughta be closed." Bibb's voice boomed through the hallway, capable of shattering concrete walls.

"My bad. I just came out. Sorry." She popped an uncomfortable smile on her face. "Did you have a good time? You look good."

"Lost thirty damn pounds with worry. I leave for a couple

weeks and the wheels come off. What are you doing in my hallway?" He fell silent but squirmed under her gaze. Taking a deep breath, he wiped his lips with the back of his hand. "I'm sorry, Salome. This door." He tapped the control-room door. "Should be locked all the time. Every door should be locked all the time."

"Yeah, they should, but you have to calm down, Sarge. Everything's fine."

"Yeah? That why we got another dead guy? Got a call yesterday about Wrubel. Spent an hour today reaming out the administration and telling them that their security sucks."

She laughed, then stopped when his face remained serious.

"After telling them 'I told you so,' which you know I loved doing, I grabbed some food." He held up a bag stuffed with two sodas and a premade sandwich from the grocery store down the street. "Forgot my peanuts, though, damn it."

Jace swallowed a chuckle.

"I said this place was lax and no one believed me and now Wrubel's dead and we're strapping Mercer in the chair so he can ride the lightning in Huntsville."

"You heard that? That Mercer did it?"

"Couldn't have been anyone else, the way I hear it." He stared at her, his gray eyes a wall between them. "Hear you're hip deep in the investigation, too."

Jace shook her head. "Not hip deep, but deeper than I want to be. Von Holton asked me to document a few things."

"Asked?"

"Well . . . demanded. He ordered me to do his legwork and Major Jakob just let him."

"That's 'cause she's testing you."

"I'm tired of being tested."

"Gonna happen every day until you retire."

"Yeah . . . well . . . I passed the test. I'm the one who brought him Mercer."

"Good for you." Bibb pointed to the control room. "I'll take a look and see what I can see on the hard drive. Maybe we can get you some actual evidence to take to him."

Jace smirked. "Sarge, Conroy didn't catch anything on the hard drive. He's barely able to open the doors."

"Yeah, the boy is a moron."

"Anyway, the investigation's basically over but I'm not sure I'll be off Von Holton's radar any time soon."

"Yeah?"

She pulled tonight's flyer from her pocket. She'd known there would be one waiting because she had pissed Von Holton off so badly. This one had five officers trying to handcuff bad guys while a crude depiction of Jace—no breasts and a huge butt—pointed the five officers out to a stick figure with a Texas Rangers badge pinned to its chest.

Bibb nodded. "I've seen 'em around."

"Von Holton's one of them."

"I heard that, too. 'S probably good information."

"He didn't deny it."

For the first time, a tiny smile cracked Bibb's face. "You 'fronted him? Knuckle up, worm." He held his fist out for her while his smile grew.

Grinning like an idiot, knowing she was basking in the glow of his approval, she tapped his fist with her own. "I probably shouldn't have done it."

"He deserves to get his shins kicked."

"By the way, that whole worm thing? I'm pretty much done with that."

"Hah. I'm not." He paused. "So what happened with Wrubel." His fist banged absently against the control room door. "Christ, I can't believe there was another one. Just proves what I've been saying, doesn't it? We'll be lucky if the Southwestern Jail Commission doesn't step in and take us over. Or shut us down completely. Damn it. We gotta get better about security, we want to keep people from dying. Or maybe fire your ass."

"Excuse me?"

He looked at her, stricken, and just blinked. "Crap, Salome, I'm sorry; that was stupid of me. It was just a joke. Shit. I'm really sorry." His head lowered.

Anger poured through her. Her hands balled to fists and her teeth ground against each other. "How could you say that?"

"Jace, really, I'm sorry; it was—You know I don't have no social skills. Hell, I lived with my parents 'til I was thirty. I only moved out when Dad died and Mom had to go to a home. I never learned . . . it doesn't matter. It was stupid and I apologize."

Through gritted teeth, Jace slowed her breathing. "It's fine, I guess. You are, after all, the guy who stares at my chest and ass, all in the name of protecting me. That's just you. Like a puppy who can't learn to pee on the newspaper."

His brows knitted together. "Uh . . . thanks?"

They both managed a nervous laugh and she showed him the five-pound bag of unshelled peanuts and the Mountain Dew. "Welcome back, Sarge."

"What's that?"

"Uh . . . five pounds of nuts? From me and Rory. The Mountain Dew is from me . . . just because I thought you might need one." She held the gifts out but he didn't take them. "Superficially, it's a welcome back. But I think it's more of a thank-you. For not letting me die."

"Oh, that. Whatever."

Eventually, Bibb took the gifts. His face was thinner than it had been, and it fit unevenly on his bones. Puffy and blotchy cheeks were now gaunt and angular though his skin was still pale. His jowls were gone and a nose that had once been nearly lost in the middle of a marshmallow face was now an alpine ski jump over a pile of rocks. In fact, his entire body was lost in a memory of what it had been just a couple months ago.

"Cruz was at the meeting. Asked me to look at the video," Bibb said.

"You won't see anything until after Deputy Ezell found the body."

"I'm pretty good."

"I know you are, Sarge, but if there's nothing there, there's nothing there. I'd think this is going to throw a kink into Cruz getting those new contracts."

"Ya' think?" Bibb nodded. "He's babbling bullets about it right now. Hard to convince the inspectors your procedures are safe when your assistant gets killed. The Travis and Taylor County guys were at that meeting, too, and they didn't look none too happy."

"I'll bet."

"Should'a heard Cruz. 'Wasn't medical's fault,' and 'That was facility security, not ours,' and all kinds of other crap."

Again, Jace felt the disconnect between what she'd seen of Cruz the night before and what other people told her. Vernezobre said Cruz was a gentleman and that was all Jace had seen, but shuffling blame off on the jail staff was a crappy thing to do.

"Has to save his company, I guess."

Jace hesitated, then said, "Are you sleeping at all?"

He said nothing for a long moment. "Not really. Getting better, I guess. Can't get the inmates outta my dreams, though. They run all over the damned place and every single one of the idjits looks like Badgett."

"Yeah." Jace had told Bibb of her dreams. "Me, too. The go-between and that damned shack sort of morphed into each other. Kind of hard to tell where I am sometimes."

"You and me both, Salome. Welcome to law enforcement. Now get outta my room."

CHAPTER 14

Every location. Show him every step Mercer took in this jail.

By her next shift, Jace had decided to overwhelm Von Holton with details. She would show him every place Mercer had been housed at Zachary County Jail, and where he was—and was supposed to be—the night Wrubel was killed. Dillon wasn't happy she was doing Von Holton's job. He complained up the food chain but had gotten ignored. He wanted her to get Von Holton's information as quickly as she could and get back in the jail rotation.

She would start wherever Mercer was living now and make copies of all the in-pod logs and work backward to when he came through the sally-port door. Next, she would document each and every trip out of his housing pod to medical or the yard or wherever. Then a trip to medical to document exactly when he was seen and for what, and when he was released.

When she was done, she could compare all that to Mercer's master log, which was a log generated by data entry of everything relating to an inmate for that particular stay, including all visitors and phone calls, all commissary purchases, all disciplinary procedures and court appearances.

—moving one . . . E edward to D david—

E Pod was old men and the infirm. D Pod was discipline. Jace chuckled at the thought of an old man getting over on a jailer enough to be moved to the discipline pod.

Ten minutes later, after a check of the main computer, Jace

keyed her mic. "Control from 479 . . . ad-seg outer."

Immediately it popped open. When it closed behind her, the ad-seg inner door popped open and she stepped inside.

"Schlomo besties, senorita," Jimmson said from the jailer's desk. "Urrea's been teaching me Mexican. Paying him a few bucks here and there to teach me."

"Well, first of all, it's Spanish, not Mexican. Second of all, it's *como estas,* not schlomo besties, and third of all, get your money back."

Jimmson grinned. "Meaning?"

Jace laughed. "Where's Croft?"

Jimmson pointed to the pod's bathroom. It was in the day-use area and meant for prisoners when they were locked out of their cells during the day. Given that the toilets were for prisoner use, Jace had never been quite able to put her bottom on one.

She headed for the desk, slipping around the backside of one of the large load-bearing posts because of a table and chairs that had been left out. Mostly the chairs were gathered around the table, though a few were scattered elsewhere. A checkers game, half-finished with four black kings against none for white, had been left on the table.

"Fuck you, you fucking bitch!"

Mercer screamed and pounded his cell door. The boom exploded through the pod, less than a foot from Jace. She jumped, her heart in her throat, and fell over one of the chairs.

"Jimmson!"

Her feet got tangled in the chair and for a split second—for a heartbeat—she was sure it was attacking her. She would feel metal fists, metal feet, a headbutt from a metallic aggressor. She tried to kick it away, certain Mercer was headed for her.

Where is Rory?

She hit the ground hard and bit through the tip of her tongue. Warm blood coated her tongue and her shoulder screamed as her arm got wrenched backward.

Where the hell is she?

Blood filled her head, heated and scared, and her legs were above her, caught in the chair's legs and arms. She couldn't see everything at once but she knew they were coming for her. They'd come from over there, and over there; from behind her and over the top of her. Inmates would beat her and kick her, stomp her out of existence. After that it would be the ERTs taking control of the pod. After the feet and fists of inmates she'd get batons and shields of fellow officers.

This can't be happening again.

"You ain't railroading me." Mercer screamed and pounded against his cell door, his fist punctuating every word. "I didn't fucking kill nobody."

"Mercer," Jimmson yelled. "Shut the hell up. Ain't nobody listening."

"I didn't kill no freakin' doctor."

Jace kicked the chair. Bolts of pain rocketed up through her duty boots. The chair blasted away, bounced off Mercer's cell door.

Mercer laughed madly. "Take more than that. You can't shut me up that easy, bitch."

Scrabbling away from the chair, Jace tried to get her feet under her, to get up and fight back, but none of her limbs seemed to work right. They had minds of their own and they ignored her commands.

"Jace. Take it easy. Everything's cool."

"Everything ain't cool. I ain't taking no shot for killing nobody. Bitch, you ain't railroading me."

Get hold of yourself. If they're coming for you, you have to protect yourself. Get hold of yourself.

She pushed away from the cell, away from the attacking prisoner, shoving herself across the floor until she was under the checkers table. The adrenaline dump was molten metal in her blood.

Remember what it does to you . . . cuts your breathing . . . narrows your vision . . . makes you paranoid.

Under the table, feeling somehow safe, like a puppy in a box with his back against two sides, she managed to breathe more deeply. Cool air chilled her throat and her head. She made a point of swivelling back and forth to see the entire pod.

The chair was just a chair. None of the inmates were out, cell doors were not popping open. No one was coming for her. There was no shrieking alarm calling the ERTs to smash her and make her piss herself.

Certain she was safe, she lay on the floor, staring up at the underside of the table. She heard Jimmson come to her while Mercer continued to howl from behind his locked cell door. Her chest heaved painfully.

"Can I move the table?"

She started laughing. Long and loud, loud enough to cover Mercer's yelling.

"What the hell?" He moved the table and stared down at her. "Are you dead? That why you're being hysterical?"

Her laugh petered out and she breathed long and deep. Her vision cleared and she felt her heart slow down. Eventually, she sat up. "What an idiot."

"You or him?" Jimmson pointed to Mercer.

"He scared me to death. I'm such a dumbass." She laughed again and knew it was the last bit of adrenaline slipping away from her. It was a nervous laugh and even that struck her as funny. "I knew they were locked down."

"Have been since before I got here. That's how efficient I am." Jimmson helped her up. "You okay?"

"Yeah, yeah." She tried to laugh it off again even as she tasted humiliation on the back of her throat and felt it in the embarrassment filling her cheeks. "Just me being stupid."

"Stupid? Hardly. I thought that son of a gun had gotten out." Jimmson's voice rose on the last word. "I thought he was killing you. Holy crap—scared me to death." He chuckled. "Well, not killing you because, obviously, you're so tough."

Jace shook her head. "You know, I hear the right words, but I think I hear a bit of . . . sarcasm?"

"Maybe."

"All fun and games with you assholes?" Mercer pounded on his cell door again. "I'm telling you I didn't kill the doctor. You can't pin it on me."

"Okay, Mercer. We hear you. Nobody's pinning anything on anyone. Now shut up."

"Fuck you. You can't tell me what to do." He fell silent and stared at Jace. "You ain't sticking me with this killing, I don't care what you think; I didn't do it."

Jace stood slowly. "I don't think anything, Mercer. I'm just doing paperwork."

"Bullshit." Mercer's voice rose. "You're investigating me. He told me so. Told me you were gonna put the needle in my arm yourself."

The walk to his cell door was a short distance, maybe twenty feet, but she took it slowly. Her legs were weak, her knees watery, her hands still shaking. "Who told you that?"

She stopped about two feet beyond his cell door. It wasn't barred, like in the movies, but was solid. There was a chuck hole about halfway down through which items could be passed, and a narrow window about halfway up.

"Who told you I was going to execute you?"

"That fucking detective. I don't know his damned name."

Jimmson said, "Von Holton was in here when I got here, talking to Mercer."

Von Holton had talked to Mercer? Anger bit Jace from the

back of her throat, nipped at her heels like a small, yappy mutt. Von Holton had set her up, filling Mercer's head with crap. Even had Jace never come in here for records, Mercer would have been looking for her. Maybe he'd have come after her in the yard or while going to court or back to medical. Von Holton had put Jace squarely in the sights of a man who'd already shown he was capable of murder.

Jace tried to keep her voice calm. "Mercer, I'm not a detective. I don't pin anything on anyone. Von Holton asked me to gather some paperwork, yes, on you, and deliver it to him. He's the one looking into this mess."

Mercer's face was as tight as a drum, his shirtless torso slick with sweat. "That's crap. You're trying to put it off on him."

"Mercer, come on, you're smarter than that." Jace stepped up next to the door, as close as she could get to his face. She wanted him to see her as plainly as possible. "How is a jailer, and I haven't even been here a year yet, going to take an investigation over a detective who's got . . . I don't know . . . thirty years on?"

Mercer was silent, though Jace could see one of his fists through the window. It hovered at his chest.

"Jimmson. How long have I been here?"

"Since April."

"And Von Holton?"

"Forever."

"Does he let anyone take his cases?"

Jimmson laughed.

"Mercer, listen to me. Von Holton came to talk to you because he's the investigating officer and he thought he'd have some fun with me at your expense. Do I think you did it? Yes. Am I the investigating officer? No."

"I didn't do it." His voice had gone soft, almost delicate. Gone was his anger and screaming. Gone was his fist, now it was just a hand that played at the back of his neck. "I didn't kill nobody. I'm just in on a cheap warrant. I ain't a player and I didn't kill nobody."

Jace took a deep breath and gave Jimmson a small nod. Jimmson returned the nod and wandered back to the jailer's desk.

"You think I did it?"

"The evidence says you did."

"The evidence is bullshit, then, 'cause I never even left medical. What . . . I'm gonna get out of holding, out of the pod, down the hall, knife him, come *back* to medical, get back in the pod, and put myself back in holding? They put me in holding after you guys came storming in and they didn't let me out until the day after he was dead. I. Never. Left. Medical."

Jace chewed that over. It was, basically, the same argument she'd used on Von Holton to convince him it couldn't be just any inmate. "You threatened him."

"Yeah, I did that. I was pissed off. He wouldn't give me my meds. Every time I get picked up I go through this crap. I never ask for anything but my asthma meds and every damn time it has to get approved. Hell, I'm up in this bitch just about every other month. Just keep what I need in that meds cabinet; you guys know I'm coming back."

"I hear you, I really do." She tried on a small smile. "Dude, I *work* here and they won't stock the soda I like so what are they going to do for you?"

He chuckled. "Ain't that the shitting truth. Look, I got mad and yelled and knocked the computer over and whatever. That's fine . . . charge me." He stood up straight and faced her dead on through the door window. "But I didn't kill him. I'm not a killer."

She waited for his eyes to leave hers, for him to sweat or fidget or fill in the silences. She watched for all the things guilty inmates did but she saw none of it. After a few seconds of star-ing at each other, wariness crept into his eyes.

"Ask."

"Huh?"

"You got a question. Ask."

She swallowed, unsure. "I keep hearing about drugs being smuggled into the jail. I wonder if you can help me with that."

A smirk slipped across his face. " 'Cause I got a bit of a problem, you mean? Got myself a little addiction?"

"I'm not judging." She leaned in close. "Look, I'm trying to work my way up, you know? That's why I'm doing a little work for Von Holton." She winked. "Got to suck up to move up, you know? So I'm just wondering if you can help me notch my belt a little."

He laughed. "You guys are all assholes. Don't want to give me my meds but have no problem asking me to rat. I ain't no rat, but I'll tell you this: You wanna stop some of the smuggling and selling? Don't be looking just at inmates. Be looking higher up the food chain, know what I mean? Not way far up, just a little up."

"Mercer, just tell me."

He laughed. "No, thanks."

Eventually, she nodded. "Tell you what; I'm going to gather the paperwork that Von Holton asked me for, but I'll sit down with him. I'll tell him you never left medical and he'll look into it. That's the best I can do. I'm just a jailer, remember."

"That ain't gonna get'cha any more information."

"These are two separate things. One does not affect the other."

He nodded. "You promise you'll talk to him? 'Cause I didn't do it."

"Absolutely. You have my word."

Again his gaze descended on her, harsh and brutal and tough, but also vulnerable. It reminded Jace of Mama and for a moment, Jace couldn't breathe.

Eventually, Mercer nodded. "Fine, then. Good night, Deputy."

"Good night, Mercer."

CHAPTER 15

Rory, badge number 456 and RC30, bounced into the break room, light on her feet. " 'S up?"

Jace plunged right in. "Mercer said he didn't do it."

Rory's step stopped mid-bounce. She spun, a rusty pirouette, from her ballet days as a little girl, and bowed deep from her hips. "He didn't." She rose. "I did. Took my little girl-scout pocket knife and sliced him all to pieces."

Jace frowned. "What are you talking about?"

Sitting, Rory became serious. "Jace, everybody says everything. You know that. You've been doing this long enough. Everybody in the Zachary County Jail is innocent, didn't you know that?"

Jace shook her head dismissively. "Yeah, yeah, I know, what I'm saying is . . . I believe him."

"Why's that?"

"Because of you." Jace explained how she had watched for Mercer's tells: for fidgeting and sweating, for increased breathing, for his jugular pounding harder with an increased heart rate, inability to speak clearly without hesitation, all those tells Rory had taught her to watch for. "I didn't see any of them."

"Just means he's a better liar than you. Look, there is a possibility he didn't do it. But he's the most logical suspect right now. You follow that string out until you prove he didn't do it, then you jump on the next suspect and follow that out."

"You know Von Holton was in there talking to him."

"Von Holton's a detective, that's what they do. Talk talk talk-talktalktalk."

Jace shook her head. "No, ma'am. He told Mercer I was the investigator, the one sending him to Huntsville to death row."

Rory frowned. "What?"

"Yes, ma'am."

Finally, Rory shrugged. "Not how I would have done the interview but I can see that. He's tossing you under and trying to work Mercer into coughing up more information. Kind of a good-cop, bad-cop thing."

Jace took a deep breath. "Or."

"Or what?"

"If Mercer didn't do it, who did? And why is Von Holton trying to put a target on my back?"

Rory stood and slammed the chair up under the table. "No. Absolutely not. This doesn't happen to you twice, Jace. You're seeing crazy shit, just like you did last time."

"Last time I was right."

"Which is why you won't be this time. It's not a cop . . . *again* . . . Jace. We're not all bad people. We're not all out to kill inmates or staff."

"I never said any such thing. I'm following the evidence . . . like you just told me to do."

"You're not following anything. You have an inmate, who's been charged with murder, telling you he didn't do it, and suddenly you think the detective in charge of the case did it. Show me what evidence you're following. Show me a shred of evidence. Not something you think, but something you can touch and feel. Evidence, actual physical evidence."

Rory waited, the break room filling with silence as deep as the surrounding desert. Doors popped and banged, squads took off with sirens loud, jailers laughed and argued. It was as though the building itself had a sound; low and mournful, both afraid and confident, the sound of hunter and hunted; the certain and uncertain.

Jace was both of those. Still learning to trust her gut, but fully cognizant that she wasn't as critical a thinker as she wanted to be, that she could be taken in, at least to a degree, by earnestness.

"There is none," she said finally.

—479 from control—

Jace's gut tightened. "Go ahead, Sarge."

—come see me—

"As soon as I can."

—come see me now. Bring her, too—

"Sarge, I'm—"

—now—

Two minutes later, they stood in the Pig Pen. Peanut shells were everywhere as though Bibb had never been gone. The screens flickered, black and white images of the jail at ebb tide. A handful of deputies wandered the halls, in and out of administrative offices, to and from the sally port. Two deputies hauled a cuffed woman into booking. In a far corner of the secured part of the facility, Sheriff Bukowski leaned against a wall in an empty hallway and chewed his cigar, his head back and his eyes closed.

—456 from 434—

Rory rolled her eyes. "I'm working B with Urrea. Must be getting lonely. Go ahead."

—gonna work this pod tonight?—

"Be there in just a minute."

—tick tock tick tock—

"Two bits of video for you." Bibb's fingers, shockingly thin, pounded the keyboard and a second later footage from the medical pod popped up on one of the fifteen screens.

The date and time stamp put the footage at 1:57 a.m.

Christmas Day. About twenty hours before Wrubel was killed. Initially, it was just the pod's outer door. No one in or out. Through the glass flanking either side of the door—thick enough to withstand an enraged inmate pounding against it—Doc Wrubel and Big Carol were plainly visible. Jace shivered. She'd seen the video of Thomas getting killed and she was pretty sure that was at least partially what fed her dreams. Seeing Wrubel now, before he was killed, impacted her like a fist dead center of her chest.

Bibb sped the footage up. "Watch the outer door. Ain't nothing happening inside."

Ten or fifteen seconds later, though they didn't hear it, the outer door popped and through it came Mercer with Deputy Croft just behind him. The door closed, then the inner door popped open and they went inside. A moment later, Wrubel and Big Carol came over and the four began talking. A few seconds later, the conversation became animated and shortly thereafter, the ERTs entered the pod from off-camera near the back where the war doors were. On screen, Mercer was on the ground, just as Jimmson had described, and Laimo was already laughing, leaning over Mercer and pointing a finger in his face.

"God, I hate that." Jace's jaw ground hard, grinding pain into her head.

"Don't sweat her, worm."

Jace looked at Rory, then sideways at Bibb. "I don't want to be her. I don't want to become what she is."

Bibb shook his head. "You won't. You don't have the same . . . uh . . ."

"Brutality and sadism?" Jace said.

"Well, I was going to say nastiness but yeah, we can go with your answer." Bibb turned back to his screens. "To the task at hand, this is where they take Mercer into a holding cell in medical. You can see it, barely, in the upper left corner through the glass. Then there ain't nothing for twenty-four hours. I've watched the entire thing. You can watch it if you want, or I can just forward it."

Thinking about her conversation with Dr. Vernezobre, Jace asked, "Does Big Carol ever fall asleep?"

"What? Uh . . . no, I don't think so. No; I'd'a remembered that."

"Maybe she took a nap in one of the exam rooms."

Bibb shook his head. "I checked all the cameras. Every room in medical is taped because there have been attacks in those rooms. Plus, we've had inmates say doctors did something or didn't do something and the footage is a pretty good reporter. No, Big Carol didn't fall asleep. I don't like her, but she's pretty responsible when it comes to her job. Why you asking?"

"Fast forward it, please."

Bibb punched some more buttons, the screen froze for a beat or two and then the time stamp was about twenty hours later. Doc and Big Carol wandered inside the pod, hands full of clipboards and bottles and various tools of their trade. After a few minutes, Doc Wrubel left the pod and something inside Jace broke.

"Don't worry, Salome. We can't see it. Hallways aren't recorded . . . as much as I have asked for them to be . . . for this very damned reason. Anyway, it ain't about the murder. We know that happened. It's about what happened at this end."

More than fifteen minutes after Wrubel left the pod, Big Carol jumped up from behind the desk and went to the pod's inner door and checked that it was locked. Then she strained to see out into the hallway.

"The alarm just went off, didn't it?"

Bibb tapped the time stamp. "At that exact moment, Rory."

Big Carol keyed the radio she wore at her hip. Her lips moved and Jace remembered the woman had said only that medical was locked. But Jace remembered it was less her words than her tone. Her tone had put everyone in the facility on edge. And now, seeing that the woman was pale and dancing nervously from room to room inside the medical pod, squeezed a tight fist of fear around Jace's heart.

A few seconds later, Big Carol spoke again, and told everyone Doc Wrubel was not locked down in medical, that he was somewhere out there. Jace shuddered to think that even as everyone heard Big Carol speak, Wrubel was already dead.

"Mercer never left." Jace took a deep breath.

Rory stared at the screen for a long moment. "It's kind of hard to see, but I think maybe you're right."

Bibb grinned. "Ever the skeptic. And hence to video number the second."

His finger blasted over the keyboard again and this time, the view was from a high corner of medical holding. The time stamp was just about the time the ERTs got called into medical. After the scuffle, which was unseen, two ERTs hustled Mercer into medical holding and closed the door. Mercer paced back and forth for a short time, then sat on the bed. After about ten minutes of sitting, he lay down and fell asleep.

"Every watch someone sleep in fast time? It's hilarious."

Bibb sped the footage up and Jace shook her head at Mercer tossing and turning, legs up and down, arms all over the place. At one point his head lolled just slightly off the bed. Then he was awake and wandering in a circular pattern around the room, then sitting, then eating when a meal was brought in, then sleeping again.

And then suddenly awake when the alarm went off. He jumped to the locked door and stared out the window.

"What's he seeing?" Jace asked.

"Big Carol get crazy and not know what to do. Maybe he can hear her telling everyone Wrubel's out of pod, maybe not."

"He was sleeping," Rory said. "When Wrubel was getting killed, Mercer was locked down in holding and sleeping. He didn't do it."

"Not by a damn sight," Bibb said.

Rory thumped Jace on the shoulder. "*That's* evidence, worm."

On the monitor of the here and now, the sheriff continued to lean against the wall in the hallway.

CHAPTER 16

Through the rest of her shift, Jace documented everything: where Mercer had been housed, her conversation with Mercer. She completed her written report and made multiple copies of Sgt. Bibb's video. When she was done, she sat at one of the computers in the squad room, three or four roadies scattered around the room like buckshot, each finishing their reports, and thought.

She was disappointed in herself for not realizing earlier Mercer couldn't have done it. In hindsight, knowing where he was at the moment of the attack seemed so basic. How would she ever be able to have faith in her decisions when she missed easy clues and cues like that? Where he was should have been her first question. That would have led her directly to the video and none of the rest would have been necessary.

"How's it going?" Ezell asked.

"Hey, how are you?"

He shrugged. "Banging reports. The bane of my existence."

She laughed. "Me, too."

"Wha'cha got?"

"Finishing the investigation on Wrubel."

Ezell frowned. "You're doing it? Thought that was lazy-ass Von Holton's."

"Technically it is, but he asked me to do a few things for him." She tried to eat back her grin.

"Spill; wha'cha got?"

"Well, between us?"

He made a cross over his ballistic-vested heart.

"He's focused on Mercer."

"The guy who Wrubel was fighting with."

Jace nodded. "It wasn't Mercer."

Ezell said nothing for a few seconds. Then he looked around to make sure they were semi-alone, and leaned in close. "No, it wasn't."

Jace stared at him. "What?"

"Mercer never left medical holding and Von Holton knew that. Or should have known. It's basic. Investigation 101: where was the suspect at the time of the crime?"

An image of the flyers, splayed all over her second bedroom wall, burst into her head. Bloody Jaces, bloody rats, bloody inmates, all topped by SuperHeroCops with huge chests and thighs the size of a well-grown burr oak tree hammering down the bad guys and keeping society free and clean and functioning.

Von Holton was one of the flyer boys. He'd made no secret of it, almost dared her to accuse him of it. He hated her, hated anyone who went after cops. Of course he knew Mercer wasn't the guy, and of course he'd used her inexperience to make her look like an idiot.

"Listen, don't take it so hard, okay? You figured it out, right? At least from what I heard . . . Bibb talks a lot. He loves you, by the way. Thinks you're brilliant."

"Bibb loves watching my ass."

Ezell shrugged. "Sure, that, too. But you got where you needed to be. Learn from it and move on." He patted her shoulder. "Don't play Von Holton's game. All he does is try to make people look bad. Let him make himself look bad."

While they'd spoken, everyone else had left. Ezell sat with her a moment longer, then clapped her on the shoulder. "I got to get back to it, see if I can find some traffic stops. Don't sweat it and don't worry about him . . . he's a sweaty ball sack."

Then the room was just Jace, her packets of information, and her anger.

CHAPTER 17

Twenty minutes after her shift, Jace saw Major Jakob in the parking lot.

"Good morning, Deputy Salome." Major Jakob blew across the top of a coffee. It was from a local coffee house, fancy cup and thermal lid. A wisp of steam rose through the tiny opening. She held a book under her arm. "How goes the investigation?"

Jace took a deep breath, stared out into the neighborhood around the jail, a neighborhood just beginning to come to life. A few cars here and there; an old white, work pick-up truck, the driver eating a burrito and aimlessly watching Jace and Major Jakob and the roadies going in and out. Near the courthouse a van from Texas Department of Criminal Justice waited, two prison guards in front and a single inmate, maybe brought back on a writ or wanting to ask a judge for a new look at his case, sat behind the guards, separated by a metal cage. Later, when the street fully awakened, it would teem with bail bondsmen, lawyers, courthouse workers, court clerks, advocacy counselors, counselors for addictions to alcohol or drugs, to sex, addictions to whatever might break a person's spirit and leave them staring through the thin windows of the Zach County Jail toward the counseling centers.

"Well, I used Detective Von Holton's case number and filed my report as a supplemental."

Jakob smiled a harsh little sneer. "Except his isn't done yet, is it?" Jakob waved away Jace's hesitation. "And you discovered

Mercer is our boy, right?"

It was a split second of hesitation but Jace knew the major saw it. So Jace faced the major fully and squared her shoulders. "No, ma'am. Mercer is not our suspect."

"No, in fact, he's not."

"You knew that."

Jakob nodded. "I was fairly certain, but there's always a chance, Deputy, that something turns up. That's why you never stop asking questions." She sipped her coffee. "Some kind of thing with vanilla and cinnamon and I don't know what all. Should'a just got coffee. Plain old coffee. So tell me what you found, Deputy."

She told the major about everything she'd found and about Mercer giving her an earful.

"You talked to Mercer?"

"Yes, ma'am."

"Good for you. He scared you and you got right back up on the horse. So to speak."

She left the videotape for last. "There is no way, from two different viewpoints, that Mercer killed Doc Wrubel."

"Well done, Salome. Very well done. So . . . who's my murderer?"

"I'm not a detective, ma'am."

Jakob laughed into her coffee cup. "My mother and I always had problems. She was a strait-laced Catholic who hated everything about everything. Used to tell me I was a bad girl because I wasn't as worshipful as she was. 'No, no,' I'd say, 'I'm not a bad girl. I'm a good girl.' " Jakob laughed again. "I was absolutely a bad girl, and it's what drove my mother into an early grave." She looked thoughtfully at the rising sun. "I wonder why you and I feel the need to deny our nature."

"Deny our nature? That's a little heavy for this early in the morning. I'm just trying to finish an assignment."

Jakob smiled disarmingly. "Absolutely, Deputy."

Jace squirmed under the woman's gaze. "I was asked to track where Mercer was housed while he was at the jail and I did that."

"Yes, you did."

"Yes, I did. And I think you already knew where he'd been housed."

"Yes, I did. Von Holton told me. He didn't tell you because he's an asshole. Don't look shocked, Salome. I'm brass but I'm not oblivious. He's an ass who runs with those guys who put nasty flyers in your locker. He wanted to watch you chase nothing."

Jace forced herself not to clench her fists.

"Except you didn't do nothing, did you?"

"Ma'am?"

"You tracked down some video that showed something quite interesting. Von Holton didn't think about video so you have that above him."

"Well, that wasn't me."

"It was your team."

"Excuse me, ma'am, but I don't have a team."

As they spoke, two black Lincoln Towncars pulled into the lot. They pulled into a no-parking zone near the employee entrance. Two drivers jumped out and seconds later, Dr. Cruz, along with six men, headed for the entrance. All except one were in uniforms or plainclothes with pistols and badges on their belts.

"Another of his tours," Jakob said.

"Who's the guy with no gun or badge?"

"An administrator, I'd guess."

The man's hair was perfectly combed, raked back to a jet-black slash over his skull. He took the lead toward the entrance, ahead even of Dr. Cruz. His suit was a deep gray and from here, Jace thought it might be a double-breasted, pinstriped thing. Walking with confidence, even aggression, he made a handsome picture as they disappeared into the jail.

Jakob looked at Jace. "Your team is the two deputies you've surrounded yourself with. Sgt. Bibb is as creepy as the day is long, but he's *damned* good at his job. Bogan is a scrapper. She wants to do the job well. She's too excited right now but when she calms down she's going to be just as good."

Jace said nothing for a minute, surprised that anything she or Rory had done was noticed by the commander of the lab. "So who's the suspect?"

Jakob shrugged. "Don't have one yet. Figure it out for me." With eyes swimming in sadistic delight, Jakob watched her. "Worried about Von Holton? Screw him. *I'm* giving you this assignment. And a bit of information . . . that better not go any further than you and me for right now. There were two sets of stab wounds, Deputy. The ones you saw? On his chest? Those big, raggedy wounds were made by the shank, but that's not what killed him. They would have, but the other set killed him first." She poured the remaining coffee out. "Two sets. One from the shank, one from something else."

There'd been so much blood, and she'd been so far away, it would have been impossible for Jace to see a second set. "From what?"

"Something sharper. Much more precise than a shank. Could be anything."

Jace thought. "So you've got a missing murder weapon?"

Jakob nodded. "I prefer to think of it as unrecovered but basically you're right. So what do we do about that?"

"Lockdown." Jace said it without hesitation but immediately saw the problem. "No. Lockdown announces to everyone something is going on. The murderer will assume it has to do with him. He'll jettison that weapon and we'll never find it."

A sturdy smile slipped over Jakob's face and Jace found herself bathing in it. She liked this woman. Even with the vaguely condescending way the woman forced Jace to think situations through, Jace liked her. Jakob carried herself with absolute confidence and spoke the same way, but managed it without sounding arrogant. The strength in her jaw, a product of nothing more than genetics, seemed to advertise a self-assuredness that Jace had never felt in her entire life. This woman, Jace was sure, knew exactly where her path in life was and how to navigate it.

She's the antithesis of Mama.

"Listen to me, Deputy Jace Salome. Only three people know about the murder weapon. Me, a lab rat, and you. No one else is going to know with the possible exception of Sheriff Bukowski, as much of a waste as that is."

Jace squirmed at the sentiment. "What about Von Holton?"

When Jakob smiled, the warmth was gone, replaced by a predator's leer. "When you talk with him tonight—"

"I'm off tonight. And tomorrow."

"Well, then, next time you're on. That bit of knowledge will keep. After all, I haven't yet finished my report, have I?" She flashed her predator's smile again and then it was gone. She stuck a stray bit of dark hair up under her knit cap. "So next time you talk to him, I want you to jam the murder weapon so far up his bazoo he tastes it."

"Uh . . . 'bazoo,' ma'am? I'm not familiar with that term."

"You oughta be, as much as he's been putting it up yours." The woman buzzed to be let inside the facility. "Oh, before I forget, this is for you."

She handed Jace the book. *Techniques of Crime Scene Detection.* "Barry Fisher wrote it. Good guy. Good book. Take your time with it. Get it back to me whenever."

"Wow. Uh . . . okay. Thank you, ma'am; I appreciate it."

"Well done, Deputy, well done."

When the door closed, Bibb's voice slipped from the intercom speaker. "Making some friends, worm?"

Jace laughed at the overhead speaker. "Damn it, Sarge, why are you still here?"

"I could say overtime . . . but mostly it's just to annoy you."

"Yeah . . . well . . . I guess your work here is done."

But as she drove home, the book between her legs, Jace smiled.

CHAPTER 18

That morning, Jace slept better than she'd thought she might.

While she had gone through the ritual, it had lasted but a moment, just long enough for her to feel a sliver of victory before closing the door and locking the two deadbolts. She hadn't gone into her second bedroom, painted with flyers, though she'd felt the pull in an almost primitive way. She'd resisted, had undressed and climbed into bed. She pretended she didn't hear the flyers calling her with their schoolyard mockery. She pretended, too, that the dreams of the house on cinder blocks with broken walls and windows wouldn't come for her.

Those dreams, night after night, frequently made it difficult to sleep. But this morning, after her conversation with Major Jakob, she'd read a bit of the book, and then slept nearly five hours. When she woke, she lounged under the blanket for a bit, thinking she might get a few more minutes. Eventually, she realized that wakefulness was playing in her head like edgy free-form jazz. Finally it annoyed her out of bed and she filled the apartment with Frank Morgan's sweet alto sax as she showered and dressed.

Major Jakob wanted a suspect and Jace wanted to give her one, but she had no idea where to turn. With the other small investigations she'd done in the jail—thefts within a cell block, scammed phone cards, fights and rapes—there had always been something for her to follow. This time, everything had evaporated when Mercer had.

She cracked a Dr Pepper and drank half of it, the fizz stinging her throat and making her eyes water pleasantly.

If there was no evidence, what else was there? As she drank,
her gaze fell to a prescription for antibiotics she'd had after a
prisoner bit her during a wrestling match, and something in her
brain clicked.

Dr. Vernezobre had been adamant about Mercer as unrepen-
tant killer. He'd said Mercer threatened to kill Wrubel, and
while that might have been true, it was equally true that Dr.
Vernezobre, late of Cuba and giving medical care to the poor of
Zachary County, had been incorrect to the point of lying. Big
Carol hadn't been asleep nor had Mercer escaped medical.

"So why'd you work so hard to convince us otherwise?"

A quick call and half hour later they were in Rory's Monte
Carlo.

After passing the park where Zachary City asked residents to
put their old Christmas trees and Christmas garbage, Rory said,
"Christmas pretty much gets funky after it's over, don't it? All
the crap, I mean. Decorations and trees and lights. See, before
Christmas, everything's nostalgia and what you remember as a
kid and everything. After, it's just garbage and lots of trees
without needles and tons of wrapping paper. Like Times Square
after New Year's."

Jace laughed. "Have you ever seen Times Square after New
Year's?"

"Well . . . yeah . . . on TV and stuff."

"What I remember of Christmas is Denny's. The rule was
that I could play with anything Santa left out and whatever was
in my stocking. But I couldn't unwrap anything until after
breakfast. Everybody had to get up and get dressed and then
we'd go eat at Denny's. So Christmas to me is pretty much the
smell of eggs, overcooked bacon, coffee and pancakes, and

drunks left over from the night before."

Rory looked at her. "Wow, and you think *I'm* the cynic? So where we going?"

"I want to know why Dr. Vernezobre lied to us." Jace laid it out quick.

"He's a helluva guy, Jace, biggest heart I've ever seen." Rory spoke in sorrowful tones.

"Yeah, but—"

Rory held up a hand. "Yeah, I think he lied to us."

They headed toward The Flat, on the opposite side of Highway 80, and a world away from Zach City's Garden District. The Flat lay on the south side of the rail line that sliced Zachary City in half like a ragged scar, and it was home to most of Zach City's blood clubs. That blood both rained and reigned was as inevitable as the summer dust storms and every night, on a dance floor or in a bathroom or in a parking lot, someone bled. Frequently, they died. This area of town was steeped in violence. Though there were good places and good people who lived down here, the seductive odor of violence held absolute dominion, covering even the stink of cattle and oil.

Violence wasn't The Flat's only attraction. People came for booze brewed in bathtubs hidden in basements, for drugs grown in Mexico or Afghanistan or sometimes the rural parts of Zachary County. They came, too, for the sex. A five-spot or the cost of a single room could easily score the entire breadth of human depravity: young and old, fat and thin, fetishes running from bugs underfoot to diapers on hips. It was a seething mass of humanity that Jace knew far better than she wanted. It was, at once, both the pinnacle and pit of those who called Zachary City home.

Dr. Jesus Vernezobre's office lay in the middle of The Flat, as though it had been dropped from a plane that had gone badly off course and shoved its cargo out in a blind panic. It was a glass-front building and looked as though in a previous life it had been a laundromat. The windows were dirty, streaked with lines of dust and liquid long since dried to a crusty stain. The door was open, propped with a rock that had a picture of Jesus painted on it, and plywood nailed over a small window where Jace presumed there had once been glass.

"What?" Rory shut the car off.

"Nothing. Just doesn't seem like the man I met."

"Don't judge the cover by the book."

"Book by cover."

"Yeah, well, whatever. I'm saying, shitty office or not, this is where Dr. Vernezobre gets his pass to Heaven."

Standing on the cracked sidewalk, Jace saw Vernezobre through the front window. At just after one in the afternoon, the doctor was bent over an elderly woman while three other patients waited in plastic folding chairs. "Not much of a castle for a man of Cuban royalty."

"Rich people don't need his medicine." Rory shrugged. " 'S what he tells me, anyway."

Inside, they waited until he was finished with the woman. She nodded while he spoke rapid-fire Spanish and then handed her a sandwich bag of pastel-green pills. Nervously, she glanced at Jace and Rory but Vernezobre calmed her with a few whispered words. The woman shoved the pills in her purse and hobbled out. The other visitors never stood to take their turn with the doctor. Instead, they kept their eyes on the portable TV or in one of the gossip magazines strewn about the place like dead party favors.

"Ladies." Vernezobre bowed. "Good afternoon. I am honored to see you. How can I be of service?"

"We need to talk, sir," Jace said.

The doctor's smile faltered but he immediately ushered them into the office.

Rory swallowed. "Dr. Vernezobre, you know how much I respect you and your work."

"I do, and I thank you for all the help you've been. But, Miss Bogan, are friends to stand on ceremony? How can it be that, given the ground we've traversed together, you hesitate to ask something of me?"

"Yes, sir. Well . . . uh—"

"You lied to us." Jace held his gaze.

For a long moment, Vernezobre said nothing. His gaze hardened and moved between the two women. His jaw tightened and the muscles across the back of his shoulders tensed.

"Doctor?"

Then it was gone. Like the air from a tire, he deflated and sat heavily on his exam table. "Yes."

"Why?"

Rolling his shoulders, he spread his hands. "Who knows why I do anything, Miss Salome. I am an old man who's spent his life helping those who couldn't help themselves and—"

"Doctor, please; I don't need the pity party, just the truth."

"Jace, dial it down."

"Do not scold, Miss Bogan. In trying to help Francis, I have probably impeded your investigation. I was going to say that I've spent my life helping those who couldn't help themselves and in Dr. Francis Wrubel, I have—had—a dear friend who could not help himself. In telling you what Dr. Cruz told me, I was attempting to ensure someone paid for Dr. Wrubel's death."

"Even if it was the wrong man?" Rory asked.

"I did not know it was the wrong man. When I spoke to you, I believed, as fervently as my dear mother believed that salvation lay through the Father, the Son, and the Holy Spirit, that Mercer had killed my friend."

They were interrupted by a frail woman. Her face was as white as wedding lace though her hair was steel gray. She was in obvious distress and to her, Jace and Rory did not exist. *She has too many other things to care about,* Jace realized. When she came in, Rory and Jace were immediately forgotten to Dr. Vernez-obre. He and the woman hovered together near the corner of the office and then the doctor went into a tall file cabinet near the window. He pulled out a sandwich bag similar to the one Jace had seen earlier except these pills were tiny and white and there were few of them. He handed the bag to the woman by wrapping her tiny hand in his giant ones. He then kissed the top of her head and she left. The entire transaction took less than thirty seconds and everything they needed to say had been said silently.

The doctor watched her leave, then nodded to the other waiting patients. "Her daughter is a lovely woman. I did not expect her to survive so long."

"What's she have?" Rory asked.

"Heart disease. Quite advanced for someone so young. Three heart attacks so far, each worse than the previous. She will not survive a fourth." His face was filled with some measure of hurt for his patients but also with a self-knowledge that there was nothing else he would do with his life.

"What are the meds?" Jace asked.

"Nitroglycerine. It will not help."

Jace frowned. "Then why?"

"Because this is what I do, Miss Salome. Because I am a doctor and I tend to the sick. And because—for her daughter, those pills are the last thing she has. She believes they will save her and if that is what she needs for comfort at the end of her life, then that is what I will do."

"Will they save her?"

He shook his head. "Her heart is too damaged. When the next comes, it will most likely kill her."

"False comfort?" Jace asked.

"Perhaps. But it helps the patient and, to be brutally honest, Miss Salome, no one else matters in that equation. She will die but perhaps I can ease that knowledge." He eyed her. "It is, after all, what we do with those who are terminal."

Rory spoke quietly. "Jace's grandfather died of cancer."

Jace bit down her anger. She wanted to know why Vernezobre had lied to her about Mercer; she didn't want to go mucking about in her own past.

"Indeed."

"I don't want to talk about it."

"Certainly, but I'd ask you to look into your memory and compare that woman's daughter with your grandfather. Was there some last thing that comforted him, as useless as it might have been?"

The truth was that the entire thing was a blur to Jace. Grapa had been the strongest man she'd ever known and then, seemingly overnight, he was reduced to chairs with blankets over his legs and then beds and sunken cheeks and constant bouts of nausea. She remembered him putting his head in his hands and saying he was tired, before making a trip to the hospital. They could do nothing and so released him. He spent two more days at home before dying. Then it was Jace and Gramma and a sad memorial affair with a few friends.

"Miss Salome, I am sorry about your grandfather, but you understand, better than most non-patients who come through my door, exactly why I do what I do."

"I don't. I do not believe it's better to lie to someone."

"Yeah, she does," Rory said. "If she ain't a cop? She'd be a social worker or maybe stealing meds off the back of a truck and handing them out to poor people who can't afford to pay."

Jace blinked. "What?"

Doctor Vernezobre shook his head. "Well, Miss Bogan, let me address your contention of medicines stolen from a truck. I do

145

not know what you're talking about. Secondly, my patients can afford to pay; they simply do it in unconventional ways. Just last week, a woman whose husband I treated cooked a delightful lunch for myself and the four patients who happened to be here at the time."

Rory grinned. "Uh . . . okay, you don't know about stolen meds. That's fine . . . whatever."

Jace pressed on. "I want to know about what you told us Dr. Wrubel said to you."

"Yes, ma'am."

As they spoke, a middle-aged man came to them. He looked at them but said nothing. Eventually, the doctor spoke to him, frowned, took a small bottle of pills from his desk, scrawled his name and the date across a blank label, and handed the bottle to the man. The man disappeared.

The doctor sighed. "Sometimes, medicines that come from trucks that are not . . . how shall I say . . . noticed by the government, are not the best medicines."

"You mean less than full strength? Or maybe not exactly what you're told they are?"

Dr. Vernezobre shook his head. "They are always what I'm told they are. If not—" He snapped his fingers. "I do business elsewhere."

"So you do know about stolen meds."

"I do not know about stolen medicines. I have never, in my life, given a patient stolen medicine. I have always paid for the medicines I give my patients." Color flooded into his face but he stood as tall as his impressive frame allowed. "However, rarely do I pay full price. But yes, to answer your question, sometimes the strength is that of an old, weak woman, rather than a robust young man."

Rory said, "So you said Mercer had threatened to kill Wrubel. Other than that night in medical, is that true?"

"Were there other threats, you mean?"

"Yes."

"Francis told me of no specific threat from Mercer." A pained expression crossed Vernezobre's face. "Dr. Cruz told me of the incident."

That surprised Jace. "When?"

"When he called me about Francis's death. The morning I had the good fortune of making your acquaintance at Alley B's. I believed that by saying Francis spoke to me directly, I could give you some urgency."

"Mercer didn't do it." Jace took a deep breath. "But we spent a day working on him. Dr. Vernezobre, that time should have been spent looking for the real killer."

The doctor lowered his head. "I understand completely, but I honestly believed him to be Francis's murderer. Ladies, is there anything I can offer beyond an apology? I believed I was helping, though it seems I made the situation more difficult. I see, now, that I became one of those who you deal with daily; I become one of the liars, though my intentions were good."

Jace tried to soften her glare. The man hurt, it was obvious, and was trying to help a friend. He had not meant to slow them down and, for that, Jace couldn't fault him. "So who did do it?"

"Miss Salome, please believe me when I tell you it tears my heart desperately that I do not know." He touched a black and white picture of a doctor and nurse standing in front of a severe-looking government building. "My father was a doctor and my mother, a nurse. In Cuba. They were good people and I fear I have dishonored them with my lies."

"No, Doctor, you just made a—"

"Miss Salome, there is one other thing I can tell you, though I have no idea if it has any bearing." His eyes, so strong and brown that morning at Alley B's, were now weak and tired. "Dr. Cruz told me, a few days before Francis's death, that a scalpel was missing from medical."

Rory's eyes bulged. "What? I hadn't heard that."

Jace swallowed. *An inmate walking around with a scalpel?*

"Francis said nothing. It was found within a few hours. He believed it never left medical."

Rory, frowning, said, "Doesn't matter what he believed, it matters that—"

"Where'd he find it?"

"He didn't; Dr. Cruz did. He told me that he and Francis had a terrible argument over it. Dr. Cruz believed Francis lost the instrument."

"You don't believe he did?"

Vernezobre took a deep breath. "I believe that whoever killed my friend took the scalpel."

"But you said it had been found? So it was accounted for when Wrubel died?"

"Perhaps, but that is not to say the missing scalpel wasn't supposed to be the weapon. Apparently, Dr. Cruz found it before it could kill Francis. The killer simply found something else."

Two sets of stab wounds, Deputy. One from the shank, one from something else . . . something sharper . . . more precise.

And that second weapon, the sharper, more precise one, was still missing.

Unless it had been used and put back into the medical inventory.

Could Major Jakob check the scalpels for blood? Could she check for Doc Wrubel's blood and DNA?

In the silence, the trio heard a baby crying from the cramped lobby. When Jace looked, she was surprised to see the place had filled for the afternoon with patients.

"Ladies, I have made your job more difficult and I will atone for that in any way possible. But can it not wait until my office has closed?"

"Uh . . . yeah . . . no problem," Jace said.

Digging a twenty from her wallet, Rory set it on the desk. "Thank you, Dr. Vernezobre."

"Bless you, Miss Bogan. By the by, *American Buffalo* is opening at the Zach City Theatre in two weeks. Perhaps you will accompany me? It concerns a robbery."

Rory laughed. "Everyday stuff for me. Call me when they do a love story."

"You are ever the romantic. I will surely call you."

CHAPTER 19

"Theater?" Jace asked when they were gliding along in Rory's Monte Carlo.

Rory shrugged. "We go sometimes. Symphony, too."

"Right . . . music with rules."

"As opposed to your music . . . where they play whatever they want."

"They don't, but that doesn't mean you're not a philistine."

"Philistine? I'm a Texan."

"Again, the razor sharp wit."

But both women smiled as Rory navigated the streets of Zachary City. She drove confidently. The Monte Carlo's motor thrummed, steady and certain.

"So who did it, then?"

"Beats the hell outta me." Rory changed lanes seemingly without regard to those behind her. Her speed continually crept up over the limit and at least once, as she passed a Zach City officer, she held up her wallet badge, flipped open so the badge was visible.

"You always keep that ready to flash?"

Rory giggled. "Just since I started working in Rooster. The older guys there do it all the time. Seems like a decent perk."

"Yeah, hey, why not? Now I'm the law so these pesky laws don't really apply." Jace huffed.

"Now you're getting it." She glanced in the rearview mirror. "I'll make a road deputy outta you yet."

"No, thanks. I'm perfectly comfortable in the jail."

Rory grinned. "Sister, you're uncomfortable all the time and everywhere, but I get what you're saying. Listen, come with me tomorrow tonight. It'll be fun. You'll love it."

"Thanks, but I just don't think I'm interested. It just . . . I don't know . . . just doesn't seem like something I want to do."

Rory gunned the car into the right lane. "Yeah? Then why are you putting so much effort into Wrubel's killer?"

Jace's hesitation was uncomfortable. "Well . . . because it was an assigned case, I guess."

"Bullcrap. Could'a dumped the whole heaping pile on Von Holton and been done with it. Hey, I'm all for showing Von Holton up; that's an admirable goal. But I've seen your face. When you thought it was over you were disappointed. When it didn't go down, your face lit up like a crack whore when poppa comes calling."

The silence grew this time, even more uncomfortable.

"A crack whore? Thanks."

"Look, babe, all I'm saying is that you like the investigation and the hunt. You hate most of what we do but you love that part."

"I don't hate most of what we do. I hate the physical violence." She turned sideways in the seat to face Rory. "And I tell you this: I really hate the emotional and spiritual violence that people like Laimo dish out to people."

"Laimo? What's the she-beast got to do with any of this?"

"I don't like how she treats people."

"Bah. Don't worry about her. She's weak and scared and so she covers it by getting over on weak and scared people. Someday someone's going to come along and put her in her place."

"Getting over on people who are weaker by nothing more than circumstance."

Trey R. Barker

"She didn't rot far from the tree, you know."

"What? Her mother is not that kind of a person."

"No, Major Jakob is tough and strong and amazing." Rory shook her head. "Major Jakob's ex-husband . . . Laimo's daddy? Not so much."

Jace couldn't have been more surprised if Rory had told her every rainbow came from Laimo's heart rather than a pot of gold or the refraction of sunlight through water.

"From Major Jakob's first marriage." With a shrug, Rory grinned. "What's more . . . you know him. And he ain't one of your favorite people, either. At least not right now."

Rory's eyes held tight to Jace's and eventually, with Rory smirking, Jace's jaw dropped.

"Gonna catch flies in there."

"Von Holton?"

"Married thirty years ago for about thirty-seven seconds. Neither of them has ever forgiven the other." Rory laughed. "Or maybe themselves. Hell, I've had bad boyfriends I haven't forgiven myself for."

That little nugget of info certainly explained the animosity between them when Jace was in the Pulpit and why Jakob was so insistent about Jace working in Von Holton's face.

"She's using me to make him look bad."

Rory inclined her head. "Ahhh . . . probably not. She hates him, no doubt, but she's about solving cases and empowering women."

"A three-fer, then. Empower me, solve the case, and make him look bad."

"Hah! Maybe." Her eyes flicked to the rearview mirror, then back to the road, which she sliced and carved with ease. "Has to be an inmate."

"Why?" Jace asked.

"Because of the shank."

152

"Unless someone was using the shank as a cover."

"Huh?"

Jace told her what Jakob had said. Rory frowned when Jace mentioned a weapon sharper and more exacting than a jailyard shank. "That was what killed Dr. Wrubel, not the shank."

"And she doesn't know what it was?"

"Said she didn't but who knows."

"And Dr. Vernezobre said there was a scalpel missing."

"Which he said they found."

Rory nodded. "Yeah, but still."

Jace yanked her phone out and called Jakob. "Major? Deputy Salome. I have a question. Do you have the capability of checking all the scalpels in medical for traces of blood?" She paused. "So you could tell if it was Wrubel's blood or DNA?" Another pause. "Well, I was just thinking that maybe whoever killed him, if they did it with one of those scalpels, maybe they got it back to medical before anyone realized what was going on."

Jace pulled the phone from her ear so Rory could hear the long pause. "Well done, Deputy. We've already done that. There are ten scalpels in stock. Seven of them were still in factory-sealed packaging. Two were clean with no trace evidence. One had a bit of blood. Not enough to type the DNA but enough to say it wasn't Dr. Wrubel's blood type."

"Oh. Well, it was just a thought."

"You and Rory make a good team," Jakob said. "Keep going. Find me a suspect."

"Yes, ma'am."

When Jace hung up, she glanced at Rory. Rory's smile took up the largest part of her face. One hand was banging the steering wheel in a rhythm only she could hear. "That's a good day, Jace. Jakob noticing us? That's a damned good day."

"Yeah, it is." Jace grinned at her friend's delight. "She told me this morning we were a good team."

"Yeah? Very cool."

After a moment of silence, Rory frowned and said, "So someone was pretending to be an inmate. Using the shank, I mean."

"Who better to look guilty than four hundred guilty people?" Jace chewed it over. "You're saying a cop."

"Civilian staffer? Lotta those in the jail."

"A medical staffer could get a scalpel but Jakob said none of them was the murder weapon. But a staffer would end the question of how an inmate got out of the pod, wouldn't it?" Jace took a deep breath. "There weren't any staffers around, at least not that I remember."

With a sidelong glance, Rory said, "Hell, you don't remember anything . . . you were too freaked out." Again, her eyes drifted to the mirror. "Got something else might freak you out."

As she looked behind them, the spit in Jace's throat dried. There were four or five cars and some trucks, but to her they all looked like regular morning traffic. "Which one?"

"The beat-to-crap pickup. White and rusty." Rory pushed the speed a bit and moved over a lane.

"The one right behind us? Too obvious. Plus, why's he following us?"

Months earlier, she'd been followed and run off the road, and remembering that nightmare put a cold ball deep in her gut. But, as scared as she'd been, she'd learned something that time. So instead of panicking, which is what her gut wanted to do, she started looking for the license plate. "Maybe he's following us because we are two extremely lovely women and he hasn't had a date in . . . like . . . years."

Rory sighed. "Great, another creep. You'd think simple percentages would give me a winner some time."

In spite of their attempts at humor, fear bubbled deep in Jace's soul. She breathed deeply, trying to keep adrenaline at bay. From experience, she knew it would narrow her vision and speed her breathing. It would steal her fine motor coordination and leave her with only the most basic of skills. But mostly, it would make her paranoid.

Calm down. It's not happening again. This isn't a thug Badgett sent. His thugs are gone. He's gone.

Except her sleeplessness and tangled dreams demonstrated that the fear was not gone completely, not in her head and heart. Not being able to simply enter her apartment, snapping at Gramma and Preacher when they invited her to play dominoes, told her the experience still had its thorns deep in her soul.

"Hang on." Rory eased their speed, yanked the wheel hard left, and got them into a turn lane at the last minute. A car somewhere in their wake honked, but the pickup behind them managed to make the turn, too.

"Shit." Jace grabbed her phone and tried to see the plate.

"Don't call. Not yet."

"You have to stop, Rory."

"And do what? No, let's see how this plays a little first."

"No, you have to stop."

"Ain't stopping just yet."

Rory hit another turn, this time to the right and pushed the car harder. Her Monte Carlo rocketed west along Front Street. The abandoned two-room train station slipped past in a gray blur. Every pothole was as large as a crater. The car bounced and howled its protest.

"He's still coming. Rory, please. Just stop."

Rory came off the gas, went on the brake, then on the gas again. The car lurched, dodged, and fishtailed around another corner. The pickup truck followed, though now the driver looked apprehensive.

"Who the hell is it?"

"No idea. Some punk kid, probably."

"Go to Industrial Loop."

Rory nodded. "Good. Lotta warehouses and alleys."

Thirty seconds later, Jace pointed down an alley. "There. Maybe he'll miss it."

But he didn't. Raggedly, his truck came around the corner and bounced over some trash cans.

Rory tossed a hard glance at her friend and rounded another corner. "Man, what is it with you and car chases? My insurance rates are gonna go up . . . seriously."

"Rory, I can't see the plate."

"What?"

"No front plate."

"Doesn't mean anything. All kinds of cars ain't got no front plate."

"Stop."

"Jace, I'm not stopping to call anybody or—"

"Just stop. Right now. In that lot. I'm done." Anger spiked her throat and her volume filled the Monte Carlo.

"Jace—"

"Stop."

Rory blasted into a dirt parking lot and slammed the car into a power slide. It came to rest in a shower of gravel and dust and then swam in the cloud. Jace yanked Rory's shirt up and jerked her Glock from her waistband. Rory looked stunned while Jace jumped from the car and strode through the dust.

The truck stopped at the lot entrance. The engine rattled and the windshield was cracked, a long spider's leg reaching across corner to corner. It was a work truck, with a faded logo of an animal on the side. The driver, a white male who ran maybe mid-thirties, made no move to get out.

"Here I am," Jace shouted and raised the pistol. "Whatever you think you want . . . here I am."

Behind the wheel, she saw the man's eyes widen and his lips flap. Jace moved fast and the guy froze. When she was nearly at the truck, he gunned it, spun it, and shot down the street, trails of black rubber behind him like adrenalized fear.

"Jace." Rory dashed from the car and clapped her hard on the back. "Holy crap. Did you see that? Holy crap. You scared the shit outta me. *And* him. Holy jeepers. What were you thinking?"

"Huh?" Her hands shook and she could feel her heart slowing. Her breath was hot and fast in her throat. Her vision had shrunk to just the truck but now was opening up. She had peripheral vision again. She looked at Rory. "Holy jeepers? What kind'a jeepers are those . . . specifically?"

She handed the gun back to Rory and walked unsteadily back to Rory's car, where she leaned on the hood, fear and violence sloshing through her like bad booze. It was all going to come up; the doubt, months of anger, years of uncertainty, of being alone. It would come out here and now, on a cracked parking lot shot through with weeds and broken bottles and lost pennies. Here where so few footsteps left an impression, with a closed-down Redi-Mix concrete plant hovering over them, with a barely open auto-body shop and the stink of oil and cow shit heavy in the air, she would be sick and leave everything that had poisoned her since Mama left on the gray asphalt.

Will that let me sleep at night?

"Damn, girl, you okay?"

Jace hadn't been thinking at all. The world, and the man chasing her, had been screaming at her, red-faced and fists swinging. Red anger, maybe, or black or maybe even sickly yellow. Mindless fury had been her response.

"Man, that was outta sight." Rory danced a little jig. "That got me all juiced up and ready to rock and roll." She frowned as she repacked her gun in her waistband and drew her shirt down over it. "How'd you know I was carrying?"

"You should wear looser clothes."

"Well, whatever. That was great."

"No, it was stupid." Jace took a deep breath and her head began to slow down.

If the driver had been armed, he could have killed her. Or he could have run her down. A million possible scenarios and all of them ended with her dead in the dirt. Her breath caught in her lungs and came out in hitches, percussive like a hard bop jazz drummer from the Fifties . . . strung out and pounding his kit until it bled music. The bitter taste of burned adrenaline sat on the back of her tongue and made her gag. And she couldn't quit blinking.

She'd been thinking nothing and that bothered her.

In her short time at the jail, she'd seen too much of that, from both inmates and cops. Those were boots she didn't want to wear. If she needed anger or violence she wanted to choose it. She wanted a conscious choice rather than being led.

So now the girl wants you to use violence. You waved a gun, Jace. What if he'd gotten out of the car? Shoot him? Violence doesn't fix anything.

Gramma's sentiments. Not her words but what she believed to the core of her soul and what she'd tried to teach Jace in the years since Mama was killed.

Jace swallowed. Maybe Gramma was right.

"Hey, you okay? You're kind'a pale. Don't pass out on me, okay? Come on, let's hit the road."

Jace stared at the empty lot. "No back plate."

"What?"

"No front plate . . . no back plate."

Rory frowned. "Son of a bitch."

CHAPTER 20

That night, she fell asleep in her second bedroom. Curled on the floor, fetus-like, staring at the walls towering above her. At first she wallowed in the violence of the flyers, fantasized about hitting back at those who left them, thought about flattening their car tires and putting sugar in their gas tanks; her brain filled with an entire universe of juvenilia to hurt them. Eventually, she closed her eyes but that only seemed to magnify the flyers' power. Perhaps it was the power of what was in shadow and hidden. It was waiting for her, regardless of whether she looked at it directly or tried to hide herself.

Eventually, when she did sleep, she dreamed of the house that morphed into the go-between; then it was the house again and she still had no idea whose house it was or even where it was. She had no idea, awake or sleeping, what it meant to her and why it had only bubbled up recently.

Now there was something new, too: the truck that had followed her and Rory, the truck with no license plates at all. It drove around the house endlessly, kicking up dust from the gravel, never stopping while Rory ate endless Skittles.

She hated the entire dream: the go-between, the house, and the truck.

Because they scared her.

Most of the next day she spent with Gramma.

They cleaned the entire Sea Spray. Gramma had a cleaning

159

service that came in every day, a few older women who cleaned rooms for the transient guests, those who came and stayed a few days and left. But for the regulars, those who chose the Sea Spray as their home, it was Gramma and sometimes Jace who did their cleaning. Jace spent the time with the old woman, both to be with her and in hopes that the togetherness might ease the worry etched deeply into Gramma's face. They filled boxes with the soon-to-be-departed year's tax and occupancy records, and opened up a new box for the coming year. They filled the hours with plumbing and vacuuming and replacing light bulbs, but, mostly, they filled those hours with near total silence.

"Much more laundry?" Jace asked.

Gramma spent one day a week doing laundry for her older live-in tenants, those who had trouble getting up and down stairs or lugging baskets of dirty clothes to the laundry room. She charged nothing for the service, but almost always got some sort of thank-you. One of the old men fancied himself an artist though all of his pictures were drawn from his time as a tunnel rat in Vietnam. At least once a year he gave Gramma a painting. A woman, who'd been here as long as Jace could remember, had spent her life keeping the books for a number of bars around town. Once a year, she marched—as well as one could behind a walker—to the office with a pencil behind each ear and demanded to do the hotel's books as a thank-you for the laundry service. Gramma always acted so pleased and cracked open the books. But the woman had done most of her work for men who tried to keep most of their work off the books. Gramma tried never to show too much alarm at the shortcuts the woman suggested, and then always had the books and taxes redone.

"Not much, little girl." Gramma's voice was soft and helpful. "Thank you for all your help today. It's your day off. Shouldn't you be out hunting boys and getting ice cream and going to the movies?"

Jace laughed. "Sure, if I were fourteen."

Gramma set down the basket of laundry. "Well, I guess you'll always be fourteen to me."

"Even when I'm behind a walker?"

"I'll be long dead by then."

"Cripes, Gramma, you're going to outlive everyone."

"Holy shit, I hope not. Stuck in bed, crapping myself, drooling all over, eating pureed soup." She shook her head. "Get me outta here long before that. Maybe in the arms of the all-time ultimate lover. He gets me off in such a huge way that my poor old heart just stops plunking then and there."

"There's an image I needed."

Gramma smiled. "Good, then. Seems my work here is done." She grabbed the laundry basket, had Jace grab a tool box, and headed out. "Next up? Mrs. Evans. Cranky old bitch but she makes me laugh."

Jace opened her mouth, thought to ask Gramma about the house with the broken windows, but in the end said nothing. For now, she would keep her nightmares to herself.

CHAPTER 21

The next evening, after the sun had fallen over the horizon and the New Year's Eve chill had taken stronger hold, Jace sat uncomfortably in Rory's Rooster County cruiser. It was a hulking Impala, filled with radio gear, a shotgun over her head, citation books, and maps of nearly forgotten Rooster County back roads.

After Rory's fifteen-minute equipment check of all the cruiser's gear, eating red Skittles incessantly, they headed out onto Rooster's roadways.

"Just the reds, Etta?"

"Strawberry is my favorite. Why the hell you call me Etta?"

Jace snickered and hunkered down in her seat, snapping the seat belt over her.

Jace had managed to grab a decent nap after helping Gramma yesterday and today they'd done a bit more. Then they'd spent a few hours leisurely playing dominoes with Hassan and Preacher. Hassan, an old timer who had been at the Sea Spray since Grapa was still alive and spry, had been full of questions but Preacher had shushed him and the afternoon had pleasantly stayed away from the Zachary County sheriff's office.

After Jace had some beef soup, and while she was head-deep in Jakob's crime scene book, Rory had shown up at Jace's apartment and demanded she go with her.

"What's this stop for?" Jace asked as Rory turned the car

around, flipped on her emergency lights, and stopped a gray Toyota.

"Cracked windshield."

Rory radioed to dispatch, ran the plate, and waited for the response, her butt wiggling in the seat. "I love traffic stops. Never know what you're gonna get. Maybe a warrant. Maybe an open container. Maybe the driver's smoking a doobie."

"A doobie?"

"A joint."

"I know what it is, just never heard anyone use that term. Except the old guys at the motel."

"So I'm an old guy at a hotel."

The license plate came back clear and valid, and Jace saw Rory's shoulders deflate just a little. Then Rory hopped out and approached the car as though it held Al Capone himself: slowly, eyes on the driver, hand on her gun, tight against the car. In a few minutes it was all over. The car belonged to an elderly woman who'd let her grandson drive it and he cracked the windshield. Rory wrote a warning but no ticket.

"I love stopping them, but I'm not going to hammer an old lady 'cause her grandson is an idiot. I'll make that stop every time, though."

And so it went for nearly two hours. Rory stopped everything that came past them if she could. Speeding, crossing the center line, rolling through a stop sign, no turn signal. She wrote no tickets but came back to the cruiser laughing almost every time.

"Why are you always laughing?" Jace asked when Rory climbed back in the car during a motorcycle stop.

"People make me laugh. Rooster County from R30 . . . 10-27."

"10-27? License check?"

Rory grinned. "I'll make a roadie outta you yet."

—R30 go ahead—

"Last name Sayles . . . sam-adam-young-lincoln-edward-sam. First name Michael. Middle is G-george. 10-27-66."

—10-4 . . . clear and valid—

"Hang tight." Rory went back to the bike, talked to Sayles for a minute and then came back, shaking her head and grinning. "Guy says he was speeding because he had a date."

Jace looked at her.

"Right? Had a date and ran out of denture glue. Rattled his dentures around so I could see. Rushing to Wal-Mart for some glue or whatever." She snorted. "I told him his girl might like—"

"Stop! Yuck. Don't want to think about that."

Rory cranked up the squad and glanced at her watch. "We should start watching for the drug van."

For the next while, the two kept to the westbound lane of I-20, moving about 45 miles an hour. A number of trucks passed, but none with the right coloring or plates. Each time a van passed, Rory ground her teeth a little.

"So I've been thinking." Jace stared out the window, at the passing vehicles, at anything other than Rory.

"Yeah? Always a step forward."

Jace frowned at the car behind them. It had slowed to the same 45 they were doing. "What's that about?"

Rory grinned. "See those other cars? All passing us right by, ain't giving us no kinda extra thought. They're good, they know what the speed limit is and they can go that fast. Doesn't matter what I'm doing. But that car behind us? They're not so sure and they probably have something they'd rather we not know about. Open booze. Warrant. Drugs. Something." Rory banged back a mouthful of red Skittles.

"You notice them more because they're staying behind."

"Pretty smart for a jailer."

Jace laughed. "You're a jailer; don't forget."

"Not in Rooster County, I'm not."

"But you're going to pass on the obvious murderer fleeing from Dallas because you're looking for this truck, right?"

Rory nodded. "So you were thinking . . ."

"About Jakob's sharper and more precise weapon." She hesitated. "And what Dr. Vernezobre told us. And the guy following us."

"Well, the guy following us was nothing. No plates just means west-Texas redneck. Probably hasn't had them renewed since dear old W. was president. Don't sweat him. As for the other?" Rory frowned for a second and Jace could see her digging the information out of her head. "The scalpel."

"Maybe. And Wrubel maybe being an addict and maybe selling."

"Except Dr. Vernezobre told us the scalpel was found and returned."

The car behind them finally came around and passed them. It was an elderly couple. She drove and kept her eyes on the road while the gentleman waved at Rory and Jace. Rory returned the wave and glanced in the rearview mirror.

"But he heard the story second-hand from Wrubel," Jace said. "If Wrubel was an addict or dealer, he sure as hell wouldn't have told Dr. Vernezobre everything. Or maybe Wrubel didn't know it all. Maybe there were two scalpels and only one was found."

Rory looked again in the rearview mirror. "Maybe, but that doesn't put you any closer to who done the deed."

Above them, the moon stubbornly refused to show from behind banks of clouds. It left the night dark, lit only by the stark, rare orange glow of arc sodium lamps every few miles. Cars passed slowly, quickly, and constantly. Jace was amazed at the life on the highway. She'd been on the highway before, even at night, but had never paid attention with the intensity that Rory was bringing to bear. Vehicles everywhere; even when there weren't many, it was a never-ending flow of metal. Beyond the highway, cattle wandered through fields empty of everything but animals and hay bales. In the distance, like the hinted-at background in a painting, were the occasional head- or taillights of a cotton farmer's truck on a back road.

Rory took a deep breath, her eyes glued to the rearview mirror as she turned on the digital recorder hanging at the top of her windshield. "Here we go."

What Jace saw when she turned was an exact description, delivery via Shelby and Force Chrome from a dealer's brother, of the white van. It came on quickly and suddenly slowed when it was just a few car lengths behind the squad. It made no move to pass so Rory eased off the speed until the cruiser was down to less than 40. The van stayed behind them, the driver with his hands locked on the wheel at ten and two. Rory slowed further. Eventually, the van signaled into the next lane and crept to their side. As he passed, the driver kept his hands on the wheel while rigidly never looking at them.

"Son of a bitch is scared to death," Rory said.

So am I.

Jace had watched Rory make traffic stops for a couple hours but realized she had no idea what to do if things got out of control. Nothing in training for a jail—or working a jail—gave her a single tool for an interstate traffic stop, but she also knew, now that she was here, she wanted to see what was in that van.

Because it's the next question.

Sheriff Bukowski had told her months ago that the next question was the only thing that drove Jace; a need to make sure someone asked all the questions. At the time, she thought his theory simplistic, but Jakob had said much the same thing while blowing on her fancy coffee. There was truth in that simplistic theory and, right now, she wanted nothing more than to see what was in that van.

It's the drug war, Jace, a useless waste of money that attempts to cut supply rather than demand, which then raises the price of supply because the demand is still there.

In her mind, there were no more questions to ask about the drug war.

She gritted her teeth. There *were* questions to ask about this little sliver of the drug war in the van next to them. Plus, there was that little chili-pepper burn of excitement deep in her throat.

The hallmark of an adrenaline junkie.

"Calm down, sister."

"Why do you always say that to me?"

" 'Cause you're so high strung. Cut a loud fart and you'll have a heart attack."

"Fart? That's ladylike."

"Okay. Cut a loud fluff and you'll have a heart attack."

"That is total psychological projection. You're amped up, Miss Candy, not me. On a Skittles sugar high."

Grinning, teeth bared like a feral dog, Rory nodded. "Damn straight." She grabbed the mic. "All right, gangsta, let's see what you're all about. Rooster from R30 . . . 10-28."

The plate came back valid and registered in California. They followed the van for another two miles before the driver gave Rory a reason to pull him over. Rory called in the location, reran the plate, and let dispatch know they were out with a single driver and white van.

"So let's see what we've got."

"Uh . . . should I come or stay or what?" Jace hadn't gotten out on any of the other traffic stops.

"You stay in this squad car . . . and I'll be sorely disappointed. This is the show. This is why we're here. Let's dance!"

Rory hopped out of the squad and Jace trailed a few steps behind. Traffic rocketed past them, some vehicles moving to the far lane and some not. Rory paid them no mind at all. She crept to the driver's door, hand on her gun, hugging the side of the van tightly.

"Good evening. Deputy Bogan, Rooster County sheriff's office. Can I see your license, registration, and insurance, please."

Jace came up on the passenger side and tried to stay out of sight while getting a look at the driver. A skinny, middle-twenties kid, not unlike what she dealt with in the jail. Hispanic, with a wisp of dainty mustache and definitely scared.

"Did nothing wrong." The driver handed over a license and a confused pile of papers.

"Arizona? Where'd you get the truck?"

"Huh? Uh . . . Arizona. No, California. I don't remember; been a long drive."

Jace swallowed and felt the constriction of her sharps vest. It was for knives, for the jail, and wouldn't stop bullets on a traffic stop but it made her feel safer.

"You don't remember? Huh. Okay, well, there's a lotta trash in the foot well there. Drinks and food wrappers and stuff. You driving straight through?"

"Why you axing me all these questions? I ain't did nothing wrong."

"Calm down; I'm just making polite conversation."

"No, you ain't; you profiling. That's illegal. You stopped me 'cause I'm a Mex."

"No, you're a man who was riding the shoulder."

"Bullshit."

Rory smiled and pointed to her squad car. "Wanna see the video? Didn't think so. Any reason you were riding the shoulder? Maybe a medical problem? I can call an ambulance if you need it."

He held a cell phone up. "Calling my boss."

"Yeah? What's your name?"

He pointed to his license in Rory's hand.

"Right. But what is it?"

The man's face twisted, his eyes darting from Rory to the windshield. Jace saw fear come fully into his face. Rory was pinning him down to a name he didn't remember and that wasn't going to match any of the paperwork.

"Lemme get the 'surance."

He reached across the truck and Jace saw his ass scoot away from the driver's door. He leaned across and opened the glove box with Rory watching him intently. His butt again scooted further from the driver's door.

Or closer to the passenger door.

He looked out the passenger window toward the darkened field beyond the highway.

He didn't see Jace. She was dead still in the shadows. Even as he reached for the glove box, his eyes were fixed on the distance. The box popped open and a ream's worth of papers fell out.

"Hang on . . . it's here."

And still closer to the passenger door.

He's grabbing a gun.

"Gun! Rory . . . gun."

The door blasted open and something heavy smashed into Jace's chest. She stumbled backward.

"Got a rabbit." Rory's voice boomed.

He was running and Jace tried to close the door on him, but he was already a blur, blasting out of the truck and disappearing into the very darkness he'd been eying since the traffic stop began.

"Rabbitrabbitrabbit." Rory's head was tilted toward her shoulder-mounted portable radio mic. "South off'a I-20."

—Rooster County to R30 10-4 foot chase—

Jace hesitated only a second before leaving Rory in the tangle of paperwork. The driver was already fifty feet ahead, moving quickly, and Jace bolted into the empty cotton field after him.

169

"Stop. Police. *Policia.*"

The bang of his feet on the hard ground was in her ears like handclap jive, but it was fading as though moving away from her, like he was on a float in a Mardi Gras parade, clapping in time to the music but getting further away as the entire parade slipped down the street.

Except this wasn't a street, lit by neon or giant blue-white street lamps, where she could keep him in sight. This was a dark, empty cotton field and if he got too much further away, she'd never find him.

"Stop."

Where the hell was Rory? This was her stop . . . her arrest. Why was she making Jace do all the work?

The guy's gray sweatshirt melded into the dark and the passing traffic overwhelmed the sound of his feet.

"Son of a bitch. Rory. Where the hell are you?"

The man was still visible ahead of her but everything was fading into darkness. She kept running, the mesquite whipping at her legs, sometimes tall enough to grab at her arms, hundreds of tiny nicks eating into her skin, stinging ever more and more.

"Stop, damn it." Her voice was gone, ragged and hoarse.

As she ran, her feet bobbled, sometimes landing on flat ground but sometimes not. She pulled in, suddenly afraid of stepping into a gopher hole or tripping over a mound left by rodents. The last damned thing she needed was a twisted or broken ankle.

Damn it, where was he? Lost in the darkness? Had he slipped away through her hesitation?

"Rory . . . where the hell are you? I need some help on your damned arrest!"

The squad car's motor screamed. The noise wound up through the air a split second before Jace heard the car bounce off the interstate shoulder and roar into the field. Then light as bright as a high desert noon stabbed the dark and in that light, harsh and stark, the truck driver was perfectly visible. He was directly in front of Jace, maybe thirty feet away, facing her. He wasn't running, but standing, his face hard and angry, lined with fear and adrenaline.

A pistol in his hand.

"Stay away." His voice was high and scared. "I'll shoot. Swear to Christ I will. I ain't going back to prison."

"Wait; don't get ahead of yourself." Jace slowed to a walk. "No one's going anywhere. We're just talking here."

When he fired, Jace saw the flames but heard nothing. She ducked as he fired a second time. More flame but still no sound.

The squad car, a metal monster somewhere behind her, bearing down on her and the truck driver, was silent now, too.

The world was silent and she wondered if she was already dead; shot twice but too stupid to lay down and die?

"You son of a bitch. You shot me?" Jace shouted, did not hear her own voice, and blasted toward the driver with every ounce of juice left in her. Her thighs screamed through the buildup of lactic acid. "You killed me? I'll beat your balls off."

The driver looked startled. His mouth opened and closed as he dropped the gun, and turned to run. But he was off stride, his balance gone. His arms flailed at the air.

Jace pumped her legs hard, a hot lance stabbing her side and a painful howl deep in her thighs. She jumped a clump of dead cotton and stumbled through a wide washout. Light from behind her blasted the driver, highlighting him like a spotlight. He was close now and his shirt flapped behind him. Her fingers brushed it. She stretched, almost had him, and then lost him. Her center of balance was gone and her feet tangled up in themselves.

She fell but somehow managed to grab the flap of his shirt and yank him backward. She hit the ground hard and he crashed down on top of her.

"Don't shoot." His voice was a scared squeak. He flailed on top of her and she kept expecting to feel the pain of a punch. "Got no gun no more."

"Don't . . . resist."

"Ain't resisting."

The squad slid to a stop and kicked a pile of dust into Jace's face. Rory jumped out and hammered the guy's back with her knee until she had him cuffed. She jerked him off Jace and said, her voice still and steady, "You're under arrest."

Jace let go of his shirt. "Ye . . . ye . . . yeah." She lay, the sky spinning above her, her heart pounding so hard in her chest it hurt. "Under." Hot, fiery air burned her lungs while dirt stung her eyes. "Arrest."

"Jace? You dead?"

Instead of answering, she waved a hand and tried to catch her breath.

"So that means . . . dead? Or not dead?"

". . . piss . . . off . . ."

"Not dead, then."

Laughing, Rory put the driver in the back of her Rooster County squad, then helped Jace into the passenger seat.

CHAPTER 22

The man, name unknown, didn't move. He sat on a simple chair, his hands knotted together in his lap, his shoulders slumped, as though the sculptor had carved away too much of him. His breath was fast and shallow and sweat broke on his forehead, glistening under the blue-white light of the humming fluorescent bulbs.

Rory sat near him and Jace watched through one-way glass, the Rooster County sheriff at her side. He was a surprisingly young man with fiery red hair. He had told Rory it was her bust and therefore her interview. Right now, he stood with his hands on his gunbelt, watching intently, the smell of aftershave heavy on him. They stood in a small room next door to the interview room. It had been a closet at one point, but the previous sheriff had put in a small window so it could be used for observation. The interview room had once been the observation room for Rooster County's single indoor shooting lane, where deputies watched other deputies shoot. The shooting lane was long since closed and had become an overflow evidence room. From where they stood, Jace and the sheriff could see through the interview room and into the old shooting lane, now piled high on each side with boxes and bags sealed with red evidence tape, tags hanging off like gift tags on forgotten presents.

Rory had asked his name. He hadn't answered, instead looking down at his hands, and she had let that silence linger for nearly three minutes.

Eventually, she nodded. "That's fine. I can charge you just as well without your name. We'll John Doe you and it'll be fine. But why would you let someone else let you take the weight of this? Meth, weed, heroin, a ton of 'script pills. Cash. Maps. That doesn't make you just the delivery driver, but a player. And we both know you're not."

"Playah. Gangstah."

Rory shook her head. "You're smarter than that. Gangsters are idiots. They got nothing for you except fear. You're smarter than that."

He shook his head in a tiny arc, his voice as soft as a summer rain. "You playing me now . . . playah."

"I don't play. If I thought you had nothing to offer or were too stupid to offer it, I wouldn't be here. You'd be locked up, prints on the way to Austin, and I'd be hanging with my girl eating barbeque." She sighed theatrically. "Ain't my skin in this game. I got a great arrest for my stats. Possession with intent to deliver, fleeing and eluding, attempted capital murder of a peace officer."

When he looked up, his face was pained, his hands clenched to fists and suddenly on the table in front of him. "Wasn't attempted murder of no cop."

The sheriff stiffened beside Jace.

"It wasn't attempted murder? You shot at my partner."

He shook his head violently. "No, I didn't. I mean, yeah, I did." He banged a hand on the table. "I shot but wasn't no cop. Damn it, I wasn't trying to off no cop." Again his fist hammered the table, the dull thud echoing through the speaker system into the other room.

The sheriff's hands came off his belt. "He better calm his ass down."

"You. Shot. At. A. Cop." Rory leaned back in her chair. "How do you not understand that?"

"I didn't know you was cops, is what I'm saying."

Rory laughed. "Didn't know we were cops?"

"No." The man's voice thundered up through the room, banged at the glass through which the sheriff and Jace watched. "How was I gonna know that?"

Rory's voice rose as well. "The flashing red and blue lights? That maybe give you a hint?"

"Damn it, don't talk to me like that, bitch. I didn't *know*." He shoved away from the table, stood, and kicked the chair out behind him. He stumbled over it and ended up near the far wall.

"Sit the fuck down." Rory's voice was hard but controlled.

"Ain't sitting shit. I didn't know you was no cops. How many times I got to tell your dumb ass?" He came at the table fast, both hands in tight fists, his eyes hard on Rory. The sheriff moved toward the door but Jace blocked him. "Hang on, Sheriff."

"That's my deputy in there."

"And my friend. She's fine."

Rory never moved. She sat in her chair, her eyes hard on the man who hung over her. His face was blood red, his hands near Rory's face.

Rory spoke slowly, softly. "Sit down. Please. Explain it to me."

The sheriff watched, his hands ready to shove Jace out of the way.

Jace tried to put reassurance on her face, though her insides were on fire. "This is what she does, Sheriff. I've seen it a thousand times in Zach. Let her do her thing."

The sheriff looked again at Rory and the arrestee. They still hadn't moved. The man breathed hard, Rory didn't. She kept her hands on the table, unclenched and relaxed.

"Tell me how you didn't know we were cops, okay? Make me

understand."

Eventually, he backed up. Moving slowly, he raised his shirt. An ugly, gray scar ran from the base of his neck across his chest and down his abdomen until it ended just above his waist.

"The cops. In Mexico."

"The cops did this to you?"

"Dressed as cops, but not cops. Enforcers. *Sinaloa.* You think I want to run drugs? You think I want to smuggle dope across the border to do to Americans what they done to *mi hermana*? She was a junkie and sold everything we had to feed it. Her body, too, and then she stole when no one would buy her body."

He sat, his voice soft again, his breath ragged. "I am an American citizen." He thumped his chest. "A Texan. But I go back to see my family. The cartel forced me to drive to repay Maria's drug debt even after she died, and when I refused, they cut me open, left me to bleed to death on the sidewalk. I survived and refused. I don't care if they kill me, so they took my mother and grandmother. If I don't drive, they will kill them. So I drive. Simple."

Shaking his head, the sheriff looked from Rory and the arrestee to Jace. "Hire the right people, then trust them. That's what the former sheriff told me when I got elected. Sometimes I forget that."

"Well, you're a big, strong, west-Texas man. It's in your DNA to help a woman."

He looked at her, a flash of confusion in his eyes. When he smiled, he nodded. "Yeah, that's probably true. Gotta remember she's good on her own."

"Plus? She'll kick your ass if you foul up her play."

He laughed. "Yeah, there's that." He clapped Jace on the shoulder. "I'm glad you were out there tonight, Deputy Salome." He pointed at the tip of her ear. After cleaning and bandaging it, there was only a sliver of pain. "Let that be a lesson to you."

"Thanks for letting me ride, Sheriff."

"Almost anytime, Deputy."

He left the room and when Jace turned back to the window, Rory was staring at her. The arrestee had his head in his hands. On the outside of his right hand, Jace saw a tattoo, the letters *T* and *S* twisting into each other.

"Say that again," Rory said.

"Not everything is bad. I don't bring just death. I bring some life, too."

Rory kept her gaze on Jace. "What does that mean?"

"I told you already."

"Tell me again."

"Some'a them drugs go to poor-people doctors."

"And you were going to Zachary City?"

"Yeah."

"Delivering to who?"

Looking up, he said, "No. Ain't going to get a doctor in trouble to save my skinny ass. He do good work; you don't need to know who he is. You got his drugs, that's enough."

"But I want to know who's making a profit off your back. Who's making the benjamins?"

The man laughed. "Ain't no benjamins. Doc trades most'a his services. He ain't getting rich no how."

"How'd he afford smuggled drugs, then?"

Now the man laughed, though the sound was shot through with sadness. "I buy 'em for him. Take whatever they gonna pay me, which ain't too much, and buy some extra. I give them to him."

Eventually it dawned on Jace. Dr. Vernezobre. That was the name no one was saying. Deep in her gut, Jace felt emotions split two different ways. Disappointment that he bought smuggled drugs. But an odd kind of pride that she knew someone who stood so tall for what he believed.

"What's your name?"

The man took a deep breath. "Absalon Bustillo. I been down in Lynaugh. On a dime. It's in Fort Stockton."

"For?"

For a moment, he said nothing. Eventually he nodded. "Possession. Intent to deliver."

"And the other scar?"

It ran from the base of his neck up toward his right ear. He sort of smiled, a pained and lopsided thing. "Got this in a yard fight. Dude cut me. Tried to kill me."

"Not a fan of *Sinaloa* soldiers?"

"Nigger won me in a poker game and I refused. I got turned out soon as I got there . . . *Sinaloa* soldier said I was pretty. He lost me in a poker game and I was tired of it so I . . . just . . . refused."

Rory shook her head in admiration. "How are you not dead?"

He shrugged. "Just lucky. It is what it is, I guess."

"I guess." Rory patted his hand and stood. "All right, Mr. Absalon Bustillo. Hang tight and let me see what I can do."

"Nothing," he said. "You try and I'm grateful, but there's nothing. I'm down for this one."

CHAPTER 23

An hour later, as they left, Jace was deep in her head about Dr. Vernezobre and Dr. Wrubel. Paying no attention, she came around a corner and bumped into a trusty.

"Excuse me, ma'am." The trusty shoved the mop bucket out of her way.

Jace smiled apologetically. "Sorry. I didn't see you."

He waved it away. "No problem, Deputy." He grabbed the sleeve of his jail-issue black-and-white striped uniform. "Damn near makes me invisible."

"Better place to be usually," Rory said.

He winked. "No doubt there."

"Hey, have a good night."

"You, too, Deputies."

As they went out the door, Rory munched an assortment of Skittles and Jace turned back to the trusty. He was bent over his mop, the yellow bucket just a few feet away, a flop of brown hair over both eyes.

Invisible.

He glanced at her, a quizzical and somewhat uncomfortable smile on his lips, but kept mopping.

CHAPTER 24

Jace's balcony was on the east wall of the second floor of her apartment at the Sea Spray Inn. It overlooked a broken bit of asphalt that ran like a hard, gray river behind the Sea Spray building. Once upon a time, according to Gramma, that alley had been back-door access to some of the rooms. Now it was just forgotten.

Invisible, Jace thought.

"Christ, that was great." Rory whooped softly, though midmorning had already passed.

"Why are you whispering?"

"Because you got nothing but old people here. They sleep . . . like . . . twenty-four hours a day."

"First of all, we don't have just old people. Second of all, they don't sleep all day. Third of all, most of them can't hear anymore anyway."

Rory laughed loud. "Good enough. You see the sheriff?"

Jace chuckled. "Yes, Rory, I saw the sheriff."

After watching the interview and helping to catalog the haul, the sheriff had loudly praised Rory and had harassed his two night deputies for not making the same kinds of arrests.

"Ahhhhhhhh." Rory leaned back in the chair and raised her face to the noon sun. A chill bit the air but it wasn't too bad for the end of December in west Texas. "Basking in the glow."

"Dork."

Rory grinned. "And your point is?"

"So do they always do that?"

"Do what?" Rory finished off her beer and went for another in Jace's fridge.

"The deputies and town cops. Do they always come in to hear the story while you're doing evidence and reports? If they hadn't interrupted, we'd have gotten out of there an hour earlier."

"It's not about getting out earlier, worm. It's fun telling your stories. Everybody laughs and hangs out. It's about . . . well, the camaraderie, I guess. Sounds kind'a cheesy but it is. Having stories to tell is gold in law enforcement."

"The currency of the realm."

"Uh . . . okay. You and your big words. All those stories prove that you're part of the family, Jace. You know that. Hell, you've got some of your own already." Rory snorted. "What annoys the crap outta me is that everybody's favorite part was you chasing ass after him."

Jace shook her head, ran a hand over the bandage on her ear, and drank. "It was stupid."

Rory plopped down next to Jace. "Wasn't any stupider than snatching my gun yesterday and just about chest bumping that truck. Like some badass Old West gunslinger."

Holy crap, am I an idiot. Double idiocy . . . twice in two days. Next thing she knew, she'd start knocking on the doors to all the shooting galleries and identifying herself as a cop, just for the adrenaline rush.

Getting to be a junkie, she thought. *Getting to like that rush.*

It was the last thing in the world she wanted. She did not want to turn into a road deputy always looking for the high-speed chase or the shootout or the bar fight, unable to get off with anything other than excitement.

"You know, if you'd gotten shot, I mean real shot, not just a flesh wound on an ear you don't use much anyway, I would

have cashed in your life insurance and gone to the Caribbean."
Rory sighed theatrically. "It would have been a worthy cause so
I'm a little disappointed here."

Jace chugged back a long swig of Corona as a white work
truck, old and beat up, meandered slowly down the alley. "I'm
basking in your warmth and love."

"Hehe . . . was just a joke. I don't want you dead. I mean . . .
I don't think I do."

"Nice. Thanks." Jace took a deep breath and the air smelled
of winter and exhaust from cars and trucks on the highway, of
greasy breakfasts served up and down this stretch of the I-20
frontage road, what Zach City residents still called Highway 80.

Most of those cars and trucks are invisible.

They came and went and did their thing and no one really
ever saw them. Like the truck that had just passed under her
balcony, the driver with a soda in one hand and a sheet of paper
in the other, a knit cap loose on his head because of the chill in
the air. *He goes to work every morning, slipping in and out of traffic
and no one sees him except those who need to: the guys he works for,
or the guys he delivers to, his family. Otherwise, he is invisible.*

"So do we have to do something about Dr. Vernezobre? Buying smuggled drugs?"

"Well, we don't really know anything, do we?" Rory's eyes
were downcast. "We have a smuggler telling us that, but he's a
con, been a guest of Texas prisons at least once. Probably more.
Works for the *Sinaloa* cartel. So really, we have the word of a
POS and Dr. Vernezobre is high dollar in Zachary City." She
shrugged.

"Well, the doctor pretty much admitted it."

"Yeah, he did. I don't know, Jace, I really don't."

At the end of the alley, under Jace's gaze, the white truck
turned right toward Midkiff Drive. On the right side, as it was
disappearing from view, Jace saw it.

The logo. Faded and almost impossible to see, but the same giant round shape that she'd seen before.

And no rear license plate.

Son of a bitch.

"That was him." Pointing down the alley, Jace jumped up and dropped her bottle to the balcony. Beer spilled out and foamed all around her feet. "Damn it. That was him."

"Who? What are you talking about?" Rory looked at an empty alley.

"The guy who followed us. That white truck. That was it. That was him . . . driving past my damned apartment."

"What? Are you sure?"

"Rory, he turned right toward Midkiff. We'll never find him now."

Midkiff Drive was one of the larger arteries in Zachary City and, at this hour, it was bursting with traffic. Slipping onto Midkiff was tantamount to a single person slipping into a football stadium during a game.

Invisible . . . again.

"Hang on, Jace. How do you know it was him?"

"When he turned right, I saw the logo. Black outline of what looked like a circle. Old and faded or maybe sort of painted over, I don't know. Plus, he didn't have a rear plate."

Rory looked down the alley, then up the alley as though he might magically reappear on a geographic loop. But the alley, as forgotten as Gramma always said it was, was quiet and empty.

"Who are you?" Rory asked, as quiet as the alley.

"The hell are you following us is what I want to know." Jace leaned over the railing and stared hard toward the houses and businesses, as though she could see the truck through them. Useless, she knew, but panic ate at her, hot and sharp. How had he found her apartment? "He's coming after me? Rory, he came to me."

Reaching out, softly, Rory hugged Jace and held on until the woman's shaking stopped. "Yeah, he did, but who cares. He obviously didn't have balls enough to stop so piss on him. He won't do anything."

"You don't know that."

"Yeah, I do. I know bad guys. He had a chance the first time and just now, and he didn't do anything. He's a coward. We'll see him again and—"

"I don't want to see him again."

"Yes, you do, because every time you see him, that's one more chance for us to grab him. Plus . . ." She pulled out her cell and dialed. "Mr. Balsamo. How are you this lovely day?" She grinned and nodded at Jace. "I'm sorry to see Manchester United had such a terrible season."

Balsamo was an Anglophile who ran the records department at the sheriff's office. Rory never got tired of giving him grief. Now she laughed.

"Come on, don't talk nasty to me. Listen, I need a favor. Huh? Sure, next time I'm there during the day, I'll come down and let you look at my bum. Can you call your buddies at the court clerk's office and see if anyone in the county has written a registration ticket for no back plate to a white work truck. I know, I know, and that's all I can tell you. Check back about six months or so? You funny man." She kissed the phone and put on a British accent. "Thank you, love."

"You think that'll get us anywhere?"

Sitting down, Rory shrugged. "Worth a shot."

They fell silent for a few minutes, the sounds of industrial Zachary City in their ears. The light-industrial area was just across the railroad tracks from the Sea Spray Inn, and from early morning until deep into the night, it was banging with life. The thump and smash of trucks being loaded and unloaded, of things being made and shipped out via rail to the far corners of everywhere, of things being fixed and broken and refixed and maybe broken again. The smokestacks snorted an assortment: black and tan, white, white tinged with orange, gray. That smoke was one of the economic barometers. Oil and gas production were the cash crops, but those were out in the field. A local company might have twenty producing wells, but they were all over the state, maybe scattered up through Oklahoma and Kansas, Colorado and Wyoming. The stacks and their smoke were here and visible. When they painted the wide-open sky, times were good. When the smoke was weak and spotty, when the air was clean and clear and the environment happy, times were rocky.

Invisible.

In other words, when things were invisible, when there was no smoke . . . the situation was bad.

"What are you thinking about? Since you tend to massively overthink everything. The chase? The white truck? What?"

Jace shook her head. "Wasn't overthinking anything."

"Oh, you totally were, but you tell the story however you want."

"I was thinking about invisibility."

"Again with your big words."

A series of knocks boomed through the apartment. "Jace? Answer the damned door. I know you've got that freak in there with you." More booms. "Get her ass out here."

A second later, Shelby barged in. "Had to call me, huh? I give you the info so *you* can make the arrest and I don't have any paperwork and you call me anyway. I tell you I'm old and tired and you call me anyway." He trudged through Jace's apartment and sat heavily on the balcony between the women. "The two superstars."

"Yes. Yes, we are," Rory said.

"Beer? Instead of Skittles? You're always eating candy. You

sick or something?'"

Candy? Jace frowned. Shelby's mentioning of candy rang a distant bell in her head.

Rory pleasantly gave him her middle finger.

"Good enough. So got another beer?"

"Uh . . . Shelby? We have to work tonight." Jace glanced at her watch. "I need to get to bed soon for a nap."

"Bah. That can wait." He tossed them some computer printouts. "So Mr. Bustillo was surprisingly cooperative. He gave us a few people, I assume no better than low level since he's scared to death of the *Sinaloa*s. So I then spend, like, days and days tracking down a couple of those low-level people and wha'd'a I get?"

"Bupkis?" Rory asked.

"That would have made my day easier. No. Turns out one of the names is actually a dealer and that dealer gave us more than a few of his customers. Guy name of William Milner. Street name Billy Milly. Turns out Billy Milly has been convicted in Texas before . . . twice, in fact . . . and he's got a warrant outta Bexar County for distribution. Had a little problem in San Antonio. So he's extremely eager to work off some of the debt he suddenly incurred last night, along with a little of the San Antonio debt. He's ready to deal up and down the food chain."

Rory smiled and nodded and handed Shelby her beer.

"That's good, right?"

"Yes, Miss Salome, it is very good." Shelby knocked back the last of it and handed the bottle to Rory. "A dead soldier. Time to breathe life into a new one."

With a laugh, Rory headed for the kitchen. "Aren't you still on duty?"

"Taking some personal time."

"Is that what they call it?"

Shelby gave Rory a middle finger. "Seems Mister Billy Milly

has some friends in Mexico and New Mexico and Chicago that he's willing to name for our friends at DEA and DHS, but he's also willing to hand over his customers to Force Chrome and the Zachary and Rooster and Midland and Ector *and* Bexar County sheriff's offices."

Jace whistled. "Wow, that's quite a haul."

Rory handed him a beer. "A new soldier, General."

Shelby pointed at the list he'd handed Rory. "So what I wonder from you guys is how many of his customers do you know from the jail. Who might be workable?"

"If you have their dealer, what else can you work?"

He grinned. "There is always something to work, Jace. Always something else to discover. 'S just like working in the jail: wheels within wheels within wheels. Most junkies don't work and if they do, we're not talking about high-paying jobs. So how do they feed their habits?"

"Burglary. Theft."

He nodded. "So if I can work the junkies, maybe I can clear cases." He sighed. "Or give those cases to people who aren't as old and tired and—"

"Crotchety," Rory said.

"I was going to say curmudgeonly, but okay." Shelby took a long pull from the beer.

On the first few pages, there were no names she recognized. But on the fourth page, Jace's gaze stopped. She pointed out a name to Rory.

"Damn." Rory looked at Shelby.

"Who?"

"A friend of mine. Dr. Vernezobre." Looking at Jace, she said, "We sort of heard his name from Bustillo, and there've been rumors for years."

Rumors you alluded to yesterday when we spoke to him, Jace thought.

187

"Yeah . . . well, your friend's a bad boy." Shelby finished the beer in just a few swallows, grabbed another beer in the kitchen, and popped the top.

Rory got defensive. "He's a good man. Gets pills as cheap as he can and gives them free to poor people." She gave Shelby a long look. "Is there anything we can do about this?"

"You asking me to lose evidence of a crime?"

Jace thought about it. "Has there been a crime? A name on a computer that belongs to a dealer? Could be your dealer had some medical problems. I'm not sure there's a crime anywhere to be found."

Shelby grinned again and Jace liked the grin. It was lopsided and toothy, but warm with a hint of mischief. "Trust me. The man's been buying black market for thirty years. Hell, I think even the circuit judges know him. If I charged him, the DA wouldn't prosecute and if he did, the judge would toss the case and even if the judge didn't toss the case, I guarantee you most everyone on the jury would know someone he helped. They'd acquit. Don't worry about him." Shelby winked. "Plus, seeing as how he knows some of the mopes in the county, he's helped us from time to time."

"Good." Jace thought of Preacher. The old man's body ached in more places than Jace's body had and Preacher was as down and out as anyone Jace had ever known. For years, Preacher had gotten his painkillers from back-alley dealers and that was the best he could afford. Yeah, he was breaking the law and yeah, she knew it, but she didn't care. The world wasn't black and white and neither should the law be. The letter of the law shouldn't crush the spirit of justice, as freaking corny and clichéd as that sounded in her head.

"Anyone else?" Shelby quaffed half the new beer in a single swig.

At the top of the fifth page, Rory frowned. "Well, lookit here."

"Who's that?" Shelby asked.

"Dr. Wrubel."

Shelby's eyes bugged. "What?" He grabbed the sheaf of pages. "Holy shit. I gave the list a quick look, didn't see his name. So you're telling me Dr. Wrubel, who was killed in the Zachary County Jail, was a drug addict?"

Jace took a deep breath. "Why am I thinking about candy?"

" 'Cause you're about half crazy." Rory looked at Shelby. "Yeah, that's what we've been hearing. Maybe dealing, too. Hell, probably dealing."

"I saw Kerr in the hallway a few nights ago," Jace said. "He told me that if we wanted to stop drugs coming in, we shouldn't focus on inmates so much. He said we should focus higher up the food chain. His exact words."

Shelby stared at her. "And why was he telling you that?"

Jace felt hot blood flood her cheeks. "Well, I was trying to find out if he knew if Wrubel was selling but I didn't want to say Wrubel's name if I was wrong. He said look slightly higher up the food chain but he wouldn't give me any names." They said nothing, just stared at her. "So I asked him if he'd help me put a notch in my belt so I could move up."

Rory grinned. "You did not. Put a notch in your belt?"

"You played him?"

Jace squirmed under the gazes. "Well . . . yeah, I guess I did. I was just trying to get information."

Shelby raised his beer. "Cheers to the newbie worm. Well done."

Rory laughed and slapped Jace's knee. "Damn, you're good. Played both Kerr and Mercer. Getting good at this, worm." Rory suddenly looked shocked. "Damn it, I'm not sure how much longer I can call you worm."

"How about never? Does never work for you?"

"Lemme think . . . uh . . . no." Rory's smile disappeared.

"What if Wrubel's not an addict? What if he was buying drugs on the cheap like Vernezobre?"

Shelby rubbed his bristled cheek. "Could be, but if he were buying on the cheap, like Vernezobre, was he buying for Vernezobre? That doesn't make sense because Vernezobre can buy his own and I don't think Wrubel had his own practice, did he?"

"Maybe as a sideline?" Jace said.

"Or buying for the jail? Maximize profit?"

Jace frowned. "He and Dr. Cruz argued about missing meds. So maybe he's taking from the pharmacy and then replacing them?"

Shelby shook his head. "Too risky. Why do that when he can just take the smuggled meds? Not have to worry about getting them into the jail. A sideline? That could be a maybe." Taking back the printouts, Shelby stood and yawned. "Again, thanks for calling me after I told you explicitly I wasn't interested."

"You're always interested, General."

With a grin he winked. "True that. Always working it. All of us had a great night so . . . here's to me and my master plan." He saluted the ladies and left.

They sat for a while, silent, and let the sounds of the afternoon come to them. A touch of warmth had taken hold from the morning frost, though it was still nippy out. Eventually, things would warm up to a decent mid-50s probably. Not quite warm enough for Jace, but not too bad. Then, as she and Rory headed in to work tonight, it would cool down all over again.

It came to her suddenly, like a blow from a fist.

Candy.

Invisibility.

Barry Ezrin, a captain with the Texas Rangers, had once told her Bobby liked his candy.

. . . his family was gone one night, he robbed the house, looking for candy money.

When Ezrin said candy, he meant drugs. And when he said Bobby, he meant Inmate Bobby.

"Son of a bitch."

"Jace?"

"I misread Inmate Bobby."

"How'd we get to him all of a sudden? Come on, this is a great day." She waved a hand in the direction of the jail. "Piss on that place. Give it a rest."

Wrubel had been an addict, or had been selling, or both. Had Inmate Bobby been selling? He was an addict, too, and Kerr had told her to look up the food chain but only slightly up. Who was up from an inmate, but only slightly? A trusty. Up from there was civilian staff, then jailers, then roadies, then administration and the sheriff and the judge.

"Misread him about Wrubel's murder," Jace said.

Rory wiped the condensation from her beer bottle, let it drip from her fingers. "What are you talking about?"

Invisible. Mercer had never left medical but Inmate Bobby had been within a few feet of Wrubel's death. Invisible in his jail uniform and with his jail mop bucket. Had Inmate Bobby stabbed Wrubel with the scapel, hidden it in the mop water, then jammed the shank into the doc before Jace ordered him into the go-between? Then later dumped the scalpel somewhere in the huge custodial room, with so many places to dump it, and gone on to his cell for the night?

"I think it was Inmate Bobby."

"What?" Rory's head snapped around. Her eyes dug hard into Jace.

"Preacher says everyone is a killer given the right context."

"That crazy old man is probably right. Everybody *is* a killer, things roll the right way." Rory played with the bottle. "But this?"

Jace put it all out while Rory slowly pulled the label off her beer. "It could be that Wrubel and Inmate Bobby got crosswise about something in medical; something legitimate. Inmate Bobby wanted something or thought he needed something and Wrubel wouldn't give it."

Silence answered Jace.

"Or maybe everything we've heard is right . . . maybe they're both selling to inmates and Wrubel was cutting into Inmate Bobby's profit." Jace shook her head. "I'm not sure I believe Wrubel was selling drugs but if he wasn't, then a drug thing makes no sense. Records would tell me if Inmate Bobby has ever been in medical."

"Maybe they met in the hallway."

"A casual hallway meeting isn't motive for murder."

Rory sighed and her gaze slipped away from Jace and into the winter sky, as though the answers were hidden behind clouds and if she looked long enough, west Texas would blow everything clear. "Bobby's in on distribution. Not the first time, either." Rory set the beer bottle aside, a last few swallows left in it. "Wrubel's name is on a drug list and Bobby's down for distribution."

"Dr. Vernezobre's name is on that list, too."

"And Inmate Bobby was near the body." Rory stood, stretched, yawned. "We could have ourselves a winner, folks, in the Please-Send-Me-To-Prison-For-Murder category."

"I want to talk to him."

"No." Rory's hands went to her hips and her head shook vehemently. "Absolutely not."

Jace nodded. "He's never lied to me. He'll tell me straight."

"Never lied to you? You've never asked him to let you stab him with a death needle. Think that might change things? You're not getting in and questioning Bobby about a murder. What if you screw it?"

"Thanks for the vote of confidence."

"Jace, listen to me. I know you're good, and someday I think you're going to be great, but that day ain't today. Or tomorrow or next week or even next month."

Silently, Jace ground her teeth. She wasn't ready for this, she knew, but something dug at her. She had pointed everyone toward Mercer and she had been completely wrong about that. She didn't want to point everyone toward Inmate Bobby and be just as wrong.

"Sorry, Rory. I'm going to talk to him. I'll be delicate, I promise, but I can't throw him to the wolves if he's not the right guy. I did that to one man already; I won't do it again."

Rory took a deep breath, nodded, and left.

CHAPTER 25

After Rory left, Jace went immediately to the jail. When she arrived at the employee entrance, the afternoon sun was limping higher in a cold, cloudy sky.

The door's electric lock popped open and she stopped at the security desk. "Do I need to sign in?" she asked the desk clerk, a uniformed deputy she didn't recognize.

He never looked up from his shooting magazine. "You wanna?"

"Your door, your procedure."

"Ain't my damned door or my procedure. I'm just here."

"Ah. Well, okay, then."

Records was staffed by civilians, including a man who led the department and believed himself to have been an English king in a past life. Jace had called before she'd left the Sea Spray and told the clerk, Pat, what she needed. Now Pat handed her a thick manila folder.

"The entire file."

"I appreciate it, Pat."

"No problem, babe. Way I hear it, this'll help you take Von Holton down a peg or two."

"You heard that, huh?"

Pat winked, her hazel eyes flashing in the light. "Sad thing is, I been here a long time and I can remember when he was a decent man. Now he's caught up in . . . I don't even know what . . . wanting to be on top, I guess. Word is he'll run for sheriff next election." She sighed. "When you get up there, floating around in that rarefied atmosphere, you better damn well remember the little people down here."

With a smile, Jace grabbed the file and headed out. "What little people? Everything I've done, I've done on my own."

"Kiss my ass, ya' wench. When we going to lunch?"

"Anytime you want. Text me."

"10-4"

There was a different deputy on duty at the back door as Jace left. "The other one get fired?"

The man whistled. "My winner of a lunchtime replacement."

"They give you guys lunch?"

"Once a week, whether we need it or not." He winked. "Get it more often when I work courthouse security."

"Wow. Maybe, if I work hard, I can get a lunch break someday." She held out her hand. "Jace Salome."

The man watched her while he shook her hand. "Salome, huh? Heard of you." Eventually, he relaxed. "Tell you what, way I heard it? I'm not sure I'd'a had the eggs to do what you did with Badgett." He shrugged as though embarrassed at his own honesty.

"To tell you the truth, I mostly didn't have the eggs, either. If I'd had a chance to stop and think about it? Hell, I'd have gone to Aruba instead."

He laughed again. "I'm Billy Kemp." He pointed at the logbook. "Don't forget to sign out."

After signing and being let through the door, she sat in her car and let the local college radio station give her a solo piano version of Duke Ellington's "Mood Indigo." She scanned each page of Inmate Bobby's file and by the end hadn't found a single reference to medical services. What his file did have was pages and pages of exemplary work reports and decent housing reports and fairly boring commissary reports dating back more than seven years. There were two minor disciplinary write-ups, one for smoking and one for offering a deputy a sip of cell-brewed hooch Inmate Bobby had purchased from another inmate. The file also included a commendation for performing the Heimlich on a deputy who'd been choking on a pastrami and rye while they were together in the sally port.

"Deputy."

She recognized the voice and tried not to suddenly shove all the papers back in the folder or cover the folder with her hand. "Sheriff."

"Anything interesting?"

She stared at him a long minute, trying to decide how much to tell him. They'd had conversations before, more than the sheriff and the average deputy probably had but still she was uncertain around him. "Well, he got caught smoking in the jail once . . . just like you."

His laugh might once have been a bellow and full of the expanse of west Texas, but anymore it was as worn as his face. "Did you cite him . . . just like me?"

"Aw, hell no, Sheriff. I only write tickets to people who can derail my career."

Another breath of laughter. "Career, huh? Seems like not that long ago you was gonna quit."

"It wasn't that long ago."

"Guess that's changed."

"As far as you know."

His grin faded as he bundled his coat up a bit more tightly. A slight wind had come up. The coat wasn't one she'd seen before. It might have been an old navy pea coat, but it was hard to tell given the mileage it had on it. Whatever it was, it definitely wasn't the coat she'd seen him wear at political rallies. She said so.

"Well, sometimes you gotta tailor a little bit to the audience.

I'm more comfortable in this thing, fits me better, but ain't nobody gonna vote for me if they see me wearing it."

"The plain folk might vote for you, one of them and all that."

"Ain't no such thing as plain folk. They might wear the same ratty coat, but that'll just make them think I'm as poor as they are, or as uneducated. That's fine to have a beer, but people want to look up to whoever they put in charge. They want to believe that person can solve all their problems. Plus, those people wearing a coat like this? They ain't got no money to help me along. I gotta wear a nice coat to get the nice money, otherwise I'm out on the street and ain't helping nobody." He nodded to Inmate Bobby's file. "Bobby's your boy, now?"

After a hesitation, she said, "I don't know. I don't want to say until I'm sure."

He shook his head, looking past her and the truck into the Zachary City skyline. "I'm almost never sure of anything anymore."

"I was sure of Mercer and sent everyone running after him."

"Bullshit. No one ran anywhere. Von Holton knew it wasn't Mercer when he sent you on that stupid goose chase."

"And Jakob? Did she know?"

"Jakob's a good woman. A damned fine officer and a good woman. She believes there aren't enough women in law enforcement."

"There aren't."

"Maybe, but she loves her little tests for the good ones. Seems you made her list and passed the test. But that's not why you haven't said anything about Bobby yet."

"No."

He waited.

"He hasn't had a single medical contact," Jace said.

"Meaning?"

"Maybe he's telling the truth, maybe he's not."

197

"State of the world, Deputy." Turning his head away from her, he closed a nostril and blew hard until his sinuses were clear. "You know, Bobby had at least one medical contact. I'm sure it ain't in there."

"Huh?"

"Dr. Cruz interviewed him for medical trusty. Ol' Bobby can't stand the sight of blood. Bobby said he could do whatever else, but sure as shit didn't wanna be around when there was blood."

"It's good Kerr came along, then, isn't it?"

"Guess God shining down on Cruz. Doesn't get the inmate he wanted but lookie here, here's someone else even better qualified."

Jace looked at him, something tight in her head. "What are you saying, Sheriff?"

"Not a thing. Just thought you oughta know Bobby and Cruz had a conversation."

Closing the file, Jace set it beside her. "I looked like an idiot. That's why I haven't said anything about Inmate Bobby yet."

Nodding, he pulled a cigar from his pocket and lit up. He blew the smoke away from Jace as his gaze wandered the parking lot, stopping for a minute on the bail-bond shops near the jail. They lined the street like soldiers in an ongoing war and most were open twenty-four hours a day. "Lotta bail money moving through those doors."

She looked over her shoulder at the businesses. "Trying to keep up with all the arrests, I guess."

"You ever notice how rarely we arrest the rich?" He dismissed the thought. "So . . . that bandage on your ear . . . that your first foot chase?"

"Yes."

"You'll remember it forever. First time you arrest a domestic, first time you make a traffic stop with a warrant or drugs." His dark eyes were as intense as summer thunderstorms. "First time you arrest a drunk driver . . . save someone from getting killed."

She looked away.

"My first foot chase was a disaster. There used to be this little gas station, Illinois and Midkiff. Great old shop. Go in there off duty, buy homemade hooch. Best I ever drank, God rest his soul. Had a collection plate on his counter, church soup kitchen. Getting gas one night—off duty—and this mope walked right up while Walt was in the back. Took that plate off the counter.

"Chased that son of a bitch five blocks through a damned sandstorm. Couldn't see crap. He was pro'ly ten years younger than me. Felt like his head start was about a mile. I was wearing boots. No gun or badge or stick. Nothing. Might as well have been naked for all the good I could'a done."

"So it turned out well, is what you're saying, because you could have been killed?"

"A disaster. Tripped over a tricycle. Broke my leg. He got away clean."

"Wow, that's a really uplifting story, Sheriff. Thanks for sharing."

"You ain't hearing me. I pissed off my sheriff with that stunt. He believed I had no business doing it and I believed otherwise. Sometimes you gotta do what you think is right, don't matter who you piss off." He chuckled and the tension drained away. "If you're pissing them off, though, helps to be right. But sometimes there's somebody up there you can trust, who gives you cover. Use them to give you the power that you won't have until you've got some years under your belt."

"And you're my guy?"

"Me? Hell, no." He spat and sucked deeply on his cigar. "I can't stand you. Ain't no chick oughta be in law enforcement."

"You don't believe that so let's talk like adults, shall we?"

The slightest twinge of a smile broke at the corners of his mouth. "The man who ran that gas station was a war man, fought them Nazis and could tell you every single one he killed up close. Believed that was the only way to kill a man. 'You gonna kill him,' he used to say, 'you do it close.' Believed a man—or woman—should understand exactly what they were taking from whoever they killed."

"Have you killed people, Sheriff?"

"Just worms who write me smoking tickets." He pulled his coat more tightly around him. "Yeah. A few. More than I wanted to, less than probably needed it." He looked sideways at her. "You wanna kill somebody?"

"Thought about it when I fell chasing the drug dealer."

"At embarrassment or pain?"

She thought. "Well, it didn't hurt too much." Then, after a moment, she said, "I wanted to kill Badgett."

For a long while, the sheriff said nothing. He smoked his cigar down before dropping the butt to the parking lot and stubbing it out. "Wouldn't have been a crime."

"No, sir."

"You talk to the attorneys yet?"

Though the Badgett affair was only a few months behind them and the official investigation, being done by the Texas Rangers, wasn't yet completed, the lawsuits over the deaths had already started flying. The sheriff's office, the sheriff personally, the jail staff, the administration, the academies that had hired Badgett, the deputies he'd trained. The families of the dead men were looking far and wide for anyone with money to try and cool the raging anger at what they thought the system had done to their loved ones. But Jace believed it hadn't been the system that killed their loved ones. Jace believed the system had stopped the killers.

"Not yet, sir."

"Get to it. Soon." He glanced at his watch. "Bobby ought to be coming outside in a few minutes. Probably at the fence like every day. Him wanting to breathe air that don't belong to the jail. Good timing . . . if your intention was to talk to him."

"Yes, sir."

" 'Sir.' You blowing me, ain't you?"

"Absolutely, sir."

Then he was gone, disappeared in the chill breeze that had wrapped west Texas like an obsessive lover. The back door popped open and he slipped inside.

CHAPTER 26

"Bobby, tell me the truth."

"Sheriff Jace, I didn't do it."

"Please don't call me that."

"Deputy Salome, I did not kill Dr. Wrubel. I didn't even know him. Never met him. I saw him around, sure, but I didn't kill him."

"You selling to the johnnies?"

His gaze darted away, maybe to the same bail-bondsmen's shops Bukowski had looked at. "Huh? I . . . uh . . . what kind'a bullshit is that? I ain't selling. Why would I sell inside?"

"Why wouldn't you? Got a captive audience, many of whom need their ganja fix."

"I ain't selling to nobody."

"So anyone who says you are is lying?"

He fidgeted, bouncing from one foot to another.

"You cold?"

"Huh? Well, yeah, it's cold out here."

"Must have just now gotten cold, I guess. I believe you were selling and someone was cutting into your profit."

"Deputy Salome, you know I like you. You've always treated me good, better than most. But I ain't talking to you no more. You ain't going to bother to get to the truth. You going to go along to get along. I didn't think you were like that."

"I'm not. I'll follow the truth where ever it leads me. Right now, it's leading me to you."

"Leading the wrong direction."

"No, it's not."

He grinned but it was full of teeth and anger. "Yeah, oh yeah, it is." He jingled the keyring at his belt. "Got some chores need doing." He turned and walked away. "I ain't talking to you no more. Have a good day."

"Chill, chick; she'll call." Hassan, a 67-year-old dealer of gourmet ganja, winked. "Ain't got to get all worked up and lathery and slippery."

"Slippery? Don't ever use that word around me again."

He grinned. "Because you get all worked up and lathery when I do. I know it; ain't got to lie to ol' Hassan about Ol' Willie."

"Stop it. The less I know about your named parts, the better."

"Give her some time. She gotta get over the shock of me calling her. Thought she was gonna get a little Hassan." He held his hand across his heart. "Very sad it wasn't about me."

Hassan was one of Grapa's Hot Five. The group was down to just three now: Gramma, Preacher, and Hassan. Grapa had passed and Galena Brown, a stripper who'd seen her best days in the Fifties, had walked out without a word years before. Every few nights, they got boozy and crazy on dominoes, and then insulted each other until they yelled at each other.

Hassan got serious. "She wasn't too happy—"

Jace's phone rang. "Carol? Thank you for calling me."

There was a long pause. "I owe Hassan a favor."

Jace waved *goodbye, Hassan.* He grumped but left. "Well, I appreciate it. It's no big deal, really."

Carol choked out a bitter laugh. "Wrubel's dead, Bobby's a murderer, you're making Von Holton look bad, he and Jakob are *still* pissing on each other, and more than a few deputies hate that you sided with a Texas Ranger over fellow cops. So no big deal. Really."

Jace swallowed.

There was a pause punctuated by Carol's heavy breathing. Eventually, she apologized. "It's been a bad few days. Doc Wrubel was my friend."

"I didn't know him so well, but I liked him."

"So what's your question?"

"Where'd you hear that Inmate Bobby had done it?"

There was a long hesitation. "Didn't you tell me?"

"No, ma'am."

"Well, I don't remember. Somewhere."

Jace let the silence hang between them. When it became obvious Carol wasn't going to fill it, Jace changed tack. "Why is the doc dead?"

The nurse, who'd been with the jail for years before becoming a Cruz Medical employee, hesitated. "I guess . . . uh . . . Bobby wanted him dead. Why does anyone kill anyone?"

"So Inmate Bobby did it?"

"Didn't he?"

Jace paused. "I keep hearing Doc was selling to inmates. Or was an addict. Or stealing from the pharm. Doesn't seem like the man I knew."

"Sometimes people are hard to see."

"So he was selling?"

"No, no, no, of course he wasn't."

"Dr. Cruz thinks he was."

"Damn it. I don't—I don't know anything about that."

"Please, I'm trying to help."

"The man is dead. Leave him be."

She's scared.

Jace had heard scared inmates, usually first timers who had no idea what being in jail meant. Carol's stuttering, rushing and then denying, reminded Jace of that fear. She'd heard it, too, from Inmate Bobby when she asked him straight out if he'd killed Wrubel. Fear about the murder, not about selling drugs to inmates.

"Carol—"

"No." She breathed hard and angry. "Look, why would he do to other people what someone did to his family? Why would he do that?"

"He wasn't selling?"

"Hell, no, and anyone who says he was has got an axe getting grinded."

"But what about—"

"Look, missy, ever'body has demons. Maybe Doc's were bad enough that he'd do it to himself but he never hurt nobody else. Ever. But what the hell do I know? I'm just a fat old nurse who needs a job because her husband has a bad back and never made enough cotton farming to sock anything away. Don't ask me about this anymore."

Carol was gone, in a blast of sudden silence. Then the electronic beep of Jace's cell phone losing the signal.

CHAPTER 27

That evening, just before work, Jace stood at her window. The sky darkened as dusk fell over Zachary City and it matched Jace's state of mind. She'd been wrong about Mercer and had misread Inmate Bobby and was in a dark mood. She shook her head at the metaphor. She'd always thought the weather was too cheap and easy a metaphor for life but sometimes it simply couldn't be avoided.

There wouldn't be a winter storm, though the weathermen were calling for it. There would be cold that got into bones and cracks and crevices, but there wouldn't be any rain or snow, nor any blasting winds that left ice in her blood. Tonight there would be only dark skies.

Beneath the clouds were the downtown skyscrapers that tried to puncture them. Those spires were three or four miles distant, deep in the city's heart, but were visible from nearly everywhere, as was so much in the almost mind-numbingly flat west-Texas desert. Twelve miles from here there was a four-corners stop; eastward would take a traveler to Tarzan and Lenorah, while west led to Andrews. But if a traveler stood at that four corners, where the black ribbon of state routes 349 and 176 collided, and stared south, those downtown buildings would be perfectly visible.

There was a hamlet a little north of that crossroads, too small to even be considered a village, called Patricia. It had three or four old buildings whose best days were a century gone and a few nearby dirt farms. It also had a garage that did very little business in cars but a thriving run in machine soda. Visible from nearly a mile down the road outside of town was a Coca-Cola machine with bright-red, electric skin. That machine did business by the truckload when drivers stopped and jammed in a handful of quarters.

That road was the way to Lubbock, and it was the road Mama and Jace traveled every time they made the trip. And every time, without fail, Mama stopped and bought a single sweaty can of Coke to split with her daughter. Nowadays, the machine was half-liter bottles but regardless, there had been something about the ritual of coin-coin-can that always left Jace with a radiant warmth. Since Mama's death, Jace had stopped frequently, even making the drive with no reason other than the machine. She'd realized only a couple of years ago that, with Mama gone, the sodas not only didn't conjure up any particularly strong memories, they barely scratched the surface of nostalgic. Standing there, dust in throat, soda in hand, Jace had realized with a startling bitterness that it was just a soda machine in the middle of the desert.

"Babygirl," Preacher called through her closed door. When she opened it, the old man stood there with a sloppy grin on his dark face, his pipe emitting its usual spicy, orange odor. Without waiting for an invite, he entered, set his briefcase on her coffee table, and tapped a withered finger against it. "Ain't understanding that boy's homework."

"I wasn't much of a student, but let's take a look."

Robison's death had broken something in Preacher's heart and head. He believed, with an eagerness and sincerity that sometimes scared Jace, that Robison would be back someday, and when the boy came back, he would need to finish school. To that end, Preacher tried to keep up with what his head told him was Robison's homework. In reality, it was a sheaf of pages marked with Preacher's own chicken-scratch handwriting and kept in his briefcase. But it made the old man feel better and connected to his dead son, and who did it hurt?

Preacher snorted. "Ain't much of a student . . . tha's just a lie."

When they sat, Preacher handed a few sheets of paper to Jace. She stared at the incomprehensible writing and furrowed her brow, as though deep in thought. During her academy training, they'd had a few courses on mental illness. So many of the country's jails were short-term housing for the mentally ill, her instructors told her, that she had to have at least a general understanding of mental illness. "You will see it," a particular instructor had told her. "You will see it and it will scare you and you won't have any idea what to do. It will embarrass you and frighten you and eventually anger you."

"Why?" Jace had said. "No reason to get mad at someone who's sick."

"When the shit's hitting the fan, it won't be someone who's sick, Salome, it'll be someone—in crisis—who's not listening to your orders. It'll be someone who is, at best, ignoring you and, at worst, threatening you."

Preacher had never threatened her but she knew his was different. Preacher's illness was soft and sad but at the jail it would be violent and scary. Yet Jace always felt a bit of guilt with Preacher. Not only was she doing nothing to help his illness, she was actually hurting him by playing in his melancholic world. She knew that only reinforced his sickness but she also understood it made both him and her feel better to believe in a world where the dead might come back and repair life's broken glass.

"I don't know, Preacher, this looks pretty tough to me. Can I think about it a while?"

"Ain't nothing but a thang." He stuffed the papers back into the briefcase. "Got a few days yet before I have to turn it in." He would forget about it before the day was through. "So, how's jailing?"

Jace grinned. "Helping with a case." The grin dissolved into a frown. "Thought I had it solved yesterday. Turns out I had the wrong guy."

"So that how that work?"

"What do you mean?"

"You remember that carnival St. Anne Catholic used to put on? Had the rides and hot dogs and dart throws?" He chuckled. "I 'member the first time I let Robison go by himself. He met some girl there, Elicia something. Boy had it bad for her; tightening his pants he had it so bad. Well, they met and ate some food and went on some spinny ride and after they done? Robison threw right up. She runned away so fast I felt for that poor boy." Preacher winked. "It'll be a'right, though. When he get back, she'll still be waiting on him. She had it hard for him, too."

"Yeah?"

"Oh, yeah, young'uns and they hormones. Anyway, what I was saying was is it like them dart games? Where you just keep throwing and throwing and eventually you hit the right balloon? Your cases like that?"

The analogy didn't please Jace at all. It made her efforts seem nothing more than a poker game or a spin on the roulette wheel. "Well, that's not really how I see it, Preacher. I look at the evidence and follow it. Sometimes I don't have all the evidence at the beginning. Then when I get more evidence, things sometimes change."

"Yeah, yeah." Preacher nodded. "I getcha, little girl. Like knowing half the Bible, maybe you understand this verse or that chapter, but when you add it to some other book, you understand it better."

Jace nodded. "Yeah, Preacher, maybe kind of like that."

"So now you got all the verses now? Gotcha all the chapters you need?"

Maybe, Jace thought. This time, she was certain it was the right person, as much as she didn't want it to be. Inmate Bobby was the only person with access, or so Jace told Major Jakob late this afternoon when she called the woman after talking with Carol. It had been a tense phone call and after Jace gave her Inmate Bobby's name, there was a long pause. Jakob asked if Jace was certain, and then asked her reasons for believing so. Jace went through the entire thing twice. Once for herself and once for Major Jakob.

After a pause, the major had said, "Well done, Salome, very well done."

Jace had pocketed her cell phone gently, both angry at Inmate Bobby and disconcerted by the glow she felt at Jakob's approval. When Jace had started the job, she'd thought she might be good at it, but she didn't delve too deeply into any motivation beyond that. Yet now, with a few months behind her, with a few small cases and one huge case tucked safely in her experience, she found herself with an appetite she hadn't expected.

"Ain't cain't be nobody else, then gotta be him," Preacher said as he hugged her lightly. "Done good, babygirl. But you ain't looking so happy."

"What? No, I'm fine. It's just . . . I'm surprised at who the bad guy is."

"He playing a good guy?"

Jace thought about that. He hadn't ever said he was a good guy—he owned the crimes that landed him in jail—but this did seem a step up for him. "I didn't think so, Preacher, but I don't know now."

"What flavor bad is he now?"

"Murder."

The old man's grin slipped away. He sucked long and hard on his pipe and a spike of orange filled the apartment. "Yeah? Another inmate get himself killed?"

"The assistant doctor. Guy named Wrubel. Worked nights in the medical pod. An inmate stabbed him a few nights ago."

Preacher frowned. "You didn't say nothing."

"No." Maybe she hadn't wanted to worry Preacher or Gramma. Maybe she had been all too aware of what Gramma's response would be and she'd wanted to avoid it. She shrugged. "Lots of things go on in that jail I don't mention. It's nothing, Preach, just the job."

"Uh-huh. So death ain't no big deal."

Jace cleared her throat. "Anyway, we thought it was one inmate because he'd had an argument with the doctor. He wanted some drugs or something—"

"Drugs?"

"Well . . . asthma medicine."

"High-dollar narcotics."

Jace felt herself color and tried to bite back her defensiveness. "Preacher, you can't just have anything you want; it's jail."

"Ain't doubting that, little girl. Just don't seem like no big deal to me . . . a little inhale make a man feel better." He took a deep drag on his pipe, held the smoke deep in his lungs, then blew it out over Jace's head.

"Well, regardless, it turns out it wasn't that guy. I was asked to do some legwork on the suspect and I managed to discover—" She was unable to stop the swell in her chest. ". . . that he couldn't have done it."

"That's my babydoll. Damn straight if you didn't save a man's life keeping that murder noose from around his neck."

"Yeah, Preacher, I guess I did. Now I've got a major who likes me, I think. She's fourth or fifth from the top in the command staff. Big cheese."

"And she's got her eye on Jace Salome. World winking at you right now, ain't it?"

"Maybe . . . for now."

"But you wearing your missing-Mama face."

Jace shook her head as though she could empty it. "I always miss her, but that's not . . . I don't know. I'm sad at who killed Dr. Wrubel. I thought he was a decent guy. A criminal, yeah, but a decent guy generally. I read him completely wrong."

Inmate Bobby had actually been a help since she'd started the job. He and she had connected during her first night on duty and they'd had an easygoing relationship since. Yes, he'd been convicted. Yes, he'd been sentenced to eleven months in county. But he was unfailingly polite and had even guided her a few times to this or that location. And he'd been in jail so many times for minor things, what Rory called misdemeanoring, that he knew the jail better than Jace did and helped her with the little things that fell through the cracks in her training. So the image of him stabbing a man repeatedly was a cognitive disconnect for her. It simply didn't reflect who she thought she knew. Yet she also understood that she didn't really know the prisoners—or a prisoner's psychology—well enough to be able to wear their skin.

"What'sa matter?"

"I look good and he goes to prison for murder. Doesn't seem like the scale is balanced on that one, does it?"

"Well, decent ol' boy or not . . . do the murder, do the time."

"Yeah."

"How that sleeping coming?"

"PTSD takes a little time."

"You be aw-right." He snorted. "Back in the day, didn't call it no PTSD. It was just fucked-up. Got counseled with a bottle of Thunderbird . . . Cuervo on a good day."

"How'd that work out?"

He smacked his lips. "Well . . . mighty tasty either way."

They sat in silence for a few minutes, Jace's eyes on the book Jakob gave her, then on Preacher. He'd said everybody changes everybody. She wasn't sure she'd believed it, but it came up in Jakob's book, too.

Every contact leaves a trace.

Locard's Principle . . . that every perpetrator left something of himself at a crime scene and took something from that crime scene with him.

For Jakob, it was about hairs and fibers, DNA and finger-prints, but maybe Preacher was right and it was that way with life. Maybe every contact Jace had, with criminal or cop, changed her in some slight, nearly undetectable, way.

How long before I don't recognize myself anymore?

She nodded thoughtfully. "Preacher?"

"Yeah?"

"I have to go to work, but do you think maybe we could go look for Robison, maybe when I get off."

He beamed. "You bet, babygirl. That a fine idea. He might be home when you get off, though."

"He might be at that, Preacher."

CHAPTER 28

That night, Sergeant Bibb buzzed her in. The intercom boomed with his voice. "See if you can foot chase your way over to a particular cell."

"Foot chase?"

"I hear that's what you're good at." His laugh was heavy even through the intercom. "Congrats, baby cop."

"This the cell I think it is?"

"Yeah. Adam 1 and Lincoln 1 have been waiting. I think your fav dick is there, too."

The door lock popped and she stepped into the jail. The deputy sitting on the sign-in desk grinned at her.

"What's up?"

"Stock in Jace Salome, sounds like." He pointed to the bandage on her ear. "Come back and tell it all." He banged a fist against the desk. "Been here six years and never had a foot chase."

Law enforcement was a small community and everyone knew everyone else's business. It was, Jace thought, much like living at the Sea Spray, with the same support and jealousies and prying eyes and ears that heard everything but admitted to nothing.

"That wasn't anything," she tried to say. "It was just—" She stopped. It was a foot chase that ended in a two-shot gun fight and a mass of felony charges. There was no way to dress the night down.

"Salome." Bibb's voice was impatient. "The cell . . . now."

The deputy behind the desk winked.

Most trusties were housed in administrative segregation because it was easier, with so many of the ad-seg inmates on 23/7 lockdown, to shuffle trusties in and out for their work assignments. Most trusty cells were left open 24/7 and trusties came and went, to a degree, when they needed. When she arrived, the entire pod was locked and a batch of people stood around the jailer's desk. Sheriff Bukowski, Major Jakob, Detective Von Holton, with Sergeant Dillon between them, along with two B-shift jailers—Smit and one Jace didn't know—and one of the lab techs Jace had seen working Wrubel's body.

The sheriff passed her on his way out.

"You're not staying?"

"Naw. Now that you're stuck here, I can go smoke this." He held a cigar between two fingers.

"Sir, if you light up, I'll know it."

He nodded, tired. "Yeah, you probably will. Good luck, Deputy."

"Thank you, sir."

When she got to the desk, Jace rubbed her hands together, amazed again at how nerves and excitement could work on her at the same time.

Von Holton tapped his watch. "Can we finally get started now?"

She wanted to laugh at his transparent grin. *Let him make himself look bad,* Ezell had said. The man was supremely satisfied at how he'd played her. "Sure, now that I'm here."

His grin faltered and Jace caught a twitch on Jakob's mouth.

"Bobby's cell, please," Jakob said to the jailers. One of them touched the computer screen and a door on the bottom tier near the war doors clicked open.

Dillon keyed his radio. "Control, you got this recording?"

—10-4—

"For whatever we might find," Dillon said to everyone. "Control, keep the subject wherever he is right now."

—which is?—

Dillon thought for a second. "Give me a 21; let's keep this off the air as much as we can."

Half a second later, Dillon's cell phone rang. "He's probably still mopping. Hallways or the kitchen. He's working on the sally-port thing, too. He's been sleeping out there sometimes." He sighed. "Guess we ought to end that, huh?"

Jakob nodded. "Probably."

Dillon snapped his phone closed, and as the group moved toward Bobby's cell, Von Holton smirked at Jace. "Good job on this thing. Took you too long, but at least you got there."

Don't rise to the bait, Jace thought. Just eat the anger and wield Jakob's information as precisely as a surgeon's scalpel. "Least I found what I was looking for. You crib up that murder weapon yet?"

"What?" His eyes narrowed. "That's classified information."

Inwardly, Jace grinned. *How's that feel . . . up your wazoo?*

"Got a source in my lab, Deputy?" Jakob asked smoothly. "I can't have information leaking out. When we are finished with this investigation, I expect a visit."

Von Holton's eyes darted to the major, then back to Jace, a glimmer of understanding sparking on his face.

At Inmate Bobby's cell, Von Holton and Jakob went inside while everyone else waited. They took a cursory glance and Von Holton poked around Inmate Bobby's toiletries and food. Eventually, he motioned to Jace.

"Shake it."

"Sir?"

"Shake it down and find my murder weapon. We'll step out because too many people in a cell is a crowd and like you said, the jail ain't my kingdom."

For a second, Jace stood in complete surprise. She'd been so terrified of Von Holton when summoned to an interview, but in reality he was a little man wearing cheap bravado like a bad toupee.

—*405 from control—*

"Go ahead."

—*no on the hallways . . . going kitchen—*

"10-4"

With a deep breath, Jace entered Inmate Bobby's world. It was a standard cell, built for one. It measured eight feet by ten and included a metal-framed bed along one side bolted to the wall. On the opposite wall was a desk and chair, each bolted to wall or floor, a sink, and a shelf, each metal and bolted to the wall. Over the door was a light fixture behind a thick face of deeply scratched plastic.

After putting on a pair of examination gloves, Jace stood in the middle of the cell and tried to acclimate herself to how Inmate Bobby kept his life ordered. *Where's the scalpel?* But the question was about more than location. It was also about safety. If she went too quickly or blindly through the shake, there was a reasonable chance her hand would resemble what the butcher left on the floor.

"Might not even know it," she said. " 'Til I saw the blood."

"Salome?"

"Uh . . . nothing, Major."

"Not sure what you're doing?" Von Holton asked.

"Kiss my ass," Dillon said. "She's one of the best."

Jace ignored Von Holton and looked at Dillon. "Nice and slow. Nice and safe."

"Damn straight." Dillon nodded. "For God's sake don't chop off a finger or something. Christ, I'd have a ton of paperwork to do."

"Always thinking of his people."

—*405 . . . nada in the kitchen*—

"10-4. Check the sally. Gets his phone time in the yard sometimes, too."

—*10-4*—

At the academy, Jace had been so uncertain of doing shakedowns that she'd created her own mental map and slavishly followed it. Doing it the same way every time insured she forgot nothing. It began at the door and moved to her right, eventually coming back to where she started. This time, she spent more time inspecting the walls than she usually did. She wanted to ensure there was no loose material that could be pulled out to house a weapon. Then, feeling the heat of their gazes on her back, she moved to the bed and removed the thin sheet. She snapped it like a towel before checking the sewn edges for anything hidden inside them. *Squeeze those edges, don't slide*, she thought. *Keep yourself out of the medical pod or Zach City Memorial.*

When she was certain the sheet was free of contraband, she handed it to Dillon and lifted the thin mattress to the floor. Under the mattress were five small, clear plastic bags.

"He a chef?" Von Holton asked. " 'Cause that looks like oregano to me. A whole lot of oregano. Maybe thirty grams worth." The detective laughed as Jace stopped and allowed the crime-scene tech to take pictures and collect the evidence.

"Field test it," Major Jakob ordered.

"Yes, ma'am." The man dropped some of the contents from one of the bags into a small vial filled with liquid and shook it. Less than thirty seconds later, he nodded. "It's weed."

"Bingo." Von Holton looked satisfied. "Motive to whack Wrubel. Cutting into his profit. Now find me the knife."

Jace went back to the bed. It was built like a serving tray, with a squared figure eight as the frame. The tray was empty so she went to her knees and focused on the mattress. Ignoring the sweat on her upper lip, she began to check the seams, but then stopped abruptly.

"Salome?" Dillon said.

There was a small brown spot on the floor. It was slightly elongated, as though the spatter had come from an angle. How the hell had she missed it? "Major?"

"Yes?"

"I think it's blood." Jace backed carefully away from the spot.

"Double bingo," the detective said.

The lab tech came in, his hand already full of a cotton swab and a bottle of chemical reactant. On one knee, he peered at the spot, but rather than spraying, he gave Jace a sideways glance. "Hershey's."

Von Holton pressed forward. "What?"

"Sorry," the lab tech whispered to Jace. He then cleared his throat and spoke loudly. "Chocolate. But it could have been dried blood. Sometimes brown is chocolate, sometimes it's sh— feces. Sometimes it's dried blood."

Von Holton snickered. "One of the best, huh?"

Jace pressed a finger to her temple. *Damn it, Bobby, what'd you do with that knife?* "Seams are good." She tried to keep the anxiety from her voice even as her stomach twittered. "All sewn up."

Their collective gaze was as stony as a quarry, except for Dillon, who gave her a tiny, approving nod.

—405 from control . . . no on the sally port . . . no on the rec yard—

Jakob cast her gaze over to Dillon.

"Where's our boy?" Von Holton asked.

Dillon waved the question away, as though it were a silly thing to ask, but Jace saw a tiny knot of tension worrying Dillon's eyes. "10-4. Check medical. 405 to dead shift. Keep an eye out for our subject. Do not—repeat, do not—bring him home. And be careful; if he knows he's up, he might lash out. Corporal Kleopping?"

—10-4 405—

Kleopping was running roll-call tonight while Dillon was here. The last unspoken command had been for the corporal to let the entire dead shift know who the subject was. Thus far, Inmate Bobby's name hadn't been uttered over the radio and Dillon wanted to keep it that way.

Where'd you go, Bobby? Are you invisible again?

"Maybe visitors?" Jace looked at Dillon. "I've found him asleep there before."

Dillon passed the message on to the control room.

"Sounds like your boy has the run of the place," Von Holton said.

"Oh, he's my boy now? He was our boy a few seconds ago." Dillon sniffed loudly.

"That was before you managed to lose him."

"You know what, Von Holton, you can suck—"

"Sergeant," Jakob said. "Leave it be. Salome, get on with it."

"Yes, ma'am."

Jace moved over the mattress's entire surface, pressing down with one hand while she bent the mattress over the pressing hand.

"Aren't you going to roll it?" Von Holton asked.

"Why?" Dillon said.

"Mattress won't roll with a knife hidden in it. Quickest way to discovery."

"Maybe . . . if the knife is big enough or in there head to toe," Jace said. "I always check for the smallest thing. By doing that, I can find the big thing. If, instead, we check for the big thing—"

"I've got it," Von Holton said. "Don't treat me like a . . . worm."

"Worm's doing pretty well at this point," Dillon said.

"Except for the chocolate . . . excuse me, the blood."

Trying to slow the freight train booming through her, Jace returned the mattress to the bed. Before moving on, she wiped the sweat from her face.

"Salome?"

"I'm okay, Sarge."

Dillon came to her side. "Take a deep breath, concentrate on your job. On this job, I mean."

"What's that mean?"

He imitated a running man with two of his fingers. Dillon chuckled. "You did a great job last night, and you're doing a great job now. Do it the way we always do it. Don't change anything because you have this audience."

"Yeah, but does that son of a bitch have to watch this?"

Dillon cracked a smile. "You're making him look like an idiot. Enjoy it."

"Gee, great, boss. I might cut myself to pieces but as long as he's an idiot . . ."

"Wounds are easy. Healing is hard."

Jace frowned. "More of your non-sequiturs?"

"Don't cuss at me."

She chuckled and some of the pressure disappeared.

"Good job calling Jakob, by the way." Dillon winked at her. "She filled me in. I think you're exactly right. Mercer wasn't our guy but Bobby . . . ?"

"You think he did something stupid? I mean . . . really?"

"I don't know, but nothing surprises me anymore."

Jace hesitated. "Does Inmate Bobby have any medical problems?"

Dillon shrugged. "I have no idea . . . not that I remember."

"Not on any drug regimen?"

Now her sergeant gave her a curious eye. "Why?"

"Maybe he took some pills and they put him to sleep somewhere or something."

He narrowed his gaze on her. "Uh-huh. You hear that?"

"What?"

"Your own wheels, turning and turning and turning. Spill."

"Nothing to spill, sir. Uh . . . not yet."

"But when there is?"

She batted her eyes at him. "Why, sir, you'll be the first to know."

His face went blood red. "Get back to work, worm."

Jace continued around the walls. There were no cracks or holes and nothing inside the light fixture. On the shelf, Jace carefully went through the handful of books and food from the commissary list—most of which was unopened packages of those small chocolate donuts he loved—and found nothing. Then she took a look at the spigot and water controls, and the underside of the shelf and the sink. All were as they should be.

At the jailer's desk, Smit and the other B-shift jailer watched intently. Jace laid her hand flat, palm up, and waved it back and forth in front of her. A moment later, Smit brought her a mirror. It was attached to the end of a long handle and allowed jailers to see what was under lower-set fixtures without having to get on hands and knees or blindly slide their hands or fingers along those frames.

—405 from control . . . coming up empty . . . need some fresh ideas—

"Unbelievable," Von Holton said. "Where is this guy?"

Panic bubbled deep in Jace's blood. Dillon shook his head. "Get back to work, Salome."

"Uh . . . yes, sir." She nodded at the jailer. "Thanks, Smitty."

"You betcha." When he turned for the desk, he bumped hard

into Von Holton. "Excuse me, Detective, I didn't see you there."

"Fucking jailers."

"Detective," Jakob said. "That's enough."

"Well, Major, this is bullshit." His nostrils flared and his teeth bared. "They're pissing all over me and they—"

"Give what we get," Dillon said.

"—can't even find the prisoner." Von Holton grabbed the mic at Dillon's shoulder, keyed it, and shouted, "Where the hell is Bobby? Goddamnit, find him."

Dillon twisted away, his face a rictus of rage. "If you ever touch me again, we'll go 'round right there."

Von Holton laughed.

"You got a question about it?" Dillon stepped up to Von Holton, nose to nose, and very nearly put his hands on the man's chest. "How about now? I don't hear any laughing now."

Jace jumped between the two men, just as one of the other jailers did, too. Gently, Jace moved Dillon backward. "If you're going to get suspended, let it be for something not quite as . . . useless."

"Fuck you, bitch," Von Holton said.

"Detective Von Holton." Major Jakob's voice came down like a sledgehammer. "Another word and I'll suspend you here and now."

He grinned at her. "Yeah? Without a board of review? That'll look good to the union."

"You think I care about the union? I will let you know when you and Adam 1 and I will sit down and discuss this incident."

"And I'll bring a union rep, *Major* . . . so there are no misunderstandings."

"Not a problem."

The group stood like that for a moment, as though everyone were trying to decide if they could move on. Eventually, Dillon and Von Holton each backed away a few steps.

"I think what the sergeant meant to say," Jace said calmly, "is that if Bobby can hear a radio, you've just told him we're looking for him. If he had the murder weapon on him, he's tossed it."

Breathing heavily, his face as red as a sunburn blister, Dillon snarled. "Not even close to what I was saying." His hands were still balled to fists. "If any of my people get hurt because of you . . ."

"Take a breath, Sergeant," Von Holton said. "You guys have been talking about him over the radio for a half hour."

"Actually," Jakob said, "they've been neutral. No names, if you'll remember."

Breathing hard, Dillon stepped even further away from the group, his face toward the ceiling as though Bobby might somehow be hanging there. As he did, Jace's phone rang.

"Don't forget the lawnmowers," Rory said.

"What? Oh, right. Good." Jace hung up. "Sarge? The tool shed? We told him to do some maintenance on the summer tools, remember?"

"Right." The relief was obvious in Dillon's voice. "I forgot all about it." He radioed control. "That's gotta be it."

"Unless he's gone to ground." Von Holton sighed. "If I screwed the pooch and he knows we're looking for him, he may be in the wind."

" 'In the wind'?" Jace asked. "How's that possible in a jail?"

With a resigned nod, Dillon said, "It's possible, Salome. There are more nooks and crannies in this place than I care to count. And in the old section? Forget it, he could be anywhere."

"Not to mention the old tunnel," Jakob said.

"Tunnel?"

"There's a tunnel between here and the courthouse. Used to use it so inmates weren't above ground going over. I guess there was a mass escape about a million years ago. So the tunnel got built. We haven't used it in forever. It's boarded up at both sides, but who knows."

Jakob pointed back at Bobby's cell. "Let Sergeant Bibb do his job and let's return to ours."

Von Holton nodded and for a split second, his face cracked and Jace saw something beneath. For just a heartbeat, his face had the same mileage that most other officers at the sheriff's office had, rather than his infuriating ego.

Manipulating the mirror, Jace checked the underside of the toilet and bed frame and found nothing. She was both relieved and disappointed. "There's nothing here."

"No," Dillon said. "Major? Detective?"

Von Holton shrugged. "He's got it on him." He paused. "Unless he dumped it." He banged a fist against the cell door. "Damn it. I shouldn't have—"

"No, you shouldn't have," Jakob said. "But we'll get it done. All right, Deputy, step out and let my lab guy spray his magic."

Jace came out as the tech went in. He winked and began spraying around the sink and toilet. Almost immediately, the spray around the sink turned a brilliant bright blue.

"Luminol," Jakob said to Jace's unasked question. "Tells us if there's been blood."

"It's talking pretty loud." Von Holton nodded to the tech. "Good job." After a second, he looked at Jace. "You, too . . . worm."

The sink was awash in the blue chemical stain. Bobby had washed his hands or cleaned the knife and now blood residue, translated into blue smears, covered the inside of the sink and splashed to the outside of the basin. There were also tiny splashes crawling a few inches up the wall just behind the sink.

"You want to over-spray the backsplash and wall?" Jakob asked her tech.

"I think so. Just in case."

With a nod, Jakob herded everyone out of the cell. "Your scene . . . your call."

While the tech worked, the group sweated. Dillon constantly checked his watch and tilted his head in case his shoulder mic squawked news on Bobby. Jakob stood alone, making notes on her phone while Von Holton paced. Behind the jailer's desk, both B-shifters collected their gear slowly, their eyes never far away from Jace and the shakedown. One gave her a thumbs-up and, with a grin, she shrugged. In a few minutes, the dead shift would appear and the four would pass some information and maybe a joke or two, then the dead shift would be in charge.

The pod was absolutely silent, save for the sound of a spray bottle.

"Holy shit."

More spraying.

"Uh . . . Major."

More spraying.

Major Jakob stepped in. "Jesus Mother Mary." She motioned everyone else over and for a moment, maybe the rest of her career, Jace couldn't move. Her legs were frozen but even if they hadn't been, her feet were concrete. Dillon and Von Holton peered inside the cell and the color drained from Dillon's face. Von Holton stared, bug-eyed.

"Deputy," Jakob said.

Breathing heavily, Jace dragged herself to the cell door. At that instant, between the first and second thumps of a single heartbeat, when her eyes simply couldn't register the sheer volume of bright blue smeared across three of the cell's four walls, Dillon's radio crackled to life.

—control to all call: lock it down—

The alarm began shrieking and, as ever, the sound was a woman's scream or the long, anguished wail of a Sonny Rollins tenor saxophone and Sergeant Dillon moved so slowly, his head

226

to his shoulder mic, his eyes roving toward the pod doors.

—*lock it down NOW . . . zebra four*—

"Son of a bitch," Von Holton said, his voice nearly lost in the howl of the alarm. "That fucker's gone."

—*zebra four . . . possible escape . . . repeating: possible escape*—

CHAPTER 29

Dillon's voice cut through the explosion of noise. Into his shoulder mic he said, "ERTs station beta."

—ERTs beta—

Kleopping confirmed Dillon's orders. Station beta was a series of two-man posts around the jail from which ERTs could quickly respond to any place they might be needed.

Von Holton ran to the ad-seg inner door and yanked on it. "Open up."

The lab tech, his face as white as a summer cloud, stepped out of the cell. Jakob pushed him back in. "Keep working. Document absolutely everything. If there are less than a hundred pictures, you're going on report."

"Get me outta here," Von Holton called across the pod.

From behind their doors, prisoners suddenly woke up and stared with wide and scared faces.

"No one in or out, Detective," Dillon said.

"Sarge," Jace said. "What do you want me—"

He cut her off. "Detective, you're—"

"If Bobby's gone, I gotta get on it." Von Holton jerked on the locked door again.

"No." Dillon shook his head. "You're here to stay."

"Goddamnit, open the door."

Dillon turned away from Von Holton as the alarm continued to jar its way into Jace. She tried to eat down the fear that rose from deep in her gut. "Sarge, what do you want from me?"

Dillon waved her off. "Bibb, get everything in record."

—done, baby—

"Phones, too."

—got it—

From behind their desk, the B-shift jailers were a whirl of motion. One went quickly to the lower tier while the other went upstairs. They yanked on every door to ensure it was closed and locked, and they peered through every cell-door window to account for every prisoner.

"Dillon, open the door. I've got to—"

—A Pod locked—

—locked in B—

—discipline locked—

—we locked? Yeah, E is locked—

—locked in females—

—medical pod is locked—

"We're good, Sarge," the jailer on the second tier called.

"On the radio, everyone needs to know."

—ad-seg is locked—

—two in booking, both locked . . . ERTs enroute to station beta—

"Control, kill the alarm."

The silence was as instant as a bullet to the head and in the burst of quiet, Jace had the sensation of suddenly being at a precipice with one leg over. But in that silence, the facility took a breath, and so she did, too. She put both feet back on the safe side of the cliff.

Licking his lips, Dillon shifted his body inside his sharps vest. "All right. Okay. Everybody chill out. We're good. We're good." After another deep breath, he keyed his radio. "Every pod that's locked and secured coughs up a jailer. Jailers search everything . . . you guys are the bloodhounds. ERTs will not search, under any circumstances. ERTs are the shotguns. Everyone under full jail arms. Two people per team. I find anyone in the halls alone,

229

they'll get thirty days no pay and both my boots in their ass."

"Patrol?" Major Jakob asked.

Dillon nodded. "On it, ma'am. Control, let Lt. Beem and Lt. Silverman know what's going on. I want five of their patrol deputies working a perimeter around the jail, looking in every hole and shadow they can find. Ask them to send some cars to his known haunts, too. I have no idea how long he's been gone."

—10-4, Sarge. Soon as I get that, I'll dig up vid, see if I can nail down a time—

"You're a good man, Sergeant Bibb."

—yes, I am . . . and my birthday's coming up—

Von Holton had come back to the group, his face was swollen with anger. "Dillon, listen: if Bobby has taken a powder, I've got to get on top of that. I can't do my job from this pod. Let me outta here."

"Step the hell off'a me or we're going to be back where we almost were a few minutes ago."

"Sergeant, I need—"

"Detective." Dillon's voice boomed across the pod. "As far as I know, I have an escapee . . . one who is your murder suspect. We know he's violent and we know he's killed and I've got no guarantee he won't do it again. You are unarmed and I will not have anyone unarmed in my halls while I'm looking for someone who stabbed a doctor twenty or thirty times." Dillon held up a hand to stop Von Holton's protest. "We are in lockdown until we know what's what. I know it's a pain in the balls for you and for that I apologize, but my priorities right now don't include you. No one moves. I don't care who it is."

Von Holton chuckled but it was a sound riddled with anxiety. "Right, protocol. Bet Bukowski ain't locked down."

"Adam 1 from 405." Dillon stared at Von Holton.

—405 go ahead—

Jace recognized the sheriff's tired voice. To her ear, the depth of it always put her in mind of Zeus from atop Olympus, though perhaps a Zeus who was ready to turn Olympus over to a new tenant.

"Sir, where are you?"

—locked in my office, Sergeant . . . you better send me a god-damned pizza or something—

Though a chuckle was on his face, Dillon kept his voice straight. "Yes, sir." He looked at Von Holton but softened his tone a bit. "The better I do my job, the sooner you get outta here."

Reluctantly, Von Holton acknowledged Dillon and stepped back.

"Same for you, Major," he said to Jakob. Her face became stony, but she said nothing.

"Sarge, what about me?" Jace waited until Von Holton was out of earshot. "I need something to do."

He nodded. "456 . . . what's your 10-20?"

—D pod . . . I was headed out to search—

"Negative. 10-25 ad-seg hallway. You and 479 will search the tunnel. Full jail arms for you."

—Yes, sir—

Once, when she'd been young, maybe eight or nine years old, Jace and Mama had gone to a Halloween spook house down the road in Stanton. It was in an old mansion—money long since made from cattle and wildcat oil wells and gone from God knew what—and was their first visit. Before Mama finished parking the car, Jace knew she was scared. She had giggled to cover her fear, but then lost the laugh when she and Mama got to the entrance. It was a walkway that led from the county road up to the front door and where once it had been covered in honeysuckle and ivy, it was now covered with cobwebs and bats and blood. A man took their money, then grinned—with bloody teeth—and held the curtained doorway open for them. Beyond that black curtain was a tunnel that was about a hundred miles long.

Jace tried to keep her face neutral. "Tunnel?"

Dillon eyed her. "It's one of the nooks and crannies."

Jakob shook her head. "It's about a million of the nooks and crannies. Happy New Year."

CHAPTER 30

It wasn't a shiny darkness, like that of a deep west-Texas night when the lights from countless oil rigs competed with a deep blue-black blanket of stars. This was muted, the kind of flat pallette reminiscent of the black primer that stared from between smears of hand-applied gray on Grapa's long ago battered pickup. But it was more than simply black; it was a breathing darkness, its breath overpowering from deep in the tunnel. It shoved its way into her throat and coated her lungs as though it were a powder, ground fine by years of disuse.

Hearing the muffled sound of the world above, the clank and bang of it, but seeing only dark was unnerving. Jace's and Rory's radios crackled in their ears, popping to life every few minutes with a quick blast of chatter before falling silent again.

—from 405—

—sweep team—

—go—

—got somebody's dinner at the back door . . . Chinese, I think—

—send 'em back, Bibb—

"Signal's getting bad." Jace turned up the volume.

"Be gone soon." Rory's flashlight limped out in front of her, a weak beam trying to cut open the darkness. "We'll be on our own. Let's don't get separated."

"You're the boss, sister."

"Pro'ly ought to scare you."

Jace breathed out hot, scared air. "It does."

233

Pipes ran above their heads, the sound of rushing water clear. There was also a low-volume moan that could have been anything from the harmonic resonance of earth held back by cracked concrete walls to a Hammond B-3 organ playing soulful jazz. Regardless, it and the rushing water came together as an angular and jagged music that played relentlessly and sideways, just as Mama's friends' well-intentioned pronouncements had after Mama's memorial service.

—456 and 479 status—

Rory keyed her radio. "10-6, control."

Jace imagined this place was what Mama would have seen had there been an actual burial; this darkness that deepened when Jace and Rory played the bluish swath of their flashlights over the tunnel's walls. Instead of a burial, there had been a service attended by a handful of friends, by her and Grapa and Gramma, by a few old high-school chums, conducted by Preacher.

—4 . . . 6 and . . . status—

"Control," Rory said. "We're fine."

Both women stopped and listened for a response.

"Control, 10-6."

A crackle came back, punctuated by remnants of Bibb's voice.

—did . . . say . . . 6?—

"10-4"

There the reception died, with an audible, rattling last breath like that of a wounded animal.

"He's gone."

Jace focused her flashlight into the tunnel. After no more than ten or fifteen feet, the dark ate the light. "I'm starting to freak out a little."

"Take it easy."

Jace's boot kicked the leg of a rusted and bent chair, decades old. She stepped around it and they continued on, their lights back and forth, trying to see everything while actually seeing almost nothing, and hoping Inmate Bobby didn't come out of some hidden shadow.

"Hey," Jace said. "What's 'full jail arms'?"

"Everything you're given to work the jail. Baton, OC spray, Taser, whatever."

"Don't we already have all that?"

"Not everyone. Some jailers haven't been certified or recertified on something."

"And 'full arms' would be firearms."

Rory nodded. "That'd be a pretty extreme situation."

In the yawning dark, which lent itself to a moaning silence, Jace felt fear bulge in her like a tumor closing her throat. She tried to ignore it, then to swallow it down but it went nowhere, impervious to her attempts. "I keep thinking about the locks."

"Me, too."

There was a series of doors, each secured, that led down through the basement and the sub-basement to the tunnel. Each lock had been opened as though it were a child's puzzle that, after having been opened, lost the attention of the child.

"Who'd'a thought Bobby was paying enough attention to snick some keys and get his ass outta here."

Jace kept her feet in as straight a line as she could, though the darkness bent her sense of direction. "True, that. Shouldn't we just go back to Dillon? Let him know what's what?"

"First of all, we don't know what's what. We have some opened locks. Maybe it's Bobby. Maybe it's custodial services."

"You don't believe that."

"No. It's Bobby. But he's already gone."

"Tempting fate, aren't you?"

"Haven't had a date in a while . . . at least I'm tempting somebody. Look, he killed Doc and boogied outta here through the tunnel when he realized we knew it. Probably already got out the other end. Operations has cars around the jail and heading to his places. Our job—as I see it—is to go back to Dillon with all the answers he's gonna want. Which doors and what route and blah blah blah. Don't matter what happened, we're going to do our jobs damned well and look good to Dillon and Major Jakob and the sheriff while we do it."

Rivers of sweat traced lines along Jace's face and neck. She wiped it away and tried to ignore walls that, regardless of her flashlight, stepped closer to her. "You like her, don't you?"

"Jakob? She's righteous, Jace. She is who I want to be."

"Forensics?"

Rory kicked a rat out of her way. It thumped against the wall and scurried into the safety of the darkness. "She didn't start out there. She was a roadie. Years ago. Wanna talk about tough? A woman in this county on the road twenty years ago? Fighting drunks and arresting wife-beaters? And you know she didn't have much backup. Had to prove herself to the boys every single minute. Doesn't get any tougher than that."

"So you don't want to test semen samples; you want to be tough."

"Hah. I am tough."

The basement of the Zachary County jail housed Records, the repository of every sliver of jail-produced records, both paper and digital, that state statutes demanded be kept. On the far side of that brightly lit room was a door Jace had never before noticed. Through that door, which was sometimes locked and sometimes not according to Rory, there was a stairway—lit by a string of yellow incandescent bulbs—that led to the sub-basement. Jace hadn't known that area existed and was shocked to find even more records.

"Hundred years back maybe," Rory had said.

The room was also a messy final resting place for bits and pieces of equipment. Ancient radios and gunbelts with leather so old and dried that much if it had cracked to pieces where it had been left. There were worn boots and, to Jace's shock, they were actually cowboy boots rather than Gore-Tex or zippered duty boots. There were also scrapbooks put together by long-ago deputies highlighting some retiring man's career or car chases and shootouts. On the far side of that room was another door, also unlocked. Through that was a last gate, then a short stairway down to the tunnel that connected old jail with old courthouse. Both the door and the gate had been unlocked, the rusty padlocks sitting on the floor like forgotten bullets.

They stepped carefully and tried to see anything Bobby might have stumbled against in his headlong rush toward the courthouse. The women traced their lights in a pattern: Jace in the nearness and Rory deeper in the tunnel.

The lighting has gotten dimmer, Jace realized.

In the hallway upstairs the lighting had been almost too bright, a splay of harsh blue-white fluorescent. In Records only a few of the overhead fixtures had been on because the office was closed. The two fixtures gave just enough light that, in the morning when the clerks arrived, they'd be able to see to get behind the counter. Each next place had fewer lights and they'd gone from the fluorescent to a handful of single bulbs, then to a single bulb. Each step put Jace and Rory deeper in the black, until, at the tunnel entrance, there was no light but what they had.

"I asked Dillon about Inmate Bobby's medical."

"Yeah?"

"He didn't know."

"Didn't know what?"

"What meds Bobby might have been taking."

Rory stopped, cocked her head slightly, and listened. After a drawn-out second, she started walking again. "Which would mean what?"

"Well, I thought maybe Wrubel was getting Inmate Bobby some drugs for a medical condition."

"That's not it."

"No. Wrubel and Bobby were both selling and Bobby killed him."

"Yeah. If you think about it, what better place to sell than a jail? Or a damned jail hospital." Rory held up one finger. "Patients," and a second finger, "junkies. It's perfect."

They had walked about another fifteen minutes when Jace's ears twitched.

"What?" Rory kept her eyes ahead of them.

"Probably shouldn't be hearing anything in here, should we?"

Rory turned into the tunnel. "Uh . . . no."

In the distance, someone cried. A weak sound that, to Jace's ears, was full of mourning. They moved cautiously, their flashlights arcing back and forth. Within a couple of minutes, they saw the blood.

"Shit." Rory swept her flashlight along the blood. It had splashed, then sprayed, and then there were drops as big as quarters heading deeper into the tunnel.

"Cut himself?"

"Lotta blood for a simple cut. And what would he have cut himself on?"

"The scalpel. I didn't find it."

Even in the dim light, Jace could see Rory grit her teeth. "Damn it."

"Bobby? You okay?" Jace's voice echoed in the tunnel. She walked faster, trying not to let panic overcome her. "Bobby? Come on, it's Sheriff Jace. Talk to me. What's going on?"

"Jace?" Rory was two steps behind. "Whiskey tango foxtrot?"

"I think he's killing himself."

"Crap."

Rory took off at a jog, faster than Jace was comfortable with, but not anywhere near as fast as Jace wanted to go. "Bobby? It's Deputy Bogan . . . Rory. Where are you?"

The dark grew deeper, darker. It tightened on them with every step. The light moved slower, too, shrinking and slipping behind them. The walls came in, concrete and aggregate, chipped paint and cobwebs, and slipped around them like a cold, hard blanket.

"Bobby?"

There was no answer. The crying stopped, then started again.

"Bobby? Where are you? Do you need a doctor?"

On the floor, the blood spatters got smaller. Moving faster? Or bleeding out?

—*. . . 456? Do . . . py?*—

Rory grabbed her shoulder mic. "Yeah, yeah, we're here. Send me a doctor. I got injuries."

—*. . . say again . . . you're injured?*—

"Inmate injured. Send a doctor. Now."

—*. . . 56 . . . breaking up . . .*—

"They're never going to hear us, Rory."

"Damn it, we need some help."

The crying got louder, almost within reach. If this was suicide, it wasn't over yet.

"Damn it, Bobby. Where are you?"

When they rounded a bend in the tunnel, they found him. Peering through the slashes of light, they saw a face streaked in red, almost an angry grin that reminded Jace of a clown's huge mouth. A scalpel was in Inmate Bobby's right hand. Covered in blood, it melded into his hand and then his arm until all three were a single instrument. Blood ran down, then sideways, then back up toward Inmate Bobby's face.

"Holy God." Jace stopped, frozen by the violence.

He'd been standing up when he slit his own throat. Probably back where they found the first spray. He walked here and lay down and the blood ran down his neck toward the floor. Then he struggled against the pain, or sudden regret, and turned his head until the blood seemed to rise into his face and eyes and stain his forehead.

Rory knelt next to Inmate Bobby and felt for a pulse. She spoke into her radio, though that was probably useless. "Control . . . 10-22 the doctor. Get me the JP."

—*456 . . . Justice of the Peace?*—

"Yeah, damn it. The JP and Major Jakob."

—*. . . 10-4 . . .*—

"And a detective. And some damned lights, I can't see anything. Adam 1 if he's available."

—*. . . 56 . . . break . . . cannot copy. Will . . . Jakob . . .*—

"Yeah. Whatever, whatever." Rory had already let go of her mic.

"Damn it." Jace backed up a step, then another. Her lips trembled and she bit them, hard, to stop it. She'd seen death, though more since hiring on at ZCSO, but this was someone she'd known. Murderer or not, drug dealer or not, she'd known Inmate Bobby. She'd bought him his little chocolate donuts when he'd done good work, had passed conversation with him when things were slow, had locked his cell at night a few times when work was finished. She wanted to say something to Rory, to ask what was going on, to find out why the world had tilted so precariously out of balance and so many people were dying, but she couldn't find any words.

Rory gently moved Jace backward. "He killed Wrubel and couldn't live with it and so killed himself. Jace, you're a professional police officer, you have to remember that. Like him or not, and I did, we have a job to do. Now back up and secure the scene for when the others get here."

Jace wiped her eyes and nodded. "Yeah, yeah, I know." She backed up, started looking at the scene from an evidentiary standpoint. It would need to be marked off from at least fifty feet before where they first saw the blood. Who knows what Inmate Bobby was doing before he cut himself and what evidence he'd left. And dead in front of them or not, Major Jakob would want the end of the scene marked off another fifty feet beyond Inmate Bobby's body.

When she looked back toward his body, Rory was on her knees, looking closely at Inmate Bobby's bloody left hand.

"Rory?"

"Yeah?"

"What are you doing?"

Rory stood, took a deep breath, and said, "He's got a deep cut on the palm of his left hand." She held her left hand up near her neck, mimicking the wounds. "If it's in a straight line with his neck, why would he cut his own palm?"

"Maybe it's not in a straight line. You're assuming one wound. Maybe it's two."

"Okay . . . say it is. Why cut his palm first? Or second? Or even at all? Makes no sense." Rory shook her head. "Seems like a defensive cut, not a hesitation cut."

Jace leaned her head back and stared into the darkness, away from Inmate Bobby's body, stunned at what she was hearing. As she did, an arm blasted out of the tunnel's darkness and hammered around her throat. It yanked her sideways, quick and harsh, and she dropped her flashlight. It popped off, leaving only Rory's light.

CHAPTER 31

"What the hell?"

"Shut up."

Rory turned instantly, her light in Jace's eyes. "Jace? You okay? Who the hell—Kerr? What the hell are you doing?"

"I didn't kill him."

"Let Deputy Salome go."

He tightened his grip and Jace's hands automatically went to his arm. "I didn't kill him."

"Let her go. Now. And I mean right the hell now."

"Yeah? Wha'choo gonna do? I got your woman, right here. I'll snap her in half."

"What are you talking about? This isn't you."

"Everything is me, damn it, except the murder. I didn't kill him."

"Kill who?" Rory took a step toward them.

Kerr tightened his hold around Jace's neck. He leaned back, putting her off balance. "Not another step. And I mean Bobby. I didn't kill him. I found him."

Jace saw Rory swallow, heard her take a deep breath, and saw her free hand come out, palm down. "Kerr." Rory spoke quietly. "Don't let this go bad, okay? We can talk about anything you want to talk about, but first, you have to let her go."

"I don't have to do shit."

"Easy, boy." Jace's voice was a croak. Kerr was cutting off her air supply but not completely.

"Don't tell me easy." He yanked Jace backward, fast enough that she lost her feet. She yelped and stumbled and tried to fight being dragged, but Kerr's right arm was a steel band around her neck. His sweat was sour, like a high-school locker-room stink, and she gagged as he dragged her.

"Kerr." Jace forced a casualness into her voice. "Don't do anything crazy."

"I didn't do it."

"Kerr, don't do—"

"I *didn't* do it. Didn't kill Wrubel, either."

Jace worked her fingers between his arm and her throat. If she could get some space in there, she might be able to keep him from choking her. If he blacked her out, God knew what would happen.

"Stop it or I'll snap your neck." He jammed his knee into the back of her thigh and pulled her further off balance until he was the only thing keeping her upright. "I don't wanna hurt you."

Jace dug her fingers into the meaty part of his forearm and used that for leverage, both spinning herself and tearing skin. He grunted and she faced him full. When she leaned back, his eyes went wide with surprise.

"His nose, Jace. Take out that son of a bitch's nose."

"Salome, no, I—"

Jace blasted forward, her eyes nailed to a spot on the bridge of his nose. Just before she struck him, Kerr jerked his body to the side. Her momentum took her hard into the wall. He hammered his arm across the back of her neck and crushed her against the cement.

"The hell are you doing?" His bellow was like a brick to her head. "I'm not gonna—"

She shoved off the wall and at the same time, kicked back and up, hoping to catch his scrotum with her foot. Instead, she connected with the outside of his thigh.

Without missing a beat, he shoved her back against the wall and jammed a scalpel near her eyes. "You want this? This what you want? I'm trying to tell you—"

Jace jerked her head left and low and shoved out against him again. Somewhere in the dark, she heard Rory's footsteps pounding toward them. Pain flared bright and hot in her cheek and she saw a flash of red on the blade. She bit back a scream and stopped fighting. She put her palms flat against the wall. "I'm not moving, Kerr. Not moving. I'm done."

"Stop, Bogan," Kerr said. He growled and laid the scalpel against Jace's cheek.

Rory stopped. "Hang on, Kerr. Don't make this any worse."

"I'm not even supposed to be here and now there's all this shit."

"I don't know what that means. What shit are you talking about?"

"All this shit. All I'm trying to do is get on down the road. I got kids I gotta provide for."

"You won't get down the road by assaulting two officers."

Their breath was heavy and loud, roaring in Jace's ears along with the white noise from the pain in her cheek.

Kerr said, "I didn't kill Bobby. And he didn't kill Wrubel."

His words lay there, roadkill brought to an elegant dinner table. But his body had stiffened when he spoke, his breath more ragged.

"He did kill Wrubel. His cell was covered in blood. The evidence is pretty clear."

He laughed and mumbled.

"What?"

"I'm telling you Bobby didn't kill Wrubel."

"Yes, he did."

"You found him, Deputy; was he bloody? They was blood everywhere. I had to clean it all up, I know how much was there. How Bobby gonna gut him and no blood get on Bobby?"

He's lying. I don't hear any deputies coming to save us and he's lying.

Bibb had heard some version of a call for help. He'd heard some version of injuries, though he might not know if it was officer or inmate. He'd heard something and Bibb wouldn't let them down. Bibb wouldn't assume it was okay. Bibb would assume the worst and send the armies of the world to save them.

Until then . . . we're alone.

Rory had once told Jace, in Jace's very first hours on duty, that if Jace was ever completely alone, it would be because Rory was already dead. Across the room, her face nearly lost in the darkness, Rory was not dead. Instead, her eyes were pools of anger and helplessness, but no fear. She was thinking, Jace understood. *Figuring out how to save me.*

Jace almost laughed. Rory was absolutely convinced of her own invincibility. A dash of ambition didn't hurt, either, and despite the fear gnawing in Jace's gut, watching Rory made her feel safer.

"Bobby was my friend. I've known him since we were in high school. He done a lot of bad stuff, but not that."

Jace pointed at Inmate Bobby's body. "That looks like remorse and regret to me."

Kerr looked. His eyes misted and his hands loosened on Jace. "That's my fault. I killed him. Shouldn't'a called." He stood tall and took a deep breath. "I killed Bobby."

"Kerr." Rory took another small step.

With a flick of his wrist, the blade nipped at Jace's cheek. There was no pain and Jace assumed it slipped into the first cut or her adrenaline was overpowering it. "I'll kill her." His voice boomed through the tunnel. "I'll fucking kill her. I'll do her up like the fucking Christmas turkey."

Rory stopped. "No you won't."

"Yeah? You sure about that?"

"Yeah, I am." Rory lowered her voice, forcing him to strain to hear her. Behind Jace, he leaned forward the slightest bit. "Because that's not you. Failure to pay child support? Come on, that's not a murderer."

"You don't know me."

"No, I don't, but I know you have a medical degree. I know you want to get outta here and get back to your older kid and the one on the way. I know that a man who wants to make good for his kids doesn't kill cops."

"Shut the hell up. You don't know shit."

"Kerr . . . I see the intake files, I know what's what. You work cash jobs. Why? So you can give your son cash and so you can buy him clothes and food and whatever else. You do it that way so your ex can't garnish your wages."

"She's a junkie," Jace said. "We all know that. And you're doing the best you can do for your son. If she gets your wages, she shoots them into her arm. You are not a violent man. A man who works healing people is not a violent man."

"I told you I killed Bobby."

"I'm not worried about that right now. I'm worried about you killing me, okay? Straight up, that's as honest as I can be." Jace took a deep breath. Warm blood ran from her cheek, down her neck, and cooled between her t-shirt and vest. "And don't cut me anymore, okay? You know I'm a wuss when it comes to pain. If I stub my toe, I'll be out for six months."

Kerr snorted back a laugh and the pressure on the blade decreased. "Why they searching Bobby's cell? He didn't kill anyone. That blood ain't Wrubel's. I heard that cop tell everyone to find Bobby."

Biting her lip, Jace silently cursed Von Holton.

"Bobby's been gone for a while. None of you high-powered cops even fucking knew. He's been gone. Sometimes he comes down here."

"Why?"

"Same reason I do, I guess. Sometimes I just gotta clean the jail outta my head."

It was, Jace realized, the same thing she and Rory did at Alley B's. The ladies got banana splits and the boys got a place to hide while still locked away from society.

"We come down here to do that cleaning in our heads." He sighed. "I didn't kill him. I found him dead. But it was my fault."

"Why do you say that?"

" 'Cause I can't keep my mouth shut."

"Kerr, you have to let Deputy Salome go. They're coming for us and you don't want them to find you like this. Remember what those ERTs do when they hit a room."

The man nodded. "I know; I been on the shitty end of that stick." He jerked his head toward the tunnel. "I'll hear 'em."

"How'd you guys get down here?"

He thrust his hips forward into Jace. Between them, she heard the jingling of his keys. "Bobby's top trusty and I'm in medical. They give us keys to just about everything. I didn't kill him."

"Gotcha. Well, killing me isn't going to help your case."

He hesitated. "I couldn't kill you, Deputy Salome; you the only one's ever treated me decent. And her sometimes." He nodded toward Rory.

"Sometimes? Dude, I got you yard duty when it was thirty damned degrees outside. Right at the fence line so when your son had his birthday your baby momma could drop him by for a *very* unauthorized visit. I could'a been suspended for that."

Kerr chuckled. "Yeah, you did do that."

"You've got me pinned against the wall," Jace said. "You say you couldn't kill me but you've already cut me twice and threatened to do me up like the Christmas turkey. Tell me again how you can't kill me."

"It doesn't matter. None of it matters. Bobby didn't kill himself or Wrubel. You guys are all wrong. I'm scared shitless and it doesn't matter what we do here. Okay? There it is. I'm scared like a titty baby."

Though he still held the scalpel toward her, he pivoted away until his back was against the wall. "Damn it. I'm sorry, Deputy Salome. You, too, Deputy Bogan. I'm just a fuck-up."

The scalpel's not toward me, it's toward the room. Toward Rory and the tunnel and the jail. He's got my blood on him but he's trying to protect himself.

Her blood spattered his jailhouse-blue shirt, like bad pop art from a high-school student. For a split second, it amazed her how much blood there was from a cut that had already gone from a sharp, piercing pain to a dull roar.

"Well, how about you and I figure it out together? Not out there." She waved a hand dismissively toward the jail. "But here and now. We don't walk out until we've got a handle on it, okay? That's the best I can do for you right now."

Relief came into his eyes. "Yeah. Thank you. But what about—" He indicated her bloody face.

She shrugged it off. "I'll tell them Deputy Bogan did it."

Both Rory and Kerr chuckled. "They'll believe that?"

"About her? Absolutely. She's crazy."

Rory rolled her eyes. "I am."

He laughed but the scalpel still hovered. It was coming down, still only a few inches from Jace but moving in a steady, slow arc to his side. As soon as the knife was down, she'd stomp his toe, which would lean him forward. Then she'd knee his face and send him backward, hopefully out cold. It was harsh and brutal but, in spite of her calming words to him, she wanted him unconscious. More than that, she realized, she wanted to hurt him as much as he'd hurt her.

Rory said, "You said the blood in Bobby's cell wasn't Wrubel's. How do you know that?"

"Bobby wasn't the only one with access to that cell."

"Come on. A conspiracy?"

"Ask Deputy Croft; he was on that night. Look, Bobby ain't no killer, Deputy Bogan. He deals and eats. You catch him, he'll do his time fair and square, no hassles. He gets out and he'll sell again and if you catch him . . . fine. We all know what the game is." He looked at the scalpel. "Wrubel wasn't selling to nobody and Bobby wasn't no killer."

"Then how did the blood—"

"The hell should I know? He said he got home last night? Maybe two nights ago, whenever, and the whole place smelled like cleaner. He didn't have any idea why."

Jace shook her head. "Kerr, you're not making sense."

"The night after Dr. Wrubel was killed, when everybody thought Mercer did it." He laughed. "He's another one ain't no murderer. That next night, Bobby said everybody was locked down and his whole fucking cell smelled like Pine-Sol. He told me last night when we was working the sally port together."

"We clean with Pine-Sol."

"I know that; I smell it every day. But Bobby hated it so he cleaned his cell with bleach. He didn't like smelling no forest. Said 'Gimme the city and the dirty streets and the crack whores and syringes in the damned gutters.' That was Bobby's people."

Rory took a deep breath. "All that aside, whose blood is that in the cell?"

Licking his teeth, Kerr said, "I don't know." His eyes danced and caught nothing but refused to alight on her. The scalpel stayed up but his free hand crossed his chest and stayed there, holding the opposite shoulder.

"You don't know?"

Kerr shifted from foot to foot. "How would I know? I'm just

an inmate."

Jace jammed a piece of steel into her voice, stood up straight, and took a step directly into Kerr, shoving the scalpel out of the way as though it were no more threatening than a watery swear from a drunk. "Listen to me."

"But—"

"Shut up."

Kerr's mouth snapped closed.

"Don't bullshit me. You're going to stand here and cut me— twice—and demand I do some sort of investigation and then lie to me?"

"I'm not—"

"People lie to me constantly and you've never done that. But right now, with who knows how many deputies racing down here ready to go to war because they think we're dead, you haven't told me everything. You want something from me but you're not willing to give me anything in return. That's not how we play. Give to get. Otherwise, I'll snap your ass down for attempted murder of a correctional officer, kidnapping, assault, unlawful possession of a weapon, and whatever else I can think of."

The threat hung naked between them and while Jace stared hard at Kerr and tried to pry him open, she understood—with a stark clarity that left 50-grit sandpaper in her throat—that she had crossed a line. She was horrified at Laimo's laughing at Mercer but what she had done with her threats didn't feel all that different.

The scalpel was at Kerr's side. He looked at it, shrugged, and handed it to Jace.

"Whose blood was it?" Rory asked.

"I promise I don't know. I swear to Christ that's the truth. But I can tell you it was planted."

"Planted?" Jace shook her head. "You can't plant that much

blood, Kerr; that's ridiculous."

"Sure you can; easy peasy."

From deep in the hallway, they began to hear the bang of feet against the concrete tunnel floor. Moving quick but not running because of the dark. Jace looked behind her and saw the dim glow of flashlights bobbing as the ERTs ran to save her and Rory.

"How?" Rory asked.

"Every living thing's got blood, Deputy Bogan. Gut a deer or something, drain the blood, fill some containers. Easy peasy."

"And bring it into the jail?"

Kerr shrugged.

"Where'd you see it?"

"I got no idea—"

The footsteps were getting louder, the flashlights brighter, though Jace still heard no voices. They weren't far away.

"That's crap. Don't jerk us around. Where was the blood?"

Rory grabbed his chin, jerked his head to face hers. "Damn it, tell us. They're coming."

"I don't know." Kerr's voice was a plaintive wail. Tears stood in his eyes. "What about my boy?"

"Tell us."

"I don't know—"

"Answer me now because—"

"I cain't—"

"—you won't get a chance when the ERTs get here."

"Stop yelling at—"

"Kerr, damn it."

"The blood."

"I don't *know*."

"Tell us."

"I don't—"

The feet were louder, the light brighter.

"What about Bobby?"

Jace jerked him toward her. "I'm not playing around."

"I cain't. He'll—"

"Bogan! Salome!" Dillon's voice. Angry. Scared. Amped up.

"Now, Kerr."

"The blood—"

"Tell us what—"

"—kill—"

"Who did it?"

"Everybody on the ground." Dillon's voice boomed in the confined space.

"—me."

"*On the ground.* Now."

The ERTs exploded around the bend and into the tunnel.

CHAPTER 32

In the split second it took for the place to swarm with ERTs, Jace yanked Kerr to the ground. She fell as fast as she could. A ballistic shield jammed painfully against her back, wrenching her head sideways and pressing it into the floor.

A shield hammered down on Kerr but he said nothing. His eyes closed and Jace saw, reflected in the dim flashlight, tears wetting the floor.

"Sarge, wait—"

Laimo slammed hard into Rory, cutting her off. Rory fell backward and her head bounced off the concrete as Laimo landed fully on the shield on top of her. She stared at Rory through the clear plastic, a grin all over her doughy face.

"Gotcha now, bitch."

"Laimo, shut the hell up." Dillon's voice was huge in the enclosed space.

Boots pounded the concrete, every ERT silent, as they spread out in concentric rings, expanding their hold on the tunnel. Two ERTs went forward beyond Bobby's body as another ERT pressed a shield against the corpse. Jace assumed two more were behind them, acting as rear guard.

They brought everyone. There're more than six ERTs here. They cleared out the entire booking room.

She'd never seen that many people involved in an ERT call-out and Jace froze, suddenly slung back into the pod on her first night on the job, reaching back until Thomas's dead eye

253

stared at her.

Stop it. Let go of it already.

Near her, she saw Rory move her fingers and give Laimo a pleasant middle one. Laimo pressed her shield down harder on Rory and Rory bit back a laugh.

Ahead of them, Inmate Bobby was also pinned, his body twisted beneath the shield until the slash of his throat was a second mouth, opening and asking for mercy. His eyes were open like Thomas's had been.

I don't want to see him. Or Thomas. Damn it, I don't want to see the dead.

Jace closed her eyes, shutting out Thomas and Bobby and Wrubel and maybe the after-image of Mama. Had her eyes been open or closed when she died? Had she seen her own death? Had she seen the man who ran her down, so drunk he didn't stop for miles and then told Lubbock County deputies he thought he'd hit a deer?

Jace's gut rumbled and a moment later, she threw up. Hot ropes of vomitus spewed across the concrete even as it clung to her lips and cheek.

"Sarge," Jimmson said. "She's getting sick over here."

"Hang on," Dillon said.

"But she's throwing up."

Laimo looked over, smirk on her face, though she kept her mouth shut.

"And I said wait."

Embarrassment, as hot as the vomit, flooded her. Last time she'd been pinned she'd pissed herself. At this moment, she hated this job and its violence. She hated seeing the dead in her dreams and the flyers left in her locker. She hated that Rory loved the job so much and hated that Gramma had been right.

But mostly she hated that Sheriff Bukowski had refused her resignation.

Everything held silent and steady forever. Her vomit cooled against her skin and time became elastic. They were not moving until Dillon was satisfied that the entire area was secured. Minutes or hours or even days, nothing would happen until Dillon said so.

"Gimme some damned light."

Every flashlight snapped on, each holding on a different spot, until the tunnel was dim with diffused light.

"Holy balls." Dillon said it with a ton of air, stringing the words out until they rang forever in the tunnel. "Is that Bobby?"

No one answered.

"Bogan, is that Bobby?"

"Yes, sir."

"Are you guys hurt?"

"No, sir."

"Salome?"

She coughed. "No, sir."

"You okay?"

"Yeah . . . uh . . . yes, sir."

"Who's that?" Dillon went to Kerr and raised the shield. "What the hell is he doing down here?"

"I was looking for Bobby. He's my friend."

Dillon stood. "Is there anyone else here?"

"No, sir." Kleopping's voice was steady. "I count three and a body."

No one moved.

"Sarge?" Rory tried to twist her head around but the shield held her. "No one here but us. You can let us up."

He said nothing.

"Sarge? Really? Let us go." Rory's voice had slipped up a bit, not scared or panicked, but wary.

"Not yet, Bogan."

"Why?"

An eternal three minutes later, Sheriff Bukowski, Major Jakob, and Detective Von Holton came around the bend in the tunnel. Bukowski had a cigar in his mouth, unlit, while Jakob's face was set hard as stone as she approached Bobby's body.

"That my murderer?" Von Holton asked.

"He didn't do it." Kerr's voice was pinched.

"Shut up." Von Holton looked at Dillon. "Guess the jail commission will be dropping in. Or maybe Salome's friend the Texas Ranger, Captain Ezrin. Maybe we can get him to sniff around, root out the bad cops again. Ezrin. Christ, Dillon, how . you've kept your job I don't know."

"Detective, watch your mouth or I'll cut your damned tongue out."

Von Holton sneered at the sheriff. "Yeah? Guess this puts the nail in the coffin for your next campaign. Somebody new'll be signing my checks."

Bukowski nodded to Dillon and a moment later, Jace and Rory were free. Kleopping kept a knee in Kerr's back, holding the inmate still. Laimo walked away from Rory but Jimmson held his hand out to help Jace up. She sat, willing herself not to cry.

"Don't worry about it," Jimmson said in her ear. "Happens to all of us."

His words, meant to be soothing, slammed into Jace's ears and head like railroad spikes. She didn't want to be soothed. She wanted to lash out, to give her humiliation something tangible to feed on.

Don't let it become you.

She breathed in and out, long, deep breaths, for a few minutes, letting her anger cool. Eventually, she looked up at Jimmson, still standing next to her. When offered his hand, she took it and stood.

"Get him to holding," Dillon said. "The rest of you secure

from Zebra 4, get back to your posts." Dillon tried his radio a couple of times but got no response. "Someone let Bibb know what's going on."

Kleopping cuffed Kerr while the man was still on the floor. He lifted him up and, with the rest of the ERTs, headed back toward the jail.

"Bogan, tell me what's what," Dillon said as Jakob examined Bobby's body.

"We were searching, heard someone crying. I thought it was Bobby. When we saw the blood back there, we assumed he was trying to kill himself. When we got here, we found Kerr, and Bobby dead."

"Did he do it?" the sheriff asked.

"Of course he did," Von Holton said. "Nobody else was down here. Where's my murder weapon?"

"Over here." Jimmson pointed at the scalpel Jace had dropped.

"Don't touch it. My guys'll bag it."

"It'll have my prints, too. He gave it to me."

"After cutting you?"

"That was an accident."

"Bogan? Salome? Did he do it?"

Jace, her mouth foul-tasting, spat and said, "I don't know, Sheriff. He said he didn't." She kept her eyes on the man who threatened to have her brought to work handcuffed if she actually tried to quit. "The detective is right; there wasn't anyone else down here as far as we know."

The sheriff nodded. "Anything else?"

"No, sir," Rory said immediately.

Jace opened her mouth, unsure.

"Salome? Got something to say?" Bukowski chewed his cigar.

Von Holton and Jakob looked at her. So did Dillon and Rory.

"Don't light that thing," she said, hating the strained and

weak sound of her voice.

Bukowski stared at her for an unnervingly long time. "Yes, ma'am."

CHAPTER 33

Big Carol, the overnight nurse, had put a small butterfly bandage on the superficial wounds on Jace's cheek and neck. Dillon talked to them again, as did Von Holton, and they wrote their reports on the incident. By the time they wrapped up, they'd stayed more than an hour over the end of their shift.

In the parking lot, Jace called the sheriff's direct line. "Yeah?"

"You said Dr. Cruz interviewed Inmate Bobby but then Kerr came along."

"Yeah."

"Kerr told me this morning he wasn't supposed to be here. It got me to thinking."

Silence.

"Kerr was a first offense failure to pay child support. Why's he in jail?"

"Society's punishing him so he learns his lesson and supports his whelp."

"Not on a first offense. That's probation and a hand-slap. How'd he end up in jail instead?"

"Crappy lawyer? Deputy, you've already given me a long night. Please don't add to my day. All I wanna do is decide whether or not to run again and smoke my cigar. Have a nice day."

A Zachary City dump truck, already full of dead Christmas trees, rumbled by on the street. While she'd been on the phone with Bukowski, Jakob had come to them. "You guys know what you're doing?"

"What's that, ma'am?" Rory leaned against her car.

"You heard me. You didn't tell us everything and—"

"Ma'am, we did but—"

"Don't lie to me, Bogan. You either, Salome." She held their eyes hard with her own. Steam rose from her coffee. "I don't care that you didn't tell me everything. Von Holton has screwed you around and I'm happy enough to let you guys run with the entire thing. But it's getting big now so watch your damned step. Two murders and I promise you Von Holton is right: the jail commission will be here soon. Bobby's killing changes everything. They might shut us down, they might take over day-to-day operations, they might do nothing."

"Why are we still investigating this?" Jace asked. "Two murders. We're just jailers."

"Yeah?" Jakob glared at her. "I thought I had two cops on my hands. Cops who wanted to break the big cases and move up the ranks. Maybe I was wrong."

Jace shook her head. "You didn't answer my question."

Jakob stared at Jace, never moving her eyes, as the steam from her coffee rose and curled around her head. It reminded Jace of smoke from a chimney rising and catching the slightest breezes until it curled and disappeared.

"No, I didn't. My reasons are straightforward. I want you to hammer my ex-husband. That may be petty and vengeful but it's how I feel. He needs to be put in his place." She smiled innocently. "If two women can do it, so much the better, especially if one of them is Jace Salome."

"Please." Jace turned away from Jakob, embarrassed and disgusted.

"Salome, do not underestimate his hatred of you."

"What'd I do to him?"

"Not to him . . . to Will Badgett."

"He knew Badgett?" Jace's gut tightened.

"Knew him, trained with him, drank with him." Her upper lip sneered. "Whored with him."

Jace took a deep breath. "You're no better than Von Holton."

"Because I'm using you?"

"Yeah." That knowledge set Jace's nerves on edge.

"The difference is he's using you to make sure you look bad. I'm using you to make *him* look bad and—"

"But—"

"And because I want you to look good. Both of you. I saw your face in the tunnel and I know you tried to resign but Bukowski wouldn't let you. Well, I won't, either. Either of you. You're both staying right here. Stop coming to work and I'll drag your asses back in cuffs."

She finished her coffee and crushed the Styrofoam cup in her hand. "Now, I have some information for you. First, Deputy Ezell checked the other end of that tunnel during your search. It's in the courthouse basement and it was open."

"What?"

"The gate had been opened and the plywood covering over the entrance moved. It was all put back but there were footprints in the dust and a new lock on the gate."

"Which means they cut the original lock off."

Jakob nodded. "Ezell found no other evidence of entry to the courthouse so that means someone with after-hours access. I had my guys do a rush typing on the blood in Bobby's cell. I'd hoped it would come back a type match for Wrubel."

"It didn't," Rory said.

Jakob looked surprised.

"An animal, probably," Jace said. "Deer?"

"Well, aren't you two ladies in the know. The blood of swine. I'll tell you something else. I only looked for a minute, and aside from the defensive wound you found, Bogan—well done;

that was a good catch—Bobby's neck was slashed right to left."

There had been so much blood Jace hadn't taken a long look. Even if she had, she wasn't sure she would have known what she was looking at.

"Meaning?"

"A left-hander, Jace," Rory said.

"I need more coffee. Ladies, have a nice day." She looked at them. "I'm here if you need anything, but I can't keep Von Holton out of it forever. Get it done. Quick. And don't be wrong or we're all going down."

CHAPTER 34

In her head, as they drove away from the jail, Jace kept hearing the same riff. A Duke Ellington thing, from "Black and Tan Fantasy," over and over in a way that didn't exist in the actual piece. Insistent and unrelenting. But it wasn't bringing her back to Inmate Bobby's cell or the blood or either of the killings. Rather, it kept bringing her, round and round again, to the courthouse.

"Night-time access? What does that mean?"

Rory changed lanes, as always without looking or seeming to care. They were headed to Alley B's. "Well, it's a public building and during the day, the public entrance is open. Have to go through security. Employees have to go through the employee door; have to punch their access code in. During the day, all the daytime workers have access they don't at night because there's no reason for them to be there."

"What if they have a reason to be there?"

"Their supervisor calls us and we give them access for that night or that time period or whatever. But then there's a night crew, too. Cleaning and court clerks doing all the data entry from day court. They have night-time access only unless they go through the public entrance."

Jace nodded as they turned a corner, headed north now on Big Spring Street. Rory's tires squealed a bit and Rory grinned.

"Mario Andretti," Jace said.

"Andretti? Who the hell is that? I'm Tony Stewart."

Jace tried to fit a smile over her face but it felt odd.

"So I'm guessing there are people who have total access. The sheriff. Maybe the command staff."

"Yeah. Medical, all the jail shift sergeants, the courthouse security deputies." Rory changed lanes again, gave her purple Monte Carlo a bit of gas, and looked in the rearview mirror.

Jace pulled out her phone and called the jail. In a matter of seconds she was talking with Billy Kemp, the deputy she'd met a few days earlier. "Hey, it's Salome."

"Hey. Wondered if I might hear from you."

"Why's that?"

He laughed. " 'Cause I knew you'd want to know who was in the courthouse last night."

"Well, anyone unusual, anyway. Anyone who shouldn't have been there."

"I got the screen up right now."

"Knowing I'd call."

"Knowing you'd call." He hummed while he checked the list, a pleasant tenor voice. "I don't see anything. No one unusual. Deputy court clerks, janitors, the regular people."

Jace thought as Rory dashed around a slow-moving oil-field supply truck. Her eye caught the rearview mirror again. Jace took a quick look but didn't see anything. "Well, what about people who came in around the time of death?"

"Which was?"

Jace shrugged. "I don't know. I came on at eleven, we shook the cell and that probably took half an hour. Started the search then. Searched for fifteen or twenty before we found him. Blood was tacky but not dry. So anyone in after ten thirty? What time do the night people come in?"

"Court clerks at seven, janitors usually about eight. Never seen anyone come in as late as ten thirty except during election season when polling judges are in and out. Hang on."

He hummed again while Rory bounced back and forth between the two lanes. They passed Johnny's Barbeque. Some of the taller office buildings crowded them, then thinned out for the squat low buildings of food joints and check-cashing places.

"Cruz came in last night," Kemp said. "About ten thirty."

Something tickled the back of Jace's brain. "Why him?"

"Uh . . . incident report says one of the janitors got sick or something. Didn't need an ambo. I guess Cruz was in the jail so he went over."

"Okay, thanks. Sorry to bother you."

"No bother at all. Good copping is what it is. Von Holton hasn't called me yet." He chuckled. "Later."

She hung up. "Cruz was in about ten thirty last night. He was at the jail and a janitor had some kind of medical issue so he went over."

"Well, part of being a good cop is running down all the possibilities, even if they don't pan out." Rory frowned. "I guess I'm wondering how someone got into Bobby's cell to plant the pig blood. And who."

Planted blood had been an absurd thing for Kerr to say, or so Jace had thought until Jakob said it was pig's blood.

"But why clean it up?" Jace asked. "Why not just spread it all over the cell and leave it?"

"If you leave it, Bobby sees it right away, as soon as he gets back to his cell. Calls us and we know it's a set-up because he's been out mopping whatever."

The killer, Jace realized, had needed time to build his case against Inmate Bobby. There had to be sufficient time for the right stories to go into the right ears. "Whole thing is overkill. Why put all that blood in there in the first place? It's too—"

Theatrical, she was going to say, but the word hung up in her throat.

"Jace?"

"Nothing."

Dr. Vernezobre had said he loved a good theatrical flourish, but Jace couldn't see him involved with whatever the hell this was. Plus, he never visited the jail as far as Jace knew. But he'd known both doctors, two of their names were on Shelby's list, and all three of their names kept resurfacing, like sharks hiding beneath placid water before suddenly splashing violently into view.

"It's got to do with the doctors," Jace said. "I keep hearing their names, and it's always about drugs. Cheap drugs, illegal drugs, drugs in the jail, drugs for poor people."

Rory looked in the rearview mirror again. "Remember how nervous Wrubel was when he came to see us after Mercer?"

Jace remembered the nervous looking around, the sweat on his forehead in spite of the winter chill. "So?"

"Ever wonder why? We were talking about Cruz and the contracts and drugs for inmates and then—" Rory stopped, frowning, and looked at Jace. Then again at the rearview mirror.

"Rory? Then what?"

"Then you mentioned doctors selling drugs to johnnies."

"Yeah? And?"

Rory swallowed. "Maybe we were wrong. About the drugs. About all of it."

"I'm not following."

"I've never believed Wrubel was selling drugs. Maybe self-medicating—he had a lot of issues eating at him—but not selling. But what'd we keep hearing, over and over? Selling selling selling. Like a freakin' political ad."

"A smear."

Rory nodded. "Trying to convince us he was a bad boy. Everybody who told us that heard it from the same source."

Jace sucked in a breath. "Dr. Cruz."

"Seems like."

Jace sat back heavily in the car, let the miles whir past her in a smear of a midmorning, colorless winter sun. There was no vibrancy in the colors, no earnestness. Everything was washed to a dull yellow, like the color of old paper, bleached by time and the disinterest of winter.

Was Dr. Cruz the man behind the curtain, pulling the levers and strings? Why? What could he possibly get out of Wrubel's or Inmate Bobby's death?

"No, no, we heard it from Kerr, too," Jace said.

"Kerr . . . who works as a medical trusty and who told us he was going to get a job with Cruz Medical once his sentence is done? That Kerr? And let's not forget about our truck in Rooster County. Weed and H and all the rest, but also knock-off pharma. Trade up, driver to dealer, and stumble across Dr. Vernezobre and Doc Wrubel."

When Rory looked in the mirror again, Jace looked, too.

"Sooooo . . . remember how I'm Tony Stewart?"

The white work truck was about a block behind them. When Rory changed lanes randomly, it did, too, though a few seconds slower.

"Son of a bitch." Jace banged a hand against the dash.

"I am getting so tired of this punk. Eat my dust, asshole."

Rory hammered down the accelerator and the Monte Carlo jumped forward.

Jace should be scared, she realized. This guy, who'd followed her and been at the Sea Spray and who knew where else, was behind her again. She should be scared but the only thing she tasted on her tongue was anger.

And violence.

Rory ground her teeth together. Her eyes were narrowed and her breath tight through her nose. One hand was on the wheel while the other was clenched to a tight fist in her lap. She sped up and traffic began to slip behind them. More than a few drivers gave them angry glares. She rocked in and out of lanes and put some distance between them and the truck.

The truck kept with them.

The Monte Carlo hugged the inside lane of Big Spring Street. It was two lanes either direction but in the next block or so it would widen. Still two lanes but with a gigantic turn lane. Between where they were and Alley B's, which was on the edge of Zachary City, the turn lane was almost two lanes wide.

Rory shot the car toward that turn lane.

Traffic was always heavy, but this was Zachary City's rush hour, when a majority of the city's 125,000 people went to work. Many of them filled Big Spring Street to get through downtown to the northern outskirts and the professional office parks.

The truck was still with them, the driver yanking his wheel left and right, trying to keep up with them.

The Monte Carlo dashed around a tandem semi with oil pumpjacks painted on the side. The driver honked loud and long. She maneuvered the car left and slid into the turn lane. One block up, a car sat, waiting to turn.

"Rory."

"I got it."

Jace looked at the driver in the truck, trying to commit his face to memory. He bobbed side to side, his face plainly showing panic.

At the last second, as though playing chicken with the turning car, Rory yanked the wheel right and came back into a traveling lane. The other driver started screaming and hitting his hands off the steering wheel.

Behind them, the truck was lost to sight, behind a wall of metal; semis and oil hands' trucks, which were almost uniformly huge, crew-cab pickups.

"Dangit," Rory said. "Come on, catch up."

"You want him to catch up?"

"There you are. Come to Mama." She eased back into the travel lane and slowed down a hair.

The truck roared up, directly behind them now.

Ahead of them, traffic emptied out as they reached the edge of Zachary City. To their right was the strip mall that housed Alley B's. Just beyond that mall was the Zachary City minor-league baseball field.

After that, seemingly an afterthought to the current development, was the original Zachary City cemetery. Closed decades ago, it was still open to visitors, but had only one way in or out. Metal and brick fencing surrounded it while 125-year-old trees hid the entire thing from the sight of passing drivers.

Rory blasted in, taking the corners fast enough that the rear end of her Monte Carlo fishtailed. She flipped the wheel and hit the brakes to straighten out on the main drive of the cemetery. It was paved and she left trails of rubber dancing behind them as the truck entered.

At the edge of the cemetery, the road turned right but Rory went left onto a maintenance track that was gravel and weeds. Dust spewed up behind the car and it fishtailed again, driving over a couple of flat stones.

"Rory."

"I know, I know. They're dead; they won't notice."

The cemetery was filled with thousands of graves, each in neatly lined sections, just as neatly lettered with signs. Many of the stones were flat but most were odes to settler families and stunningly successful oil wildcatters or ranchers who'd run ten thousand head. They stood tall, almost phallic in their symbolism, and every time the car grabbed a pothole or large rock and slid one way or the other, Jace was sure they'd slam into one.

The truck had to slow for the turn, but managed it. It came on fast as Rory whipped around another turn and brought them eventually back to the main road, this time headed for the exit.

She slowed for a split second, letting the truck catch them just a little, before she stood on the brakes and put the Monte Carlo into a power slide. They stopped broadside across the main road.

The truck was closer than Jace realized and it swerved to avoid them. It yawed left in a spray of dust, rumbled over a couple of flat headstones. Tools and cans bounced around in the truck's bed.

Rory jumped out of her car and headed for the still-moving truck.

The truck drifted left and bumped through some bushes. Bits of brown and dead yellow caught in the grill. The driver yanked the wheel hard back in the opposite direction and the truck swerved to the right, smashing into a headstone. It cracked through the deceased's name and fell backward as the truck came to a stop.

"Get out," Rory yelled, running to the truck and pulling the Glock from her waistband. "Get out now."

The driver raised his hands, his face as pale as a winter moon. Rory jerked the door open and yanked him out, throwing him to the ground. She shoved a knee in his back and twisted his right arm around behind him.

"Don't shoot. I ain't gonna hurt you."

"Shut up."

"Please, don't shoot—"

"Shut up." Rory gave a yank to his arm and he squealed. "Just stop talking. Okay?"

"Yeah, yeah, okay."

Silence hit the cemetery hard, like the volume suddenly muted on a TV. It ricocheted around, bouncing off the headstones and trees, losing its power as it came back at them. Eventually, the silence was peaceful and calm, what Jace imagined it to be normally.

Slowly, her skin hot with sweat and her head on fire with fear and anger, Jace walked to the driver and stood over him. "Who are you?"

He said nothing.

"She asked you a question." Rory yanked his arm.

"Ouch. And you told me not to say anything."

"Well, now you can talk. Who are you?"

"They call me Ty."

"That's not what I asked you, dumbass. I asked who you were." Rory yanked his arm again. This time he winced but made no sound. "He's toughening up, Jace . . . excuse me, *Deputy* Salome."

"Yeah, yeah, I know you're cops. That don't scare me."

"Really."

"Why are you following us?" Jace asked. Her hands shook and anger sat heavy in her throat. "Why the hell were you at my house?"

"This is an illegal search," he said.

Rory grinned. "You idiot, this isn't an illegal search, it's a . . . eh . . . maybe semi-legal detainment. When I go through your truck, *that'll* be an illegal search."

"You ain't going through my truck."

"Why are you watching us? Why were you at my house? Why'd you follow us the other day?"

He laughed. "I've watched you a lot more than that. Saw you outside the jail one day, too."

"Sounds like a stalking confession to me." Rory grinned. "This really is an easy job when they're so stupid."

"Yeah, *I'm* the stupid one. You fucking bitches have no idea what kind of shitcan you opened."

Jace went to her knees, put her face right next to his, spoke through clenched teeth. "What's your problem?"

He chuckled. "I ain't talking to you."

"So tell me this, Einstein," Rory said. "What were you going to do with us when you caught us?"

"Caught you? If he'd wanted you caught, you'd have been caught."

"He who?"

"Kiss my ass."

"Who?" Jace was on the edge of that precipice again. She wanted to yell and shake him, maybe to head butt him, to make him tell her everything.

"I ain't telling you that, idiot."

"Idiot?" Jace scooted close enough that she could see her spittle covering the distance between them. "We're the idiots? You're driving a truck that will tell us everything and we're the idiots? That VIN'll tell me exactly who you are."

He smirked. "Sure. Whatever you say."

"Jace, in my glove box is a pair of cuffs."

A few minutes later, they had him cuffed and Rory was on the phone with dispatch, running the VIN because the truck had no plates. She stared at the guy while she listened.

Leaning on the hood of Rory's car, he began to fidget. He looked around the cemetery. He pulled away from Jace just a bit.

Jace released his arm. "Do it," she whispered. "I haven't had a good foot chase in two . . . three days." She pointed at her ear, no longer bandaged, but scabbed. "The guy who did that is in federal custody." She pointed to the bandages on her cheek and neck from Kerr in the tunnel. "That guy's going down for attempted murder of a peace officer."

"Dougie? Bullshit." The guy spat. "Dougie ain't got the balls for that."

Jace stared at him. "You know Kerr?"

The guy shrugged. "I been around."

"Around the Zach County jail?"

His eyes darted away and he sniffed. "Arrest me if you gotta, but you got no case. I was here to see my mama. You and that freak blocked me in and attacked me for no reason."

Rory sauntered over. "So you get that truck from your boss? Looks like a work truck to me."

"I ain't telling you shit."

"Good." Rory winked. "Makes it easier for me that way."

Uncertainty flitted over the man's face. "Meaning?"

"Well, no plates, the VIN comes back to a little old man in Kermit, Texas; last legit registration was nearly ten years ago. So as far as I can tell, you're driving a stolen truck."

"Stolen? I bought that fucking thing from a guy five years ago. It's mine."

"Okay, so where's the registration? Or title?"

His face became stone.

Rory grinned. "Possession of stolen vehicle it is, then. No more nice afternoon drives for you, homie." She looked at Jace. "No name, but I'd guess he's Ty Campbell . . . who got a ticket for no registration from DPS just a couple of weeks ago, according to Balsamo. He's been down a few times."

"He's also good, good friends with Mr. Dougie Kerr." Jace walked over to his truck. It was an old Chevy, rusted through in most places and Jace wondered what held it together. She noticed a brown stain that had leaked out of the bed. It had run between the truck and the bumper.

Hershey's.

The lab tech's words.

. . . *sometimes brown is chocolate, sometimes it's feces, sometimes it's dried blood.*

"Rory?" Jace looked into the bed. "Rory?"

"Yeah?"

When Rory came over, she looked in the truck bed and

whistled. "Isn't that interesting."

Near the bed of the truck were bits and pieces of a mutilated pig.

CHAPTER 35

They never made Alley B's that morning.

After Zachary police arrived, two officers in shiny black Chargers festooned with all manner of strobes and emergency lights, and hauled the man away for possession of a stolen truck, Jace asked Rory to take her home.

Now, two hours after a short nap, Jace was edgy and unable to sleep. The dream had awakened her again, but this time with music that her dream-self thought she recognized but that her waking-self couldn't quite hum. That was new, yet another piece that might explain the dream to her, or detritus that meant nothing.

She went to Preacher's room. On the way there, she saw Gramma walking along the second-floor walkway. When the woman looked up and saw Jace, she smiled, then immediately scowled.

"Gramma?"

The woman stopped, her hands clenched to fists. "Damn it."

"You okay? What are you doing? Let me help." Jace assumed Gramma was in the middle of her daily hotel chores.

"No. I don't need your help, Jace. Thank you." The thanks was an obvious afterthought. Breathing deeply, Gramma turned away. She sniffed and wiped her face and then looked out over the parking lot. "Two bandages? Your cheek and your neck? And wasn't your ear bandaged just a few days ago?"

"It's nothing."

"Yeah, well, the nothing on your cheek is bleeding." She pulled a handkerchief from her pocket and tossed it to Jace.

Surprised, feeling the heat of Gramma's angry stare more than pain from the wounds, Jace pressed the handkerchief to her cheek and came away with a tiny spill of blood. "No big deal. Just a thing at work."

"Right."

Gramma already hated what Jace did. It was a bad job, warehousing people, and the violence was ever-present.

"Happened with your Mama like that. Just a thing at work."

"Work didn't get her, Gramma; a drunk driver did."

"Drunk driver took her body. Work is what killed her." The woman snorted. "Work. Can't even call it that. Stripping. Taking her clothes off for sweaty men."

Mama had done a slow strip to old jazz standards. That was part of where Jace had found her love of jazz. Mama had worked those gigs in the early 1990's when most dancers were using hair metal and hip-hop. The jazz, and her stage name, Salome, had made Mama different. Late at night, when Jace was vulnerable and missed her mother, she could believe that Mama had been something more than just a stripper. Gramma had never been able to make that distinction.

The old woman cupped Jace's face in withered hands and whispered, "Don't let it win, Jace; it'll take your soul."

" 'It' what?"

Gramma kissed Jace's forehead and hugged her tightly. "All of it. Good guys and bad guys and cops and robbers and . . . the violence."

"Gramma, I'm fine."

"Listen, just because you're part of violence's world don't mean you have to let the violence be part of your world. Violence begats violence."

"Begats? You've been talking to Preacher? Letting him read

Genesis during the dominoes games?" Jace tried on a smile but knew it didn't fit well.

Gramma ground her jaw. "Damn it, Jace, don't ignore me. I lost my daughter to stupid shit and I'm not going to lose my granddaughter, too. You never got hurt a day in your life and now you've always got bandages. That place is killing you, and I don't give a stone's shit in hell what that crazy old Bukowski says; you wanna quit then you walk out the door. Come home and let's run this place together. There's enough work; you won't be bored. We'll run it together, then I'll die and it'll all be yours."

"Gramma." Jace held tightly to the woman's hand. "I love you more than you'll ever know. After Mama died you were the only thing that kept me whole, you and Grapa."

"You kept us whole."

"We healed each other, then. I am never leaving you; I will always be here." She indicated the Sea Spray. "And here." She touched Gramma's heart. "Always and forever, but I like this job. Yes, sometimes it's a bad job, but it's a good bad job."

Gramma harrumphed. "That doesn't even make any sense."

"I'm helping."

"By getting hurt."

"No, by helping. Von Holton was going to string Mercer up and I figured it out. Yeah, I had help, but I figured it out. Me."

"I know, but—"

"Listen to me. I might be good at this job. Might not; I don't know yet. But if I am, it'll be the only thing I've ever been good at. The video store? Porn to creepy old men and teenagers trying to pass for men. The music store? How many times can I sell the sheet music for 'The Power of Love' for weddings without going completely batty?"

Gramma sighed. "I know all that. You were lost and unsure and afraid of the world after your mama died, but this—"

Gramma looked away, held her hands together in front of her. "Is a scary job."

Jace waved her hand dismissively. "Couple of cuts. No big deal. What happened with Badgett doesn't happen again. Every officer gets their big case. Mine happened my first night."

"Jace," Gramma said sharply, her voice like a blade. "Don't patronize me. This job is dangerous and unpredictable."

"I'm sorry; I wasn't trying to be patronizing. Yes, this can be a dangerous job, but I'm strong and I'm smart and I promise you I'll never let it get between us. I will keep this job away from you. I promise this with all my heart."

"Bah. Whatever."

Jace laughed. "You're turning into quite the crazy old lady, aren't you?"

Without a grin, her face set and tight, Gramma headed down the stairs. "Probably."

Twenty minutes later, Jace and Preacher stood at the corner of Lee Street and East Industrial Avenue. Preacher had asked a few times how her days were going—he could always tell when something had gotten inside her—but she ignored his questions with jokes so weak they limped from her mouth.

Lee Street was one of two or three north-side entrances to The Flat, which spread from the south side of Zachary City like a pool of spilled gasoline. When Jace was little, there had been more streets that crossed from the old Highway 80 to The Flat, but the city fathers, startled at the sheer amount of brown and black they saw every time they drove past on their way to City Hall, had closed two of the main streets that crossed the highway and railroad tracks and snaked into The Flat. There had been an outcry, community activists and residents and everyone of the belief that cutting the trade routes with the larger Zach City would weaken the local economy. Outwardly, it had. There were fewer cafes and convenience stores and video stores and liquor shops. But behind the boarded-up storefronts, there was a thriving economy, and that was the economy Mama had reveled in. She'd always bought her booze and tobacco down here—home-brewed liquor, cigarettes hijacked from trucks in Dallas or El Paso or Oklahoma City and sent to the seedier areas of Texas towns to be sold from under even seedier counters.

As Jace and Preacher strolled The Flat's aged sidewalks, black and brown faces stared back at them. Sometimes those faces were angry and sometimes they were guarded, but always they were curious. The challenging eyes and body language didn't intimidate Jace. She believed she understood the fragrance of the area's humanity. Most everyone down here was just trying to boogie to their own tune and get on with their own lives as best they could. Not too damned many of them gave a crap about some white chick wandering around with a lunatic black preacher while flashing a picture of a dead black kid.

They were on South Lee Street, about ten miles east of the Sea Spray Inn. Four blocks north of them was Highway 80 and the railroad tracks, and another two blocks north from there was the county courthouse and the jail. Between where they were and Highway 80 were six or eight small businesses lined up like prisoners to be searched. When she started to go inside one, Preacher stopped her with a nod toward a man on the sidewalk. He was older, his dirty hair gray, his clothes torn. He lay against the brick of a video store, in the fetal position, and he shook.

"He's been got," Preacher said.

"By what?"

" 'On't know, little girl. Drugs. Booze, maybe, or just a broken heart. But something's got him powerful hard." Preacher's eyes welled up. "Maybe he lost his boy."

"Preacher?"

"I'm'a be killed," the man said, his voice thick with phlegm.

His eyes cast over them but Jace didn't think he saw anything. "He'll kill me . . . kill me. Stabmeshootmechokeme burn in hell forever." He smacked lips worn out by age and heat, cracked and swollen. "He'll kill me."

"Go on ahead, Jace, maybe I can talk to him."

Inside, the man behind the counter, as old as the surrounding desert, was unable to quash the sadness that washed through his eyes when he saw her. "Ah, *chica*. No Robison today."

"*Gracias,* Arturo. You will call?"

"*Si, si.*"

She stood, lost in hesitation, and finally took a different photo from her purse. It was frayed at the edges, the colors faded. In the picture, Mama's grin was tight and muted but there was a spark in her eyes that Jace saw every time she thought of Mama. "I know I keep asking . . . but maybe you've remembered her? Maybe she bought something?"

Arturo made a show of studying the picture but Jace knew he'd never seen Mama. She snatched it back. "I'm sorry. I shouldn't have shown you that."

"No, *chica,* I am sorry. I wish I had known your *madre*. I wish I could tell you she bought flowers or something sweet for her little girl."

"Thank you."

The delicate bell hanging over the door tinkled as she left. She stood outside the door and willed the tears not to fall. It was a battle she always lost so, just like always, she gave in and let herself cry. Finally, she wiped her face, rubbed her eyes, and realized Preacher was standing next to her.

"Ain't seen them?" His voice was soft and soothing and understanding and Jace loved him ferociously.

Sniffling, she linked her arm in Preacher's and they strolled north, enjoying the bit of warmth in the winter air. "What had him?"

"Got himself a bugaboo about pills. Cain't live his days without 'em. Got some this morning but they ain't working for him so he hurting." Preacher seemed wounded by the childlike moan coming from the man.

"He's building up a tolerance."

"Maybe is. His needs gotta jump a higher fence every day."

"Who's going to kill him?"

Preacher shrugged. "Boy talking crazy. Had a card could'a got him some pharma but it older'n me. Expired years ago."

"For what?"

"Some pharmacy drugs."

. . . knock-off pharma . . .

Shelby and Rory had both said that.

Jace stopped, thinking about what some of Dr. Vernezobre's patients had to go through every once in a while. Maybe, in his zeal to show investors solid financial sheets, or in an effort to pull as much profit out of Cruz Medical as he could, Dr. Cruz was the endpoint user on a pipeline that delivered weak drugs.

Rory should test the pharma pills they found in the truck, see what the strength was.

So was Wrubel killed because he was selling . . . or because he knew about the pipeline?

If the pipeline even existed. It was a stretch to say Cruz was using smuggled drugs with no potency. After all, they hadn't found his name on a dealer's list, just Wrubel and Dr. Vernezobre's.

. . . he'll kill me . . .

The junkie's word, a man lost both on the street and in his own head and addiction. But why did his words ring a bell?

She realized, when she stopped walking, that she hadn't been paying attention to her surroundings. She and Preacher had crossed Highway 80, only four narrow lanes that this time of day didn't have much traffic, and were standing near the courthouse. All the way around the giant square upon which the courthouse stood were bail-bond businesses, copy shops, pawn shops, an old mom-and-pop diner. There were more than a few lawyers' offices, though they had tattered and dirty awnings if they had any at all, cracked windows, and roll-down storefronts that rarely got used because the attorneys lived in these offices and were available 24 hours a day.

But as Jace looked, and thought about someone going through the courthouse to the tunnel entrance in the basement, she realized there was a bodega directly across the street from the courthouse's employee entrance.

And there were at least two security cameras posted on the outside of the building.

CHAPTER 36

Her phone rang. It was Sheriff Bukowski.

"I get one free indoor smoke behind this."

Her breath held.

Preacher led the way back to his truck.

"Spoke to a couple of black robes. Kerr's first offense. There were no deals yet but it was looking like probation. Then he gets nailed down to a year in county."

"What changed?"

"Dr. Ernesto Cruz."

Jace's grip tightened on her phone.

"Cruz came across Kerr's pre-sentence investigation; don't know how that happened. Saw that Kerr had some medical training, went to the presiding judge, made a deal." Bukowski laughed. "Judge told me he asked Cruz what if Kerr kills somebody, doing medical procedures."

. . . he'll kill me . . .

Again, the old junkie's words, but someone else's, too.

"Made a deal? With a judge?"

"Election time's coming, Salome. Cruz Medical is a big company; maybe threw some donations the judge's way. Told the judge that a year in county would be perfect punishment and training for Kerr and that, afterward, Cruz would hire him at Cruz Medical. Hey, everybody wins, right? Cruz gets an assistant, Kerr gets a job, Kerr's kid and kid-to-be get child support. It's a win-win."

Then she knew. Kerr's words. In the tunnel. Jace hadn't put them together because she and Rory had been yelling and Kerr had been crying but he'd said it. He couldn't tell them what was what because some unknown *he* would kill Kerr.

"Shit."

"What, Deputy?"

"Kerr told us in the tunnel that if he said anything he'd be killed."

"Said anything about what?"

"I don't know. Never gave us a name, either."

The sound of the man's breathing, heavy and strained, was clear though the phone. "Well . . . damn."

CHAPTER 37

The bodega was small, just an afterthought that had been there for decades, probably handed down from father to son and then to grandson. Its stock was small and precisely targeted for the customer base. Cigarettes for the clerks and cigars for attorneys and judges; flavored coffees for courthouse workers who couldn't afford the upscale coffee shop down the street; newspapers spread from Midland to Lubbock, Dallas, Austin, a few copies of the *Wall Street Journal;* homemade sandwiches filled with pork or brisket, chicken fingers fried in lard; a few pre-made salads, and scores of sanctuary candles decorated with Jesus and the saints for those who wanted to light a candle over their loved one's misfortune with the legal system.

Jace stepped up to the counter, Preacher outside, and popped open her wallet. Her badge, something she still loved looking at, gleamed in the light. "Do your security cameras work?"

The clerk, an older man with wisps of gray hair lonely on his head, looked at the badge, at Jace, at the cameras. "Wouldn't do no good otherwise, am I right?"

"You are." Jace put her badge away and held out her hand. "I'm Deputy Jace Salome, Zachary County sheriff's office."

With a grin, the man held both his hands out. "Cuff me up, take me away. Three squares a day and no responsibilities? Cuff me right up."

Jace laughed as though the joke weren't ancient and was still funny. "Maybe, but before the cuffing, I wonder if your cameras caught anything last night between ten and midnight."

The man shook his head. "We close about seven and had no trouble. No break-ins or anything."

"I'm more interested in what they might have seen across the street."

The parking stalls on the street were angled and both of his outdoor cameras were pointed in such a way that would probably catch cars and license plates if need be.

The man glanced toward the courthouse. "Trouble over there? An escape?"

"No, no, nothing like that. Actually, it was someone going in. We've been having problems with our access code system recently. One person comes in but the computer says it's someone else. You know . . . software and computers." She rolled her eyes, feigning exasperation.

"I got one but I hate it."

Together they checked his footage and fifteen minutes later, Jace walked out. She'd had to show the owner how to burn a copy of the footage for her, but she had it and it left smoldering embers in her head.

Who in the hell are you?

"Jace? You okay?" Preacher had been sitting and studying Robison's homework while she was inside. Now he stuffed the papers inside his briefcase and stood.

"I'm not really sure, Preacher." She was certain the video showed Bobby's murderer; she just had no idea who the man was. "How about you?"

His face, lined with so many years of missing his son, seemed even more anguished than usual. "I miss my boy." He wiped his eyes and started walking. "Hoped today maybe we'd see him."

They walked back to his truck, hand in hand.

CHAPTER 38

The rest of the afternoon and evening, Jace slept. Her dreams were crowded; cells and inmates screaming "Murder!" while alarms shrieked; dead men wandering through tunnels while they sold prescription drugs to Sheriff Bukowski and Major Jakob; Detective Von Holton madly punching the button on a copy machine and letting it spew thousands of flyers.

But it was also crowded with the small house, up on cinder-blocks as though waiting for a truck to haul it to better days. The young girl that she was in the dream hated the brown paint on the walls. Spots and drips and, in some places, large brush-strokes. Holes in the living room walls, torn and stained carpet in the bedroom, smashed windows everywhere through which a hot wind blew and scalded her, a broken mirror staring at her with ragged glee in the bathroom.

But that little girl also knew, with the preternatural knowledge one finds themselves with in dreams, that those windows faced west.

And blazed with an early-morning sun.

The little girl knew, too, the song she'd heard the last few times the dream crowded her. It was one of the songs Mama danced to . . . at least, the little girl thought it was.

Jace woke, scared and sweating, her entire body tight and coiled and defensive. She yanked open a curtain to let the half-moon bleed into her room and wondered if the sun now rose in the west.

287

Hershey's.

Not particularly that brand, but chocolate. She hadn't known that until the tech had sprayed Inmate Bobby's cell. Now she knew that dried blood could be mistaken, sometimes, for dried chocolate.

Or brown paint, maybe?

So maybe, in this tiny house in her recurrent dream, the brown wasn't paint at all. Maybe it was blood, spattered and stained and once wet and dripping, but now dried into the house's memory of violence.

Before she left for work, she stopped at Gramma's and hummed the bit of song for her. Gramma smiled and shook her head. "Can't believe you don't know that one. 'East of the Sun (West of the Moon).' Grapa and I danced and . . . uh . . . stuff to it."

East of the sun, hence the sun rising through west-facing windows.

"Did Mama ever dance to it?"

Gramma frowned, gnawed her lip. "I think so. I don't know what all she danced to, but I think that was one."

"Thanks, Gramma."

"You're welcome, baby. Be careful tonight, okay? No bandages?"

"Deal."

Later, after roll call, she said to Rory, "There's blood on the walls."

Rory looked at her.

"In my dream house. The sun rises in the west because Mama danced to 'East of the Sun,' and there's blood on the walls."

"Whoa . . . hang on. What are you talking about?"

Jace shivered. "It scares me, Rory."

In the locker room, with no one else around, Rory held Jace's hand. "That dream can't scare you; you're Jace Salome, Super Worm." She squeezed her hand. "Maybe you have that dream because you feel locked down here. It's that house and it's the go-between so maybe it's your brain telling you that you want to go to the road and get out of the jail." She cracked an impish smile.

Jace shook her head. "This is serious, Rory. I don't think that's what it's saying."

"I do. You want to get out of here and see what real life is all about. You may not realize it yet, but you want to go to the road. Your mama didn't just dance in Zach City, right? She went all over west Texas? On the road? See what I'm saying? What's more . . . you want Von Holton's job and someday you'll have it. You may also want world peace and free Skittles for life, but that can probably wait."

Jace, anxiety flooding her like a white-hot tropical disease, shook her head, muttered that Rory was a doofus, and left. Jace was assigned floater status tonight, which meant she'd spend the night moving from place to place helping with minor problems. If there were none, and usually nights were quiet when it came to the floater's position, she'd be able to catch up on her paperwork.

If it were quiet, she would figure out exactly what the footage from the bodega meant; footage that had a man Jace recognized, though she didn't know from where, going into the courthouse about ten thirty the night Inmate Bobby was killed and coming out less than a half hour later. Night-time light around the courthouse was spotty, and the betweens were filled with a darkness that was perpetually deep, regardless of moonlight. The tall buildings kept the spaces between streetlights and building lights hushed and dark. On his way in, the man had stumbled and as he tried to regain his footing, he'd stepped into light from both the building and a walkway lamppost. His head was turned slightly away from the camera but it was a good picture of his face. Bibb would probably be able to grab a good still from it.

The footage didn't prove the man had killed Inmate Bobby, or even that he was in the tunnel. But it did prove that someone who was obviously not Dr. Ernesto Cruz had entered the courthouse after hours.

How'd you get Cruz's access code?

Why did you kill Inmate Bobby?

One of the second-shift detectives Jace had gotten to know had worked a case two months earlier that involved a 64-year-old man trying to have sex with a 14-year-old girl. The girl had been texting the man, whom she'd met on social media, and had gotten scared by the sheer volume of sexual talk. She'd told her mother everything and her mother had come to the sheriff's office. The detective had taken over the girl's account, texted the man as the young girl, and had been there to make the arrest when he showed up for a scheduled date, his truck full of candy and condoms and sex toys.

After the arrest, the detective interviewed the man and he'd claimed he was there to save the young girl, just as he had the other two girls, from making bad decisions in life. He'd gone silent at that point, perhaps realizing what he'd said. Immediately after he'd bonded out, the 64-year-old had gone home to Lubbock and shot himself to death.

The questions in that case, including who the other two girls were and how many others there might have been, immediately became null. There was no defendant, therefore no charges, therefore no case. The search warrants for the defendant's electronic devices were quashed, the subpoenas to internet service providers were dumped, and any information was basically put in the case file and forgotten. The detective had been furious and had told anyone who cared to listen, and quite a few who didn't, that the justice system was wretched indeed if it wasn't even interested in other possible victims.

Was that Inmate Bobby's death? Killed to stop questions? Questions, with unknown answers, crawled on Wrubel's and Inmate Bobby's deaths like maggots. Questions about drugs inside the jail, about buying and selling among johnnies and maybe staff members, about prescription drugs smuggled in from Mexico. And over it all, Dr. Cruz and his new jail contracts.

Or was the first half of the equation as simple as Inmate Bobby killing Wrubel for profit? And if that was the case, what about the second half of the equation? Who killed Inmate Bobby and why?

Except Big Carol said Wrubel wasn't selling.

At nearly midnight, Jace saw Von Holton. He was headed to the Pulpit and passing through the jail to get there, a sheaf of papers in his hand. He gave her a neutral stare.

"Good evening, Detective. How goes your case?"

"Fine, Deputy, just fine." A bit of color leaked into his cheeks and he licked his lips. "I made some missteps but I'm on track now." He handed her one of the pages. "Bobby's outgoing calls. Nothing all that interesting."

It was a computer printout from Balsamo in Records. It listed every outgoing phone call Inmate Bobby had made. That was standard procedure. None of them were recorded because trusties generally had looser restrictions. Regular inmates had every call recorded, and huge red lettered signs at every phone in the pods announced the recordings. The numbers and names of those called were all provided by the phone-services company, which charged what Jace thought to be exorbitant rates for inmates to make calls.

Perusing the list, Jace saw an end user identified as "pharmacy" four or five times. Her gut tightened. She took out her cell phone and texted the number to herself.

"What're you doing?"

"Just answering a text from Rory."

"Don't understand people being so glued to their phones. Guess I'm just old."

"I guess."

He cracked a vague smile. "If I were in charge? No cells in the jail at all."

"Guess you should run for sheriff, then."

He eyed her, seemingly unsure if she was poking him, and took back the page. "Thanks for your help on this thing, I appreciate it. Glad it's done."

"Yeah? Bobby killed Wrubel and then himself?"

Walking away, he nodded. "That's about how I see it."

Then you're not seeing very well.

"Hey, Croft, how's it hanging?"

"Low and left, Bogan, low and left."

Rory laughed, stuffing as much genuineness into the thing as she could. "Well, not that low; I mean, they only dropped last week."

"Funny girl. Why you in my pod? I thought you were in A tonight."

"Traded with Jimmson. He was floating and I had some things needed doing." She cocked her head as though deep in thought. "I got a question for you."

"Yes, I will go out with you, but you have to wear some sexy boots. And a gunbelt." He paused. "And nothing else."

"Wow, there's an image. I'd probably give you a heart attack and then I'd have to do mouth-to-mouth."

He stared at her, his expression completely flat. "I'm good with that."

"Uh-huh. So you were in ad-seg a few nights ago? The night before they searched Bobby's cell?"

"Yeah."

"Anything funky that night?"

"Funky how?"

She gritted her teeth. She'd wanted to do this quietly, but Croft, nice kid that he was, wasn't the brightest knife in the cookie jar. "I don't know. Anyone odd in or out? You now those trusty cells . . . open all day. Like a freakin' flea market in there sometimes."

He laughed. "My mom used to run a flea market. Called it a trading post."

"Yeah, huh. So anyone around?"

He turned toward the computer in the jailer desk, double-checked the locked cell doors. His partner tonight was Laimo and she had run to the break room to grab her dinner. When he looked back at Rory, his brows were knitted.

"Well, we had some plumbing issues so the shit-man was here. Sheriff came in a couple times looking for someone to clean up the front lobby. Dr. Cruz came in once, looking for Bobby."

Rory kept her face even and neutral. "Yeah?"

"Bobby wasn't around but his cell was open. Doctor said he had to drop some meds. Bobby had an allergy or something. I don't remember. Cruz said he was going to wash down Bobby's house with some new cleaner and see if that helped." His frown deepened. "Don't remember anything else."

"Okay. Well, thanks; I appreciate it."

"Wha'choo doing?"

Rory grinned. "You know how Jace is always hammering the sheriff for his cigars?"

"Yeah?"

"Well, I'm her little cigar spy, keeping tabs on the man."

Croft laughed. "Well, ain't no cigar stank in here, though the wash Cruz used 'bout killed me."

"Yeah?"

"Smelled like Pine-Sol."

"You don't like the forest, Croft?"

"Hell, no. Gimme the stink of cows any day."

Rory turned to leave, then turned back. "Oh, yeah, who was in here the night of the search?"

"Smit. Second shift."

"Okay. Thanks."

"Smitty, it's Rory."

"Seriously? It's like . . . I don't know . . . three in the morning."

"Hell, I figured you'd just be getting home from some hot date."

"We never left. I've got one of your cohorts right here."

"Yeah? Who's that?"

"Shhhh . . . super secret." Smit laughed quietly. "She's in the bathroom. Rooster County detective."

"Well, since there's only one Rooster County dick who's a female, and that one is married, I'll assume you have some other county investigator in your house."

"Assume all you want, but I can tell you she's quite good at . . . ah . . . investigating things."

"Whoa. Way too much information."

"My house, my phone call, my information. What do you want?"

"You were in ad-seg the night of the search of Bobby's cell."

"So?"

"Anybody go into that cell before Jakob locked it down?"

There was a long silence but behind it, Rory could hear Smit's wheels turning. Then she heard a female voice, whispering. "Yeah, now that you mention it. Kerr did."

Rory was confused. "What was he doing in there?"

"I don't know. I asked Bobby if Cruz had found him and he didn't seem to know what I was talking about so I told him that

Croft had told me Cruz was in his cell with allergy meds or an allergy wash or some shit. Bobby freaked out and left. Kerr came in . . . I don't know . . . fifteen minutes later or something, asked where Bobby was. I told him the little bit I knew and he got weird, too. Eyes all crazy—he's goofy anyway—and then popped a call at the phone and disappeared and like an hour later, *boom!*, you guys hop a squat in Bobby's cell."

Rory chewed her lip. "Thanks, man. Get back to your . . . whatever."

Click and he was gone.

CHAPTER 39

It was just after three in the morning. The jail had been quiet since lights out. Trusties had moved about the facility, carefully watched by both guards and Sgt. Bibb in the control room. Jailers traversed hallways almost with anonymity, heads down, conversation quiet. Few road deputies were even in the jail. Their jobs were outside, in their squads and at their off-site posts. They didn't want to be in the jail with its oppressive atmosphere.

Inmate Bobby's death was still fresh, a raw, open wound. Some deputies whispered amongst themselves that any time a convict suicided out it was a public service but most deputies were shaken. Bobby and Wrubel had been liked and now were inexorably linked, the why almost a forgotten matter.

For Jace, the night was filling out forms and signing sheets. She had escorted some trusties from place to place, had filled Rory in on Von Holton's information about the phone numbers.

"A pharmacy? That many times?" Rory wrapped her mouth around a chicken burrito.

"Yep. I want to know what pharmacy and why. Any meds he needs, as an inmate, are in the medical pod."

"So call and find out who it is."

"I'd bet Cruz Medical. All the calls were during the day and they're all on the trusty phone."

"Which means no recording." Rory grinned. "Sly little Bobby, trying to get around us."

"I'd bet he was looking for Dr. Cruz."

Jace told her friend about the video footage and Rory was both surprised and intrigued. The news stopped her in mid-chew of the last bite. "Who the hell is it?"

Jace shook her head.

"I want to see it. You didn't tell Von Holton, did you?"

"Only you." Jace unzipped her uniform shirt and pulled the disk out. Jace had looked at it four or five times, the few minutes that were on there, and still she had no idea who the man was. After handing it to Rory, she said, "I think that's who killed Inmate Bobby."

"I'll take a look. Gotta get back. See ya."

When Rory was gone, Jace called the pharmacy number from Von Holton's list.

"Hello and welcome to Cruz Medical. Our offices are open Monday through Friday, 8 a.m. until 4 p.m. For the pharmacy, please press 9 now. If you know your party's extension, please enter it at any time. For general voice mail, please press 0 and leave . . ."

She hung up and headed to medical. "Control from 479."

—go ahead—

"Medical outer, please."

The door popped almost immediately. Jace let it close completely behind her and didn't bother to radio for the inner door. It popped but she didn't move.

—Salome?—

The dream, with its go-between, flooded her head when she stepped in. This hadn't been the go-between where she fought, but they were all the same, built exactly the same, smelled exactly the same—

Like a forest because we use industrial Pine-Sol on everything.

And felt exactly the same as her dream.

—Salome? The inner is popped. Get in there. Now—

In this go-between, she could almost feel the tiny house; the shotgun shack with bloody walls and used condoms on the floor and syringes like trashy knickknacks and an early morning sun coming from the wrong direction, putting her and the house on the east side of the sun, and music to go with that wrong-direction sun. She'd been in the go-betweens before, thousands of times, but right now, something gouged at the back of her head about that house.

—*Salome. Now. Get your ass moving*—

"Huh? Oh. Right." She opened the medical-pod inner door and closed it firmly behind her.

Big Carol watched her with cautious eyes.

"I thought we could talk some more."

"Said I didn't want to."

"Yes, but you know as well as I do that Inmate Bobby did not kill Dr. Wrubel."

"Don't tell me what I know. Besides that, on the phone two damned days ago you said it was Bobby." She sat behind the counter and hadn't come out, or even stood, when Jace came in.

"Excuse me. I'm sorry, that's not what I meant."

Carol stared, her face as blank as the midwinter sun.

Jace changed tacks. "Tell me about Kerr."

Carol blinked rapidly, surprised. "Kerr? You think he's in this shit? Idiot. You couldn't be more wrong." She turned away, shaking her head. "Why all you jailers all think you're smarter than Dick Tracy."

"Carol, I don't—"

She turned back, her face as red as a serving of beets. "Kerr is a good man. Getting his life back together." She pointed to the medical pod. "He's got a job and when he gets done with his sentence, Cruz is going to hire him full time. Ain't that what we want? Offenders to become productive members of society and all the rest of the shit you guys spew? That's what he's doing."

Jace bit down her anger, tried to keep her voice calm. "I don't think he's mixed up in this at all. In fact, he's helped me quite a bit."

Carol's anger dissipated. "What?"

"Yeah."

The nurse straightened the desk of papers before moving them aside. "Helps me, too. Loves all this paperwork. Well, maybe doesn't love it, but can do it, bless his black little heart. Nothing I hate worse."

"What all can he do?"

"Basic vital signs. Temperature, heart rate, blood oxygen, but paperwork, too. I think he's trying to make himself indispensable so Dr. Cruz will have no choice but to hire him. Pretty smart plan. He knows the supply schedules and inventory control programs backward and forward. Anytime Dr. Cruz checks it, it's perfect."

—medical outer—

Jace turned, surprised at the anger in the voice. Through the inner-door window and then the go-between, she could make out Dr. Cruz standing in the hallway. He raised his portable radio and barked into it again.

—I said medical outer. Now—

With another pause of a few seconds, Bibb finally popped the door. Cruz strode through, one hand gripping the radio tightly while the other held something to the side of his face. Before the outer door had closed he yanked on the inner door.

—damn it . . . medical inner—

—procedure says once the outer is closed I can—

Cruz yelled so loudly that Jace and Big Carol heard him through the inner door. "I don't care about procedure. I need supplies and I need them now. Get this door open or I'll have your job."

—nine days out of seven, you can have it. I'll open your door when the other is closed—

Cruz crossed the go-between in three angry steps, yanked the outer door closed. Almost immediately, the inner door popped. He came through, his face red and shaking. He slammed the portable radio on the counter next to Big Carol and disappeared into the first exam room. The two ladies heard cabinet doors opened and slammed closed, drawers jerked open, the supplies in them bouncing about and spilling to the floor. Cruz muttered curses and banged more doors. After a minute or so the pod got quiet.

Big Carol sat behind her counter, her eyes wide, her hands shaking as she tried to type something into the computer. Jace heard her breath hitch as she stopped typing, and saw her put her head down in her hands.

"Carol?"

"Did you see that?" the nurse whispered to Jace, staring toward the exam room. "He was holding a compress against his cheek."

Jace frowned. She'd been paying attention to the radio and the angry walk; she hadn't seen the compress. Or the blood.

I missed it. Something that important and I missed it.

"Uh . . . Doctor?" Big Carol's voice was barely controlled. "Anything I can help with?"

The doctor said nothing and continued banging around. To Jace, it sounded like tools on the counter. Scissors or the like.

"My God." Carol was ashen. She glared at Jace but spoke softly. "You know it was that asshole."

"What?"

"Hair all swept back like a mafia ass. Been here a few times. Part of the tours but comes with the doctor, too, sometimes.

Showed me a badge once. A Mexican cop or something maybe?"

"What's his name?"

"Jorge something. He and the doctor constantly talk about how many inmates there are and how many come to medical. They talk about 'scripts a lot, too. Like do we need anything else, more of this or that drug. I thought he was a drug rep first couple of times I saw him, but—" She laughed a nervous laugh. "He never gave me any crap. I mean like free pens or notepads or nail clippers or all that bullshit the drug reps always shove off on clients."

"He's a police officer, you think?" Hadn't Kleopping said something about a Mexican officer being involved in the tours?

"I think so, but a shitty one. Shouts at Cruz. Gives me the stink eye. They talk about drugs a lot." She sighed. "God, I hate this job. Used to love it. But now—" She looked at Jace, something like hopelessness in her eyes. "My husband has a bad back. I need the benefits or I'd be gone in a flash."

"I don't understand."

"Me either because he don't talk like any cop I know. I heard him once threaten to beat up the doctor unless he cleaned up some mess. I almost punched him. I keep a clean pod, don't need some damn Mexican national telling me it's dirty." She pointed to the exam room. "Now he's beat to pieces so you tell me, Dick Tracy."

"How do you know Dr. Cruz got beat up?"

"Worked emergency rooms and jails for thirty years. I know what a beating looks like."

"How long has Jorge been coming around?"

Carol shrugged. "Two months? Three? I don't know."

"Damn it." Cruz's voice exploded from the exam room.

"Doctor, I'm right here if you need anything."

From the exam room, he said, "I think I can suture a simple wound."

301

"A suture?" Alarm spread on Carol's face. "What happened?"

He stormed out of the exam room, his face mostly cleaned. "I had a little car accident, okay? Nothing to worry about. Zach PD got it all taken care of, put a little bow on it for me." He grabbed the radio and realized, for the first time, that Jace was in the pod.

"You. You wanted to talk to me?"

"Huh?"

"You called my business. Like half hour ago? Didn't have balls enough to leave a message but your cell number was big and brassy right on the screen. Why the fuck did you call me? And what the fuck are you doing here? You have no business in here unless you are the assigned guard." His head snapped back and forth. "Where is the assigned guard? Not that you people can guard anything . . . two murders and no one's done a damned thing about it. We're about as safe here as in a firefight in Iraq. Well done, *Deputy* Salome."

Up close, she saw the damage clearly. Cruz had some stitches on his right cheek, but also a black eye, and traces of blood up near his hairline. The finger of his left hand, twisted in an accident when he was young, seemed straighter than the last time she saw him, perhaps broken.

He stepped up to her, not quite giving her a chest bump. "Not two deaths with you, though, right?"

Jace backed up a step, stunned. He followed her.

"Every time you turn around someone dies, right? Inmate . . . officer . . . your grandpa . . . hell, your grandma probably not too far from it, either, with you around."

"What?" She backed up again, trying to put space between them. He mirrored her steps. "Why would you say that?"

He crowded her until she was against the wall. "You think I'm an idiot? You think I don't hear what's going on? I hear everything, Deputy. I know what you're saying about me. I'm not selling drugs to the inmates. I'm not an addict. Bobby didn't kill Wrubel for revenge. Bobby killed Wrubel because Bobby was a cheap thug. Too stupid to stay outta jail. Who knows why he killed the man."

His voice was like razors in her ears. It ground her down and made her physically smaller. She tried to turn her head away, but he moved with her, making sure she saw him unless she closed her eyes.

I will not.

Swallowing her fear, deep in her belly now rather than at the back of her throat, she faced him fully. "And then killed himself?"

Cruz glared at her, uncertainty in his brown eyes for just a moment before they masked over and became absolutely certain. "Sure, he did. Filled with remorse. Like all rednecks. Do the deed but can't stand that they did it. If you're going to do it, man up about it." He grinned, his mouth curled at either end until he looked like one of those Greek tragedy/comedy masks the anonymous computer hacking group wore to hide their real faces.

And what are you hiding, Doctor? Why the personality shifts and one word to one person and a different word to a different person? What's behind your Greek mask?

"How do you get into the courthouse?" Jace asked suddenly.

For a long moment, he said nothing. His grin was more sneer, more anger and calculation than pleasance. "Like all the other county employees, I go through the employee entrance."

"Yes. Yes, you do. Day after day, always in the courthouse for one thing or another, aren't you? Probably working on those contracts that you told me are so utterly worthless. Hard to make money, right? Do it because you love medicine? Because you want to heal people?"

Cruz backed up a half step.

"And what about at night, Doctor? Been there lately at night?"

He sensed it, she knew; sensed the unknown, maybe ground that had suddenly become dangerous beneath his feet. He kept his face neutral, his eyes on her but with the hard edge. "I can count the number of times I've been there at night on one finger, *Deputy.*"

"Really."

"During a tour nearly two months ago. For that excursion, I used my access code. You know what an access code is, do you not, *Deputy*? I'm sure you don't have one."

"I do know what they are. Long time ago, at my apartment, the manager had gates with access codes. I gave mine to friends so I wouldn't have to go all the way downstairs and let them in."

He sneered. "An idiot *and* lazy. My code is my own. No one has it, no one uses it. I change it frequently."

"Well, good. There was a break-in at one of the offices. County clerk, I think." The lie rolled easily off her lips, surprising her. She both hated, and was glad, that it could. She'd known it wasn't Cruz who'd used his access code, but she wanted to see what he'd say. Now he was denying having been there in the first place.

"Well done, Deputy. You found a possible suspect and questioned him. I trust he passed your . . . interrogation?"

She smiled slowly. "Oh, he didn't need to pass; we know it wasn't him. Just like we know it wasn't his access code used to get in. You sure no one has your code?"

His eyes startled but he quickly regained himself. "It must have been hacked. Given the physical security around here, I can't imagine the cyber security is any better."

"Or maybe you gave it to a friend."

He worked his lips as though he were working up a mouthful

of spit. "A lie. Doctors used to be trusted. Doctors used to be part of the staff. I guess we're in different times, aren't we, Deputy?"

"Different from what?"

He raised his right hand and pointed a finger at her. His ring sat there like a fat drop of gold, squeezed carefully onto his finger. A ruby stared out at her, with a *T* and an *S* imprinted in gold on it. "When I started in medicine twenty years ago no one questioned doctors. We were—and still are—lifesavers."

His eyes caught hers and he jammed the ring up in her face. "Yeah? You looking at my ring? Medical school, Deputy, a step or three above correctional school. You and your fucking neck tattoo, looking at me like I'm some kind of leper." His hands flew out wide, taking in the entire jail. "I'm no leper. I save convicts, Deputy. I am not a baby-rapist or a burglar or a two-bit junkie or a crack ho with no teeth selling her snatch for a hit. I am better than all these people . . . all these *convicts*. I am better than you." His finger came back right into her face. "Why that tattoo, Deputy? Get your heart broken once? Grow up, bitch; life is heartbreak and fire-walking every damned day."

He grabbed the radio off the counter and demanded to be let out. Two pops later, he was moving rapidly down the hall, away from medical. Without a word, Carol, still pale and shaking, went to the exam room to clean up.

"Control from 479. Medical inner."

The door popped immediately.

Before she left at the end of her shift, Jace got a call. Big Carol, barely able to hold back her tears, hesitated. "He wasn't a doctor twenty years ago. Nine . . . maybe ten. Graduated from a university in Mexico."

"Why did he say twenty years?"

"I don't know, but he says it all the time."

"Padding his resumé, I guess. How do you know otherwise?"

"This is going to sound stupid, but he doesn't have any old stories. I've been a nurse thirty years and all his first patient stories are recent medicines or procedures. Plus? He and that guy talked about it. In Dr. Cruz's office once. I heard them. They were talking about outstanding school loans and I don't know what all."

All doctors had school loans, it should be no different for a man who went to school in another country. Maybe the guy was a relative, someone with whom Cruz was comfortable talking about personal issues. But if that were the case, why the repeated tours? Family member once, sure, to see where their loved one worked. But two or three or more times?

"What guy," though Jace was sure she knew.

"Jorge."

CHAPTER 40

Before noon, New Year's Eve, Jace stared at the wall of flyers.

They stared, too, silent but somehow still howling in their paper-language.

Why had she put them up? Why had she given cops like Von Holton power over her? Why hadn't she let their hatred bounce off her like bullets off Wonder Woman's bracelets?

Because things got to her, got under her skin, got deep in her brain. Like Mama's main song, given Jace over so many sleepless nights when she was a young girl. "Embraceable You." It wasn't a brilliant song, nor was Mama a particularly good singer. There were other songs, spanning the world of jazz, Jace liked better. There were other singers, both professional and amateur, who Jace thought had better control or deeper creativity or a wider knowledge of the music. But that song, sung in Mama's warbly alto, had gotten to Jace and burrowed into her head and heart and memory and that's what things did to her—good things and bad things.

So she kept the flyers. She brooded over them, got angry and melancholy over them.

She had come home after her shift, her head full and confused, and had gone straight to bed. She'd called and left a message for Major Jakob, intending to tell the woman about Dr. Cruz's injuries and what Jace believed was going on.

She'd then had two cups of tea and had fallen asleep on the couch. When she awoke, four hours later, Jakob had returned her call but Jace didn't call her back. Because what did she know? Nothing. She had beliefs and theories, but knew nothing.

Now she stood, naked, in the second bedroom and let the flyers needle her like a bad recording filled with static.

Her phone rang. The screen said Zachary City. She answered it.

"Salome? Captain Novotny over at Zach PD. Listen, we've been talking to Ty Campbell, your truck driver from the cemetery? Lemme ask you: Do you know Dr. Ernesto Cruz? I think he's the jail doc."

The flyers stared at her, as though just as intent on Captain Novotny. They swelled closer to her, waiting for an answer. "Yeah, he is. I know him. Why?"

"Well, turns out Mr. Campbell is his second cousin. Or third cousin. Hell, I can't remember. Got himself a bit of a habit, too. Busted a few times for possession. He's a pill popper but his arrests have been minor. He's related by marriage through Campbell's mother's brother's father's third yellow Lab dog or some crap; I can't remember. It was pretty thin, but they are related. He lives out . . . hang on." Jace heard papers shuffling. "Second cousin and he live out on 3200 a few miles north of Zach City. Actually in Martin County. Owns a hog farm. Cruz has been out there for injuries a few times. Hog farming is tough, I guess."

. . . it was pig blood.

Breath hot and scared, Jace said, "Did Dr. Cruz have an accident in the last couple of days? You guys take a report on that?"

"Hang on; lemme check."

This time, Jace heard him punching keys into a computer. Less than a minute later he was back. "If he did, he didn't report it." The captain chuckled. "You'd think a guy works for the poh-leece would report an accident. Maybe it wasn't too bad."

"Bad enough to require stitches."

"He went to the hospital?"

"No, did it himself. At the jail."

The captain whistled. "Not sure I could sew myself up. Well, we don't have anything on file. Maybe it was you guys."

It wasn't, but Jace agreed it could have been.

"Well, have fun tonight. New Year's Eve . . . lotta drunks."

"Nothing I like booking better than drunks."

The man laughed and hung up.

Jace glanced at her watch. It was just about noon. She dressed quickly and in a few minutes was headed to the Zachary County jail. On the way, she called Rory.

"I was sleeping, worm; why you calling me?"

Jace filled her in about Dr. Cruz sewing his sutures himself. She told Rory about Carol's belief that the doctor was beaten, by a man named Jorge who sometimes visited. She also told her friend that Carol believed Dr. Cruz's medical degree was not twenty years old, but closer to ten.

"Eh . . . everybody lies about their history. Building himself up. No big deal."

"It is if he's lying to administrators to get contracts. Wouldn't that be some sort of malfeasance or false pretenses or something?"

Rory laughed. "Probably. You wanna go be an investigator for the Texas medical board? What do you think he had to do with all this?"

"I don't know. So remember the cemetery guy? Ty Campbell? Guess who he is."

Rory whistled when Jace explained it. "That's the shit right there. Jakob said it was pig blood in Bobby's cell."

"Campbell likes to get a taste, too. No clue what his drug of choice is. Can you get some of the pharma from your truck arrest? Get it analyzed or whatever?"

"I don't know. Why?"

"Maybe it's less than full strength. I don't know; might mean something."

"Damn, sister. When you jump into something, you really go balls out."

"Jail balls. The ones you keep talking about."

"I'd say so."

"So I'm not the worm anymore?"

Rory laughed. "Always be the worm to me. I can hear traffic. Where you going?"

"To talk to a man about guns."

"Huh?"

"Later, sister."

Ten minutes later, she had signed in with Kemp and was walking into the yard. She tried to look calm but her insides were on fire and she was pretty sure she was going to throw up. One of the second-shift jailers asked if she needed any help. She'd said no, thanked him, made sure her badge was prominently displayed on her belt, and had the control room pop the door into the recreation yard.

It was about fifty degrees but the air was bathed in sunshine and felt warm on her face. As did the scores of eyes watching her. Most of B Pod was getting yard time right now, about a hundred inmates. Some played basketball, some stood and talked, some worked the weights in the far corner.

She headed for them.

When she was about fifty feet from the weight area, those inmates stopped lifting and stared at her. Their eyes were all hard as steel, as wary as wolves circling what could be predator or prey. Jace swallowed and felt her feet slow down. She willed herself on.

She put a mask on her face, as hard and unyielding as the inmates around her. Confident and sure of herself, unconcerned about a handful of men. A mask, but she was buoyed by it, strengthened. She could pretend to be a woman who was sure of herself, who held a deep belief in herself and what she could do.

How many of us, she wondered, *are scared behind our masks right now? Like Cruz was last night?* Probably everyone in the yard right now; each wearing a mask that made them smarter than they were, tougher than they were.

The inmate she wanted was lying on the bench, two huge steel plates on either end of the weight bar above his head.

"Tate." She nodded specifically at him and ignored the other inmates.

"Deputy . . . ? Uh . . . ?" He snapped his fingers, trying to remember her name.

"Salome," she said.

"Who gives a shit?"

"Looks like the guns are getting bigger."

"BB guns, an idiot cop told me once."

Jace nodded. She'd assumed he'd hammer her for that mistake. "Got a question."

He looked at his partners, his face blank but with tension beneath his skin, changing his mask by the heartbeat. None of them said anything. "Ask."

She looked at the other inmates. They all stared back, unwilling to move, unwilling to leave their partner alone.

It's exactly like cops. Rory and Bibb and Jakob and Bukowski. This is what they talk about . . . the camaraderie.

"What's the story with weed? Here . . . in Zach jail?"

Tate grinned and looked to his buddies. "I have no idea what you're talking about, Deputy. How can there be illegal drugs in a penal institution?"

"Look, I couldn't give two shits about who's smoking. All I want to know is where it comes from."

"Trying to snap a bust on our backs," one of the inmates said. "Fuck her."

Tate regarded her for a long while and her throat dried. She wanted to look around the edges of the yard, find the jailers bundled up in their department-issued winter coats, make sure their eyes were on her.

She didn't. She stared at Tate.

Eventually, Tate stood from the weight bench and silently invited her to lie down. For a heartbeat she hesitated and he saw it. A smirk began at the corners of his mouth. When she lay down, it disappeared. She put her hands on the bar above her head and two inmates moved to take some weight off the bar.

"Leave it," she said.

Silent but grinning, they left the weight. One of them went to the head of the bench, his crotch inches from her head. He put his hands on the bar and when she was ready, he helped her lift it straight up.

For a moment she managed to hold it, longer than she'd thought she would. It didn't come crashing down like she thought it might. She pushed with everything she thought she had, maybe a bit more than that, and she managed to slow it, but she couldn't stop the weight. It was too much, too overpowering.

It was like the bar, bending the slightest bit in the middle, was alive. It stared at her and grinned at her and laughed at her and kept coming at her, an insistent lover who played at domination, who played at putting his hands around her throat.

Strangling.

Like the job. Strangling her, transforming her into a different person. Forcing her into a skin that wasn't hers, one that she wasn't comfortable with.

Because it isn't you? Or because you haven't grown into it yet?

The bar kept coming. About a foot above her neck now.

The job was that insistent lover. It wanted things from her that she wasn't sure she could give, or wanted to give. Maybe she'd like those things once she gave them, but what if she didn't? What if she didn't like who this new lover made her become? What if she couldn't go back to who she'd been?

Except she wasn't sure who that had been. A lost girl, wandering job to job and watching the future slip into the past with only a moment between. Playing dominoes with the Hot Five, washing tenants' laundry with Gramma, drinking beer, sleeping late, never looking at a clock, never moving forward.

The bar was inches from her neck. She strained and pushed, felt the heat of trying in her face.

She was with this lover now. She'd stay with him and see where he led her . . . because maybe, way down deep somewhere, she liked where she thought they were going.

The bar touched her neck and she almost cried out. She almost screamed for help. Instead, she tried to find more gas in the tank, more fluid in the hydraulics.

There was none.

It strangled her, this metallic beast. Cold fingers around her neck and whispering in her ear while stars burst at the edge of her vision, dancing gold against a sunny sky.

—so many stars, Mama—

They'd gone to the desert all the time to watch stars. Away from the city lights so the depth of the dark could overwhelm them, always with the giant west-Texas sky above them.

—wanna go see some stars, Mama—

—just look through the window, honey—

—but, Mama—

—Jace! I'm busy—

Panic set in, stealing air from her lungs, oxygen from her

blood. Sweat coated her hands, making the beast, the strangling beast, too slippery to hold; even for her to turn sideways and maybe roll out from under it.

Then it was gone. The beast, the weight, the stars, the hazy memories of Mama. Tate and another inmate lifted it off her and put the bar back in its cradle above her head.

Slowly, embarrassed and feeling stupid for even trying to connect with him, she stood. Her breath was fast and hot in her throat. When she could breathe normally, she pointed at Tate's arms and said, "Bigger guns."

"Damn straight." His chest puffed out and he grew at least a couple of inches. The inmates around him slapped him on the back.

After a second, she pointed to the jailers around the edges of the yard, to the cameras and two guard towers. "More guns."

There was silence and for a split second, she thought she'd gone too far. But there was no new tension in the air. There were no curiosity ticklers, no hot spots. Jace was relaxed and comfortable and still rubbing her neck.

After a heartbeat, the inmates started hooting and laughing, both at Jace and Tate. His face flushed a little but he smiled and whapped a couple of his guys in the heads. "Guess that's true, ain't it?"

Jace grinned with him and let that single moment, as narrow and tailored as it was, immerse her. It wouldn't last long and two minutes from now she and Tate would again be on opposite sides, but right now the joke at his expense was okay.

Because he challenged me and I accepted. I did the best I could when he expected nothing from me. He did better. We both saved face.

His face beginning to serious up, Tate grabbed a 25-pound weight and headed toward an empty section of fence line. "Lemme tell you how to lift these weights, cop."

Jace followed. While they walked, he gave her the weight

without looking. Eventually he stopped near the fence.

"Raise it up and down, like I'm telling you how to do it."

"They'll believe that?"

"Perception, cop. Everybody talks." He shrugged. "Cain't think nobody's talking, though. Like when I was in high school. I'd go on a date and my homies wanna know how far I got. Hell, I didn't get nothing but some tit but telling the story, she did *everything* I told her to, didn't matter how freak."

"Gotcha." She raised and lowered the weight slowly.

"So you smelled the herb, huh? How come you didn't say nothing that night?"

"Tate, I don't care about the drug war. We waste too much time on weed. Frankly, I'd rather deal with guys toked up on weed than drunks. Hard drugs?" She shrugged and kept lifting. "I don't know. Seems like the whole war isn't working, but right or wrong, I could give a crap about weed."

Tate whistled. "Damn, woman, you got that speech all down and everything. Must be giving it for the Rotaries and Lions clubs and shit."

She grinned. "I'd give all you guys weed if you'd sit around eating Twinkies and watching TV all day so I didn't have to worry about having shit thrown on me."

"Why you asking?"

"Someone killed Doc Wrubel and I don't think it was Inmate Bobby. I keep hearing Wrubel was selling and I don't think that's true."

Tate shook his head, as though listening to some naïve fantasy from a young child. "Wrubel wasn't selling. Hell, I sold to him a few times when he was jonesing."

Jace took a deep breath. "Tate, I need it straight up, okay? No bullshit. Wrubel bought from you sometimes but wasn't selling?"

He stared hard at her. "As far as I ever heard, and I been up in this bitch a while now." His face flushed. "Plus a few other visits in the last few years. As far as I ever heard, Wrubel did not sell."

"What about Inmate Bobby?"

"Bobby traded a lid or two here or there, but never sold as far as I know."

"So he was a user?"

Tate shook his head. "Hell, no, not a real user. Toked up some weed but his addiction was those damned chocolate donuts."

Jace looked out over the yard. His compadres were watching and didn't care that she knew. She continued to lift and lower the weight. "So where'd you get your stash?"

He looked away, obviously uncomfortable. "Ain't looking to get anyone behind no 8-ball."

"Doing 8-balls, now, are we?"

He laughed. "Deputy Salome, knowing herself a little something about the game. Ain't 8-balling. Just some weed. Look, mine comes from an inmate; I ain't saying who, but he don't get his from an inmate. He sure don't have it delivered to the jail, either."

"Staff?"

"Drug pushers is drug pushers, ain't they?"

On her way out, Jace paused at the employee entrance, staring at Kemp.

"Yes, I'm beautiful and totally date-able," he said. "So tell your friends."

"All one of them?" After signing out, she thought for a minute. "Does everyone have to sign in and out?"

He closed a textbook he'd been reading. "They're supposed to, but . . . you know how it is. First of all, you got dumbasses like the guy who relieves me. He doesn't care because it isn't his name on the duty roster. Plus, some officers who don't believe they have to."

"Brass and command."

"Not necessarily. Sheriff Bukowski always signs in, but not everyone else."

"Why sign in?" She pointed at Bibb's video cameras, which hovered inside and outside the door.

"Cameras don't always work, and we both know that not all control-room guys are particular about doing their job. Bibb, for instance, is a tyrant about doing his job but—"

"I heard that." Bibb's voice came through the tinny intercom system.

"Get the hell outta here," Kemp said. "Quit stalking me."

"Yeah, *you're* the one I'm staring at," Bibb said.

With a tight grin, Jace gave the camera a middle finger.

"Oh, that'll look good in front of a grand jury, Deputy," Bibb said.

She added her free hand for a double banger.

"Anyway," Kemp said. "Bibb's the exception. Not all the control-room guys record who's coming and going. I promise you that'll change when the jail commission comes in. They'll take over running this place and it'll be on total lockdown all the time."

"Because of the deaths?"

He nodded.

Jace thought for a moment. "Mind if I take a look?"

Kemp shoved the book around. "Looking for something in particular?"

Silently, Jace started on December 20 and moved slowly forward. Not once, before or after Wrubel's death, did she see Cruz's signature.

"Remember, Salome, this is only one door. We've got ten or twelve throughout the entire facility. Four in the secure part of the jail. If you're looking for someone during the day, they could have used any door."

"This would have been well into dead shift."

Kemp drank from his steaming cup of tea. "This is the only door, then. Everything else closes at six. Since administrative is closed, makes no sense to keep those doors open. We funnel everyone through this door."

"Does Dr. Cruz sign in?"

Kemp's eyes flashed. "This about Wrubel and Bobby? Don't look at me like that; I hear stuff. Cruz used to sign in religiously and once a month he'd make copies of every visit."

"Documenting his hours."

"Probably. He doesn't do that anymore. Never signs in or out. Told me a few months ago he didn't have to because he was administration. It's crap. He started getting these other contracts and now his head's as big as mine. It's just ego."

Or blurring the lines of when he was here and gone, just in case.

Jace turned the book back toward Kemp. "Thanks for the help; I appreciate it."

"No sweat. Anytime. Gets kinda lonely at this door all the time."

"Why are you here? You seem maybe smart enough for the road."

He tapped his knee. "ACL injury on a tussle at a bar fight a few months ago. Isn't healing the way my doc thought it would. I'll be back out there eventually."

But Jace heard uncertainty in his voice, anxiety about his future. "Yeah, you will. I mean, I hope. I don't know, maybe not."

"Ouch!"

Laughing, she headed out. "Have a quiet shift."

"Damn it! Did you just jinx me?"

"Probably."

CHAPTER 41

Jace didn't sleep much that afternoon.

Her head moved too fast to do more than doze in fits and starts. If her skull were a record, it would be the hard bop jazz that exploded out of Minton's Playhouse in New York in the early Fifties, all head and steam, intricate harmonies, no speed limits. Her head would be Charlie Parker's sax or Thelonious Monk's piano.

And like those guys, circling around the melody and expanding it and pushing it and refining it, but always coming back to it, she came back to Dr. Cruz.

"It's always Cruz and drugs," she told Rory when Dillon assigned them both to E Pod that night. E Pod was the orange stripe on the floor and old men and infirm men in most of the cells.

"So Tate told you Wrubel wasn't pushing? Just using?"

Jace nodded as they checked each door together. By shift start at eleven p.m., usually everyone in this pod had been asleep for a while. Most of them would wake, plagued by age and unreliable bladders and bowels, and pace through the wee hours, but at shift change most of them were asleep. "Said staff was pushing."

"Who do you think?"

"The way Cruz's name keeps circling around this thing? I'd lay money on him. Plus, remember how he kept pushing Wrubel as the pusher. So I guess I'd like to know why Dr. Vernezobre told us Wrubel was selling."

Rory shook her head. "Dr. Vernezobre said he had demons but I don't think he ever said Wrubel was selling."

"So Wrubel's name was on Shelby's list because he was buying for himself?"

Rory nodded. "Makes sense. Good job with Tate, by the way. Give a little, get a little."

"I'm learning."

Rory's eyes, so light as to be almost translucent, were sad at the mention of Dr. Vernezobre. "I think he knows more than he's telling us."

They checked doors in silence for a bit, pulling each one to make sure it was secure. The computer already told them the doors were secure but it was a quiet night and they liked walking. More than one inmate waved at them. They nodded or waved in return.

"He's a good man, Jace; he wouldn't be playing around in illegal shit without a damned good reason." She chuckled. "His vaunted Cuban honor wouldn't allow anything skeezy."

"It's admirable in a certain light."

"In every light, I think. Can you dig Cruz's ego at not signing in, though? Doctor balls, I guess."

But Jace wasn't convinced. She believed it had to do with hiding tracks rather than leaving the tracks of an ego. "I think it has to do with Jorge."

"Who is this guy? Kleopping mentioned a Mexican poh-leece coming on a tour. Maybe that's him. But Carol said he's been around for a few months?"

"Yeah."

While they talked, they walked laps around the entirety of the pod. Faces, some old, some attached to bodies with issues, stared out through some of the cell-door windows.

Jace shook her head. "All of this is tied together and the ribbon around it all is Cruz."

"Maybe something Doc knew?"

"Or had. Was he giving drugs to inmates? There were the missing meds a few weeks ago."

"Giving to Bobby? Bobby was jonesing and Wrubel held out on him so Bobby stabbed him?"

Jace shrugged. "Tate told me Bobby didn't have a habit and we know he'd never visited medical or had any condition that needed meds."

"Which wouldn't explain why Bobby was killed anyway. So we're back to something Wrubel knew, and the way Cruz's name keeps floating around this whole mess, it's pretty damned safe to say it's about Cruz Medical and their new contracts or something going on in this jail."

"So Cruz killed Wrubel because he knew something? And then . . . what? Killed Bobby because Bobby saw it? What about the other guy? The one going into the courthouse?"

Rory shrugged. "I'm just spit-balling."

"Well, don't spit on me."

As they rounded a turn and came to the doors leading to the go-between and the main hallway, Rory saw Dr. Cruz pass E Pod, his body wrapped in a white coat emblazoned with the Cruz Medical logo. He glanced up and saw them. His eyes bulged and his mouth started flying, though they heard nothing.

—control . . . E Pod outer—

The outer door popped and as soon as it closed, the inner door popped. Cruz blasted into the pod, his hands clenched to fists, his eyes fixated on Jace.

"Again? Stay the hell outta my business. You do not need to know why I do or don't sign in, do you understand me? That is an arrangement between me and the administration, way above your pay grade so keep your nose out of it. If you need to know

321

something I'll be sure to tell you." He stepped up to her, chest to chest, his lips bleeding white and his eyes as fiery as a west-Texas Southern Baptist sermon. "And if you're going to investigate me, do it yourself."

"Doctor, I don't—"

"Sending Kemp to do it is weak, Salome. Shouldn't expect anything else." He snorted and thumped his chest, then stuck his finger in Jace's face. "I am *Doctor* Ernesto Reo Cruz and I'm strong enough to let my own hands get dirty. Don't have to hide behind someone else."

"Like your cousin?" Jace put her chest against his, forced him back a few steps. "Why'd you have Campbell following us?"

Cruz's face paled. "What?"

"Trying to intimidate us?" Jace shoved as much contempt into her laugh as she could. "You wanna dig your way under my skin, you'd better get a bigger shovel."

"I have no idea what you're talking about."

"Campbell tell you how I 'fronted him in a parking lot and he took off, too scared and *weak* to stand up? He tell you we caught his ass in the cemetery?"

"Bullshit."

"Why the pig blood, Doc?"

"I didn't—"

"Why'd you smear Inmate Bobby's cell with it?"

"Fuck you, I didn't—"

"Right, which was why you told Croft you needed to get into Bobby's cell. New allergy meds . . . a new allergy wash. You were washing the place with pig blood your cousin supplied."

Rory laughed. "That's a pretty lame frame-up. We cracked it in about seven seconds."

Jace moved in close, dropped her voice to a whisper. "I'm coming for you, *Doctor* Ernesto Reo Cruz. I know you killed Wrubel. And Bobby ended up dead at your hands, too, even if

322

the blood is on someone else's. I know you did it for drugs and I'm coming for you."

He looked from Jace to Rory, to the cell doors where old men watched him, laughed at him. "*Chiquita,* such big talk. You come, then."

His body shaking, he called for the inner door and within moments was back in the hallway, headed to medical.

Jace's guts were in her throat, hot and acidic and with even one more breath she might throw up all over everything. Her vision had narrowed to just Cruz, and her auditory exclusion was extreme. Rory was talking and talking, grinning and clapping Jace's back, but Jace heard nothing.

I just gave it all away, she thought. *If he did those things, if he's a murderer, I just gave away Von Holton's entire case.*

Except it wasn't Von Holton's case. Not anymore. It might have started with him, but now it was in Jace's lap and she was damned well going to see it through.

Eventually, slowly, Rory's voice battered its way through the auditory fog.

"Oh, man, where'd you get them jail balls? Those are huge!" Rory hugged her, then slapped the back of her head. "Man, that was incredible." She keyed her portable radio. "Bibb, you get that?"

—come on, Bogan, have I ever let you down . . . don't answer that—

Rory guided Jace back to the jailer's desk and sat her down. Jace's head was pounding and racing, her hands shaking and her skin sheened in sweat. "That was amazing, worm. Maybe even better than I could'a done."

"Yeah?" Jace asked, her voice unsteady.

"Maybe . . . just maybe."

Jace wasn't so sure. She'd seen the look in Cruz's eyes, felt the hot sting of his breath on her face, heard the threat in his words.

. . . you come, then . . .

Why had she mouthed off? Did she even believe the things she said? Did she believe he had killed Wrubel and was responsible for Inmate Bobby's death? Did she believe he had sent his cousin to intimidate them? Did she believe any of that or was it posturing?

Slowly, the pod coming back into focus, the voices on the radio coming back into her ears, she looked at Rory. "Dr. Ernesto Reo Cruz did it."

Rory was confused. "Huh?"

"Killed Wrubel. He was responsible for the death of Inmate Bobby."

"Oh . . . yeah, he did. That was obvious." Rory grinned. "I'm not sure I've ever known his middle name."

"Short for Robert."

Rory frowned. "Who told you that?"

Something in Rory's voice made Jace look at her. "He did."

"He lied. 'Reo' is Spanish."

"I figured that. What does it mean?"

Rory squeezed her friend's shoulder. "Culprit . . . offender. Or—"

"Convict."

As the clock slipped past two a.m., Jace received a call. It was short, the man on the other end quiet and sure, his voice thick with a Hispanic accent.

"Happy New Year's, *Chiquita.* You are causing me problems. You have been for a while now. Stop. Do you understand?"

Jace closed the magazine she'd been reading. She stared at Rory.

"What?" Rory mouthed.

"I don't know what you're talking about."

The man laughed, quiet and dark, and it reminded Jace of being out in the desert looking at stars with Mama. Mama would wander off to pee—or fix, Jace later decided—and Jace would be alone in the stiflingly quiet dark, her security blanket gone, until Mama came back.

"Yes, you do, *Chiquita*. I will tell you this only once. Stop."

"Do you know who I am? I'm the police."

The man laughed. "Yes, you are the police, but do not worry, I have my own. So go back to being a quiet jailer who does what she's told."

"Or?"

This time there was no laugh, only a tired sigh. "They always ask for the pain. What do you think the 'or' will be? What else can it be? You will stop or I will hurt you as hard as I can. I will kill your *abuela*. I will do it slowly and I will send you pieces as she dies."

Jace squeezed her phone until her fingers hurt. Her throat was dry as the desert, her skin as hot as the desert sun. "You don't scare me, Jorge."

There was a long silence. Rory's eyes widened.

"Ah, *Chiquita* knows more than she lets on."

"Listen to me: touch my grandmother and I will kill you myself. I'll track you down and kill you and feed your pieces to a hog farmer who owes me a favor."

He laughed. "*Chiquita*. You surprise me. You're tough . . . or think you are. That's fine; everyone needs to save their face. But if you ignore me, I will kill her, after which you and I will do our own dance."

Then he was gone.

"I'm going to call the sheriff."

"Jace, no, you're not. What can he do? He's home, asleep. He hasn't answered a call in twenty years. He has no gear, no legitimate training, nothing."

"But—"

"Listen to me, Jorge's a blowhard. Nothing else. He won't do squat. But if he does, you want someone good crashing in her door. I'm going to call Ezell. He'll go by and check on her. She's fine—that guy was just blowing smoke up your skirt—but Ezell will check and make sure. Then we'll go back to our old men."

"Rory, it's my Gramma."

"I know, and I know you're worried, but this is our job. People threaten us all the time. They never follow through. He's trying to get under your skin." Rory pulled out her cell phone. "You told Cruz to get a bigger shovel so he did, but it's still only a shovel."

Rory called and a few minutes later, Deputy Ezell and a Zachary City police patrol officer were on their way to the Sea Spray.

Twenty-five minutes later, Gramma called. She spoke quietly but Jace could taste the tension, the anger and fear. Gramma asked why two cops had come by her apartment. Jace told her there had been a prank call but she wanted to make sure Gramma was okay.

"A prank call?"

"Yes, ma'am."

"You're lying to me, Jace."

"No, Gramma—"

"You've never lied to me before."

"Do you want me to have someone come sit with you?"

"For a prank call?"

There was a long silence before Gramma hung up.

CHAPTER 42

Jace went straight home after her shift. No Alley B's, no talking with Rory or Dillon, no explaining her theories to Major Jakob or the sheriff. The brass had taken the day off anyway, it being New Year's Day, and would not appreciate being told that Dr. Cruz had killed Doc Wrubel and was responsible for Inmate Bobby's death and the only evidence was Jace's gut. Besides, Jace desperately wanted to see Gramma, to assure her that everything was okay, that Jace hadn't broken her promise to keep the job away from her family. She wanted to hold the old woman in her arms and revel in her strength. She wanted to eat Gramma's cooking, sleep on sheets Gramma washed. She wanted to help her fix the broken plumbing in room 216 and reglue the weather stripping around the door in 103. She needed to hear Gramma sing Mama's song, she needed to sit with her while she read and listened to her music, while she went back and forth trying to decide what to cook for supper.

Jace Salome needed the comfort of her known things, of her everyday things, that created the foundation of their lives.

What she got was dominoes.

The game was already in full gallop when she got home.

She stood in the doorway to Gramma's apartment, the winter sun just beginning to crack open the night sky behind her.

"Throw down," Hassan yelled. He stared at Preacher. "Mofo better throw down. Better gimme the goods."

Without a word, Preacher removed his fake teeth and hammered them down on the table. "Throw *that,* towelhead."

"Preacher." Gramma's voice was half an octave higher than normal, a signal of a night of whiskey. "We have to be tolerant of our less intelligent friends."

"Less intelligent?" Hassan stood and grabbed his crotch. "I got your less right here."

"Your words." Gramma glanced at her granddaughter when Jace laughed. "Jace. How are you?"

"Filled with the image of Hassan's less."

"Creepy as hell. Play the hand, Preacher." It was something Gramma said frequently when they played. Preacher and Hassan sometimes had trouble focusing.

Preacher put his teeth back in, snapped them two or three times at Hassan.

"Please, play the hand, Preacher."

"I don't feel like it."

"Then get out, you crazy, Bible-thumping drink of dirty water."

Hassan laughed. Preacher glowered. Gramma drank whiskey.

"You ask me for help and then you insult me."

"Well . . . yeah," Hassan said. "Haven't you met this woman? She's a crazy old lady."

Jace noticed Preacher sat facing the door. Usually he sat back to the door so he could see the sunrise through Gramma's sliding-glass doors. His briefcase was on the table next to him and slightly opened. "Is he pulling dominoes from his briefcase?"

"Not this time, Jace." Gramma finished off the amber in her tall glass and stood. She winked at Jace. "Pulled them outta his—"

"Whoa." Hassan waved his hands. "No, no, I don't need no image of him digging in his skivvies for dominoes."

There was a long moment of silence. Preacher reached into his briefcase and let his hand linger there.

"Skin it up, bitch." Hassan jumped up and waved his hands. "Skin it up. I'll get my M-1 carbine."

"Thought it was an AR-15," Preacher said.

"My AR-15, then."

"I thought it was an M-16," Gramma said.

"I'll get all of 'em. Mow you all down." He mimed a machine gun and blasted the entire apartment, spraying spittle everywhere.

"Well, mow 'em outside."

Hassan and Preacher looked at Gramma.

"Get out. We're done. I'm declaring myself the winner tonight. Leave your money on the table and get outta my house."

Hassan looked at Preacher as they stood. "Can she do that? Just take my money?"

Preacher shrugged. "Her house, her rules. I guess maybe she can."

"Well, that sucks." Hassan went outside and stretched before heading to his own apartment.

"Kinda does." Preacher closed his briefcase and when he lifted it, Jace heard the thunk of something heavy inside and knew it was his pistol. Preacher kissed both women and left, closing the door behind him.

Jace opened her mouth but Gramma shut it, snapping Jace's jaw closed and holding it tightly.

"Violence begats violence. I've seen it." Her eyes dropped for just a moment before coming back up. "My past has ugliness deep in it but a wonderful man, your grandfather, swept it off my porch. Jace, it wasn't a prank call. You wouldn't have sent two officers to check on me, or ask if I wanted a babysitter. I appreciate that you did. I was scared, honey, very scared. Abelardo tells me his friend was murdered and he hurts but there is nothing I can do to stop his pain and then you send the police to make sure I'm okay. I was very scared, Jace. I haven't been this scared since the Lubbock County boys called and asked if I knew Sharon Lusk."

"Mama."

"Her death was the most scared I ever was in my life . . . except for birthing her." The old woman laughed and Jace clearly saw the age in her face.

"I'm sorry I scared you, Gramma."

The old woman shook her head. "Pish. I called my boys over, we drank, we played. I'm not scared anymore. But mark my words: I've been where you're headed, little girl. I don't want you to go through what I did. It stole part of my soul and I've never gotten it back."

"I'll be careful, Gramma. I promise. And I promise this job won't come to you again."

"Don't promise what you can't promise." Gramma frowned. "But you haven't sleep-talked lately so that's good news, right? Not as stressed? Maybe not as worried about the world?"

Jace shuffled her feet. "Awk . . . ward. Actually, I moved my bed to the other side of the room."

Gramma laughed. "So I can't hear you sleep-talking."

"Nope."

"Sneaky little bitch."

"Gramma? Will you tell me about it? About the ugliness?"

"No."

Silence fell between them and eventually, Gramma opened up her giant stereo cabinet. A moment later, music floated gently across Gramma and Jace. At the first trumpet run, the first saxophone trill, Jace understood. This was the song that had filled her dreams. A spritely melody, almost a bounce, but in her dreams, it was melancholy and almost haunting.

"Your mama always wanted that dream house of love. Her own house, a perfect yard, you. Maybe a dog."

"So this song was for me."

" 'Just you and I, forever and a day,' " the singer sang.

Gramma nodded, her jaw tight. Jace knew she wanted to say something about how could a song be a gift for a child if that song was what the parent stripped to, but the old woman held her tongue.

Later, they slept in the same bed and later still, when Jace was deep asleep, fighting dreams of go-betweens and a tiny house with blood on the walls and used heroin syringes on the floor, Jace sleep-talked the song.

And Gramma, tears held tightly in her eyes, held her granddaughter until the morning slipped into afternoon and the afternoon slipped into evening.

While Jace slept fitfully, dreamt of jails within jails, and sleep-talked to her Gramma, Rory burned her cell-phone and laptop battery almost completely down. She worked backward on Ernesto Cruz. A company five years old, financed by unnamed partners and incorporated in Delaware. A medical degree eleven years old.

And way in the back, fogged by time, a string of convictions; stints in and out of various county jails and state prisons.

"Son of a bitch is a thug." She talked to herself while digging through the ZCSO computer system for the phone call Kerr made from ad-seg pod the day Bobby was killed.

"*. . . I don't know, man; how I'm supposed to know that? He's just gone. Guard told me Cruz was in here last night. The hell was he doing?*"

"*None of your concern.*"

"*Don't give me that shit. You tell me what's going on. Dude, I'm in this, too.*"

"*Where is he?*"

"*I just told you I don't know . . . you deaf? Maybe the tunnel. He goes down there sometimes.*"

"The tunnel?"

"Yeah, a whole thing they got, used to move inmates to court. Ain't been used in forever."

"Where does it empty out?"

"Somewhere in the courthouse basement."

"Get your ass down there and find him."

"Fuck you, buddy. I ain't doing that. I'm going to my cell and playing a good boy."

"No problem. I'll be sure and send you your son's head in the mail tomorrow. And maybe what's left of the unborn one."

"Dude, you ain't got no soul."

"Find him."

"Yeah, yeah, I will. Fuck off."

Just before she called Sheriff Bukowski, she watched Jace's video footage.

And recognized the man going in and out of the courthouse.

The Mexican cop.

Chapter 43

—control from Adam 1 . . . gimme A Pod outer . . . right now, god-damn it—

The door popped immediately. A second later the inner door popped, the electric locks loudly metallic and audible throughout the entire main hallway and inside most of the other pods.

"Salome," Bukowski snarled, an unlit cigar bent and broken in the corner of his mouth. "With me. Now."

He keyed up his portable radio. "405 from Adam 1."

—Adam 1 . . . go ahead—

"Salome's done for the night."

—uh . . . 10-4. Anything I need to do?—

"Just get somebody here. Now."

—10-4. 498 from 405. You're off float. Get to A Pod rest of shift—

—405 from 498 . . . yes, sir—

Bukowski strode from the pod. Bibb, obviously watching, popped the doors before Bukowski called for them. Jace swallowed, looked at Urrea, mouthed an apology, and followed her boss, anxiety hot in her throat and on her skin.

"Sheriff?" She was four or five steps behind him, almost afraid to get any closer. "What's going on?"

He said nothing, his boots loud and intimidating in the hallway. Each thud was magnified a thousand times by the concrete and brick walls, and by Jace's own fear.

"Sheriff?"

His silence sliced into her with the subtlety of a butcher's cleaver. They passed a number of deputies, roadies, and jailers, a few trusties still out cleaning, and though most of them greeted the sheriff, he acknowledged no one.

In less than a minute they were in Bukowski's suite. They passed through the outer office, which housed two secretaries, and entered his office. A huge oak desk dominated the room, covered with the ephemera of the office. The walls were awash in pictures and commendations and election memorabilia.

Sitting on the couch along the wall was Dr. Vernezobre.

"Abelardo, tell her what you told me."

Abelardo? Gramma's friend.

Jace had known Dr. Vernezobre knew Gramma but she hadn't realized it was a friendship. That the doctor had called Gramma when he was hurting about Wrubel's death surprised Jace deeply.

The doctor's face was tear-streaked. But even with that, and him sitting, he was still regal. He was still the formal man she'd talked to and who had kissed her hand. He looked at her, his lips tight and straight. "Miss Salome. I am sorry we continue to see each other in such circumstances."

"Good evening, Doctor. Gramma told me you called her recently. She said you were hurting. She was upset she didn't know how to help."

"Yes, I called her. She has such a wonderful way of seeing the world." He nodded toward the sheriff. "I called James, as well. I have called many people in the last few days, Miss Salome." He lowered his head. "I have called *mi padre,* also. None of them have been the balm I sought and now I fear that, in talking so much, I have made a terrible mistake."

Jace's breath caught in her lungs. "Yes?"

Dr. Vernezobre stood, formally and precisely. "I am a man of honor, Miss Salome. At least, I believe I am."

"Damn it, Abbie, no more self-pity bullshit," Bukowski growled. "You are a man of honor, have been since you were a pup. Ain't nobody can take that away from you."

"Though I can give it away."

"Doctor?"

"Miss Salome, I once thought Dr. Cruz to be a man of honor as well. I know now he is not. He is driven by gold and treasure, by his ego, by his narcissism. As you know by now, I frequently buy drugs smuggled from Mexico. They are less expensive. For my poor customers, this is a good thing. I realize sometimes those drugs are not as potent but the vast majority of the time, I am able to get medicines into the hands of people who cannot afford them. I have saved a great many lives that way."

The sheriff shook his head. "Abbie. Stop it. Tell her."

"Tell me what?" Jace couldn't swallow. Her throat was as dry and painful as the sandstorms that Zachary County saw each summer, sand blasting away paint and scarring metal. Her eyes held steady on the doctor and she wanted to shake him. *Stop with your courtly world manners and just. Fucking. Tell. Me.*

"I get my drugs through Dr. Cruz's friends. I use them for the poor; he uses them to maximize profit."

Jace had danced around this entire question for more than a week now. She bit her tongue hard, let the warm blood flood her mouth. She should have seen this. Cruz's comments about how little money there was in jail medicine versus what others said about how rich those contracts could be. Of course he was cutting corners; everyone knew it. Jace just hadn't realized that smuggled drugs were part of the knife used to cut those corners.

"Dr. Wrubel knew that," Jace said. "That's why Cruz killed him, in spite of their being friends."

"They were never friends, Miss Salome."

"But Cruz told me Wrubel came to dinner at his house and that they went to basketball games together."

Dr. Vernezobre shook his head. "Untrue. Francis worked for Cruz, but did not care for him. And Francis was not much of a sporting man at all, certainly not a fan enough of basketball to go to a game."

"So Cruz killed him."

Dr. Vernezobre nodded. "I believe that to be true. Francis told me he was going to confront Dr. Cruz about it. Francis had seen issues developing with invoices and billing and such. After he realized it, he came to me." The doctor's face colored. "I lied to him, Miss Salome, as I've done to you more than once."

"Why'd he whack Bobby?" Bukowski asked.

"I do not know that he did."

"He didn't." Jace told the men about the video footage of the man entering and leaving the courthouse late the night Inmate Bobby died. "He did it with Cruz's access code."

The sheriff, his face long and tired, stared at Jace for an eternity. "You ever gonna tell anybody about all this?"

"Yes, sir. Tonight, in fact. I think we need to pick Cruz up."

"Well, I guess things changed some, Salome. We're probably too late."

"Sir?"

"Miss Salome, when Dr. Cruz and I were discussing Francis's death last week, your name came up. I mentioned to him that I had known and admired your grandmother for years. I told him that she and I, and the sheriff here, used to go listen to music together."

Jace's jaw opened, closed, opened again. She looked at the sheriff though he kept his gaze on Dr. Vernezobre.

"I probably mentioned to him the Sea Spray Inn."

Jace stared at the doctor. "And?"

Vernezobre took a deep breath. "I cannot get your *abuela* on the phone."

"What?" Jace's stomach plunged to her feet. Her head swam. "I don't understand."

"Miss Salome, I beg your forgiveness, but Dr. Cruz told me how you had been investigating him. He came by my shop tonight, wanted to know about my next drug purchase. He was sweaty and disheveled. He was talking quickly. He was bruised and battered."

"Jorge beat him up."

"That the Mexican cop?" Bukowski asked.

"Or Cruz's drug dealer."

"Hell, he could be both." The sheriff sat on the edge of his desk and played with a giant gold ring on his left hand.

Jace watched it and dug around in her memory. Where had she seen that ring before? Rounded, with a red stone. "Sheriff?"

He saw her looking at his ring. "From the service."

She stared at it, unsure of why it stuck in her brain.

"When Cruz came to see me today, he was as hysterical as the young mothers who come to me when their babies are sick."

"Doctor?"

"Miss Salome, Dr. Cruz—"

"Stop calling him that." Jace said it hard. Her voice landed squarely on the doctor. He grew smaller under it. "He's a fraud and a thug and a killer." Then she remembered. "Cruz has a ring like that."

"Not like this, he don't."

"No, not military but big and gold. It has a *T* and an *S* on it, twisted together."

Bukowski stared at her. "Twisted together? Like one over the other?"

"Son of a bitch." Jace took a deep breath, felt the spin of vertigo squeeze her hard. "I know where I've seen it before."

"Sure as hell you do. Damn it." Bukowski stood. "That goddamned driver you and Rory picked up in Rooster. The one who was driving for *Sinaloa*."

Jace nodded.

"The *T* and *S* is for the Texas Syndicate, Salome. Sometimes they enforce for *Sinaloa.*"

"Dr. Cruz is a gang member?" Dr. Vernezobre looked stunned.

"He tried to frame Inmate Bobby with pig blood. From his cousin's hog farm. He had his cousin follow me and Rory—"

Dr. Vernezobre staggered a bit, grabbed the edge of the sheriff's desk for support. "Miss Bogan?"

"Yeah and now you're telling me he went after Gramma?"

"Hang on, Salome," Bukowski said. "We don't know that. All we know is Abbie mouthed off and now she's not answering the phone."

"Excuse me, James; perhaps I was not entirely clear. The phone did answer when I called, but she said nothing. There was only breathing."

"So you woke her up," Jace said, tinges of hope around her voice. "Sleeps heavy."

"No," the Cuban said. "It was a man breathing. As he hung up, he laughed."

"Goddamn it, Abbie, why didn't you tell me this?" Bukowski grabbed the phone and punched in a short number.

He's calling internally . . . within the department.

"Beem, get someone over to the Sea Spray Inn. What? On 80. Get a Zach boy or two there." He paused. "I don't know what they'll find, but tell 'em not to be stupid when they're pulling up."

"What are you talking about?" Jace sat, images of the bloody walls in her dreams full and violent in her head.

"Cruz is a convict." Bukowski pulled his sidearm, checked the magazine, and reholstered. "Bogan investigated her skinny butt off. Did a goddamned good job of it, too. Got Cruz's history and listened to a phone call Kerr made from ad-seg the night Bobby got whacked. Called me just before Abbie came in.

Cruz is a Texas boy. Been a guest of Huntsville once or twice. Went down on a nickel in Eyman, in Arizona. Sale of narcotics. Then suddenly pops up as a doctor ten or eleven years ago with some bullshit degree from Gomez U. in Mexico City or some place. There was some blood in his term at Eyman and his last one in Texas." He took a deep breath. "And the man going into the courthouse was here for a couple of the tours."

"That's probably Jorge," Jace said.

Bukowski snatched up his phone, angrily punched some buttons. "Dillon? Bukowski. Find Kerr and put the gotchas on him. Hold him in isolation until I get back. Don't say anything to him and don't let him do something stupid. Huh? Oh, yeah, he's balls deep in this. Falsifying drug inventory to start with. Thanks."

"James." Dr. Vernezobre spoke softly as Bukowski slammed the phone down. "Please help Arlene." He wiped his face with his hands. "I have made a terrible mistake in judgment. Do not let Arlene pay for my idiocy."

On his way to his office door, Bukowski stopped and hugged Dr. Vernezobre. "She ain't gonna get hurt. I promise you. She's a tough old broad, remember?"

Dr. Vernezobre nodded and chuckled through his tears. "I do, indeed."

Bukowski glanced at Jace. "Stay here with Jace and I'll call you as soon as I know something."

"Fuck that bullshit," Jace said.

"What did you say?"

"I'm going."

"Deputy Salome, I know—"

"Sheriff, this is my grandmother. Gramma. I'm going. Either with you, or as an ex-employee. The choice is yours."

He stared at her, anger boiling in his eyes like Gramma's homemade beef stew on the stove. His jaw clenched repeatedly, and his right hand became a tight fist. Eventually, he took a cigar from his pocket and jammed it in his mouth. "I'm smoking this thing and you ain't writing me up for it."

CHAPTER 44

—Zachary County from City 103 . . . two minutes out—

—City 103 . . . 10-4—

—Zachary from City 95 . . . less than a minute out. What are we looking for?—

—City 95 . . . check the well-being of Arlene Lusk, female, late 60s, manager's apartment, per Adam 1—

—Zachary from City 95 . . . 10-4—

—City 95 from Adam 1 . . . connected to 479—

—got it, Sheriff—

—Zachary from Adam 1 . . . three minutes out—

—Adam 1 . . . 10-4—

—Zachary from 248 . . . in the area—

—248 . . . 10-4—

—City 95 from 248 . . . I want someone at the door with me . . . one each on lot entrances front and back—

—No problem, Craig; I got ya' back. 103 on front . . . 112 on back—

—City 103 . . . 10-4—

—City 112 . . . 10-4—

—479 from 248—

—uh . . . 248 . . . go-ahead—

—if she doesn't answer can I—

—248 from Adam 1 . . . kick the door per me . . . get in there—

—10-4, Sheriff . . . Zachary from 248 . . . show me 10-23. Parking just off site on Frontage—

341

—248 . . . 10-23 . . . 10-4—

—City 95 same traffic—

—City 95 from Zachary . . . 10-4—

—Zachary from City 112 . . . 10-23 . . . on back entrance—

—City 112 . . . 10-4—

—City 103 same traffic . . . on front entrance—

—City 103 . . . 10-4—

—Zachary from 248 . . . we're outta the car—

—248 from Zachary County . . . 10-4—

. . .

. . .

. . .

. . .

. . .

. . .

. . .

—248 from Zachary County . . . status—

. . .

. . .

. . .

. . .

. . .

. . .

—248 from Zachary . . . status—

. . .

. . .

. . .

. . .

—248 from Zachary . . . status—

—Zachary from 248 . . . there's no one here—

—248 from Zachary . . . 10-4—

—248 from Adam 1 . . . check again . . . if I get there and she's there, I'm going to beat your ass—

—Yes, sir, Sheriff—

. . .

. . .

. . .

. . .

. . .

—Zachary from Adam 1 . . . 10-23—

—Adam 1 from Zachary . . . 10-4—

But they both knew, when they saw Ezell and the Zachary City officer come out of Gramma's front door, that she wasn't there.

Jace smashed a fist on the dashboard. "Damn it."

CHAPTER 45

Half an hour later, under a full winter sky, only a hint of moon slipping through the thick clouds, casting the world in a dull gunmetal gray, they were at the hog farm.

They'd sent an officer to Cruz's house and it was empty. After that, no one had any ideas. Rory had sent a text to Jace: *in booking. listening on scanner. hogs?*

Jace had mentioned it and now they were half a mile from the farm, everyone standing around Bukowski.

"Find her," he said simply. "Do not get her hurt. If she is hurt, I'll deal with Cruz."

Ezell said, "Sheriff, why don't you let me—"

"*I'll* deal with Cruz."

"Sheriff, I understand, but I think maybe you should let me handle him."

The only light near them was from a hook-up at a house about a half mile away. Jace couldn't see the sheriff's expression, but she could see his head turn toward Ezell and hold.

"I appreciate that, Craig. You're a good cop, but just let me do this my way, okay?"

Ezell sighed audibly. "Yes, sir. Benji, you circle around back that way. Hughes, go that way. You guys got your earpieces?"

The two roadies, men Jace had heard of but didn't know very well, did. That meant any radio traffic wouldn't go through the speaker on their portable radios, it would go directly to their ears, keeping them silent.

"Okay, everybody go to Tac-4 for this," Ezell said.

Everyone, including the sheriff, switched the channel on their portables.

"If anyone finds this lady, let me know. If you find Cruz, let me know. He killed Wrubel and Wrubel was our friend. Let the rest of us know where you are and we'll come help you take him down. Sheriff, I'd like you to do that, too."

Bukowski said nothing.

"Don't worry, Jace; we'll find her. We're pretty good at this sort of thing."

Jace ground her teeth but thanked him and with hardly a sound, they were gone.

The sheriff looked her direction. "You stay right the hell here."

"You know I won't do that."

"No problem, then. Get your ass out and go find him. No radio, no gun, no vest, no training. Damned good thinking, Salome. You keep your ass here . . . that is as direct an order as I can give."

Then he, too, was gone.

She managed to stay put for nearly a full minute, surrounded by the empty sound of winter. The summertime desert was alive with sounds and animals and breezes, but the winter chill seemed to blanket the desert, to cut off its air as though trying to kill it. Jace had hated coming to see stars with Mama in the winter because the world seemed so dead. She never asked but sometimes Mama insisted.

Because she needed to get out, Jace realized now. Sometimes, as much as Mama loved her parents, she needed to get away from them. Here, in the desert, with her parents miles away, Mama could try to find some of the peace that eluded her for most of her life.

Jace walked away from the sheriff's car, headed away from

the direction of the house and barn, both dimly lit by the partial moon and Zachary City lights bouncing off the low-hanging clouds. The guys were searching those places and, while Jace wanted to be there, Bukowski was right. She was neither trained nor equipped for it. So she walked the other direction, not far, not so far that she wouldn't be able to get back when they found Gramma, not so far that she wouldn't be able to land a punch or two directly to Cruz's nose before he was carted away.

Violence begats violence.

Jace ground her teeth. Cruz had done violence to lots of people, including her Gramma. So yeah, in this case, violence was birthing more violence.

She didn't want violence, wasn't comfortable with it, but if it came to her, she would face it straight up.

No? You don't want it? What about waving the gun at Campbell when he first followed you? And what about wanting to hurt him when you caught him in the cemetery?

The harsh truth was that she might be more comfortable with violence than she wanted to admit. It might be growing on her, a condition scarring her soul, the way a virus slides easily through a food chain or a household, leaving infections as its footprint.

The job was changing her and mostly she liked the change. She liked that she was more comfortable talking to people than she ever had been; she liked that she was learning to see situations through different lenses; she liked the feeling of belonging to something larger than herself. But maybe this casualness with physical violence, wanting to pummel Cruz, was the negative to those positives. Maybe it was the price she was going to pay for expanding her other boundaries.

Can you do that, Jace?

She walked, the ground uneven and rocky, stubbed with cactus. Her feet twisted and turned, her ankles constantly shifting to keep her upright. A dull thud began just behind her eyes and quickly blossomed into a sharp pain. Stopping, she looked toward the house and barn. There was no activity. She listened and where moments earlier she'd heard nothing, now she heard the rustle and snort of hogs. A thin stink had slipped into the air as well.

She started walking again and the sound of the hogs, as well as the stink, grew. In the near distance, she saw some outbuildings she assumed housed the hogs. She chuckled. They were as far from the house but still on the property as they could be.

There seemed to be five or six long, narrow buildings, each probably full of hogs. But there was a smaller building, too.

Holy shit . . . the size of the house in my dream.

Her throat dried. Had she been dreaming of this place? How could she dream about a place she'd never been?

She stopped, the hogs snorting and shitting, filling the air with noise and stink, and stared. A single door, a single window, maybe two rooms. An office? Way out here? Or maybe a castration room? Was the blood she'd seen on the walls in her dream pig blood? Were the syringes for the hogs, keeping them healthy with antibiotics or hormones or whatever?

She took a few steps, her head moving as fast as a tornado, and she realized there was a light on. Frowning, she got closer and decided it was probably an office and someone had left the light on.

Except, when she got close enough to look in the single window, she didn't see an office. She didn't see a desk with papers and a bookshelf with huge binders of information. She didn't see a linoleum floor tracked with mud and blood.

She saw Gramma.

And her heart broke.

CHAPTER 46

The woman was bloody.

Blood had turned her face into a nightmarishly painted clown's face. The blood was dry and even through the window, Jace saw the same brown hue as the chocolate in Bobby's cell and the blood on the walls in her dreams. Gramma was in a chair, bound behind her back, a gag stuffed in her mouth. Her feet and legs were free, but there was blood on her right thigh and trailing down her left arm.

Somewhere behind Jace, the sheriff and Ezell and the two deputies she didn't know well were scouring the place looking for Gramma. But they were nearly a half mile away and Jace was *here* and Gramma was *here*.

She quickly texted Rory, telling her where she was and what was going on. She told Rory to call the sheriff or radio Ezell or something, just let someone know. Before Rory could reply, Jace turned her phone to silent, dumped it into her pocket, took a deep breath, and quietly opened the door.

Gramma's head turned slowly toward her and when recognition lit her eyes, fear and anger did, too. She shook her head, as though telling Jace to leave and get someone else. Or silently telling Jace, "See this? I told you so."

But after a second, she stopped shaking her head, gave Jace a long, hard look, and then tilted her head toward the door on the opposite side of the room. Jace nodded and put a finger over her lips. Quietly, pushing Cruz out of her head by mentally shoving him off the top of the courthouse, Jace quickly untied Gramma's hands. They fell free as though they were dead. As she stood, the old woman rubbed them. Jace took the gag from her mouth and dropped it.

"The fuck are you doing? Where's Jimmy?"

"Shut up, Gramma. Let's go."

But even as she said it, Jace knew they weren't getting out. She heard, or felt, and simply *knew*, that Cruz was coming through the far door, gun in hand.

"You jutht can't thtay out of my buthineth, can you? You thtupid bitch. I tol' you."

His face was a riot of blood. It spattered out from his nose and mouth in angry red slashes. He held a gun in his left hand but it was limp and pointed more at the floor than anywhere. The two broken fingers of his right hand were gone, replaced by bloody, dripping stubs. The remaining fingers were tightly closed around something Jace could not see. "Yeah? You thee? You did thith. Wrubel thtarted it and you finithed it."

"Dr. Cruz, don't do anything crazy, okay? The sheriff and five or six of our guys are out there at the house and barn. They've finished their search and are coming here next. That's why I came over." She held her hands so he could see them clearly. "Because I knew they were coming. If you shoot us, you'll be caught. You'll never make it out of here alive."

Cruz opened his mouth and Jace thought he was trying to grin, but so many of his teeth were gone, broken off at the gum line, it was impossible to tell what he was doing. Maybe it was a grin. Maybe it was pain. "I'm dead. It don't matter. I owe. Don't you get it? I owe on the drugth. I couldn't thell when Wrubel thtarted fucking with me." He banged the gun against his chest. "I'm already dead."

Jace took a few slow steps, putting Gramma behind her, and keeping her hands raised so Cruz wouldn't mistake her intentions. "That's not true. We can protect you. We can talk to Shelby and the district attorney, get you some protection. The Texas Rangers. Or the feds. I'm sure you have enough in your head to get yourself a nice cushy life somewhere on the taxpayers' dime."

He laughed and coughed. When he did, his eyes rolled up and blood spattered from his broken mouth. "Wrubel knew. He knew what I wuth doing. I wuth thipping drugth." He tapped the barrel of the gun against his chest. "I'm the pipeline, bitch. Thith ith my play."

"Kerr was keeping your records. He was falsifying inventory control. That's why you wanted him as a trusty. You stopped signing in and Conroy wasn't videoing the halls. Maybe you called Wrubel or asked him to take a walk with you or something; that's how you got him out there."

Cruz shook his head. "Doan matter why whatever. Yeah, he did that but . . ." He shrugged and opened his hand. A few white pills fell to the office floor and he laughed. "Ain't gonna let nobody take me to prithon. Been there . . . ain't doing it again. Ain't going for no Thinaloa." He coughed, another spew of blood, and Jace wondered where all the damage had come from. "Already took forty or fifty. Ain't no taxpayerth for me; I'm already dead. But *I* chothe my death. Nobody elthe. I chothe it." He jammed the ten or so pills still in his hand into his mouth and swallowed. "Ain't gonna let them hurt me no more."

"Doctor?"

When he fell slowly to his knees, Jace grabbed his gun. He looked at her, something like regret in his eyes. He nodded as he slumped forward. She grabbed him and lowered him gently to the floor. Blood leaked from his nose and when he started aspirating, he coughed up a whitish-yellow froth. A moment later, his eyes rolled around in his head until finally they caught hers. They locked gazes until his eyes were empty.

She shoved the gun in her waistband and herded Gramma toward the door.

"Jace, he didn't do that to himself. He's not the only one here."

"What?"

Jorge.

"She means me, *Chiquita.*"

Jace turned and looked at the man. Jet-black hair, swept back like a Mafia stereotype, a bloody knife in his left hand. This was the man she'd seen get out of the Town Car that day at the jail, and the man on the video getting into the courthouse.

"You have caused me no end of problems."

Watching him carefully, Jace again put herself in front of Gramma. The old woman tried to speak but Jace shushed her. She could feel Gramma's hands on her back, clinging tightly to Jace's belt.

"We're not going to play games. I'm not going to stand here and explain everything and answer all your questions. I'm going to tell you Cruz's death doesn't matter. Cruz Medical has quite a few contracts and has successors already in place. There are lots of doctors; there will be lots of contracts." Jorge kicked at Cruz's feet. "This is a bump in the road."

"You're awfully articulate for a cartel chump."

The man laughed. "Good schooling."

"Paid for by *Sinaloa,* no doubt."

"No doubt. Just like Cruz's medical degree. But I went to a better school. An American school."

"Doctors, you said. You paid for all of them? All their degrees?"

"Not me personally but the cartel, yes."

And they're getting contracts, Jace thought. *They're setting up in jails, a captive audience for drugs of all kinds.*

"Pharma . . . weed . . . H . . . meth . . . whatever you happen to have on hand."

The man nodded and behind her, Jace felt Gramma grabbing and grabbing, her fingers as full of fear as Jace's head. Jace was thinking a million miles an hour, trying to stall for time and hoping someone would notice her gone from the car, hoping someone would see the hog confinements and the light on in the office.

Rory, where are you? You said if I got hurt, it was because you were already dead. You're not dead . . . but you're not here.

Jace swallowed. Rory would have been here had she been able, Jace believed that with all her heart. But in this chunk of desert, as the new year began to settle in and get comfortable, as the dead-shift jailers were getting bored in the wee small hours, Jace was on her own. Even with officers so close, she was on her own.

"You're the one who called me."

"Yes."

"You were toying with me."

"Yes."

"Why?"

"Because I am a bit of a sadist and I thought it was fun."

"And you answered Gramma's phone when Dr. Vernezobre called."

"Yes."

"How did you know he knew Gramma?"

The man shook his head. "I'm done with this. I need to finish this and slip out the back while they're stumbling around in the dark."

Jace bit her tongue, reopening the wound she'd given herself earlier. "You're a lefty. You killed Inmate Bobby. Because he'd been in the hallway? Because he'd seen it. Or maybe figured it out. You sent Kerr for him, down in the tunnel, but you got to him first. You won't get away with this."

He shook his head. "Those men—" He waved his empty right hand toward the house and barn. "Have no idea what's going on. It is why I prefer a knife to a gun. Silence." The knife high like a battle flag, he charged them.

Jace grabbed for Cruz's gun, tucked safely in her waistband. Except it was already gone. It was already firing, from a position about waist high just behind her. Shots exploded in the wall behind Jorge, then in his shoulder, then again behind him, then once in his chest and once in his face. There was no great spasm of death. He got shot; his face exploded; he dropped. Blood pooled around his head, a sanguine halo.

Jace jumped away from the gun. When she looked, Gramma held it tightly, one-handed. Her eyes were closed and one of the cuts on her cheek had reopened. Blood flowed freely down the side of her face.

"Gramma." Jace went to her side and hugged her tightly. She took the gun and threw it on the far side of the office.

The old woman started crying and leaned heavily into her granddaughter.

"Shhhhhhh. It'll be okay."

"I killed him, Jace."

"Yeah."

"I'd do it again."

Jace hugged her fiercely, took a last look at Jorge to make sure he wasn't moving, and guided Gramma outside.

"Sheriff," Jace called as loudly as she could. "Two men down. We're secure."

"Salome." His bark came from not that far away. "You're secure? Is that what you said?"

"Two men down. We're secure."

Then he was on her, close in the dark, the last bit of light from the office splaying across his face. His eyes were burning holes in his skull, his breath bubbling with anger. He looked past her into the office, then went inside. A few moments later, as Ezell arrived, Bukowski came back out. He got on his cell phone and called the sheriff's office.

"You guys okay? What happened?" Ezell looked through the window. "Holy shit. Who's the other guy?"

"*Sinaloa* soldier," Jace said. "Carries a Mexican badge to get in and out of places. He was setting up a pipeline through Cruz Medical."

"Huh?"

"Smuggling drugs into the jail through their doctors. Pay for doctors to go to med school, and then getting them in as jail docs."

Ezell whistled. "Wow."

"Salome." The sheriff hung up the phone. "You're suspended. Seven days. Disobeying a direct order."

"Jimmy, she came and got me."

"And you'll have seven days to talk all about it. Ezell, Jakob is on her way. Tape the area; start a list. Arlene and Salome's names at the top, mine next."

"Yes, sir."

Ten minutes later, the first lab techs began to arrive and soon after that, an ambulance pulled up.

"Arlene, Salome, go to the hospital."

"But Sheriff, nothing happened to me. I'm fine—"

"Wanna make it fourteen days?"

Jace stared at him, his face bathed now in white light from the ambulance and blue and red flashing light from the squad cars. Anger strode across his lines and creases exactly the way he strode through the jail's halls late at night, unable to sleep. His eyes challenged her to defy him again.

She didn't. She took a spot on the bench. EMTs had Gramma strapped to a backboard and on the gurney in the middle of the bay. One of them banged on the glass between the bay and the cab, and the ambulance started moving. Through the back glass, Jace watched the sheriff watch them until he was out of sight.

CHAPTER 47

"You really want another tattoo?" Rory looked askance at Jace, sitting in the chair, her shirt open to the valley between her breasts. "You know I can see your boobies, right? And if I can . . ." She tilted her head to indicate the tattoo artist.

"Bah." The guy was an old man with an amazingly steady hand, a head of long, gray hair, and a body almost lost beneath his own tattoos. He stopped, looked at Rory, winked in a slightly repulsive and creepy way, and went back to Jace's chest. "Ask her where her first one is."

Rory's eyes bulged but Jace shook her head. "He's full of crap." She sucked in a long blast of air when the needle touched her skin.

"Eyes and half-hearts. Goofy shit." He stared hard at the spot on her chest between her breasts as the black outline of an eye slowly came to life.

The eye was Thomas's eye. And Wrubel's and Inmate Bobby's. Maybe a little bit Cruz and Jorge's, too. Jace wasn't sure what it said to her, what the over-arcing metaphor was, if there even was one. But she did know she never wanted to forget the emptiness, the sadness and finality of those eyes in the moments before death. She never wanted to forget what it meant when someone died. It wasn't just a puzzle to be figured out; it was a life. Maybe not a good life, maybe not a bad life, but a life nonetheless.

"Maybe its Laimo's eye," Rory said softly, watching the

quarter-sized tattoo take shape. "She was laughing at Mercer's being so scared. Maybe you want to remember that everybody deserves human dignity."

"It's just a fucking eye, ladies. Don't mean shit." The tattoo man came off her chest for a minute, staring at his work. "What color you want when we get there?"

Mama's eyes had been green, so translucent that they almost didn't exist, as though Jace could see straight through to her soul. Except Jace had never known, truly, what was hidden in Mama's soul.

"Green. Translucent."

"Trans-what?"

"Semi-transparent . . . like."

Jace grinned at Rory. "Getting smart on me, sister?"

"Been smart like you. Just don't like showing it." She tapped the tattoo artist on the shoulder and when he looked back at her, she said, "Can you put a tiny star in the pupil?"

Jace frowned.

"She used to go watch the stars with her Mama."

The man looked back at Jace, shook his head, muttered "Goofy shit," again, and got back to work.

CHAPTER 48

Four people—three men dressed in conservative blue suits with white shirts and dark ties, and one woman in a pale-green suit—walked through the front doors of the Zachary County sheriff's office. Sheriff Bukowski, Chief Deputy Gaddis, Major Yancey of Operations, and Major Jakob waited for them. The four came through the metal detectors as would anyone else coming to visit the office. They stopped directly in front of the sheriff and his staff.

"You taking over?"

The woman held her hand out. "I'm Felicia Upchurch, Southwestern Jail Commission, and I guess we'd better talk about that."

ABOUT THE AUTHOR

Trey R. Barker has published a bit of everything: crime to mystery, science fiction to nonfiction, plays to novels, and a short-story collection. He spent seventeen years, off and on, as a journalist before moving into law enforcement. Currently, he is a sergeant with the Bureau County sheriff's office, the crisis negotiator for the regional special-response team, a member of the Illinois State Attorney General's Internet Crimes Against Children Task Force, and an adjunct instructor at the University of Illinois (Champaign) Police Training Institute. He currently lives in northern Illinois, though he was born and bred in west Texas.